GODSPEED

A Medieval Romance

By Kathryn Le Veque

Book Two in
The Earls of East Anglia Series

Motto: *Mors in victoria*
Victory over death

© Copyright 2018 by Kathryn Le Veque Novels, Inc.
Print Edition

Text by Kathryn Le Veque
Cover by Kim Killion

Reproduction of any kind except where it pertains to short quotes in relation to advertising or promotion is strictly prohibited.

All Rights Reserved.

The characters and events portrayed in this book are fictitious. Any similarity to real persons, living or dead, is purely coincidental and not intended by the author.

Kathryn Le Veque Novels

Medieval Romance:

The de Russe Legacy:
The White Lord of Wellesbourne
The Dark One: Dark Knight
Beast
Lord of War: Black Angel
The Iron Knight

The de Lohr Dynasty:
While Angels Slept (Lords of East Anglia)
Rise of the Defender
Steelheart
Spectre of the Sword
Archangel
Unending Love
Shadowmoor
Silversword

Great Lords of le Bec:
Great Protector
To the Lady Born (House of de Royans)
Lord of Winter (Lords of de Royans)

Lords of Eire:
The Darkland (Master Knights of Connaught)
Black Sword
Echoes of Ancient Dreams (time travel)

De Wolfe Pack Series:
The Wolfe
Serpent
Scorpion (Saxon Lords of Hage – Also related to The Questing)
The Lion of the North
Walls of Babylon
Dark Destroyer
Nighthawk
Warwolfe
ShadowWolfe
DarkWolfe
A Joyous de Wolfe Christmas

Ancient Kings of Anglecynn:
The Whispering Night
Netherworld

Battle Lords of de Velt:
The Dark Lord
Devil's Dominion

Reign of the House of de Winter:
Lespada
Swords and Shields (also related to The Questing, While Angels Slept)

De Reyne Domination:
Guardian of Darkness
The Fallen One (part of Dragonblade Series)
With Dreams Only of You

House of d'Vant:
Tender is the Knight (House of d'Vant)

The Red Fury (House of d'Vant)

The Dragonblade Series: (Great Marcher Lords of de Lara)
Dragonblade
Island of Glass (House of St. Hever)
The Savage Curtain (Lords of Pembury)
The Fallen One (De Reyne Domination)
Fragments of Grace (House of St. Hever)
Lord of the Shadows
Queen of Lost Stars (House of St. Hever)

Lords of Thunder: The de Shera Brotherhood Trilogy
The Thunder Lord
The Thunder Warrior
The Thunder Knight

The Great Knights of de Moray:
Shield of Kronos
The Gorgon

Highland Warriors of Munro:
The Red Lion
Deep Into Darkness

The House of Ashbourne:
Upon a Midnight Dream

The House of D'Aurilliac:
Valiant Chaos

The House of De Nerra:
The Falls of Erith
Vestiges of Valor
Realm of Angels

The House of De Dere:
Of Love and Legend

St. John and de Gare Clans:
The Warrior Poet

The House of de Garr:
Lord of Light
Realm of Angels

The House of de Bretagne:
The Questing (also related to Swords and Shields)

The House of Summerlin:
The Legend

The Kingdom of Hendocia:
Kingdom by the Sea

Time Travel Romance: (Saxon Lords of Hage)
The Crusader
Kingdom Come

<u>**Contemporary Romance:**</u>

Kathlyn Trent/Marcus Burton Series:
Valley of the Shadow
The Eden Factor
Canyon of the Sphinx

The American Heroes Series:
The Lucius Robe
Fires of Autumn
Evenshade
Sea of Dreams
Purgatory

Other Contemporary Romance:
Lady of Heaven

Darkling, I Listen
In the Dreaming Hour

Sons of Poseidon:
The Immortal Sea

Pirates of Britannia Series (with Eliza Knight):

Savage of the Sea by Eliza Knight
Leader of Titans by Kathryn Le Veque
The Sea Devil by Eliza Knight
Sea Wolfe by Kathryn Le Veque

<u>Note:</u> All Kathryn's novels are designed to be read as stand-alones, although many have cross-over characters or cross-over family groups. Novels that are grouped together have related characters or family groups.

Series are clearly marked. All series contain the same characters or family groups except the American Heroes Series, which is an anthology with unrelated characters.

There is NO particular chronological order for any of the novels because they can all be read as stand-alones, even the series.

For more information, find it in **A Reader's Guide to the Medieval World of Le Veque**.

Author's Note

Welcome to Dash and Belladonna's tale!

This is a perfect example of how a writer can find inspiration anywhere – this story is based on the Edmund Leighton painting *God Speed*. It's a famous painting, and very Medieval, and I've always found it hauntingly beautiful. The lady in the painting is tying her favor on the arm of a knight who is leaving for battle. You can see the distress on her face and the calmness on his. I wanted to give that painting a backstory, including that very scene, so here it is. I hope Mr. Leighton would have been proud of it.

Now, on to the characters.

Our hero is Dashiell (pronounced da-SHEEL) du Reims. He is the son of Talus du Reims, eldest son of Tevin du Reims (While Angels Slept). In *Godspeed*, Talus is currently the Earl of East Anglia and Dash is his heir, a man who had been serving his father until he came to serve his current liege, the Duke of Savernake (pronounced SAVE-ur-nāke). What was supposed to be a temporary post became a long-standing one, for one good reason – our heroine.

A little history on the Earls of East Anglia – originally, the earldom was with the de Gael family (historically factual), but in my novel *While Angels Slept*, it went to the House of du Reims. It remains with du Reims until 1300 A.D. when, in my novel *Swords and Shields*, a de Winter marries the last du Reims heiress, daughter of the last earl, Christian du Reims. Then, it becomes a de Winter title, making the de Winters powerful warlords in both Norfolk and Suffolk.

If you're keeping track of the family tree, Christian du Reims is Dashiell and Belladonna's grandson, the eldest son of their eldest son, Tobin (see the list of children in the epilogue). While it's unfortunate that the du Reims line had to die out because Christian only had a daughter, it's not so unfortunate when you consider du Reims blood mixes with de Winter blood to continue the strong bloodlines for the Earls of East Anglia. I think Dash and Bella would have been very happy with that. Also, it wasn't unusual for a man marrying an heiress to take *her* family name to continue that family's legacy, so the du Reims name could continue, after all, if the de Winter earl decided to take on that family name.

Another power player in *Godspeed* is none other than my go-to guy, Christopher de Lohr. Christopher's story is told in *Rise of the Defender*, which happens about twenty-five years before Godspeed. Tevin du Reims had a sister, Val, who married a knight named Myles de Lohr. Val and Myles are the parents of Christopher and David de Lohr, meaning Dashiell is a close cousin to Christopher and David.

You will also note that Ajax de Velt is mentioned in this novel. Ajax's story is told in *The Dark Lord* and, for a very long time, it was my best-selling novel. If you haven't read it yet, it's a must-read. In another novel, *Devil's Dominion*, Ajax and Christopher de Lohr become friends (in a funny moment), so that's another novel you should read to gain perspective on Ajax as well as Christopher.

One of the familiar characters in this story is Gavin de Nerra, the eldest son of Valor de Nerra (*Vestiges of Valor*). We have seen Gavin before, when he was a toddler, and then both he and his twin brother in *Shield of Kronos*. In this story, Gavin has taken over his father's position of Itinerant Justice of Hampshire. Also, you'll get a glimpse of my new hero, Bric MacRohan, who will have his own novel *High Warrior* in April 2018.

So many recognizable and new faces in this history-heavy book (which follows the end of King John's reign accurately), and a brand-new hero to swoon over in Dashiell du Reims. Truly, he's one of my favorites already and I think you're really going to love him.

So, without further ado, on to GODSPEED.

Hugs,
Kathryn

Table of Contents

Prologue 1
Chapter One 13
Chapter Two 29
Chapter Three 55
Chapter Four 65
Chapter Five 71
Chapter Six 94
Chapter Seven 106
Chapter Eight 121
Chapter Nine 131
Chapter Ten 139
Chapter Eleven 152
Chapter Twelve 165
Chapter Thirteen 185
Chapter Fourteen 199
Chapter Fifteen 212
Chapter Sixteen 226
Chapter Seventeen 240
Chapter Eighteen 250
Chapter Nineteen 266
Chapter Twenty 278
Chapter Twenty-One 298

Chapter Twenty-Two 312
Chapter Twenty-Three 320
Chapter Twenty-Four 324
Chapter Twenty-Five 339
Epilogue 355
About Kathryn Le Veque 363

"Speak what we feel, not what we ought to say…"
~ William Shakespeare's *King Lear*

PROLOGUE

Early December, Year of Our Lord 1215 A.D.
Driffield, south of Scarborough

"BY THE POWER of God given me this day, I absolve you of your sins, all of you, poor wretched creatures given whim to earthy sins!"

It was a loud and booming voice that could be heard over the rumble of battle. An elderly man stood amid the fighting, garbed in robes and finery, seemingly having no idea that he was in mortal danger.

On the contrary – he was blessing the men in battle with all of the pomp that the pope would bless his congregation on Easter Sunday. The only problem was that this congregation wasn't receptive to the blessing and was prepared to demonstrate that unhappy position with the swords, maces, and flails they happened to be holding.

The man giving the blessing had no protection at all.

"Oh… God." A knight in heavy armor stood over the man he'd just killed. He could see the elderly man trying to bless the combatants, only to be pushed aside or ignored altogether. He began to run towards him. "Christ, who let him run onto the field of battle?"

It was a question to no one in particular, but a question of great angst. Sir Dashiell du Reims began stumbling over the dead, trying to make haste across a rain-soaked field that was slick with blood and body parts. It was the conclusion of a skirmish between the King of England, John, and the barons who very much wanted the man off the throne.

John had been campaigning through England, laying siege to rebel barons and simultaneously trying to raise support for his cause. But he was playing a cat-and-mouse game with the rebels; the mighty Savernake army along with several other allied factions had caught the king's men just as they left Scarborough, and tore through them in devastation. The king's army wasn't nearly ready to face another battle after their siege of Scarborough and the north, and they certainly weren't ready for Savernake supported by the House of de Lohr, the Lords of the Marches.

It had been a great victory for the rebel barons, but Dashiell wasn't feeling the victory at the moment.

Only panic.

His liege, the Duke of Savernake and kin to the House of Plantagenet, was running amok on the battlefield. Normally, it would be the man's right to shout his victory, but not in this case. The man, unfortunately, was quite mad, and he cared not for his victory. He had men who minded him, but the minders were nowhere to be found as Dashiell raced towards his liege as fast as he could go.

The bloody fool is going to get himself killed!

Suddenly, Dashiell could see another knight approach Savernake, being gentle with the man and clearly suggesting that his safety was in danger. But Savernake lifted his hand to the knight and, as Dashiell watched, the knight crossed himself as one does when in church, after prayer. But after the sign of the cross given by the knight, Savernake seemed to be more than willing to do as he was asked, which was remove himself from the dwindling battle.

Dashiell slowed his frantic pace, propping his helm up to wipe is sweaty forehead. It was a gesture of relief, of frustration. He was going to have to take a stand against taking a senile duke on a battle march. The men liked to see their liege leading the army and draw strength from it, but the truth was that Savernake was a danger to himself and to others. Any man who believed he was Paul the Apostle, and therefore invincible, was clearly a danger to everyone around him.

"So he wandered into the battle again, did he?"

The question came from behind and Dashiell turned to see his cousin, David de Lohr, approach. David was the Earl of Canterbury, dressed in well-used and bloodied armor, as he'd been in the heart of the fighting for most of the day. To his cousin's question, Dashiell nodded his head wearily.

"Again," he said. "He was blessing the men."

David grunted with annoyance. "Jesus," he muttered. "He still believes he is immortal?"

"Still." Dashiell shook his head, frustrated. "He cannot come on anymore battle marches with us, David. The man is going to get himself killed. Bent had to intercept him on the field as it was, and that puts Bent at great risk. I do not like it when my knights are put at risk like that. I want to know how in the hell Savernake wandered away from his minders and they did not see him."

David cocked a blond eyebrow; handsome and muscular, he was the younger brother of Christopher de Lohr, a man deeply entrenched in the politics of England for many years. As the powerful Earl of Hereford and Worcester, Christopher commanded half of the Marches while his brother commanded a good portion of Kent. With the de Lohr brothers united, victory was assured, and the winds of politics often hinged on their support.

But the de Lohrs had a long-standing hatred for John. The family had always been avid supporters of the crown, but seventeen years of John's rule had been their limit. They could only take so much of his foolery and debauchery. Within the past year, they had removed their support from the crown. John had been devastated by their loss, making battles like this one most important.

"The duke is sly, even in his madness," David muttered. "If he wants to escape, he will. Besides... you know as well as I do that Clayton wants him dead. You know that is why he insists on bringing him and he probably paid the minders to turn their backs for a moment, allowing the duke to slip by. The husband to the heiress of Savernake would be very happy if the duke got himself killed."

Dashiell scratched his chin unhappily. "That is not going to happen so long as there is breath in my body."

"Ever the old duke's protector, Dash."

"I have been from the beginning."

"Then Clayton le Cairon is in for a very long wait. Nothing but God himself could tear you down, Dash, or cause you to falter in your duties. You are the strongest man I know."

With that, David slapped him on the shoulder, a gesture of support, and headed off into the dying skirmish. Dashiell's focus, however, was on the duke, as the knight who had removed him from the battlefield continued to move him away from any fighting.

But it was much like herding a duck. The knight motioned the duke to go one way, but the duke went the other. Moving quickly to catch up to the pair, Dashiell came up behind the knight and put his hand on the man's shoulder in a friendly gesture. It was also one meant to release the man from his burden. The young knight turned to see Dashiell with welcome relief.

"Dash," Bentley of Ashbourne, a young and powerful knight, spoke with gladness. "Our Lord was... well, he was blessing the battlefield."

Dashiell nodded. "I know," he said quietly. "I saw." Then, he raised his voice to speak to the elderly man in Bentley's grip. "My lord, you must not venture into the heat of battle as you did. We have discussed this before. It could be very dangerous."

Lord Edward de Vaston, the hereditary Duke of Savernake, turned to see his most treasured and powerful knight, the man who was in command of his armies. Though elderly, Edward was still strong and active, tall and lanky with a full head of graying red hair. But his mind had left him years ago, an unfortunate circumstance for a man who had always been sharp and vital.

Dashiell remembered the days when he had been a young knight and serving the duke had been a pleasure. He'd learned much from the kind and patient man.

Now, it was his turn to be patient.

"Ah!" Edward said, smiling broadly. "My greatest follower. Be at peace, my son."

He lifted his hand in a gesture of blessing, something he did with everyone, and Dashiell was obliged to cross himself. No one greeted or otherwise had interaction with Edward without crossing themselves. It was simply what the duke expected now that he believed himself to be Paul the Apostle. Dashiell had even seen the Archbishop of Canterbury, Stephen Langton, cross himself and kiss Edward's hand. It's simply what one did when meeting the man who believed he was a messenger of God and, as Langton put it, perhaps he really was.

"My lord, we sincerely must remove you from this battle," Dashiell said, trying to push the old man along without making it seem like he was manhandling his liege. "I promise I will bring the wounded to you for a blessing if you will simply stay to your tent. Will you agree to this, my lord?"

Edward held on to Dashiell as the man gently moved him away from the fighting and back towards the cluster of tents that signified the army's encampment. A blue haze of smoke hovered over the tents, the fires heating food and water blazing fiercely in the cold, wet weather.

"My tent will not hold all of the men requiring my blessing," Edward said. "They have much to atone for. God wishes me to be in battle, at their sides."

Dashiell had a tight hold of him. "God wishes for you to live to see another day," he countered. "You cannot walk onto a battlefield without protection or a weapon. There would be men to kill you, my lord."

"But those men must have absolution!"

"What would your daughters say if I allowed you to be killed?"

That usually brought the duke around, the mention of his three beloved daughters. Lily, Acacia, and Belladonna were the light of his life, three women who were very devoted to their father.

It was those three, known as the Trinity by those serving the duke, who kept the situation with the duke from getting well out of hand. And Dashiell wielded their names like a weapon to control Savernake's behavior. He hated to do it, but the truth was that he had little choice.

He was dealing with a madman.

"Lily," the duke murmured. "Where is she, Dash?"

"She is back at Ramsbury Castle, my lord," he replied. "She is safe."

"And Acacia. Is she near?"

"She is also at Ramsbury, my lord."

"And my baby, Belladonna?"

"Ramsbury, my lord."

He was repeatedly referring to the duke's seat, the massive structure of Ramsbury Castle. It was the power seat of Wiltshire, as the de Vaston family's roots could be traced back to the Conquest of England.

"Then I must go home to Ramsbury," Edward said as he realized his three lovely daughters had not come with him to bless the troops. "Come, Dash. We must return."

Dealing with the duke was often like dealing with a child. He made quick decisions and expected them to be immediately obeyed. If Dashiell wasn't careful in responding to his wishes, the duke was fully capable of throwing a tantrum in the form of begging God to smite those who opposed his will. Dashiell had been on the receiving end of a few of those tantrums. Therefore, Dashiell had to be careful in his reply.

"Right away, my lord," he said. "If you will go to your tent and remain there, I shall prepare the men to depart. Will you do this?"

The duke nodded, already picking up the pace as he headed towards the encampment. "Right away," he repeated what Dashiell had said. "Be quick, now. I must return home."

Dashiell was about to reply but he happened to see one of the duke's minders heading in his direction. The man looked as if he were in an utter panic. Upon his heels was the second minder, a large servant whom Dashiell trusted implicitly. His name was Drusus. Though Dashiell trusted Drusus, he didn't trust the other minder, a man named Simon. As Simon came upon his wandering charge, he spoke loudly.

"My lord," he cried. "Where did you go? You were supposed to rest!"

Dashiell wasn't sure the man sounded genuine. "He was on the field of battle again," he said as both Simon and Drusus took hold of the duke. "If I find him there again, I shall take it out on your hides. Is that clear enough?"

Simon nodded nervously, shepherding the duke back to the tent in the muddy field. Drusus was on the other side, looking after the duke with concern, but Dashiell called him back. Quickly, the enormous servant rushed to Dashiell's side.

"Drusus," he said quietly. "Did you see Sir Clayton near Simon? Have you seen them engage in conversation?"

Drusus understood. He shook his head and Dashiell was satisfied. He wasn't sure he believed that Clayton hadn't had any contact with Simon, but at least he hadn't been obvious about it. He sighed heavily.

"Very well," he said, waving a hand in the direction of Simon and the duke. "Go with them. And do not let the man out of your sight. Is that clear?"

Drusus nodded firmly and lumbered off, quickly moving after the duke and Simon. Dashiell watched them go, making sure that Drusus at least moved the duke into his tent, before returning his focus to the battle at hand. Just as he swung around, he came face to face with Christopher de Lohr.

The great Earl of Hereford and Worcester looked as if he'd just seen the wrong end of a fight. The man was battered, his tunic torn, and even his gloves were ripped. Dashiell looked at him curiously.

"What happened to you?" he asked. "Did you go hand-to-hand with a group of unruly barbarians?"

Christopher cocked an eyebrow, pulling off his helm to reveal sticky blond hair and a neatly trimmed beard.

"My horse fell," he muttered. "Some bastard cut the tendons on the fetlocks of both front legs and the horse went down. After I destroyed the man with my bare hands, I had to destroy the horse. Pity; I was attached to him."

Dashiell shook his head in disbelief. "Bloody hell," he said. "I am sorry, Chris. And your sons?"

"Curtis and Richard have fared well."

"That is a relief. But I am still sorry about the horse."

Christopher waved him off, tugging at his ripped gloves. "As I am, but it is done," he said, sounding like a man who was used to too much death and destruction. "How is Savernake? I saw Bent take him from the field."

Dashiell turned around, looking at the tent in the distance where he'd last seen the duke. "Paul the Apostle is being corralled, for now," he said as he turned around to face Christopher again. "Your brother thinks Clayton is responsible."

"Clayton is out for Savernake's seat."

Dashiell eyed his cousin; Christopher was the eldest son of his great-aunt, the sister of his grandfather, Tevin du Reims. He was also several years older than Dashiell, who, at forty years and four, was fairly old himself. David, too, was several years older than Dashiell, both of the de Lohr brothers being older knights who commanded great respect from the rank and file of England's fighting men.

They were legends.

But there was no one who respected them more than Dashiell, meaning he also greatly respected their opinions. They'd been warning Dashiell about Clayton le Cairon since he had married Lady Lily three years ago, and they continued to warn him now. Clayton was the son of a lesser land baron who was extremely wealthy wanted what that wealth couldn't buy him – a dukedom.

Unfortunately, when Savernake passed, the dukedom would revert to his eldest daughter, as the heiress, and Clayton would become the new Duke of Savernake. But Clayton was trying to hasten that day and Dashiell was trying to stop him, because the day Clayton assumed the dukedom was the day Dashiell would leave Ramsbury Castle forever.

At least, he would if it wasn't for one small thing –

A woman.

"Clayton is out for himself," Dashiell said after a moment. "You know the story – the man's father took advantage of Savernake's slipping mind and snatched a marital contract for his son. You even tried to warn the duke, Chris. I know because I was there. But he will not listen. His mind cannot comprehend anything these days but the delusion that he's Paul the Apostle, and the fact that his daughter's husband is out to hasten his demise has no impact on him. You've known for three years the trouble I've gone through to keep Savernake alive."

Christopher was, indeed, aware. Scratching his dirty scalp, he put his helm on his head once more.

"I know," he said. "You have been admirable and noble in that madhouse of Ramsbury. God help you, Dash, truly. I've told you time and time again to leave Savernake and come to Lioncross Abbey with me. You would have such a place of honor in my household; you know that. But you will not come."

Now, they were veering onto a subject that Dashiell didn't like to discuss. He could feel it coming on because whenever they brought up this subject, it always came about.

"Nay," he said, averting his gaze. "I will not come."

Christopher sighed faintly, looking at his cousin with some pity. "Have you ever told her how you feel, Dash?" he asked quietly. "Does the woman even know what you deal with on a daily basis simply to be near her?"

Dashiell shrugged. "It is not her fault that her sister's husband is a scheming bastard."

"Nay, it is not. But it is her fault that you remain because of her. And you've never even told her your feelings?"

Dashiell cleared his throat softly. "There is no point," he said. "I have told you this before, Chris. I am far too old for her. She deserves a young, fine husband. Not an old man past his prime."

Christopher rolled his eyes. "Christ," he hissed. "You *are* in your prime. You have been in your prime for twenty years. You are Dashiell du Reims, Viscount Winterton, heir to the earldom of East Anglia. You will be a great and powerful man when your father passes on and you will need a wife to carry on your legacy. Why not Savernake's youngest daughter?"

He looked at his cousin, then. "Because she is destined for greater men than I."

"There *is* no one greater than you, you dolt."

Dashiell's gaze lingered on him a moment before breaking down into a modest grin; beneath his heavy auburn mustache, it was difficult to see the straight, white teeth and big dimples carving into each cheek.

"She deserves better," he said.

Christopher shook his head in irritation. "Then I am finished with you," he declared. "To hell with you and your ridiculous restraint. I am going to go to Ramsbury myself and tell this woman – what is her name again?"

"Belladonna."

"I am going to tell the woman named after a flowering plant that poisons men that you are in love with her and she must marry you. Who would name their daughter after a deadly flower, anyway?"

Dashiell was trying not to laugh at Christopher's dramatics. "As she told me once, her mother simply liked the way it sounded," he said. "All of her sisters are named after deadly or unpleasant plants – Acacia, Lily, and Belladonna. I think it was her mother's ignorance and nothing else."

Christopher grunted. "Ignorance, indeed," he said. "And utterly disgraceful. If you do not tell Lady Belladonna that you wish to marry her, then I swear to you, I am going to do it. Heed my threat, Dash. You've been in love with this woman for the past few years and it has gone on long enough. It is not fair to the rest of us who crave a wedding to attend."

Dashiell grinned, alleviating the tension. But deep down, he knew his cousin was right. Belladonna Isobel Evangeline de Vaston was twenty years and two, a woman grown, and he first started having feelings for her when she'd turned ten years and six. He'd watched a charming, sweet child grow into a woman of magnificence. That was six years of harboring a secret love for a woman he knew he could never have.

But he had his reasons for not telling her.

"Do you really want to discuss this now?" he finally said, trying to steer Christopher off of the subject. "We've got a battlefield to assess. We've slowed the king's march south considerably and that is something to be proud of. Other allies must know of this great victory, so let us stop talking about me and put the focus where it belongs – on our victory today."

As he'd hoped, Christopher turned to the battlefield where men were now starting to disband. The wounded were limping away, or being carried away, while the dead were being picked over. Overhead, swollen rain clouds had rolled in again and a light sprinkling began.

"It was costly," Christopher said, his manner sobering. "De Winter lost one of his best knights, I lost my horse, and God only knows how many men we lost in total. I suppose we should get on with it so that I can return to my wife. I have not seen her in several months."

Dashiell knew that Christopher was very attached to his lovely wife. "Indeed," he said. "Then let us move on with this quickly so you can go home."

They began to walk towards the field, which was on a slight incline, and the rain began to fall in earnest, creating rivers of red as the blood was washed down the slope. Just as they reached the crest of the hill, surveying the gruesome scene beyond, Christopher spoke quietly.

"I will ask you one question about your lady, Dash, and then I will say no more."

Dashiell was looking at the macabre sight before him. He didn't relish plunging into that mess, but it had to be done. Christopher's statement distracted him for the moment.

"What is it?" he asked.

Christopher turned to look at him, his sky-blue eyes intense. "Take it from a man who was able to marry the woman he loves," he said. "I cannot imagine my life without her. If you do not marry your Belladonna, she will become someone else's wife. Can you really stand the thought of that?"

He didn't even wait for an answer. Without another word, he headed out into the muddy, bloody field, leaving his last question ringing in Dashiell's ears.

Can you really stand the thought of that?

He couldn't.

CHAPTER ONE

March, Year of Our Lord 1216 A.D.
Ramsbury Castle, Wiltshire

IT WAS AN explosion of puppies.

Someone left the door open to the shelter where two big hunting dogs, bred by knights of Ramsbury, were nursing their young pups, and suddenly there were puppies running all over the kitchen yard in the rain and having a marvelous time.

Belladonna de Vaston suspected it was a planned move, because when she ran outside after hearing the cook's cries, she saw several children belonging to the servants rushing about with the puppies, all of them getting muddy and wet.

Puppies were wagging and licking, the children were giggling and playing, and it all seemed like great fun except for the fact that the army had been sighted on the horizon not a half-hour earlier and were quickly approaching. The knights wouldn't like to see their valuable puppies rushing all about in a crazed bit of fun.

"Hurry!" Belladonna was rushing about, trying to corral both the puppies and the children. "Put the pups back with their mothers! The army is approaching and we do not want them to see that we have released the hounds!"

Servant children were picking the puppies up, who were actually quite large, and carrying the licking, squirming beasts back to their home. Belladonna stood at the door to the shelter, preparing to shut it as soon as all of the puppies were returned, hurrying the children along.

All of Ramsbury was in an uproar with the returning army. It was a bright winter's day, with blue sky and scattered clouds overhead, and mud and filth and a dead-cold earth beneath.

Ramsbury Castle rose in the midst of this dead land, like a beacon of gray stones and grace and honor. It sat in the middle of a plain, with forests all around it in the distance. There was a small village nearby, the small wooden structures of the village seemingly cowering in the shadow of the massive castle walls.

There was an equally enormous bailey within those walls, with an array of outbuildings including the great hall, stables, and troop houses. And then a nasty moat in the center of the bailey with an island in it. A massive keep rose forth on the island.

The keep was unique in every way. Shaped like a four-leafed clover, it had three stories rising out of the island, with an open courtyard in the center of the structure, the heart of the clover. It had several large rooms on all floors, plus a myriad of smaller chambers, alcoves, and hidden stairwells to get from one floor to the next. The first Duke of Savernake had the place designed by Savoy artisans and built from local stone. He'd had a large family and valued his privacy, so his logic was to build more rooms to keep his children away from him.

But his massive keep had lasted into its second century, and now it was filled with the current duke and his family, including Belladonna. It was her home, but it was also a place of routine and traditions. It had the odd feeling of being both a revered family structure and military fortress.

At the moment, Belladonna was focused on the latest tradition, something her father had come to expect since he'd awoken one morning and declared that he was Paul the Apostle. Since then, everything had to be a certain way, especially when he was returning home from battle.

Once, the old duke had read in the bible about palms and Palm

Sunday, when Christ was welcomed back to Jerusalem. He'd wanted palms to welcome him home, but there were no trees with palm fronds in England, so he had to settle for rushes.

Now, with the army approaching, every man, woman, and child was turning out to see the return of the army with boughs of leaves in their hands. If Jesus was given a hero's welcome those centuries ago, then surely Paul the Apostle was deserving of one, too.

But nothing could happen until the puppies were put away. When the last mutt was put into the shelter, Belladonna closed the door and bolted it, breathing a sigh of relief. She could hear the soldiers on the battlements taking up the cry and she knew that the portcullis must be lifting. Everyone seemed to be running in that direction.

"Bella!" A woman in fine clothing suddenly appeared in the kitchen yard, her pale face alight with excitement. "Papa is home! You must hurry!"

Belladonna rushed towards the woman, pulling off the apron she was wearing and smoothing at the expensive dress underneath. She tossed the apron into the open kitchen door, knowing the cook or another servant would pick it up.

"I am ready," she said, smoothing her reddish-blonde hair off her face, trying to straighten up the heavy braid that hung over one shoulder. "How do I look?"

Acacia de Vaston eyed her younger sister; how did she look? Beautiful, like she always did. But Acacia was so jealous of the woman's beauty that she would never tell her that. Besides… beauty was pure vanity, and Acacia didn't indulge vanity. As a woman preparing to enter the cloister, vanity had no place in her life.

At least, she pretended it didn't.

"Like any other woman," she said, annoyed, as she grabbed her sister by the hand and the two of them began to run. "If you are not there when Papa enters the bailey, then he will become angry. Hurry!"

She was tugging on Belladonna enough to pull the woman's arm from her socket. Belladonna finally had to pull free from her sister's grip simply to save the wear and tear on her arm.

Passing through the kitchen yard's fortified wall, they ended up in the main bailey of Ramsbury, a vast stretch of property that contained outbuildings, trades and other various structures. It was full of people now that the soldiers at the gatehouse were starting to lift the dual portcullises, and the front line of the army was entering.

There was excitement all around, as the army had been gone for almost three months. Wives, lovers, children, and servants had turned out to welcome the army home, waving rushes because that was what the duke demanded. Paul the Apostle always returned to a hero's welcome, and that was what he was given.

As Acacia and Belladonna rushed across the compound, another young woman joined them. The Lady Lily de Vaston le Cairon, the eldest of the three sisters, had a handful of rushes, extending them to her sisters. Acacia took a branch, followed by Belladonna. As Acacia rushed forward to make sure she was the first of the sisters to be seen by their father, Lily and Belladonna hung back. In fact, Lily hung back so much that Belladonna turned to the woman curiously.

"Lily?" she asked, reaching her hand out to the woman. "Come along, sweetling. Your husband is returning home."

Lily wasn't the least bit excited or impressed by that. "I know," she said, eyeing the gatehouse as the army began to come through. "We received no word that he had been killed in battle, so I suppose that means I must face the man."

Belladonna stopped trying to pull her sister along. She came to a halt, holding Lily's hand, feeling the impact of her words.

She knew Lily didn't love her husband. Everyone knew, including her husband. Lily was a lovely, curvy woman, much-accomplished, and she'd been forced to marry a man whose only ambition in life was wealth and title. Lily had no desire to marry Clayton le Cairon because her first, and only love, was Bentley of Ashbourne.

She'd fallen in love with the knight when he'd come to Ramsbury, but the duke's senility had been taking hold at the time and Clayton's father had been able to convince the duke to marry his unworthy son to the heiress of Savernake.

It made for a horrible situation, even worse three years later. Lily and Clayton hated one another, while Lily and Bentley's love remained strong. But they never acted upon it, mostly because Bentley was an honorable knight and would never demonstrate his feelings to another man's wife.

Belladonna had watched her sister go from a lovely, vivacious woman to an embittered, miserable creature in those three years. She knew that Lily didn't want to greet the incoming army because she didn't want to see Bentley and she most certainly didn't want to see Clayton.

There was misery all around.

"Be brave." Belladonna squeezed her sister's hand. "Mayhap Clayton will not even care that he has come home. Mayhap… he will leave you alone this night and seek his comfort elsewhere."

Lily snorted. "I could only be so fortunate," she said. "He wants a son, you know. He will not pass up any opportunity to get me with child."

Belladonna could hear the desolation in her sister's voice. "He still does not know about the pessaries you use?"

Lily shook her head at her dark little secret. "Nor will he," she said. "As long as I use the pessaries, the apothecary promised I would not conceive a child. My only hope is that I remain barren and Clayton annuls the marriage. But, alas, that would be too much to ask. He wants the Savernake dukedom too much."

Belladonna simply squeezed her sister's hand again. She didn't know what to say, as this was a topic of conversation they'd been having for three years. Clayton wanted a son and forced himself upon his reluctant wife whenever he could. But Lily had gone to an apothecary in Marlborough and obtained pessaries, small pebbles of ingredients, guaranteed to prevent her from conceiving. That was her rebellion against the marriage Clayton had forced upon her. But she was quite certain that if he ever found out about the pessaries, he would beat her soundly.

It was, therefore, a secret to be held fast, by both sisters. Belladonna continued holding Lily's hand as she turned to the gatehouse, noting that the bulk of the army was now entering, including their father. He rode a tiny palfrey because he was convinced that Paul the Apostle would ride such a thing and not a fine horse, so the little palfrey was moving its legs furiously to keep up with the big warhorses that surrounded it.

The moment the duke came through the gatehouse, he pulled his palfrey to a stop and climbed off. Everyone greeting the incoming army began to cheer wildly and wave their rushes about, and the duke lifted his hands in a gesture to bless the crowd. The roar was nearly deafening as people cheered him on, and he walked past them, blessing them, receiving kisses to his hands, and generally accepting their accolades.

Lily wasn't watching any of it; she kept her gaze averted, unwilling to see her husband in that crowd and not wanting to see Bentley, who had dismounted his horse and was walking along behind the duke. But Belladonna was watching everything closely.

It was difficult for her to see what her father had become. The madness that gripped his mind had come on very quickly around the time that Clayton's father came to seek Lily's hand in marriage for his son. It was as if one moment her father was completely sane and in the next, he believed himself to be Paul the Apostle. There were moments that Belladonna swore she saw her father as he used to be, the calm and loving man she adored. But those moments were far and few between. Lately, it seemed as if they were gone completely.

So, she was left with a father who believed he was an apostle and a family in turmoil. Lily hated her husband, Acacia was a bitter shrew who was determined to join the cloister because she did not wish to marry at all, and then there was her…

"I see Dash, Bella," Lily said. "See him? He is handing off the horses to the stable servants."

Belladonna's heart jumped at the mention of the man's name. *Dash.* Straining, she caught a glimpse of him as he moved through the crowd, heading towards the duke, who was blessing an ill child held aloft by a servant. As he stood next to the duke and pulled off his helm revealing his cropped auburn hair, Belladonna simply stared at him from afar.

It seemed that all she ever did was stare at him from afar.

"Bella?" Lily said softly, now squeezing her sister's hand. "It is good to see Dash, is it not? He looks healthy and whole after battle."

Belladonna didn't dare look at her sister, the one who knew all of her secrets. What was the use of rehashing what they both knew? Belladonna harbored a secret love for a knight who was unattainable, the heir to the earldom of East Anglia and a man who had been with Savernake for twelve years. Literally, half of Belladonna's life. What good was it to discuss the man she'd been in love with since the moment she saw him, a twelve-year-old girl who was awestruck by the big, handsome knight who had come to her father through an alliance with the Stewards of Rochester?

A knight who still viewed her as a twelve-year-old child.

"I see him," Belladonna sighed, a resigned gesture. "He does look healthy."

Lily placed her head on her sister's slender shoulder. "Mayhap, you should go and greet him," she suggested gently. "I am sure he would be happy to see you."

Belladonna pulled her hand from her sister's grip. "As Bentley would be glad to see you," she said in a cruel jab, which she was immediately sorry for. "I am sorry, Lil. I did not mean it. It is simply that there is no use in greeting him. It only makes me… hurt."

With that, she turned and walked away, heading towards their father but trying to steer clear of Dashiell, which was difficult considering he was following the duke. Belladonna simply wanted her father to see her and then she would go anywhere that Dashiell wasn't.

It wasn't as if she hadn't thought about the man, every moment of every day since he'd been gone, because she had. It was more that it was becoming increasingly painful to see a man who had no interest in her. It wasn't that he ignored her, because he didn't. He was as kind and attentive and polite as Dashiell was capable of. To everyone else, he was the gruff, hardened commander who ruled the Savernake army with an iron fist. But to Belladonna, he was the handsome, slightly awkward knight who always went out of his way to be polite to her.

Perhaps that was why she loved him so.

Even now, she stole a glimpse of him as he stood behind her father, protective of the duke as he always was. Dashiell was a tall man, but she'd seen taller. He was, quite simply, a very big man. He had enormous shoulders and arms, and big hands that were scarred from fighting. His auburn hair was stiff, with a natural curl to it, and he kept it closely shorn against his scalp. He was usually clean-shaven except for a big mustache he kept neatly groomed, and he told her once it was because he had a scar on his upper lip that he covered up.

Belladonna had never seen the scar, but she couldn't imagine it would make the man any less attractive. He may have been older, and sporting a face with some lines in it but, to her, he was the most handsome man in the entire world.

She was so caught up in her daydreams that she didn't really notice when her father turned in her direction. Suddenly, he was moving in her direction, his hands lifted to greet her. But all Belladonna saw was Dashiell turning towards her. He was coming in her direction, too, and she very nearly bolted until she heard her father's voice calling out to her.

"My darling!" he called happily, arms extended. "My darling lass!"

It was too late to run. Deeply embarrassed that she'd been caught staring at Dashiell, who had more than likely seen her, Belladonna smiled wanly at her father as the man put his arms around her and hugged her tightly.

"Papa," she said, hugging him in return. "Praise God that you have returned to us."

Edward kissed his daughter on both cheeks before pulling back to look at her. "Grace," he murmured, touching her face. "You grow more beautiful by the day."

Grace. That was Belladonna's mother, long dead these past eight years. "Papa, it is Belladonna," she said, firmly and loudly, because sometimes he had a difficult time hearing. "It is not Grace, Papa – it is Bella."

Edward started at her for a moment or two before recognition dawned. "My baby," he said, touching her face again. "My beautiful Bella."

Belladonna forced a smile as he moved past her, heading towards Acacia, who was standing several feet away. Belladonna watched him go, the smile fading from her lips, feeling sad that her father couldn't even recognize her. Every day seemed to show his worsening madness. As she stood there, she heard someone clear his throat, softly.

"Greetings, my lady," Dashiell said politely. "I hope you have been well during our time away."

Startled, Belladonna turned to him, her gaze drinking in his handsome face. She always found it fascinating that the man had eyes so blue they were nearly lavender. He had the most beautiful eyes, at least to her. It was a struggle not to react giddily at the sight of him, a man she didn't want to see, but now a man she was very glad to see.

It did her heart good.

"I have been well, thank you," she said. "And you look as if you have come through unscathed."

"I have."

"And my father?" she asked, tearing her eyes away from Dashiell to watch her father hug Acacia. "Did he fare well?"

Dashiell glanced at Edward also. "Well enough," he said. "But, in the future, I believe it would be better to leave him here at Ramsbury. You and I will have to insist upon this to le Cairon the next time he wants the duke to ride at the head of the army. The battlefield is no place for your father these days."

Belladonna turned to him, studying him for a moment. "Did he wander out onto the battlefield again to bless the dying and the wounded?"

Dashiell sighed heavily as he nodded. "Aye," he said. "I am genuinely fearful for his safety these days, my lady. It would be far better if he remained here the next time the army moves out."

Belladonna's gaze drifted over Dashiell. "You are concerned for him."

"Verily."

Belladonna smiled faintly. "You have always been concerned for him," she said. "I cannot tell you how grateful I am for it. My father would be far worse off were it not for you, Dash. You care for the man as if he were your very own father. In fact, I believe you are the son he always hoped to have."

Dashiell returned her smile; he couldn't help himself. But in that gesture, he could feel all of the walls of self-protection go down. That always happened with Belladonna, his feelings for the woman razing whatever attempts he made at putting up a wall around his fragile heart.

It *was* fragile when it came to her.

"You know how I feel about your father," he said simply. "Next to my own father, the duke has been the greatest influence on me. I will protect him until my death."

Before Belladonna could reply, there was a great commotion near the gatehouse. People were screaming and trying to move swiftly out of the way as a knight on a big, brown warhorse came charging through them. He knocked over a man, who had to scramble out of the way to avoid being trampled.

Sir Clayton le Cairon had made an appearance.

Belladonna's features darkened at the sight of him. Clayton was tall and lanky, with protruding teeth, a receding hairline, and eyes that seemed to hold a perpetually surprised expression. He was a very sharp man but transparent in his wants and desires. There wasn't much he hid, so everyone knew him for what he was, which could be both a blessing and a curse. It was those attributes that singlehandedly made him the most hated man at Ramsbury.

"So," Belladonna muttered. "He has returned. A pity."

Dashiell looked at her, hearing the loathing in her voice. But, as always, Dashiell remained emotionless about Clayton, one way or the other. He had to fight with the man and he didn't want to be watching his back any more than he already was if le Cairon suspected his open hatred.

Even now, things with the man were dicey at best. Clayton saw him as direct competition, especially since he commanded the duke's armies, and the man was crafty. The only real saving grace was that the army and the knights were fiercely loyal to Dashiell, while Clayton had very little support. Dashiell did his best to keep the balance of power in that mode because once Clayton gained in strength, it would mean trouble for them all.

"Aye, he has returned," he said, shifting the subject because he wouldn't waste his breath on Clayton le Cairon. "Your father's army was victorious against the king. It was a fine showing, my lady. Your father should be proud."

Belladonna's gaze moved from Clayton back to Dashiell, which was much more pleasant viewing in her opinion. As the duke began to head towards the keep, Dashiell and Belladonna followed.

"I am sure he would be, if he realized it," she said. "But, of course, you lead the armies, Dash. To you goes the credit."

Modestly, he shook his head. "Not this time," he said. "There were many armies involved. You know that we headed north because the king's army was laying siege to some of the northern barons. North of Lincoln, we met up with the de Winter army out of Norfolk and my father's army from Thunderbey Castle and traveled with them all the way to Scarborough. It was a massive show of force."

"Oh?" Belladonna said with interest. "Did you see your father, then?"

Dashiell shook his head. "Nay," he said. "My father's health prevents him from traveling with the armies these days, unfortunately. I thought that I would like to see him after this particular campaign. I've not seen him in several months."

"You should go," Belladonna agreed. "I am sure your father would love to see you."

Dashiell's gaze moved to Clayton, who was several feet away, dismounting his frothing steed as he moved to greet his wife.

"Mayhap, I will see him at some point," he said, his gaze lingering on Clayton. "But now is not the time. There is much happening with the king and his barons. I cannot take a leisure trip to Suffolk to visit my father, not with so much happening."

Belladonna could see who he was looking at. She knew, as they all knew, that Dashiell would never leave Ramsbury with Clayton on the prowl. It wasn't merely the tension between the king and his barons, but the tension at Ramsbury with Clayton's disruptive presence.

As she and Dashiell watched, Clayton couldn't have said more than two words to Lily before coldly brushing her off. Ignoring the family completely, the man headed for the keep, alone.

He behaved as if he didn't want to be part of the de Vaston family. There was always a palpable relief when Clayton was out of sight. Once he was gone, Belladonna turned to Dashiell.

"Did he lead my father out onto the field of battle this time?" she asked quietly.

Dashiell came to a halt, looking at her with a furrowed brow. "Why should you ask such a thing?"

Belladonna sighed impatiently. "You need not pretend, Dash," she said. "I know you believe you have been protecting my sisters and me from the truth, but you do not need to do that any longer. The rumors fly fast around here; we have heard that Clayton is trying to kill my father. We have been hearing that for a while."

Dashiell simply looked at her, with no particular emotion on his face. It was true that he'd been trying to protect the daughters of the duke from Clayton and his motives, but he knew, at some point, others would speak of the man's behavior. Rumors had already started, whispers he couldn't control. He couldn't protect Belladonna and her sisters forever, as much as he wanted to.

"You will let me worry about that," he said quietly. "You need not be troubled, my lady. I will always protect your father. And you. And your sisters, of course."

He said the last few words quickly, as if realizing what he'd said sounded a bit too personal. Even so, there was something in his voice when he spoke to her, something soft that Belladonna didn't hear when he spoke to anyone else. Only her. It was enough to give her giddy heart hope that, perhaps, the softness in his tone indicated his feelings towards her. But she knew that was too much to ask.

"You used to call me Bella," she said after a moment. "Why is it that you have become so formal with me, Dash? I can remember all through my younger years, you would call me Bella. I can even remember you calling me 'lamb' from time to time. What has happened that you no longer address me so? Have I done something to anger you?"

Something flickered in his eyes, something liquid and warm that was just as quickly gone. "Of course not," he scoffed quietly. "You could never anger me."

"Then why…"

"Because you are a maiden of marriageable age now, and it is not right that I should address you informally," he said, interrupting her. "You are an adult, as am I. As an unmarried man, it is greatly frowned upon that I should have any familiarity when addressing you. Some might even view it as bold and lewd. Therefore, I will not risk that with you. I have been addressing you formally for the past year or two, at the very least."

"I know."

"And you are only just asking me this now?"

Belladonna suddenly felt very embarrassed. It was almost as if he were scolding her, explaining to her that, clearly, he had no intention of ever being informal with her again. She had seen twenty years and two now, and was quite old for an unmarried woman. Dashiell would never do anything unseemly towards her, the honorable man that he was.

But, sometimes, she wished he would be bold and lewd. God, she wished it with all her heart.

"Then you will forgive me for asking," she said, feeling her cheeks flame as she turned away. "I would not wish for you to do anything improper or against your wishes. You will excuse me, my lord. I must tend to my father."

She rushed off before Dashiell could stop her. His heart sank as he heard anger in her words, anger directed at him. He hadn't meant to offend her, but it was the truth. He didn't want to be viewed as taking liberties with an unmarried daughter of a duke, no matter how much he wanted to.

And he wanted very badly to.

With a heavy heart, Dashiell watched her approach her father and take him gently by the arm, directing him into the keep where she would help tend to his every need. She was a good daughter that way. Dashiell only wished she understood that what he did, he did to protect her and her reputation. Given the choice, he would not only be informal with the woman, but he might even tell her how he felt about her.

Dashiell came to a halt just before entering the keep, watching the rest of the family and a few servants go inside. He didn't go with them because he had an army to disband. So with the duke safely indoors, Dashiell headed back into the bailey where men were already underway in moving the provisions wagons back to the stables and the army over to the troop house. As he moved into the dust and noise of the dissolving army, that was when the gruff, no-nonsense knight came out.

"What are you doing?" he boomed to one of the wagon drivers, who drove his horses right into the back of another wagon. "You slop-eyed fool! Pull back on those beasts and let the other wagon pass!"

Dashiell du Reims commanded presence and the insults that went with it were legendary. He'd been known to insult his army into hysterics at times, but the men moved more swiftly because of it. Long ago, they'd learned that du Reims only insulted as a way of motivation. If he insulted you, then he liked you. Woe betide the man he did not insult, for that was a man quickly on his way out of Savernake's army.

Therefore, the insults were normal in their world and it made the men want to work harder and faster when he did so. It was the odd way Dashiell du Reims had earned the respect of his men, at least for the most part, but he'd mostly earned it for his skill and strength. He was a giant among the powerful knights of England.

But that powerful knight had one weakness, and she was currently tending her father inside the keep of Ramsbury. Dashiell tried not to think about Belladonna's unhappy face as he went about his tasks, hoping that her anger against him would cool by the time the evening meal came. And then, he might – but only *might* – try to explain to her that he didn't address her formally not because he wanted to, but because he had to. Perhaps, she would understand.

Perhaps not.

God's Blood, it was dangerous for him to try and explain his position on anything personal when it came to Belladonna. But having not seen her in two months, the last thing he wanted was for her to be angry at him his first night returned. But more and more, he was coming to realize something – the more time passed, and the more his feelings deepened, the more difficult it would be for him to refrain from telling her.

And that would be a disaster for all concerned.

Dashiell remembered Christopher's offer for him to serve at Lioncross Abbey with the de Lohr army. It had been an offer Christopher had given him many times but, at this moment, it was the first time he'd actually considered it.

Truth was, he wasn't entirely sure now much longer he could remain with Belladonna and not tell her what he was feeling. Christopher had asked him how he would feel if the woman married another man – it would be the worst day of his life.

Unfortunately, it was a very real possibility unless he did something about it.

CHAPTER TWO

"DRINK THIS, PAPA." Belladonna held the pewter cup for her father as he slurped. "That's right, drink all of it. It will help you sleep."

Edward pulled the cup away, licking his lips. He was seated on a lavishly carved chair in the middle of his equally lavish bower, as his servants dressed him after his bath and his daughters fussed over him.

As always, Belladonna took the lead with her father. When he was home, she supervised his waking hours, giving orders to the small army of servants who tended him, including the two minders that Dashiell had assigned to him. Belladonna had a kind manner about her, but a firm one, and the servants respected her a great deal.

Even as Belladonna looked after her father, it was Lily who had taken over duties of chatelaine for the duke's castle when her mother had died. She, too, was very skilled in her household duties. So between Belladonna seeing to the comfort of the duke and Lily seeing to the details of the castle, Ramsbury was run quite efficiently.

Acacia, the middle sister, also had her function in the house and hold, although she tended to be an elitist when it came to any work. It was an attitude that would not serve her well with her intention of joining the cloister. Belladonna had tried to tell her that, as had the priest from the cathedral in Marlborough, but Acacia wasn't one to listen. She seemed to think that the nuns of Amesbury Abbey, her chosen destination, would simply let her do as she pleased given the fact that the Duke of Savernake was a patron and also because Acacia's sizable dowry would be donated to the abbey upon her commitment.

All Acacia wanted to do was read her bible, or sew the lace she was so fond of, or walk in the garden. She really had no ambition more than that. Compared to Lily's quiet beauty and Belladonna's magnificence, Acacia was tall and slender, with bright red hair and a plain face, and Belladonna had always suspected that the woman simply felt unmarriageable and embarrassed against her two sisters. Men would always look at Lily and Belladonna, but never Acacia. Much like her namesake, a bitter and thorny tree, Acacia was, indeed, bitter and, at times, thorny.

Even now, as Belladonna coaxed her father into drinking a sleeping potion and Lily made sure the servants freshened his bed, Acacia made no move to help other than to sit in front of him with her bible in her hand, slowly reading the passages from the book of Esther.

Acacia had been educated, as her sisters had been, but she wasn't a very good reader. Her slow, monotone voice filled the air as everyone else around her was moving with a purpose.

"… and all the king's servants who were at the king's gate bowed down and did obeisance to Haman; for the king had so commanded concerning him," she read. "But Mordecai did not bow down or do obeisance. Then the king's servants who were at the king's gate said to Mordecai, 'Why do you disobey the king's command'?"

Before she could continue, Edward leaned forward and patted the beautifully drawn pages of her expensive bible. "Read to me of the modesty of women, my child," he said. "Why is *your* head not covered?"

Acacia looked up from her reading. "It shall be, soon enough," she said. "Remember, Papa? I am going to Amesbury next month. I will take my vows soon."

He simply looked at her as if he had no idea what she was talking about. "I must speak to your husband," he said firmly. "He should not permit you to display yourself so. It is against God's wishes, my child."

Acacia sighed heavily. "I have no husband, Papa. I am due to join the cloister next month."

Edward simply wagged a finger at her in a disapproving manner and sat back in his chair, yawning because of the sleeping potion he'd been given. The man couldn't even join the feasts in the great hall any longer because he completely disrupted them with his rages or his blessings, which physics had told the family were symptoms of his madness. It was far easier to feed him in his chamber and put him to sleep for the night, watched over by his minders.

As the duke was showing his disapproval to his middle daughter, Belladonna was making sure his tonic was measured out in case he awoke in the middle of the night. His sleep was sporadic, at best, and the physics had prescribed a poppy powder mixed in wine to create a tonic that would see him sleep soundly, at least for a while.

But even as Belladonna mixed, she was listening to her father and his clear disapproval of Acacia, who lacked self-confidence enough that she didn't need her senile father kicking her down further. Acacia was patiently trying to remind their father that she was cloister-bound, but Edward didn't seem to think a woman who was not modest was good cloister material. As Belladonna listened to them argue, Lily came up beside her.

"Are you finished with his sleeping draught?" she asked.

Belladonna nodded, stirring it well as she took a glance around the room. "All of these people must leave," she said. "Why so many servants? They only agitate him, Lily."

Lily was already nodding. "I know, but they brought his baggage up from the wagons," she said. Then, she turned from her sister and clapped her hands sharply to get everyone's attention. "Everyone must leave immediately. The duke must rest and he cannot do it with an audience. Go, now."

Servants and soldiers alike began moving for the chamber door, a great arched doorway with an intricately carved corbel. The panel itself was made from cedar wood, brought all the way from Rome, and it was quite beautiful.

Drusus held the door open for the soldiers and servants to leave, clearing the chamber in short order as Lily and Belladonna followed behind them, making sure everyone was pushed out and their father had some peace. But just as the last person wandered out, Clayton wandered in.

Then, it was as if someone had dropped a curtain; the room instantly went dark and moody. Catching a glimpse of Clayton was all it took for the women to demur, turning away from a man who was genuinely hated and feared throughout Ramsbury. Belladonna saw the man as he entered, turning to Lily to see how her sister was reacting to the presence of her hated husband. To Lily's credit, she maintained a stony expression, one she always maintained when looking at the man who had ruined her life.

Lily didn't speak to him, however. She simply turned back to her duties, busying herself over by the bed as Belladonna remained next to their father, trying to coax the man into rising. But Clayton had other ideas. He went up to the old duke, still sitting in his chair, and braced both hands on the arms of the chair, preventing Edward from rising. Belladonna stiffened as Clayton smiled his gap-toothed smile.

"It was a great victory, my lord," he said rather loudly. "Your presence, as always, inspired the men."

Edward's memory of Clayton had left him long ago. As he looked at the man, he truly didn't know who he was. He simply lifted his hand to bless him.

"Go with God, my son," he said.

Clayton stared at him a moment before chuckling, as one does when ridiculing the less fortunate. Then, he stood straight as Belladonna practically pushed him out of the way in order to help her father stand up from the chair. Clayton's gaze was on his wife's luscious younger sister.

"Take good care of the duke, Bella," he said in an utterly insincere tone. "We must take very good care of the man. He is a great inspiration to the troops and we want him well rested for when we depart again."

Belladonna didn't rise to his sickly comment, but Lily did. "Oh?" she said. "You will be leaving again, soon?"

Clayton turned to her, his blue eyes glittering with what could be construed as contempt. He didn't really hate the woman, but he had no use for her. She meant nothing to him. Reaching out, he pinched her chin between his thumb and forefinger.

"Do not sound so hopeful, my sweet," he said. "You and I will have plenty of time to become reacquainted."

That wasn't what Lily wanted to hear and she had to make a conscious effort not to appear repulsed. "It was simply a question, Husband," she said as she turned back to the bed where Belladonna was helping her father climb in. "Whether you go to war or remain at Ramsbury, it is all the same to me. I care not either way."

Clayton cocked an eyebrow at her disrespectful comment, but he didn't explode at her; he rarely did. Instead, he took a dig at her, which was his way. He liked to beat her down with sly insults.

"Nor I," he said. "I do not want your love or your kindness, my pet. I've never asked for either. I already have the most valuable thing you have to offer, which is the marriage. That is all you are worth."

With that, he turned away, but not before he passed a glance at Acacia, who had been listening to the exchange. When she saw that Clayton's focus was on her, she quickly lowered her head and went back to her bible. She pretended to be focused on it as he quit the chamber. Much like her sisters, she didn't like confrontation with the man any more than they did, so it was best to keep a low profile when he was around. At least, that's what she did in public.

But what she did in private was another thing entirely.

THE FEAST TO welcome home the duke's returning army was always a grand occasion and tonight was no exception.

Since they'd received word of the army's impending arrival the day before, Lily had been able to make preparations for the meal. Fowl had been slaughtered and stewed, baked into pies, and fish from the pond in the kitchen yard had been caught and roasted over an open flame. An entire cow, which had been slaughtered weeks before and the sides aging in the cold vault, had been brought forth and prepared in a variety of ways but, mostly, it was simply roasted over the large spit in the kitchen yard, hand-turned by an old servant.

Therefore, the smells of roasting meat wafted upon the still evening air, strong enough to singe nose hairs. Dashiell had been smelling it for the past two hours and he had to admit that he was ready to eat. The first night back from a battle campaign, strangely enough, was always one of high energy and festivities. The men from the army would gather in the bailey and partake of the feast while, inside the cavernous hall, senior soldiers, knights, and the family would eat in shelter and warmth.

Men were happy on occasions such as this, happy to have survived another battle campaign, and eager to celebrate. As Dashiell walked from the knight's quarters through the bailey, he was greeting with soldiers congratulating him on their victory against the king. Dash had an excellent relationship with his soldiers, which was why Clayton had been so ineffective in the power struggle.

As Dashiell walked through the muddy bailey, dotted with small fires as the men sat around the flames and ate and sang, he was stopped every few steps by his men. Some wanted simply to talk, while others gave him gifts and pieces of tribute, mostly stolen from dead enemy soldiers. Dash was given two lovely daggers, a coin purse, and a finely studded belt before one man gave him a magnificent broadsword that had come from Scarborough, taken from a Teutonic mercenary knight fighting for the king.

It was a truly expensive and beautiful piece, with a lion's head hilt and rubies for the eyes. When Dashiell insisted the man keep it, the soldier relayed that it was a sword only a knight could use. When Dashiell finally made his way into the great hall of Ramsbury, he was loaded down with enough weapons to single-handedly take the castle.

"Dash!" a knight called to him, cup in hand and congenial, until he saw all of the weapons Dashiell was holding. Then, he came to a halt and pointed. "What's this? Who did you rob?"

Dashiell fought off a grin. "It looks that way, does it not?" he said. "Every soldier in the bailey had some manner of gift for me. I am so weighted down that I will surely sink to the center of the earth at any moment."

Sir Aston Summerlin laughed softly. A very big man with blond hair, dark eyes, and a brilliant smile, he had been under Dashiell's command for four years. Aston and Bentley of Ashbourne constituted Dashiell's senior knight command. There were three other lesser knights, very young men who mostly kept to themselves but were eager to obey, but Aston and Bentley were close to Dashiell, and he relied on them heavily.

"Let us find you and your weapons a drink, man," Aston said, slapping Dashiell on the shoulder as they made their way into the warm, stale hall. "Of everyone in this chamber, you are the one who truly deserves the chance to relax. It has been a hard few months, with you assuming the burdens for all of us."

By this time, he'd led Dashiell over to the long, scrubbed table at the base of the dais where the duke and his family sat. This was the knight's table, and only invited soldiers were allowed to sit there. Dashiell saw that the table was already half-full with senior soldiers, men Dashiell had fought with since his very first day at Ramsbury, and he approved of the guest list. But he scowled when he drew near.

"God's Bones," he muttered. "Someone left the door to the nunnery open and now all we have are women at the table. Aston, you surely should have beaten off this group of wretched females."

The table exploded in laughter as Dashiell began setting all of his newly-acquired weapons on the tabletop. The men saw all of the lovely weaponry and began to paw through it as a servant handed Dashiell a cup of wine. He took a long, satisfying drink as he watched Aston pick up the magnificent broadsword and hold it aloft for all to admire.

"That came off of a Teutonic mercenary, so I am told," he told Aston. "Stealing his weapon is the least I can do to the bastard who came to my country seeking to support a corrupt king."

"He deserves it," Aston said firmly, inspecting the blade. "This is a truly spectacular piece, Dash."

"I know."

"Do you intend to use it in battle?"

Dashiell lifted his cups to his lips again. "Mayhap," he said. "It would be an honor for a man to be killed with a weapon like that."

The men at the table heartily agreed. They continued to inspect the sword, and the other weapons, as Dashiell's gaze moved around the room. There were three big tables in the two-storied hall with a minstrel's gallery above, and an enormous hearth that burped black smoke into the chamber. The table on the dais was empty, but the other table was overflowing with tenured soldiers and men who had seniority in the ranks.

Harried servants were delivering trenchers to that table as men drank and laughed. One of them sat on the end of the table and strummed his *citole*, a stringed instrument, and sang off-key for those who would listen.

It was the same soldier who believed himself quite a musician and during the battle campaigned, had played his instrument nightly and begged men to pay him a pence for the privilege of hearing him. Men would pay him to go away, which was how he made his money. He wasn't very talented, but he had courage. Dashiell couldn't the fault the man for that.

As he drained his cup and held it up for a servant to refill, Bentley entered the hall. Dashiell watched his friend and comrade approach the table; Bentley had seen twenty years and six, a fine knight from a deeply religious and crusading family. With his brown hair and bright blue eyes, he was the object of many a maiden's attention, but the only one who had his attention had long since married a bastard of a man.

Dashiell knew that Bentley had feelings for Lily, but it wasn't something they discussed any longer. The year that Lily married Clayton, it was all they spoke of. But since the marriage, Bentley hadn't said a word. He was crushed by it but pretended otherwise.

Yet, Dashiell could see it on the man's face every time he laid his gaze on Lily. He thought it rather ironic, in truth – Bentley yearned after Lily while Dashiell yearned after Belladonna, and neither knight could ever have the object of his desire.

Sad irony, indeed.

"Bent," Dashiell called to the man, waving him over. "Come and see my marvelous collection of weaponry."

Bentley headed in Dashiell's direction, his focus on the big sword that Aston was still holding. He stopped in his tracks, blinked, and pointed.

"Where did you get that?" he demanded.

Dashiell sipped from his cup. "One of the men gave it to me," he said. "He took it from a dead Teutonic knight."

Bentley looked at him in surprise. "I have seen that sword, and it was *not* in the grip of a Teutonic knight."

"Where did you see it?"

"De Blondeville had it."

Now it was Dashiell's turn to be surprised. "And he was fighting for the king, was he not?"

"He was. And not very well."

It was a gleeful thought on a hated enemy. Dashiell laughed into his cup.

"Now his sword is mine. The man lost the battle *and* his weapon. That's a piss-poor excuse for a warrior, indeed."

Bentley took a seat next to Dashiell as more wine was brought forth in heavy pewter pitchers with the stamp of Savernake on the side. Dishes were being delivered to the tables, a sure indication that the duke's family was expected imminently.

As soldiers crowded into the great hall and more servants poured in from the side entrances with food, the duke's family and retainers finally emerged from the main entry. Immediately, men began to cheer at the sight of their beloved duke's daughters, making sure to respectfully acknowledge the women, the only heirs to a great dukedom.

And then, there was Clayton.

Clayton soaked up the adoration as if it was meant for him even though the men were clearly welcoming the women. Dashiell, Bentley, and Aston watched the procession towards the dais. When Aston glanced at Dashiell to see what his reaction was to Clayton assuming the cheers were for him, Dashiell simply rolled his eyes.

However, none of them said a word because Clayton was drawing close and they didn't want him to overhear anything that might be spoken. They had contempt for the man, but they never voiced it in front of others. Clayton seemed fixed on Dashiell as he drew closer, finally speaking to the man when he drew abreast of him.

"Join us on the dais, du Reims," he said. "Do not sit here with the rabble. There is a great deal we must discuss."

Dashiell had no idea what Clayton meant, but he did as he was asked. When the women began to take their seats at the table, Dashiell took a seat at the very end, watching as Belladonna and Lily left the duke's usual seat empty, instead, choosing to sit on either side of it.

The duke's chair was always left empty these days in silent tribute to him. Clayton had taken the seat next to his wife and motioned Dashiell to sit across from them. Without hesitation, Dashiell obeyed.

Food was now being brought out in earnest. Now that the lord's family had arrived, the feast could truly begin. Dashiell wasn't particularly eager to hear what Clayton had to say to him, but he was glad for the fact that he was sitting at the dais and across from Belladonna. He'd take any opportunity to sit near her, even if it was at Clayton's invitation. His wait to discover what Clayton wished to discuss with him wasn't a long one.

"It was a great victory at Driffield, was it not?" Clayton said as a servant poured him a full cup of wine. "The glory of the Savernake army has surely spread across England by now."

Dashiell didn't particularly like ego where a military victory was concerned. He thought it was bad luck, and an affront to God, who was behind all military successes or failures in his opinion. A man was merely a vessel.

"There were several other armies involved," he said. "It was not only Savernake."

Clayton was served his trencher first, even before the women or guests, because that was what he demanded. A steaming trough was placed in front of him and he inhaled the smell of the roasted beef deeply before replying.

"But we planned the offense against the king's army," he said. "It was our men who held the line, du Reims. We were at the head of it."

"And de Lohr and de Winter were there, too," Dashiell pointed out. He really couldn't believe he was having to speak of the obvious. "We have support from armies who, in years past, have always fought for the crown. De Lohr and de Winter are the largest of these. Their families have always supported the crown, from the time of the Conqueror, and through the anarchy, they supported Matilda. They have never wavered. But now... now, they have."

Clayton wasn't moved by the reverence in Dashiell's voice. "If they supported the king, they would be fools," he snorted. "They are simply siding with the rebels because all of England is rebelling against John. Had de Lohr and de Winter not supported the rebels, they would be fighting a losing battle. Everyone would hate them."

Dashiell sighed sharply. "No one would hate them," he said. "Men understand the strength of tradition and conviction."

"Sometimes traditions are made to be broken."

"Under the right circumstances, I would agree."

Clayton studied Dashiell for a moment before delving into his food. He knew that Dashiell was formidable, both militarily and with his sheer intelligence, but he liked to play the game of seeing just how far he could push East Anglia's heir.

The man who was the last line between him and the riches of Savernake.

"Speaking of circumstances," he said as he chewed noisily. "I have heard that John's army is moving north into Scotland."

Dashiell eyed the man. "That is old news," he said. "It is up to the northern barons to stop him. The king is moving to support the uprising in the north and he is moving to punish the Scottish king, who is supporting the rebels. The defeats we dealt him did not stop that drive, but it surely slowed it."

Clayton wanted to show how much he knew. "But he is moving north with a weakened army and when he arrives, de Vesci of Northumberland will be waiting for him. See if he is not turned back."

A servant placed a full trencher in front of Dashiell. "Do not underestimate John and his mercenary army," he said. "Northumberland will have his hands full."

"If that is true, then we should have beaten John's army into the ground to ensure he did not have enough men to go north."

Dashiell had to shake his head at Clayton's uneducated views. "The battle we fought south of Scarborough was not all of John's army," he said. "They are scattered in the north, fighting the rebels. What we fought was only part of it. Once he aligns his entire army, he will have a formidable force."

"Then why did we not go north? Why did we return home?"

Dashiell sighed heavily. "Because our army had been on campaign for months," he said. "We must return home to fortify our army and restore our supplies. We have already fought John several times in the last few months – Winchester, Northampton, and Nottingham before we took the field against him south of Scarborough. If we marched any further north after months on campaign, our army would be wearier than John's. It would be a recipe for disaster. Surely you understand this, Clayton."

Clayton did, but he was a glory-seeker. He wanted to taste the sweetness of victory regardless of the cost to the men.

"I should have insisted we continue north," he said. "If there is victory at-hand, then we should be part of it."

Dashiell didn't want to debate policy with a fool. Above all else, Dashiell's commands when it came to the army were obeyed, something that had always greatly annoyed Clayton. He felt, as he was married to the heiress of Savernake, the control of the army should be his.

But the army wouldn't follow him, and the duke knew Dashiell these days when he didn't know Clayton. That meant Dashiell's control was permanent. Therefore, Dashiell ignored Clayton's assertion as he turned to his food, using his knife to spear moist chunks of beef. He pretended to be focused on his food when the truth was that it was shifting to Belladonna, seated across from him.

She hadn't been served her food yet, but was simply sitting quietly while the men discussed their recent military campaign. When Dashiell glanced up at her, because he simply couldn't help himself, she was looking at him. Their eyes met and she smiled. He smiled.

Clayton ruined the moment by speaking.

"Things will be different when I am in command," he said. "There will be no hesitation. If there is a battle, we will fight it. Savernake is an old and powerful name, and it is right that Savernake should be at the head of any battle in England. I shall restore Savernake's rightful glory."

Dashiell was ignoring the man's prattle for the most part until the last few words. With those, he took exception.

"There is nothing to restore," he said. "The dukedom of Savernake *is* one of the oldest in England. It was born of glory and continues to be glorious."

Clayton could see he'd offended Dashiell, something that brought him pleasure. "A glorious army led by a madman," he rumbled. "We are a glorious army that is a laughing stock."

Dashiell knew the man was trying to get a rise out of him, but he kept his cool. "Mayhap *you* are the laughing stock, Clayton, but no one is laughing at me or the rest of the men," he said. "And mind your tongue when speaking of the duke. He is still your liege."

Now, Dashiell had insulted Clayton and a balance had been struck, but Clayton was far less cool than Dashiell was. He didn't like being insulted.

"I will speak of the man however I like," he snapped. "You cannot tell me otherwise. I am his heir and when I am the duke, you will show all due respect, du Reims. Do you understand me?"

It was an effort for Dashiell not to roll his eyes. He'd heard that from Clayton, many times, and he always had the same answer.

"Until that time, you are a servant to Savernake, like the rest of us," he said. "But let me be clear; if I find the duke wandering the battlefield again because his minders have been distracted or paid by you to look the other way, I will find you and I will kill you. Is this in any way unclear?"

The conversation at the table went from mildly contentious to deadly all in a matter of seconds. Over at the knight's feasting table, Bentley and Aston had heard the threat and they rose to their feet, moving over to the dais in case Dashiell needed them.

It was a show of force against Clayton, something they'd had to do before, and something that usually pushed Clayton into a tantrum. He didn't like it when men countered his wishes. But he also knew he was no match for Dashiell, much less Ashbourne and Summerlin. Therefore, it was a most difficult task for him to keep from raging.

But that didn't keep him from being nasty.

"You'll not threaten me like that when I am the duke, du Reims," he said, avoiding the entire accusation. "Someday, this empire shall be mine and you will bow at my feet if I demand it. If I want the army to continue to do battle against the king, then it shall. All of this will be mine and you will show me all due respect. Is *that* in any way unclear?"

He wasn't beyond repeatedly reminding Dashiell that someday soon, he would outrank him. It would be him in control of the vast Savernake estate. But Dashiell didn't care about that; he didn't care that Clayton would have everything once Edward died. But he did care that the men he'd worked with for many years would be under the command of an idiot. And he very much cared that Belladonna would become the man's ward. That, more than anything, concerned him.

But he couldn't let the man get to him.

"When you become duke, I shall return to East Anglia and assume my position as Viscount Winterton," he said. "Then I shall become Earl of East Anglia at the passing of my father, which you know very well. Unlike you, I did not have to enter into a marriage to inherit my title. Mine comes from a very long line of noble men. Nobility is in my blood. The only thing in your blood is too much drink and an overabundance of foolishness."

Behind him, the men who heard his insult began to snicker. No one liked Clayton, so it was always great entertainment to see du Reims beat him down. Dashiell heard the laughter but before Clayton could snap back, he continued.

"I will again say that the next time I discover you've turned the duke loose on the battlefield, I will bring you up on charges," he said. "I will have you tried and found guilty of trying to murder the man, and you can spend the rest of your life in the vault without your dukedom. Tell me you understand this before we go any further."

Clayton was starting to turn red in the face, being outsmarted and outwitted by a knight he could never get the upper hand with. But he knew one way to get to the man; he'd known it since his marriage to Lily, something only to be used when all else failed, mostly because it was a powerful weapon, indeed.

And it drew the strongest reaction.

"Your imagination is running wild, du Reims," he said. "I would never put the duke in any danger. But if the man wishes to bless the dead and dying, who am I to prevent him from doing so?"

Dashiell knew he was lying, trying to take the blame off of him. Shaking his head at Clayton's ridiculous answer, he simply turned back to his meal, silently indicating that Bentley and Aston should do the same. But what came out of Clayton's mouth next was something that was designed to jar him.

"In fact, I have the greatest concern for the duke and his family," Clayton went on, watching Dashiell's face carefully. "I am concerned for my wife and her sisters. I am concerned with what will happen to them when the duke passes away. Lady Acacia and Lady Belladonna will be my wards, you know. Lady Acacia has already sworn her commitment to Amesbury, but Lady Belladonna is of prime marriageable age. It will be my duty to find her a powerful and wealthy husband."

That was a jab, one that got to Dashiell more than the others. He knew the man was trying to get under his skin, but he didn't look up at him, nor did he look at Belladonna, which would have been a dead giveaway. He focused on his food as Clayton continued to dig.

"I already have a man in mind for her, in fact," Clayton said, knowing that Dashiell surely must be growing increasingly upset. "I would discuss this with the duke but, alas, he does not know a discussion between the weather or his daughter's future. His mind retains nothing these days. Therefore, I will simply have to wait until Savernake is mine before I make the marital contract. Mayhap you know the man, du Reims – Sir Anthony Cromford. He is a wealthy lord with property north of Nottingham. A marriage to him would be a great alliance."

With that, he dropped the hammer and waited for Dashiell to react. Clayton knew the man's secret because, one night, Lily had let it slip – according to her, Dashiell was far gone in love with Belladonna and she with him. But looking at the two of them, one would never know it. They put on polite airs when around each other and that was the end of it. Still, Clayton very much enjoyed hitting Dashiell where it hurt.

That was Clayton's secret weapon against Dashiell – his love for Belladonna. But the reaction he received to his barb wasn't from Dashiell, it was from Belladonna herself.

Seated on the other side of her father's empty chair, she'd been listening to the conversation between Dashiell and Clayton with growing concern. It seemed to her that the men were baiting each other, and she worried very much that Clayton would try to harm Dashiell somehow.

Clayton had no self-control when it came to his temper. But the moment she heard of his plans for her, shocking plans, she could no longer keep silent.

"I will *not* marry anyone of your choosing, Clayton," she said, standing up and nearly knocking her chair over in the process. "It is Papa's choice on who I shall wed, not yours. I am no concern of yours!"

Now, Clayton's focus was on Belladonna, but so was Dashiell's. And, everyone else at the table. It was Lily who tried to intercede on behalf of her younger, and sometimes very passionate, sister.

"Clayton only wants to ensure that you are taken care of, Bella," she said before turning to her husband. "It is not necessary to speak of such things at the moment, is it? Surely we want a pleasant meal and not one wrought with shouting."

Clayton was frowning at his wife's younger sister, completely ignoring Lily's attempt to ease the situation.

"You should be grateful for any man who would consider marrying you at your age," he said. "You should have been married years ago."

"Who I marry is none of your affair!" Belladonna fired at him.

Clayton slapped the table as he bolted to his feet, knocking over Lily's wine. He jabbed his finger at Belladonna.

"Who you marry *is* my affair, lady," he snarled. "You are a valuable commodity and I shall choose the man I feel best suited for you."

Belladonna was near tears. "You mean the man best suited for *you!*"

Clayton was moving around his wife, heading for Belladonna in a threatening manner as she stood her ground. But suddenly, food was flying all around, and she instinctively winced as something sailed past her face – bread or a vegetable or… something. She didn't know what it was. But she did know when Dashiell put his big body between her and Clayton.

It took Belladonna a moment to realize that Dashiell had leapt over the table to get to her, and that was why food was scattered everywhere.

It was even on her gown. Belladonna felt hands grasping at her and she turned to see Bentley pulling her away from the table as Aston went to stand beside Dashiell.

The three knights had leapt to her defense and she could hear Dashiell's deadly-calm voice.

"Lift your hand to Belladonna and you will lose the arm it is attached to," he growled. "What, exactly, did you think to do to her, Clayton?"

Clayton was faced by men who, frankly, terrified him. He tried to hold his ground, but he wasn't doing a very good job.

"I was not going to do anything to her," he lied. "I was going to scold her. She cannot speak to me in that tone, du Reims. I will not permit it."

Dashiell was finished humoring the man. He'd spent the past several months on campaign with him, listening to his ridiculous boasting, watching him undermine his command, and a host of other offenses.

Dashiell was done with him.

Men like Clayton le Cairon only understood one thing – strength overall. It wasn't about respect. It was about intimidation and who could shout the loudest. Therefore, Dashiell thumped Clayton on the chest in a move meant to frighten him.

"Reclaim your seat," he rumbled. "Sit down with your wife and I shall forget this conversation. You do not want me to hold a grudge, le Cairon. Sit down before I am forced to push you into that chair and tie you there."

Looking into Dashiell's eyes, Clayton was in a bind. He was about to be humiliated in front of an entire room full of his men. He couldn't tell if Dashiell meant what he said, but he suspected that he did.

Dashiell du Reims never said anything he didn't mean.

But he wasn't going to acquiesce to the man. It wasn't in him to obey like that. Snatching the nearest cup of wine, which happened to be

Belladonna's, Clayton took it for himself and walked away. It was the ultimate act of defiance, turning his back on a man he couldn't bully.

But this wasn't over; not in the least. Clayton had been entertaining the idea of pledging Belladonna for his own benefit and the only thing preventing that had been the very real barrier of Dashiell du Reims.

But he was hesitant no more; du Reims thought he could control the situation. Clayton was going to prove he would have the last laugh.

Ever.

Clayton sauntering away was the end to a tense situation. Frankly, Dashiell was glad Clayton had walked away. He'd come close to throttling the man. Feeling some relief that their first night home hadn't deteriorated into a brawl, he turned around and indicated for Aston to regain his seat. Then, he made his way to Belladonna, in Bentley's grip.

"Reclaim your seat, my lady," he said quietly. "I am sure he will not bother you any more tonight."

Belladonna looked up at Dashiell – that handsome face she knew so well, and those eyes, usually so hard, but now soft when he looked at her. His voice was soft, too. But she shook her head.

"I am not hungry," she said, still upset. "I will go and sit with Papa."

Dashiell discreetly jerked his head at Bentley, indicating for the man to leave them. As Bentley walked away, Dashiell held out his elbow to her.

"Will you permit me to escort you?"

A reluctant smile came to Belladonna's lips as she took his elbow. Dashiell led her off the dais and over to the edge of the room, away from the crowds of men who had gone back to their noisy meal.

They moved in the shadows on the fringes of the room where the servants usually toiled, heading for the hall entry. Belladonna clutched Dashiell's arm, allowing herself to draw strength from the man. She'd spent the past several months worrying over his safety and now here he was, firm and warm and real.

He'd stood up to Clayton and her heart had swelled with gratitude, with adoration. How easy it would be to pretend Dashiell belonged to her, for walking with him, arm in arm, was the most natural of things.

God, she wished it more than anything.

"I apologize if I upset you earlier, my lady," Dashiell said, breaking into her train of thought. "I did not mean to offend you my first day back at Ramsbury."

Belladonna looked at him curiously, having no idea what he meant until she remembered their earlier conversation when she'd asked him why he no longer addressed her by her name.

She hadn't been angry, only embarrassed, but she wasn't going to tell him that. Her anger at him cooled rather quickly, as it always did. She couldn't stay angry with him for long.

"Oh… that," she said. "You did not offend me."

"But you left rather quickly."

"I left because I am not a child any longer and that is the way you treat me," she said, trying not to sound like she was still miffed. But then, she turned wistful. "Sometimes… sometimes I wish it would go back to the way it used to be, Dash, when you would call me Bella and we would throw rocks at the soldiers on guard duty. Do you remember?"

They were nearing the entrance of the hall, passing into the dark night beyond. "I remember," he said, going back to those days when she was so young and full of mischief. He recalled them with great fondness. "I remember you had good aim with those rocks."

"Shall we do it again? I believe I have become an even better marksman since then."

He grinned, glancing at her. "I have no doubt."

"Can we wait for Clayton to emerge from the hall and then bombard him from the shadows?"

That brought laughter from Dashiell. "I would be inclined to agree with you, only…"

"Only what?"

"Only I must serve with the man. If I attack him with rocks, who is to say he would not attack me with a knife when I am not looking? Trust in battle is, mayhap, the only thing Clayton and I share."

Belladonna sobered. It was dark and quiet, the winter night sky brilliant overhead. She slowed her pace, not wanting to enter the keep. She wanted to stretch out this moment with Dashiell for as long as she could.

"Was it terrible?" she asked quietly. "The battle campaign, I mean. We did not receive much word about what was transpiring. Can you tell me what happened?"

Dashiell could feel her slowing her pace and he slowed his as well. Not strangely, he wasn't ready to take her into the keep yet. He hadn't seen her in months and, like a starving man, he had to have his fill of her.

"There is not too much to tell, to be truthful," he said. "It was relatively unspectacular as far as battle campaigns go. We went to prevent the king from raining havoc upon the barons in the north, and we met him four times in battle."

"Why did you come home?"

"Because the army was exhausted," he said. "The men need rest. We also came home because we have new recruits for the army. While we were gone, some of the soldiers we left behind scoured the countryside for men who were willing to fight for the duke. Tomorrow, I will have new soldiers to train."

That wasn't unusual. Being that Savernake was a strong military power, there were often new recruits to train. Belladonna came to a halt and looked up at him.

"I think I have seen your new recruits," she said. "They have been camping outside of the walls, waiting for the army to return."

"I would imagine that was them."

"Are you exhausted, too?"

It was a gentle question, one that seemed to make him more weary simply to hear it. As if he wanted to collapse in her arms. God, what comfort that would give him.

"I could use some rest," he admitted. "I am not getting any younger, and these drawn-out battle campaigns are tiring."

She pondered that a moment. "But it is not over, is it?"

He shook his head. "Nay."

"Will it be soon?"

"I do not know, my lady. But I have a feeling I will see battle again before it is."

"Wouldn't it be better for you to live in peace, with a normal life and a routine that was more pleasant?"

"Aye, it would."

She smiled, timidly. "Then I have something that will help you enjoy a more pleasant life."

"You do?"

She nodded. "A party," she said. "Jillayne Chadlington is having a grand party in honor of her day of birth, and everyone who is anyone is invited. I think she invited half of London. Of course, my sisters and I were planning on going, but that was before the army returned. Now, we have escorts. Will you please escort me to the party so I will not look like a sad fool with no man on my arm?"

Dashiell was surprised by the invitation. But he was even more surprised because of the very fact that while he hated parties, he very nearly gave his consent immediately. Spending the evening as Belladonna's escort was the best possible thing he could imagine. They would be together, almost as if they were *meant* to be together. He could fawn over her all he wanted and it would be expected.

But the more reasoning side closed in on him and he found himself resisting the urge to run from her very hopeful face. How could he agree to escort her, knowing it was all a lie, that he would be living something that could never be? He didn't want to taste the pleasure only to have it ripped away from him. It would be so very cruel.

"Although I am honored by your request, my lady, mayhap you should ask one of the younger knights," he said, hating that he was saying it but knowing he had to. "Bentley or Aston would be more than honored to escort you."

Belladonna stared at him and he could see the light of hope doused in her eyes. She let go of his elbow.

"Why not?" she demanded. "Dash, you and I have been good friends for many years. There was a time when you hardly left my side. But the past year… you have gone out of your way to avoid me. You will not even call me by my name any longer. You treat me like a stranger and I want to know why. If I have offended you, will you not at least allow me to apologize?"

She was hitting too close to home for him and Dashiell had no idea what to do. He was without practice in the emotional games of men and women, but this wasn't a game. It was very serious. He could see that if he didn't ease this situation, then he could very well drive Belladonna to hate him. Perhaps, she would never speak with him again.

And that would kill him.

He cleared his throat softly.

"You have not done anything to offend me," he said. "I have told you before and I shall tell you again; it is not proper for me to address you so informally and…"

She cut him off. "But there is no one around to hear you," she pointed out. "It is only me, yet still you behave as if I am a stranger to you. Why, Dash? Do you truly dislike me so?"

God's Blood… did he *dislike* her? That wasn't the problem at all. He adored everything about her. From the top of her golden-red hair to the bottom of her little feet, she was a goddess. And she had the heart of a lion.

She was perfect.

"Nay," he tried to reassure her. "I do not dislike you at all. You are my long-time friend who has grown into a beautiful, eligible woman. I cannot continue to treat you like a child. I have told you this."

Belladonna folded her arms across her chest; she wasn't having any of it. "So you treat me with polite distance," she said. "What happened to the man I used to throw rocks with? What happened to the man who would sneak me out of the postern gate on my horse when my father forbade me to ride? What happened to the man who would cheer me up when I was sad? Dash, what *happened* to you?"

He was losing ground and struggling to stay on an even keel. With each passing moment, he was becoming increasingly inclined to tell her the truth.

What happened?

Lady – you happened!

"My lady, I want you to listen carefully to me and, hopefully, this will explain my position," he said, trying desperately to salvage the situation. "You know as well as I do that anything other than formal behavior between you and me could be construed as... inappropriate. When you were younger, there was no issue, but you are not a child any longer. You are a woman grown. I would not damage your reputation so."

Belladonna eyed him as if she didn't believe him. "And that is why you will not escort me to Jillayne's party?"

"That is exactly why. People would see us together and assume... they would assume that we *were* together."

Her eyebrows flew up in outrage. "And that is a terrible thing?" she cried. "I see perfectly, du Reims. You would be ashamed to be seen with me. Now, I know!"

With that, she turned on her heel and stomped away, leaving Dashiell feeling as if he'd just been hit in the gut. All of the air left him as he watched her walk away, wishing with all of his heart he could tell her the truth.

It was killing him not to do so.

But he simply couldn't open that door – nay, he wasn't brave enough to do it and face her rejection. As he'd told Christopher, he was an old man. She deserved a fine, young husband. What would she think if he told her that he had feelings for her? He would probably come off sounding like a fool, and she would quickly come to understand that it was more than simple friendship he felt for her. And she would be embarrassed about it, embarrassed that a seasoned, old knight had fallen in love with her.

All she wanted was an escort.

All he wanted was to give her his heart.

With great sadness, Dashiell watched her disappear into the keep before heading back to the great hall and becoming ragingly drunk.

The next morning, he would pay the price.

But he didn't care in the least.

CHAPTER THREE

"Lord Christopher has asked me to relay the message, my lord. The nature is urgent."

It was dawn the next day and Dashiell, along with Bentley, Aston, Clayton, and a few senior soldiers were in Edward's great solar to receive a messenger bearing the de Lohr blue and gold standards.

It was unexpected, to say the least. Christopher had returned home at the same time the Savernake army had headed for home, so Dashiell was deeply curious about the message the de Lohr soldier bore. He made sure the servants were out of the solar and the doors were closed before he let the man speak.

"Now," he said as he turned to the man. "Tell me everything."

The weary messenger complied. "The king has defeated Alexander, King of the Scots, on the Scotland border and even now pushes into Scotland," he said. "The northern barons, including Northumberland, were unable to stop him and it is Worcester's fear that the king's strength has grown beyond reproach. He is calling a conference of the southern barons in order to address this issue, a conference to take place at Canterbury, his brother's holding. He asks that you send word to Arundel and your other allies and ask them to convene in Canterbury for this important task."

Dashiell was listening with great concern. His head was pounding with a nasty hangover, but he fought it as he listened to the serious news. Before he could question the messenger further, Clayton spoke.

"How far north has John taken his army?" he asked, astonishment in his voice.

"He is marching on Edinburgh, we are told."

The room went deadly quiet at that news. It was shocking. Dashiell stared at the messenger for a moment before turning away, his mind working furiously. John marching on Edinburgh? He could hardly believe it.

"I knew he had men waiting for him in the north, mercenaries and cutthroats, but I do not believe anyone knew just how many men," he finally said. He turned to the messenger. "Did my cousin give any indication of what he wanted to do about it?"

The messenger shook his head. "Nay, my lord," he replied. "He simply asked me to relay the news and tell you to meet him in Canterbury in a few months. May was discussed."

"Surely he has eyes up north," he said. "He must be getting regular reports."

The messenger nodded. "Indeed, my lord," he said. Then, he sobered dramatically. "But there is still more news – the king's mercenary army did not have an easy time of it. They met an army led by de Royans of Bowes Castle near Durham and they were damaged, but not defeated. However, the king's army picked up more mercenaries who had landed in Sunderland and went on to destroy the army of Ajax de Velt near Berwick. Reports tell us that the army was strong by sheer numbers alone, but de Velt fought valiantly."

Dashiell felt as if he'd been hit in the gut. He couldn't believe what he was hearing. "Ajax de Velt was defeated?"

"Aye, my lord."

"The Dark Lord's army?"

"Aye, my lord."

"Did de Velt himself survive?"

The messenger sighed heavily. "It has been reported to us that he did not, my lord. He took the field with his army but was a casualty of

John's archers. Worcester is understandably devastated by this news."

The Dark Lord was dead. The man that, thirty-five years ago, all of England feared until he met a woman who tamed him. From that point forward, Ajax de Velt had been a model citizen, a strong ally, and to Christopher de Lohr, a good friend. He was quite elderly, taking the field into his seventh decade to fight alongside his sons, and most everyone believed he was immortal. He was one of the best knights England had ever seen.

Dashiell could hardly believe the news.

"God's Blood," he hissed, turning away. His aching head just grew tremendously worse and he sat heavily in the nearest chair. "De Velt is gone."

"Those are the reports, my lord."

Dashiell was nearly beside himself as he sat there, remembering the old knight, still big and powerful, with two-colored eyes – one eye was brown while the other had been brown with a big splash of green in it. It had made him unique among men.

"What about Northumberland?" Dashiell finally asked. "How did he fare?"

"Worse than de Velt. Northumberland's army was fragmented. The king had a great many Teutonic mercenaries waiting for him at Newcastle, so when he pushed for the border, the sheer number could not be stopped."

Dashiell was struggling to absorb all he'd been told. It was worse than he'd ever imagined. After several long moments, he finally nodded his head as if to acknowledge what he'd been told and stood up from the chair.

"Go to the kitchens and get yourself something to eat," he told the messenger. "Have a servant show you a bed so that you may rest. Seek me out before you leave; I may have more questions."

"Aye, my lord."

The messenger quit the solar. When he was gone, Dashiell turned to Aston and Bentley, who were pale with shock. He shook his head with disbelief.

"De Velt was defeated?" he said. "Not merely defeated, but killed? I cannot grasp this. I truly cannot."

Aston displayed equal disbelief. "I fostered at Pelinom Castle," he said. "Jax de Velt was a fearsome but fair master. I cannot comprehend that John was able to defeat him."

"He did not merely defeat him; he overran him," Clayton said. When the others turned to him, they were surprised to see that he was remarkably subdued, at least for Clayton. "I was raised on stories of Ajax de Velt. We all were. I always thought the man could stand up to God Himself and win."

Dashiell's jaw ticked faintly. For once, he and Clayton were in agreement. "John was wholly unworthy to defeat such a man," he said. "No wonder my cousin is calling a conference. If John's army has not only defeated de Velt, but Alexander also, then it is quite possible that the rebellion against him is in serious trouble. If John brings that massive mercenary army south…"

"Then he brings it into the heart of England where those who oppose him are plentiful," Bentley said firmly. "Mayhap he was able to defeat Northumberland and de Velt, but he will run into a good deal more resistance in his own country."

"He will overrun us all," Clayton said. "If he has an army to destroy not only de Velt, but the King of Scotland, what makes you believe we can defeat him?"

Dashiell could hear the hysteria building in Clayton's voice. "Because we will be amassed by the thousands in the south," he said. "Even John's massive army cannot overrun tens of thousands of men who have taken a stand against him."

"But he overran de Velt and de Vesci!"

"I would not worry if I were you. That is why my cousin is calling a conference; to discuss John's defeat."

Clayton fell silent for a moment, wandering away from the hearth where the men were sitting and over to the lancet windows that overlooked the bailey. The solar had a soaring Gothic ceiling, an intricate feature but one that kept the room rather cold, even on warm days. Clayton folded his arms as if to ward off the chill, or perhaps to ward off the dire news they'd been given.

Dashiell had been right; he was feeling some panic.

"We cannot face such an army," he said. "It would be suicide. We must remain at Ramsbury and protect our own."

Dashiell didn't give much stock in his ravings. "We would not be facing him alone, Clayton," he said. "We will meet with Chris and discuss what needs to be done. Until then, we will send messengers to Arundel and also to de Nerra at Selborne Castle. Since the House of de Nerra is much like de Winter and de Lohr in that they always serve the crown, I will be interested to know what the Itinerant Justice of East Hampshire has to say about all of this."

"De Nerra fought with us at Winchester and Northampton," Bentley said. "They have no more use for the king than we do."

Dashiell looked over his shoulder at the knight. "I realize that, but I would be interested to know if they've heard of John's push into Scotland."

That was of great interest considering the de Nerras, by close proximity to Winchester Castle, always seemed to know of John's movements before anyone else did. Gavin de Nerra had taken over the title from his father, Valor, only recently, but he was a sharp-minded man with a strong dedication to England and Dashiell liked him a great deal.

"Would you have me deliver the message to de Nerra, Dash?" Bentley asked. "I can ride to Selborne in a couple of days."

Dashiell shook his head. "Although I appreciate the offer, I need you here," he said. "However, I will go to Selborne personally. I have a few things to discuss with de Nerra, this being among them. But the fact remains that we can do nothing until the conference with my cousin in a few months' time. So until that time, we conduct business as usual. I have new recruits waiting for me in the bailey, as I am sure all of you have duties to attend to. Let us get on with it."

Dashiell, Bentley, and Aston started to move but Clayton remained.

"We cannot conduct business as usual, du Reims," he said. "Far from it."

Dashiell suspected they were in for more of Clayton's hysterics. "Why not?"

Clayton was outraged by his attitude. "Because nothing is as it should be," he said snappishly. "John is marching on Edinburgh and when he is done with Scotland, he will surely come back to England and back to the barons who have opposed him. We must prepare."

Dashiell was growing impatient. "And we are," he said. "We prepare by allowing our army to rest, by refilling our stores, and by training the new recruits so that when the moment is upon us, we are ready to fight."

That wasn't the answer Clayton was looking for. "Fight *where*?" he demanded. "If John has a massive mercenary army, then the best we can do is lock our gates and prepare for a siege. If we go out to meet him, we will die."

Dashiell was very close to insulting the cowardly man. He didn't like men who lacked courage and, at the moment, Clayton was showing his true self. It was an effort for Dashiell to put his insult into a constructive form.

"We cannot sit here and wait for the king to come to us, and you know it," he said with veiled impatience. "Clayton, you can help us prepare for battle by ensuring our army is adequately outfitted. I know many of our men suffered greatly during the battle marches, meaning they wore through shoes and weapons and other things. You can be a great help to our future survival by making sure the army is properly outfitted. Will you do this?"

He was giving Clayton something productive to focus on, rather than giving in to his panic. Surprisingly, Clayton was a hard worker when he set his mind to it, but it was the simple matter of forcing him to focus. However, he would only do it if the job seemed important enough, and evidently, this one wasn't. He shook his head.

"I will not," he said flatly. "Any fool can see to that."

Dashiell's patience was at an end. "Then I will put someone else on the task who I know can competently complete it," he said, turning for the door. "I care not what you do, but if I hear you have been spreading the news of John's march on Edinburgh and frightening the men, I will seek you out and you will not like my reaction. Do you understand me?"

Clayton lifted his chin, turning away from him. "You cannot dictate my behavior."

"I can when it comes to the health and well-being of the men. If you upset them, you will answer to me. I care not what you do from this point on, but keep your mouth shut."

With that, he quit the solar, heading out with his men into the early morning with a good many tasks on his mind. Still, he couldn't seem to shake the suspicion that Clayton would, indeed, spread rumors about the king's strength and the fears of obliteration.

Something told Dashiell to be ready for what Clayton was capable of.

WHAT CLAYTON WAS capable of was exactly what Dashiell had feared, only worse.

Clayton didn't like to be embarrassed in front of his men. He knew Dashiell and the army was against him; he'd always known. He'd felt alone since his arrival to Ramsbury, when he'd married Lily and assumed his rightful place as heir to the dukedom. Only, no one took him seriously. They never had, and he knew that.

But things were about to change.

As heir to the dukedom, he wielded some power, power that was rightfully his. The old duke wasn't long for this world but, even if he was, Clayton knew he could assume power to a certain extent. Although he couldn't petition the king to appoint him as the new duke, using Edward's madness as evidence that such a thing was needed, he could still act in a manner that was within his power as the heir.

And part of that power was making appropriate marriages to ensure the strength of the dukedom. No one, not even the church, would argue with that. He had to show du Reims who was truly in charge at Ramsbury. He wasn't going to be embarrassed by the man any longer.

He was going to aim a proverbial dagger right at Dashiell's heart.

Summoning his clerk, a tiny man who greatly feared him, he had the man construct a missive to Lord Sherston, Anthony Cromford. It was an invitation to view the young woman who could be his future wife. In the missive, Clayton made sure to tell Lord Sherston of Belladonna and her exquisite beauty.

Although Lily inherited the dukedom and Acacia was taking her dowry to Amesbury, Belladonna inherited wealth from her mother's side of the family. Her mother was a de Lara, a wealthy family from the Marches, and Belladonna not only had wealth, but a castle as part of her dowry. Clayton recalled that the duke had told him such a thing before his mind completely left him.

Therefore, Clayton made sure to emphasize the strength of Belladonna's wealth and Sherston, like any normal man, would be willing to take a look at her based purely on her dowry and the fact that she was a duke's daughter.

But the problem was a location for their meeting. Where could the two come together so that Sherston could glimpse Belladonna? Surely, it couldn't be at Ramsbury. Du Reims would chase the man away before he even entered the gates, so the meeting had to happen away from Ramsbury.

And then, it occurred to Clayton – a buzz he'd heard as soon as the army had returned to Ramsbury from their long battle campaign. Something about a party at Chadlington Castle for Lady Jillayne. Lily had briefly mentioned it and he'd heard his manservant speak of it, also, simply because the women had been preparing for it ever since the invitation had arrived a month before. Clayton hadn't given the event any thought until now.

But at this moment, he was giving it a great deal of thought.

Chadlington…

It would be the perfect place. Belladonna would be in attendance, as would a host of other houses, and even if Sherston wasn't invited, his presence would probably not even be noticed. Better still, even if du Reims came to the party, the opportunity to introduce Belladonna to Lord Sherston could take place well away from du Reims' prying eyes.

The man would never even know until it was too late.

It was a brilliant plan, at least as far as Clayton was concerned. He was going to undermine du Reims and take delight in doing it. Later that morning, a messenger bearing Savernake colors rode swiftly from the gatehouse of Ramsbury, a messenger personally selected and handsomely paid by Clayton himself.

He told the guards at the gatehouse, guards loyal to du Reims, that the messenger was taking a missive to his father, but that wasn't the truth. He simply didn't want the guards tipping off Dashiell, and as the messenger headed off to Sherston, about a two-day ride from Ramsbury, all Clayton could do was smile.

His plan was in motion and du Reims would be none the wiser.

Aye… Clayton would have the last laugh in all of this.

CHAPTER FOUR

THE PUPPIES WERE out again.

The kitchen yard was now overrun with happy puppies and their mothers, all of them running about the muddy yard as they were out of their cages.

Belladonna stood near the enormous iron cauldron used to boil hide from bones, and other necessary tasks unrelated to cooking, as she watched the children of Ramsbury chase the puppies about, playing with them in the weak winter sunshine.

Not surprisingly, the puppies were a valuable commodity to the knights who bred them because a Ramsbury dog came from a long line of great hunting dogs, and was invaluable for protection for a fine lord. Many such puppies had been sold all over England with very satisfied results.

When the knights were away, it fell to Belladonna and her recruited gang of servant children to tend the puppies – feeding them, making sure they were comfortable, and also tending to the mother dogs.

The knights, mainly Dashiell and Bentley, hadn't been to see the dogs since their arrival. In fact, they hadn't seen the three new litters that had been born while they were away. One sire, three bitches, and a combined nineteen pups were now the sum total of the entire dog family. Dashiell and Bentley were going to get rich selling this new crop of puppies, who were rushing around the kitchen yard as the children ran after them.

Usually, Belladonna ran after them, too. But today, she didn't feel much like doing it. She'd spent the entire night weeping on and off about Dashiell and had slept fitfully as a result. When she'd awoken, it had been with an aching head and a heavy heart. Now that she had the truth out of the man, that he was embarrassed to be seen with her, she felt a great deal of shame.

But she should have suspected that Dashiell had an increasing aversion to her. He'd come to Ramsbury when she'd seen ten years, and the first several years of their association had been years of companionship. They seemed to laugh at the same things and he took a fatherly interest in her because the duke was so caught up in his own politics. Although Edward loved his daughters, he hadn't been an active father. Dashiell, for Belladonna, had somewhat filled that roll as someone she could talk to, a steady male figure, someone who was always there to support her.

But things changed when she turned ten and eight.

Four years ago, to be exact. It was almost as if the change had happened overnight. One moment, he was calling her Bella, and in the next, it was "my lady". It hadn't bothered her too much at first, and she'd even gone to France for two years to live with a cousin and learn the culture and customs of the country. But when she'd come back, Dashiell was even more formal with her.

Belladonna had returned home, older and wiser and dressed in beautiful French fashions, and Dashiell had become as attentive as a tree stump. Belladonna thought she was imagining that he was avoiding her, but she knew in her heart that it was not her imagination.

His avoidance had been real.

And her heart had been broken.

It was even more broken now, shattered as the truth of his attitude towards her had come out. It was difficult to face the truth after all of these years. As she stood in the kitchen yard, watching the puppies and children run around, she wondered why she even bothered with tending the dogs that Dashiell loved so. At one time, she'd done it because she loved the dogs, too, but now she did it because she loved their master.

But he didn't love her in return.

Lost to her thoughts, Belladonna was alerted to a runaway pup when one of the children rushed to her, tugging on her sleeve and pointing at the gate to the kitchen yard, which someone had left open. The children weren't allowed out in the main bailey, with all of the soldiers and men about, so Belladonna rushed after the escapee.

The bailey was full of new recruits for the duke's army, poorly dressed men standing out in the bright, cold weather as the knights looked them over to see if they would make good candidates. These were men who lived on the Savernake lands, farmers or tradesmen, and men who were willing to fight for the duke for either pay or a break in the tariffs the duke demanded of those living on his lands. Savernake lands were very rich, with part of them being a royal forest, so it was a densely populated dukedom.

There were very old men, old men, middle-aged men, young men, and still younger men. Tall, short, thin, and everything in between. As Belladonna walked past a group of shivering men, she noticed that a few of them couldn't have been much older than ten and two, though they were pretending to be older.

She also noticed that the puppy was in their ranks, wagging his tail and happily licking men's hands. She pushed into the group of men, picking up the dog, when she suddenly heard a sharp voice barking overhead.

"Christ upon his mighty throne!" came the very loud bellow from Dashiell. "Is this a school for girls, mayhap? I have never seen such a terrible group of recruits. Stand up straight. Show some pride or I'll throw you to the wolves!"

Men began to stand up tall, prompted by the very mean knight's shouted words. In the midst of men who were shuffling about,

Belladonna grabbed the dog and began to push her way out. She wanted to get away from Dashiell before he saw her, but the men didn't move easily. They didn't like a woman pushing them around.

It took some effort for Belladonna to finally propel herself out of the group, clutching the puppy, and the action almost thrust her straight into Dashiell. He happened to be standing just where she was emerging. Startled, she stepped sideways quickly to avoid him.

Dashiell, too, was startled to see her. In fact, he was quite confused. "My lady?" he asked. "What were you doing in the middle of the recruits?"

Belladonna didn't feel like speaking with him; she truly didn't. The sight of his handsome, rugged face brought back the feelings of disappointment and shame she'd been trying so hard to fight off. But she needed to tell him something, simply so he wouldn't follow her and demand an answer.

"The pup ran off," she said. "Have no fear; I am taking him back to his mother."

She walked away before he could respond, moving as swiftly as she could without actually running. She didn't look back to see if he was pursuing her – she simply tucked her head down and kept moving. Nearing the kitchen yard, she came across Bentley, who was coming from the stables. She almost ran into him.

Belladonna genuinely liked Bentley. He was a kind man with a polite, gentle manner about him, and she'd heartily approved the match to Lily before Clayton came along. She was well aware of her sister's longing for the man, a strong love that still, three years later, would not die. In truth, it was a sad situation all around and Belladonna forced a smile at Bentley.

"Good morn to you, Bent," she said. "Are you going to see your dogs this day? We've had three new litters since you were on your battle march."

Bentley grinned, looking at the pup in her arms and rubbing its head. "So I have been told," he said, turning to point to two little boys who worked in the stables. "Evidently, everyone wants a puppy now. I am told I have some to spare, as I cannot sell all of them."

Belladonna's smile turned genuine as she looked at the stable boys, who were grinning mischievously at her.

"It has taken an army to raise these pups since you have been gone," she said. "I have had to enlist every child at Ramsbury to assist me, and they all want a puppy. I have had to count them nightly to ensure they are all still here."

Bentley took the puppy out of her arms. He very much loved animals and he cuddled the little creature. "I cannot blame them," he said. "The pup looks wonderful. You have done an excellent job with him."

"I am glad you are pleased."

With a final squeeze, he handed the pup back to her. "I am," he said. "Have you shown Dash?"

Her smile vanished and she averted her gaze. "Nay," she said. Not wanting to elaborate on her answer, she turned for the kitchen yard. "I will expect you to come and see the rest soon. They are your pups, after all. And there are nineteen of them, all of them soon ready to go to new homes."

Bentley watched her go. "I will," he said. To him, she seemed suddenly angry. "My lady… is something wrong?"

He'd picked up on her mood shift and Belladonna came to a halt. "Nay," she said, trying to pretend there was nothing in the world amiss. "All is well. Bent… are you terribly busy today?"

He lifted his big shoulders. "I have some things to attend to, but I am not too busy," he said. "May I be of service to you?"

Belladonna thought of the party she'd been invited to, the one Dashiell was too ashamed to escort her to. He'd suggested Bentley or Aston, hadn't he? Perhaps she should take his advice. Perhaps it would teach Dashiell a lesson, proving to him that his rejection didn't matter in the least.

"I should like an escort into Marlborough," she said. "There is a merchant there I would like to visit. Will you take me?"

He nodded. "Gladly," he said. "Can you wait an hour?"

"I can."

"Then I will meet you in the bailey."

"I shall be ready."

With that, he headed out to the main part of the bailey where the new recruits were, and Belladonna headed back into the kitchen yard.

Squaring her shoulders with determination, she simply wasn't going to cry over Dashiell any longer. If the man was embarrassed to be seen with her, then she would spare him any further shame. It might take her a lifetime to get over him, but she had to start somewhere.

She would start now.

She'd already been without him over the past few months and she'd come to a certain peace about it. So, perhaps, she simply needed to continue on that path. She would push him from her thoughts and pretend he was still away. *Far* away. And when she saw him around Ramsbury, well… she would ignore him.

God help her, she had to.

Returning the puppy to its mother, Belladonna headed back into the keep, trying to be firm in her resolution. Unfortunately, deep down, she knew she was weak. Sooner or later, Dashiell would be able to break her down.

It was depressing to know that she was in for a lifetime of misery.

CHAPTER FIVE

"IF YOU ARE coming with me, then hurry!"

Belladonna was prepared to go into town, waiting impatiently for Acacia, who had wanted to accompany her. But Acacia was dragging her feet, finding other things to occupy her time, and Belladonna's patience was at an end. Just as she turned for the stairwell to go down to the bailey, Lily rushed up behind her.

"I am going with you," she said. "I must see the merchant who has threads and sewing kits."

Belladonna looked at her sister, who was fully dressed for travel.

"You knew I was going?" she asked.

Lily pulled on her gloves. "I heard you ask Acacia. She has no need to go with you, but I do."

Belladonna didn't say what she was thinking – *Bentley is escorting me*. She knew that Bentley and Lily mostly avoided each other these days, for their own sanity, but in that understanding was something Belladonna found interesting. By watching the pair, perhaps she, too, could learn to live alongside a man she loved, a man she could never have.

Perhaps, this journey into the village would be a good thing for her to experience.

Therefore, she said nothing as she made her way down the narrow stairwell and into the foyer of the keep. It was a cavernous area, two-storied, that always smelled of damp earth for some reason. With Lily beside her, Belladonna made her way out to the bailey beyond.

As promised, Bentley was waiting. He'd pulled together a four-man escort and a small gray palfrey for Belladonna to ride on. When he saw Lily with her, a flicker of surprise crossed his features and he snapped at one of the men to rush to the stables and prepare another palfrey.

Lily, too, rippled with surprise when she saw Bentley at the head of the escort. Arm looped through Belladonna's, she slowed her pace.

"You could have told me he was your escort," she muttered.

Belladonna's eyes were on Bentley, who pretended to be busy with other things. "You did not ask," she said. "Besides… he is here all of the time, Lily, and you two are able to co-exist. Surely a small trip into town will not be an issue."

Lily simply shook her head and looked away, unwilling to reply. In truth, she was secretly glad that Bentley was going with them. Belladonna was pleased her sister wasn't going to make a fuss about it until a big man in big armor, astride an enormous red warhorse, suddenly rode into view.

Dashiell appeared.

"They are bringing the second palfrey about," he said to Bentley. "You only have four men for the escort party?"

Bentley nodded. "I did not think we needed any more with two knights riding escort."

Dashiell simply nodded; it was clear he was coming along. Belladonna's heart sank into the pit of her stomach as she realized it. Here she was, so smug about putting Lily with a man she did not wish to be around, and now Dashiell had appeared to make her feel as uncomfortable as Lily did with Bentley.

Somewhere, God was punishing her for being cruel to her sister and expecting her to tolerate a situation that Belladonna was unwilling to tolerate herself. With a faint sigh, one for strength, she resigned herself to a miserable, tension-filled trip into town. She hadn't invited Dashiell to escort her, so why was he here?

Letting go of Lily, Belladonna marched up to Dashiell aboard his snappish charger. "Sir Dashiell," she said, addressing him quite formally. "What are you doing here? I have only asked Bentley to accompany me. Your presence was not requested."

Dashiell was well aware of that. And he could hear from the tone of her voice that she was still quite angry with him.

That was precisely why he was here.

A drunken, unhappy night followed by an unpleasant encounter with her this morning had forced him into joining the escort when Bentley told him about it. He still had a raging headache, and he'd put the new recruits he was supposed to manage in Aston's care, but he wasn't going to miss this opportunity to be with Belladonna and, hopefully, ease her anger against him. Even if he couldn't be honest with her, at the very least, he couldn't stand that she was angry at him.

But he could see it was going to be a tough fight.

"Because you warrant such protection, my lady," he said after a moment.

She cocked an eyebrow at him. "You should not bother. I would not wish to cause you shame to be seen with me."

Dashiell stared at her a moment before lifting his visor, peering down at her. "I have never said any such thing, my lady, nor would I ever."

Her eyes narrowed. "Do not make it seem as if I misunderstood you," she hissed. "You made your position plain enough last night. Now I am making mine."

"And what is your position?"

"I do not want you to go."

"And I do not care what you want. Two daughters of the duke warrant two knights as protection."

She took a few steps closer, avoiding the horse when it swung its big head. "Then you protect my sister," she said, her voice low and unhappy. "Do not talk to me. Do not even look at me. Pretend I am not here. Bentley will serve my needs. At least he is not ashamed to be seen with me."

With that, she turned on her heel and marched back to Lily, who was waiting near the escort.

Dashiell watched her go, feeling frustrated and hurt. Clearly, she took what he said last night and stewed on it, creating an even bigger situation this morning. He wondered if she would even listen to him if he tried to defend himself and clarify what he meant.

Lily…

He would be guarding Lily, it seemed, and Lily was a sweet woman. He'd always liked her. And she was very close to Belladonna.

Perhaps, if he told Lily what had happened, she might be a liaison between him and Belladonna. He felt like a fool for thinking such a thing but, at the moment, he was desperate. Even if he and Belladonna could never be together, that didn't mean he wanted her to hate him for the rest of her life.

He had to make it right.

IT WAS FRIGHTFULLY cold as the party from Ramsbury made its way to the bustling town of Marlborough, a mere seven miles from Ramsbury Castle and part of the duke's properties. It had a castle, called *The Mound* by the locals, that had been a royal hunting lodge and residence until the falling out with John, who was quite unhappy to have lost it to the Duke of Savernake when the man overran the property and captured it.

Dashiell had led that particular siege, which saw the aged castle fall in a day and a night. Even now, he had Savernake men stationed there. John had a fondness for Marlborough and he'd even married his first wife at the castle. Because of the royal connections to the town, Dashiell was particularly protective over it and he was looking at the visit to Marlborough as a necessary trip to check on the both the town and the garrison. He wanted to ensure everything was in order.

The day remained clear as the party made its way along the muddy road. They were surrounded by gently rolling hills, a few dead trees, and the River Kennet to the south. The four soldiers rode in a square formation, with a man at each corner, while the women rode in the middle. Dashiell was in the front, at point, while Bentley brought up the rear, and there was absolutely no conversation at all since leaving Ramsbury.

It was a somber little group. Truth be told, Belladonna was feeling awkward riding in such tense silence. She could see Dashiell up ahead on his flaming red horse and, in secret, she watched his every move. He had the broadest shoulders she'd ever seen, made broader and bigger by the protection he wore. He had a mail coat on, with a tunic bearing the shield of Savernake on it – a white background with black, crimson, and yellow colors on a tunic the overall color of crimson.

It was a recognizable shield, and all of the men in the party were wearing their Savernake tunics. Lily was wearing a travel dress made of dark red wool while Belladonna wore a brown woolen garment with golden trim and tight sleeves to keep out the cold. She'd been rather pleased with her reflection in the mirror before leaving Ramsbury, thinking she looked somewhat pretty.

Not that it mattered, however. Dashiell wouldn't notice or even care.

"Well," Lily finally muttered, breaking the silence. "This is a cozy little group. I'd find more frivolity in a graveyard."

Belladonna turned to her sister. "You did not have to come," she reminded her. "Why did Acacia not come? She told me she wanted to."

Lily shrugged. "Because spending money is a sin," she said sarcastically. "You know that everything is a sin with her. Thinking about sin is a sin. We are all going to hell, Bella."

Belladonna fought off a grin. "She is simply preparing for the mentality of the abbey," she said. "I do not take her too seriously when she tells me that my vanity is a sin."

Lily snorted. "What sin? And what vanity? Bella, you have no vanity. I've never met such a beautiful woman who had no vanity about it."

Belladonna's smile faded and she looked away. "There is no point."

"What do you mean?"

"The only person I would have see my beauty cares not for it, or for me."

Lily was listening with interest. "What are you talking about?"

Belladonna shook her head, unwilling to elaborate with four big-eared soldiers around and Dashiell several yards ahead.

"It does not matter."

"What happened?" Lily asked. Then, she leaned over towards her sister and whispered. "Has something happened with Dash?"

Belladonna shushed her, glancing around to make sure no one had heard. *Dash*. Just the mention of the man's name set her heart to racing.

"Well," she whispered reluctantly. "I suppose I have found my answer after all of these years."

"What answer?"

Belladonna was trying to keep her voice down. "You know how he will not address me by my name any longer."

"I know. You have told me."

"He used to address me by my name constantly when I was younger but once I became of age, he no longer did it."

"*And?*"

"And I asked him why. He told me it was because he did not want to compromise my reputation."

Lily lifted her eyebrows as if expecting more of an answer. "What else?"

Belladonna frowned. "And when I asked him if he would escort me to Jillayne Chadlington's party, he told me he was ashamed to be seen with me."

Lily's mouth popped open. "He didn't!"

"He *did*. He said that if he was my escort, people would see us together and he intimated that it would be a terrible thing."

Lily could hardly believe it. That wasn't the Dashiell she'd known all these years. The man she'd known was gruff, sometimes quite mean, and very intimidating, but the moment Belladonna wandered into his orbit, he turned into a lamb. Only for Belladonna did he do that. Her youngest sister had such power over the man; anyone could see that. Anyone but Belladonna. Nay, she didn't believe Dashiell could have said such a thing to her sister.

"I cannot comprehend that he should say such a thing," she finally said. "That does not sound like him at all."

Belladonna lowered her gaze, looking off to the side of the road where puddles of water had formed. "Clearly, there is nothing more to say," she said. "It matters not how I feel anymore, Lil. He has made his wishes plain."

Lily still couldn't believe it. More than that, it angered her. Did Dashiell truly intimate that being seen with Belladonna would embarrass him? Her beautiful, spirited sister had loved him for as long as she could recall. Even as a young girl, she adored Dashiell as she adored no one else. Their father, Edward, had been aware of it before his mind was robbed of its ability to think properly, and Lily was certain that Edward had approved of the match. The man loved Dashiell like a son.

And Dashiell had clearly been mad for Belladonna, but all of that seemed to change, however, when she came of age. He was polite to Belladonna, and there were times when they were still companionable, but it was as if Dashiell had a wall up, a wall preventing him from becoming too close to Belladonna. It was propriety, of course, but there was something more to it.

Perhaps, it was time to find out what that was.

Digging her heels into the side of her palfrey, Lily urged the little horse forward, away from her sister as Belladonna hissed at her. She could hear her sister, begging her to stop, but Lily wouldn't listen. She wanted to know first-hand if Dashiell had insulted her sister. If he had, then she was going to give him a telling off. But if not…

Surely, it was a misunderstanding.

Dashiell's fat warhorse tried to snap at the little palfrey as Lily rode alongside him. Dashiell cuffed the horse on the neck, nearly the only thing capable of settling the big horse down.

"My apologies, my lady," he said. "I should have muzzled him. He tends to snap at anything that moves. It is the battle horse in him."

Lily smiled weakly. "No harm done," she said. She was coming to realize that she should probably lead up to her interrogation, so she shielded her eyes from the sun and casually looked at the road ahead. "How long until we reach Marlborough?"

Dashiell turned to the road. "You can probably tell me better than I can tell you," he said, jesting with her. "You have been to Marlborough more than anyone at Ramsbury. They should start calling the town Lily-borough."

Lily's smile turned real. "It is well and good that I go to Marlborough more than anyone, since I am chatelaine at Ramsbury," she said. "I am the one who does the buying for your fine feasts."

"Indeed you do, my lady."

Silence fell between them, but it wasn't uncomfortable. Lily eyed him as she summoned the courage to speak.

"Dash," she finally said. "I must ask you something."

"Anything, my lady."

"And you promise to tell me the truth?"

"Of course, my lady. Upon my oath, I would never lie to you."

"Good." She paused. "Did you tell Belladonna that you would be embarrassed to be seen with her?"

Dashiell looked at her. He wasn't particularly surprised by the question. In fact, he welcomed it – God, did he welcome it! He'd already been planning to speak to Lily about Belladonna, asking for the woman's help to soothe whatever tension was between them, so her question was like a gift from God.

Carefully, he answered, wanting to make it very clear that he held no such opinion of Belladonna.

"Absolutely not, my lady," he said. "Although, I can understand how she could misunderstand what I said. Truly, I was only thinking of her reputation and the fact that she would surely be more comfortable with a man who was closer to her own age."

Lily could read the sincerity on his face. There was much she wanted to say but wasn't sure how to say it.

"Then… then being seen with my sister does not cause you shame?"

"God, no," he said as if it were the most ridiculous thing he'd ever heard. Realizing how he'd sounded, he added quickly, "My lady."

Lily smoothed at her dark hair, blowing in the cold breeze, before turning to glance at her sister, far back in the pack. Belladonna was watching her with great anxiety. She sighed heavily.

"If Belladonna knew I was speaking to you about this, she would disown me," she said. "What I am about to say is in the greatest confidence, Dash. Will you treat it that way?"

Dashiell nodded seriously. "Upon my life, I will. Is something wrong?"

Lily shook her head. "I do not think so," she said. "But I do not really know. Dash, I must know something."

"All you need do is ask."

"Would you…" she began, then stopped. She started again. "Would you have any interest in my sister beyond that of mere friendship? Or does a romance with my sister not appeal to you?"

For the first time in his life, Dashiell thought he might blush. He could feel his cheeks growing hot and he was absolutely mortified. Thank God for the mail hood that covered up a good portion of his face or Lily would have seen that he was flushing like a young squire.

"I... God's Blood," he muttered, trying to regain his composure. "I am an old man, Lady le Cairon. No young lady in her right mind would consider a romance with me. I am too old for such things."

Lily was watching him closely; he seemed nervous when speaking on the subject. Or enraged. "Are you angry at me for asking?"

"Of course not, my lady."

"May I ask if anything would change your mind?"

"You may ask, but I truthfully do not know. What could possibly change the facts?"

"What if I were to tell you that my sister is... fond of you."

He looked at her then, his cheeks so red that he was beginning to sweat. "Your sister and I have long been fond of one another," he said. "We have been friends since my arrival to Ramsbury."

Lily shook her head, looking at him pointedly. "Nay, Dash, not fond as in friendship," she said. "Fond as in... as in *fond*. Very fond. She is partial to you, Dash. Do you get my meaning now?"

Dashiell could hardly believe what he was hearing. Certainly, he grasped her meaning, but it simply wasn't possible. It was the craziest thing he'd ever heard.

"You... you must be mistaken," he stammered.

Lily sighed sharply. "God's Toes, Dash. She's in love with you. Is that plain enough?"

If Dashiell was astonished before, he was so stunned at the revelation that one could have knocked him off his horse with a feather. He stared at Lily as if she had frogs coming out of her ears.

"She… she…" He couldn't even bring himself to say it. Then, he burst out in a loud snap. "*What?*"

Lily shushed him, knowing that surely her sister would have heard his tone. "Be quiet," she hissed. "Do you want everyone to hear? Listen to me well, du Reims – my sister is in love with you. She has been for years. But she does not think you feel the same. If you do, then you had better make your feelings known to her. She is convinced you are disgusted at the mere sight of her. One cannot love a man and not… have him, Dash. It consumes the soul."

She sobered suddenly, thoughts of Bentley filling her brain. As she looked at Dashiell, who seemed to have lost the ability to speak, she offered a few final, and painful, words.

"If you do not love her, then tell me and I shall tell her myself," she muttered. "You need not worry about trying to ease her heart. But if you do love her… Dash, the worst thing in the world you can do is not tell her. At least let her be happy. *You* must be happy, too."

With that, she pulled back on the reins of her palfrey, turning around to rejoin her sister, leaving Dashiell feeling as if a great boulder had just been dropped on him. He could hardly breathe for the weight of it upon his chest. But it was more than the weight of the news – it was the disbelief. He felt as if he were living a dream.

Was it really true? Did Belladonna truly have feelings for him?

God, what had he done in his life to deserve the woman's love? Sweet, gentle, and beautiful Belladonna had feelings for him. *Love*, Lily had said. Nay… this had to be a dream, because there was no world in which a woman like Belladonna would love him.

It simply wasn't possible.

… but, Bloody Hell… *it was*!

Dashiell didn't even realize that, at that moment, his eyes were full of unshed tears of joy.

It was the best day of his life.

"I KNOW YOU told him something," Belladonna hissed at her sister. "What did you tell him to make him yell like that?"

They were entering the outskirts of Marlborough, passing by farmers in their fields, and the wattle and daub huts that made up the fringe of the city. Ever since Lily had indulged in the private conversation with Dashiell, which had been about twenty minutes earlier, Belladonna was hounding her sister about the discussion and Lily was finding other things to talk about.

Finally, Belladonna had enough of her sister's evasiveness.

"If you do not tell me what you said to Dash, I swear I will run right to Bent and tell him every single thing that is in your heart," she threatened. "Do you hear me?"

That drew a reaction from Lily. "You wouldn't dare!"

"Are you certain of that?"

The line was drawn as Lily tried to determine if her sister was bluffing but, knowing Belladonna, she wasn't. She didn't bluff.

"I simply told him how unhappy I was with his behavior," she said. "Must you really ask me, Bella? What in the world do you think I would *really* say to him?"

Belladonna had suspected all along what her sister had done. She'd had time to prepare for that possibility, and she wasn't entirely sure that she was peeved by it. Secretly, she was glad her sister had run straight to Dashiell to give him a tongue lashing on her behalf.

"So you told him that I told you what happened," she said. "Did you berate him?"

"Of course I did."

"And what did he say? Did he beg for forgiveness?"

Lily eyed her. "In a way," she said. "He said that although he understood how you could have misinterpreted what he'd said, he told me that he never meant to insinuate he was ashamed to be seen with you."

Belladonna frowned. "But he said…"

Lily cut her off. "Do you really think he would say such a thing to you, Bella? *Think*. We are speaking of Dash du Reims. The man would simply never insult you, so I do not know why you are carrying on so."

Belladonna shut her mouth, feeling scolded. She'd expected Lily's support because Lily was always quite reasonable, so for her sister to rebuke her so was a blow to Belladonna's anger. It was clear that Lily believed Dashiell, so if Lily believed him… then perhaps Belladonna was simply reacting to the fact that Dashiell had rejected her request to escort her to the party and nothing more.

It was her hurt clouding her judgment.

But she didn't want to be scolded any longer, so she pulled her palfrey to a halt, letting Lily and the escort party move past. Turning her palfrey around, she went to the rear where Bentley was riding astride his big, hairy beast of a horse. Belladonna reined her little palfrey alongside as Bentley smiled politely at her.

"We are nearly to town, my lady," he said pleasantly. "Where will our first stop be?"

Belladonna pondered the coming market and the stalls she usually visited. "The merchant with all manner of scarves and shawls," she said. "You know the man – the one who has a wench dance in front of his stall to attract customers."

Bentley's smile turned into a frown. "Your father told you to stay away from that merchant. The woman who dances with his merchandise has been known to… well, sometimes men return for her. I will say no more."

Belladonna's gloomy mood lifted at Bentley's prim response. "Father told me to stay away from it in the days when he could remember what he'd said," she replied. "He cannot remember that he told me to stay away from it and even if you told him that I disobeyed him, it would not mean anything to him."

Bentley gave her an expression suggesting he didn't like her choice in merchants. "Very well," he muttered. "Does Dash know?"

"He will do what I tell him to do."

"Indeed, he will, but I do not believe he wants you going to that merchant, either."

"But he has the most beautiful things in town," Belladonna insisted. "That is where I intend to go."

She said it with finality and Bentley had no choice but to bow to her wishes. He sighed heavily. "As you say, my lady."

They were traveling closer to the heart of town now, passing through small neighborhoods with the houses packed close together. Children played in the gutters and dogs ran about, barking. The smell of human habitation was strong as they passed down the muddied street and into the main market area of Marlborough.

It was a bustling berg, full of people going about their business. The king had given Marlborough a license for a market and they held one every seventh day of the week, which happened to be today. Therefore, it was quite crowded as they emerged onto the main road, which was wide and sloped slightly to the south. Mud and water gathered on the south side of the avenue, causing the merchants on that side to keep up makeshift barriers to keep the moisture out of their stalls.

The sights and sounds of the town filled Belladonna and her thoughts turned from her scolding sister, and Bentley's prudish opinions, to the very merchant in question. He was down towards the middle of the block, on the corner of a large alley that cut north and south. She spurred her palfrey away from Bentley and towards the front of the escort. She trotted past Lily, through the front two soldiers, and straight past Dashiell.

Dashiell watched with some curiosity as she went right to the merchant with all manner of silken scarves hanging from the eaves of his roof. They blew in the wind in a colorful display. But he quickly realized *which* merchant Belladonna had selected when he saw not only one dancing woman out front, but two. The women were undulating in beautiful clothing, with lovely accessories, to lure in the females in town and their purses.

Like a moth to the flame, Belladonna went straight for the gyrating women. It was like a siren's call, one she could not resist. She didn't wait for any help to dismount her palfrey; she practically leapt off and rushed into the large merchant stall.

As she disappeared inside, Dashiell brought the escort up behind her. One of the soldiers took the reins of her palfrey as Dashiell dismounted his warhorse. Removing the muzzle from his saddlebags, he placed the device over the horse's snout and secured it so the beast wouldn't try to gnash anyone. As he handed the reins over to another soldier, Bentley came up behind him.

"Shall I follow Lady Belladonna?" he asked.

The dancing girls were getting a little too close and Dashiell ignored them, even as they waved silken scarves in his face. One hit him on the cheek.

"Nay," he said, pulling tight his gloves. "I will go with her. You remain with Lady le Cairon. See if there is another merchant she would like to visit, for the look upon her face suggests she wants nothing to do with her sister's choice."

Both Dashiell and Bentley glanced over at Lily, who was still seated upon her palfrey, now with a scowl upon her face. As Bentley nodded, Dashiell pushed past the dancing girls trying to get his attention and into the merchant stall beyond.

It was dark inside, smelling heavily of incense and exotic fragrances. They pulled at Dashiell's nose but he fought it, not wanting to sneeze all over the place. Often, in the springtime when things were blooming, he could sneeze hard enough to give himself a headache, so he had that sensitivity with smells. Around him, tables contained piles of neatly arranged merchandise and in spite of the questionable dancing women out front, the place was packed with proper women shopping for something beautiful and unusual.

Dashiell caught sight of Belladonna near the rear of the stall. She was standing with the merchant himself, a round man who wore colorful clothing and a wrap upon his head that glistened with gold. He was an unusual character and not from England, as one could tell simply by listening to him speak. He had a very odd accent.

And he was quite solicitous to Belladonna, which didn't sit well with Dashiell. He didn't like to see another man being so attentive. As he approached the pair, mail grating and sword rattling, the merchant heard him coming and turned in his direction.

It didn't take a great intellect to see that the knight only had eyes for the lady who was now holding up a pale green silk scarf, embroidered with golden thread. The merchant smiled broadly as he pointed to Belladonna, who was holding the scarf against her skin to better inspect the color.

"Ah, my lord," he said, rather loudly. "Is your wife not beautiful in this color? I have told her that green is the color of angels. They surely will be jealous if she wears such a thing. And she will be the best-dressed wife in all of Wiltshire, I promise. And this!" He suddenly reached over and picked up another scarf, made with silk and strips of a very expensive and very rare fabric called velvet sewn into it. "She will be the most beautiful woman in all of England with this!"

Dashiell was watching the man drape the fabric over Belladonna's slender shoulders. He was rather caught off guard by the man assuming that Belladonna was his wife, but God… it hit him where it hurt.

Lo, that he wished he could claim such a thing.

After what Lily had told him, he seemed to be looking at Belladonna through new eyes. There was more hope in his heart than there had ever been. But before he could speak, Belladonna pulled the scarf from her shoulders and tossed it back onto the table.

"Do not ask him," she told the merchant. "He cares not what I look like, so you would do better asking a horse."

The merchant appeared uncertain with her comments, wondering if something was amiss between the lady and her knight. He started to pull forth other pieces of fabric to show Belladonna, but Dashiell found his tongue.

"Leave us," he growled at the merchant. "Go find someone else to sell your wares to."

The merchant wasn't about to argue with the very muscular, rough-sounding knight. He immediately scampered away as Belladonna looked on with annoyance.

"Why did you do that?" she asked Dashiell. "Bring him back here. I want to see other things. And what are you doing here, anyway? I told you that Bentley would escort me. I would not put you in such a position to have to…"

He cut her off with a quiet but sharp tone. "Enough," he said. "God's Bones, woman, when you get fixated on something, you beat it until it is dead and then some. Stop playing the victim to something you think I said to you. You know very well that was not what I meant."

Belladonna looked at him, but her gaze was guarded. "I know what I heard."

He sighed sharply. Then, he took the scarf out of her hand and grasped her by the arm, pulling her all the way through the merchant's stall and out the rear of it, out into a small yard that was surrounded by other stalls.

There were trunks out here, broken barrels, and other things that the surrounding merchants had thrown out until they could be broken down further or repaired. There was a big Yew tree right in the middle of the courtyard and Dashiell dragged her over to it, far enough so that their words couldn't be heard.

But Belladonna was furious with having been yanked out of the stall. She slapped at Dashiell's hand until he let her go and even, then, she slapped his arm with frustration.

"How dare you manhandle me like that!" she said angrily.

He cocked an auburn eyebrow at her. "Shut your lips," he barked quietly. "I have barely been returned to Ramsbury for a day and already, you are throwing fits and I do not even know why. Now, I will tell you that for certain that I never said I was ashamed to be seen with you. Did you truly think I would ever say such a thing to you, Bella?"

Bella. She heard her name come out of his mouth, as it used to when they were the best of friends. It was like throwing water on a fire and almost instantly, her rage was doused. Taking a deep breath, she was able to face him more calmly. Now, the level of conversation between them was more familiar than it had been in a very long time.

All because he called her Bella.

"Then why did you say that you were afraid that people would see us together?" she wanted to know. "People have been seeing us together for years, Dash. What makes Jillayne's party so different that you should not wish to be my escort?"

She's in love with you, Dash. Lily's words were ringing around Dashiell's head and it was all he could do to stop himself from gushing like a fool. *Careful*, he told himself. He had to be very careful in his response. But, God, he was so unused to speaking of emotions and feelings, and he was terribly out of practice when it came to wooing a woman. He hadn't wooed a woman in over twenty years, and that had ended in disaster.

Perhaps that was one of the reasons why he was so hesitant with Belladonna. Years ago, he'd fallen for an allied lord's daughter. The daughter of Daveigh de Winter of Norwich Castle, Delesse, had been a beautiful young woman who had bewitched him. He'd been fond of her, and told her so, which had worked out fine until a flashy knight named Summerlin from Blackstone Castle had entered the picture and stole her away.

It had been Aston Summerlin's uncle, and Dashiell had heard that the marriage hadn't been a pleasant one. But the days of Delesse de Winter still rang in his head sometimes, and Dashiell realized that her rejection had made him far too timid with women. It had for twenty years.

But now, here he was with a chance to change all of that and he was terrified to take it. But if he didn't at least try, he would never forgive himself.

It was now or never.

"I am going to try and explain my position to you," he said, "but I apologize if I am not concise. I have never been very good with words and you are aware of that. I can only promise that I will try to explain myself and I hope that you will understand. Will you at least listen to everything before you judge whether or not I cannot stand to be seen with you?"

Belladonna frowned, apprehensive of what she might hear. "I do not think I am going to like this."

He held up his hand, as if to beg her patience. "You will, if I do not make a fool out of myself first," he said. "But will you please remember one thing?"

"What?"

"I would sooner throw myself upon my sword than insult you in any fashion. Do you understand?"

Belladonna cocked her head. "I do," she said. "What must you say?"

He took a deep breath. "I want you to look at me," he said after a moment. "I am twice your age. My skin is like leather and I certainly am not the most handsome man in town. Can you not see that?"

Her pale gaze studied him as he seriously tried to spell out the way he saw himself. "Nay," she said finally. "I cannot see that. To me, you will always be Dash, my friend, and the greatest knight Ramsbury has ever seen."

"I am an old man, Bella."

"You are ageless."

That blush in his cheeks threatened again but he fought it. "I wish that was true," he said. "But now that we have taken a look at me, I want you to look at yourself – you are young and beautiful and vibrant. The young girl I know has grown into a woman of astounding beauty and poise. You are an angel on this earth, Bella."

His words flattered her and she grinned modestly. "I had no idea you felt that way."

He was losing the battle against his flush, turning his cheeks ruddy beneath the mail hood. "I have for some time," he said quietly. "Because of this, that is where my concern comes from if people were to see me as your escort to Jillayne's party. Can you understand that?"

Belladonna shook her head. "Nay."

He was becoming flustered. "Because I am old and grizzled, and you are young and beautiful," he said, trying to make his point. "I… I am afraid that *you* would be the laughing stock. There are so many other younger, more handsome men who could be your escort, men worthy of such beauty. Instead, you would go with an old man with skin as tough as hide. *Now* do you understand?"

Belladonna did. Suddenly, his reluctance became clear and her heart about broke. "Oh, Dash," she breathed. "You think that people would laugh at me *because* of you?"

"Of course they would. I could not do that to you."

She sighed heavily. "I… I am so very sorry I became angry with you. I did not know you felt this way."

"You never gave me a chance to tell you before you were rushing off in a rage."

She grunted miserably. "I have been known to do that." Her focus on him was intense. "Dash, I have known you more than half my life. We were such great friends, you and I, until I became of age. Then, you seemed to back away from me, so very quickly. You became so formal with me. It hurt me to lose my dearest friend like that. Can… can you please tell me why you did it? Was it something I said or did to make you unhappy towards me?"

Dashiell could feel his walls of self-protection going down. He was clinging to what Lily had told him, praying that it was true. Gazing into Belladonna's face at the moment, he could believe it was true. There was something in her eyes, he wanted to believe, that was meant only for him.

Only for him…

"Because you became of marriageable age," he said simply. "It would have been most improper for me to maintain such a close friendship with you. What would a prospective husband think? It might have damaged your chances for marriage. Unless I am courting you, or we are betrothed, it simply isn't proper for you and me to have such a close friendship. Surely you understand that."

Belladonna did, but they were on a subject she'd wanted to bring up with him for four long years. Now, she finally had her answer as to why he'd been so formal with her, why he'd pulled away from her. He felt himself unworthy.

He was anything but unworthy.

Summoning her courage, she spoke.

"You are Dashiell du Reims, Viscount Winterton," she said softly. "Someday, you shall be the Earl of East Anglia. But even if you were a simple knight, with no past and no future, you would still be Dashiell du Reims, a man whom I've adored since I was a girl. You would still be the most worthy man I know. Do you know that when I was younger, I used to pretend that you and I were married?"

He grinned, nervously. "Me?" he said in disbelief. "I am not usually the object of a young maiden's daydreams."

"But you were the object of mine."

"Surely you could have chosen a better husband, even for a dream."

She laughed quietly. "There is no better man in the whole of England as far as I am concerned," she said. Then, she sobered quickly, an earnest look crossing her face. "Please, Dash... will you *please* escort me to Jillayne's party? I do not care what others think. I only care that we are able to share the time together."

Of course, he couldn't resist her. "If that is your wish, then I shall escort you."

A smile of genuine joy spread across her lips. "And you shall dance every dance with me?"

He was hesitant. "I have not danced in years, Bella. You might come away with a broken foot, or worse."

"I will help you remember how. Please?"

He seemed to be doing an awful lot of smiling, at least for him. And, he folded to her wishes as if he had no spine, no mind of his own. At that moment, he would have given her the world had she asked for it.

"Aye, my lady, if it is your wish."

"Good," she said happily. "Then let us return to the merchant so that I may find some fabric to make you a tunic to match my dress. I am wearing yellow silk, so I shall hunt down something yellow for you. And... Dash?"

He was feeling so giddy at the moment that he was nearly light-headed with it. "My lady?"

Her focus lingered on him for a moment. "When we go to this party, I will still pretend that we are married," she said. "It is a dream I have."

With that, she pushed past him, heading back into the merchant stall and leaving Dashiell feeling as if a great door had just opened up between them.

Somehow, in this brief conversation, they had gone from old and dear friends to something else, something more. It was different between them now; he could feel it. He was looking at her as if there were some hope for more than simple friendship between them and she was looking at him the same way.

He couldn't stop himself from calling out to her before she entered the stall.

"Bella?"

She came to a halt, turning to look at him. "Are you going to tell me to stop dreaming?"

Oh, God, if he had wings, he would have soared into the heavens with the expression on her face being the wind beneath his wings. He could hardly breathe for the heavy beating of his heart.

"Nay," he murmured, just loud enough for her to hear him. "I was going to ask if I can dream with you."

Belladonna's face split in two with a smile that lit up the sky. All she did was nod, once, and disappear into the stall.

With a smile all his own, Dashiell followed.

CHAPTER SIX

Lily was trying not to look at him but, God's Bones, it was difficult.

Bentley was standing near the entry to the merchant shop that Belladonna and Dashiell had just disappeared into. His big arms were folded across his chest and he stood there, watching the door, or watching people pass by, looking at anything but her.

Lily should have been used to it by now. Three years of hell in a marriage with Clayton, but she'd behaved properly in all that time in spite of being in love with another man. There was nothing clandestine going on, but Lily had to admit that it was mostly Bentley's doing. He told her on the eve of her marriage to Clayton that he would not carry on with another man's wife, and Lily had tearfully understood. Three years later, she still understood.

But that didn't mean she agreed.

Clayton was horrific in bed. Their wedding night had been a painful experience with a callous lover. Every time Clayton touched her, Lily imagined it was Bentley, seeing his strong body over hers, the warmth of his touch against her flesh. Even though they'd been sweet on each other before the advent of Clayton, they had never consummated the relationship. It had nearly killed Lily to surrender her virginity to a man she hardly knew but hated already.

It had nearly killed Bentley to know that what he loved belonged to Clayton.

But they hadn't really discussed it since that terrible day. Any conversation between them had been polite and distant, because Bentley was very conscious of what others thought and would witness. He didn't want word getting back to Clayton that his wife was carrying on with a knight. It was certainly more to protect her than to protect him.

But here, there were no prying eyes, at least not like there was at the castle. Lily did so long to speak with Bentley on more than the weather or the fine presentation of a feast. She was a reasonable, moral woman and not given to giddy thoughts of romance but, at the moment, she simply wanted to talk to the man who had meant everything to her, once.

Truth be told, he still did.

As she watched, the dancers in front of the merchant's stall began to set their sights on Bentley as he stood near the mouth of the stall, waiting. The dark-haired vixens were fixed on him, dragging their silk scarves across his face as he tried to ignore them. Sensing that Bentley might need saving, and not liking that those terrible women were teasing her sweet and noble Bentley, Lily slipped from her palfrey.

"Back, you cats," she snapped at the women as she walked up. When one of the women hesitated, Lily held up a balled fist. "Did you hear me, you used hole? Get away from him!"

They women scampered. Lily watched them hurry away, pretending not to be embarrassed or afraid of the angry woman who evidently wouldn't hesitate to beat them. As they resumed their dancing at a distance from Bentley, Lily turned to the man.

"It seemed to me as if you needed someone to chase away the scabs," she said. "I hope you do not mind."

Bentley was trying very hard not to burst out laughing. "Mind?" he repeated in disbelief. "Where did you learn such terrible language?"

Lily fought off a grin. "There is much I know these days, Ashbourne," she said. "I think you would be surprised."

He shook his head, slowly. "Nay, I would not be surprised at all," he said. "You are an accomplished woman, Lady le Cairon, even when dealing insults."

Lily stood there a moment, looking at the dancers as they tried to entice shoppers. Her warm expression faded into a grimace.

"God," she muttered. "I hate hearing that from your lips."

Bentley knew that tone of voice with her, soft and sensual, and it was like a dagger to his heart. It was a tone that haunted his dreams, and now he was hearing it again. He wasn't sure he was strong enough to resist it.

"What? That you are accomplished?" He tried to feign ignorance.

But Lily sighed heavily. "Nay," she muttered. "Lady le Cairon. I have never hated it so much as I do when I hear it from you."

Bentley felt himself being sucked into something he'd been struggling for three years to avoid. He'd tried; God knew, he'd tried. But he was still in love with Lily as he had always been. There was no use in him trying to deny it, but hearing those words from her lips after all this time was painful.

"Hate it or not, it is your name," he said quietly.

"Do not ever say it again."

"What would you have me call you?"

"Lily," she whispered. "You used to call me Lily."

Beside her, she could hear him sigh. "You know I cannot do that."

"Then address me as 'my lady'. But never again will I hear that… that *name* come from your lips. Promise me."

"I promise."

A silence settled between them, one of pain and longing. Bentley found himself wishing Lily would move away but, in the same breath, he was glad she was standing next to him. He knew it was dangerous to allow himself to entertain feelings he'd tried so hard to forget but, at the moment, he couldn't help it. The shock of her taking their conversation to a personal level so quickly was something he wasn't able to adequately combat.

"Tell me something, Bent," Lily said quietly. "Are you happy?"

"Are you?"

"Nay."

"Nor am I."

Lily bit her lip, feeling tears sting her eyes. "It has been a long time since we have discussed your leaving Ramsbury," she said. "Have you changed your mind about it?"

"Do you want me to leave?"

"Of course not."

He didn't say anything for a moment. "Even if we can never be, you know I cannot leave you," he muttered. "It would tear me apart to do so. You may, therefore, take comfort in the fact that I will never leave you, not ever."

Lily was losing the fight against her tears. "I miss you so, Bent."

"And I miss you."

"Do you love me still?"

"Still, and always."

Lily put a hand to her face, quickly wiping at the tears that were falling. "And I love you," she whispered. "Until I die, Bent. That will never change."

"I know. But it is still good to hear you say it."

"And you. Are we truly so foolish to linger on something that can never be?"

"Foolish, nay. But it does make us rather pathetic creatures."

"I would rather be pathetic in this life knowing I can never have you than live a thousand lifetimes without you."

It was a difficult thing for him to hear. So difficult, in fact, that he wondered if it wouldn't be easier for her if he did leave. He had, indeed, considered leaving Ramsbury a few times, but he'd never been able to summon the courage. The truth was that he would rather be near the woman he could never have than try to live without her.

Pathetic, indeed.

"Go inside and see what is keeping your sister," he said, simply to change the subject away from something that was becoming far too heavy. "Mayhap there is something lovely you would like to purchase as well."

Lily nodded, doing as she was told, but it wasn't enough to distract her from her conversation with Bentley. She shouldn't have brought anything up; they'd been so good at letting the situation lie. All these years, she'd simply let things alone. But today... today, something in her soul needed satisfying. She needed to hear if Bentley still loved her, and he did.

They were feelings most reciprocated.

"Lily!"

Belladonna was calling to her from a corner of the merchant stall, and Lily headed in her sister's direction. Belladonna was holding up a mustard-yellow piece of fine woolen cloth, holding it up to the light.

"Look," Belladonna said. "What do you think?"

Lily struggled to turn her thoughts away from Bentley as she fingered the material. "Lovely," she said. "But it seems heavy."

"It is," Belladonna said, handing the entire section of cloth over to the merchant. "It is for Dash. He has agreed to escort me to Jillayne's party."

Lily fought off a grin. "Isn't he embarrassed to be seen with you?"

"I am not."

Dashiell came up behind them, looking between Lily and Belladonna. "My lady has allowed me to explain what I meant yesterday and has been gracious enough to invite me, once again, to escort her to the party. I have agreed."

Lily couldn't help but laugh, but it was a joyful laugh. "Excellent," she said. "Now I do not have to listen to Bella whine about you any longer. Bella, if you do not understand the next time Dash says something to offend you, do us all a favor and ask him to explain himself before you decide you are angry with him."

Belladonna twisted her lips wryly. "It was a misunderstanding and nothing more," she said, wanting to divert the attention from her. "If you are going to purchase something, then hurry. We have more places to visit."

Lily found herself being ushered around by the merchant to a section of the stall that contained garments that had been cut from cloth and loosely basted. There was a lovely pink garment there, made from damask, and she fingered it longingly. She was an excellent seamstress and she thought that she could alter the dress enough so that, perhaps, she could wear it to Jillayne's party. Even though Clayton would be her escort, Bentley would be going, too, and she very much wanted to look pretty for him.

Such was the pathetic secret they shared.

But it was of no matter. In little time, the merchant was carefully wrapping purchases from both ladies in burlap, tying them off with twine so they would be easy to carry. Dashiell and Bentley carried out packages from the merchant's stall and secured them to their saddles. When their saddles would hold no more, the soldiers had their saddles loaded up with packages as well.

The morning of shopping turned into an afternoon of shopping. Belladonna seemed in very good spirits, so Lily knew that she and Dashiell must have settled their differences. She was glad. She also wondered if anything she'd said to Dashiell had made a difference in the end, but she didn't ask. All that mattered was that Dashiell seemed lighter of heart, and so did Belladonna.

That was all Lily could ask for. Even if she could never truly be happy, she hoped and prayed that Belladonna and Dashiell would be able to find their happiness with one another.

But Belladonna's shopping hunger gave Lily an excuse to spend a precious afternoon with Bentley, away from Clayton and away from the troubles of Ramsbury. A peaceful, blissful afternoon that meant the world to her. Bentley had reiterated his love for her, and she for him and, for that, Lily was deeply grateful. It gave her the will to soldier on.

Whatever the world brought them, as long as she and Bentley remained strong, she knew that nothing could destroy what they had.

Even if that love was never to be realized.

SHE WAS GRUNTING like a pig beneath him.

Every time he thrust into her, she grunted, as if all of the air had been squeezed out of her body.

Gathering her limp body into his arms, Clayton held her by the hair as he rammed his manhood into her, again and again, pumping into her so hard that her teeth rattled. Faster and faster he went, feeling her hot, limp body in his arms, but that was the way he liked it. He didn't like his women responsive, and this one was the least responsive of the bunch. She was like warm dough, and he was able to mold her.

Acacia's legs were spread wide as Clayton's narrow buttocks thrust him into her body over and over. Clayton's hot, smelly breath filled the space between them as he heaved and gasped, sweat dripping down her neck. Faster and faster he went until he groaned loudly, spilling his seed deep into her body.

Beneath him, Acacia squirmed and he yanked on her hair to stop her from moving.

"Hold still," he grunted. "Stop moving until I give you permission to do so."

Beneath Clayton's heavy body, Acacia couldn't breathe but she knew better than to complain. On her stomach, she was buried in the mattress as he held on to her tightly as if fearful she would try to get away.

And on top of her, he remained, his body still buried in hers as his seed spread. Acacia had a nasty little secret and it was lying on top of her; this had been her secret for the past year, ever since she'd made the decision to commit herself to Amesbury and Clayton had tried to talk her out of it.

For Clayton, his reasons had been two-fold: when he became the duke, Acacia would make a valuable commodity for an allied marriage. It was also a rebellion against a wife who loved another. To punish Lily, he'd taken up with Acacia, and the plain, quiet sister was easily manipulated. No man had ever told her she was pretty, but Clayton had. Weak as she was, it had taken very little for her to succumb to his will.

Being in Clayton's arms made her feel wanted and whole, something she'd never had in her life. He'd told her that he didn't want her to go to Amesbury, that he would find her a fine husband, but first he needed to teach her how to please a man.

Being ignorant, she'd fallen for it. But finding her a husband wasn't what Clayton had in mind at all. She was only something to bed when Lily was away, something he could dominate and control, only Acacia couldn't see that. All she knew was that Clayton made her feel needed.

Did she feel guilty that her sister's husband had become her lover? Nay, she didn't. Lily had Bentley to occupy her thoughts, and poor Clayton had no one. Acacia had never mentioned Bentley to Clayton, but she was aware that he knew. Everyone at Ramsbury had known of the romance between Lily and Bentley before Clayton had appeared. But Clayton, along with his father, had worked hard to convince the duke that he would be a better husband for Lily and, in the end, he won out over Bentley. Clayton had married a woman in love with another man, and Acacia only felt pity for him.

To her, Lily was the wicked one.

Consequently, she'd been very easy to manipulate. Their affair was a secret. Clayton had told her that it was something they had to keep from Lily. Lily didn't understand him. In fact, Lily hated him, and only Acacia could comfort him and see to his needs. They couldn't let their secret be known or it might jeopardize Acacia's chances of finding a good husband if it became common knowledge that Clayton was teaching her how to please a man. So, controlled by a man who used her as his whore, Acacia kept the secret.

A dirty, nasty little secret.

"Can I move now?" she asked, her mouth muffled by the mattress.

Clayton had been dozing on top of her and was disturbed by her words. He wriggled his hips, feeling his manhood as it grew flaccid, and pushed himself off of Acacia's long, boney body. He lay there, staring up at the ceiling, as Acacia sat up in bed with the intention of dressing. But Clayton stopped her.

"Nay," he told her. "You'll not cover yourself up, not yet. Turn and face me. Let me see you."

Embarrassed that she was naked, Acacia turned so he could get a look at her naked chest. Her breasts were small, the nipples large. Clayton reached up and pinched one, causing her to flinch.

"You missed me while I was away." It was not a question.

Acacia winced as he pinched her nipple too hard. "There... there was much to do," she said. "I did not have time to miss anyone."

Clayton's expression hardened. "If you did not miss me, then mayhap you had someone else to fill your time," he said. "One of the soldiers?"

Acacia shook her head, trying to pull away from him but he still had a nipple pinched painfully between his fingers. "Of course not," she said. "There is no one else."

Clayton eyed her, finally letting go of her breast. "There will never be anyone else but me," he said. "Must I remind you of that? I am the only one who knows your needs, and you are the only one who knows mine."

Acacia wouldn't look at him. Moments like this always made her feel uncomfortable and confused. Clayton had promised her so many things and he hadn't followed through on one of them.

"Someday, there will be someone else," she said, summoning her courage. "You have promised me a husband. My family still believes I am going to Amesbury next month, so now would be the time to announce a betrothal."

The conversation often followed this path. He hadn't been around Acacia for a few months, so he wasn't surprised this subject was coming up again quickly. The woman was pledged to Amesbury and he'd been putting off making any move to secure her a husband. It was so nice to have a woman who bowed to his wishes that he simply didn't want to think about the eventuality of him actually having to follow through on something he'd told her.

"We will put off Amesbury," he told her. "You will write to them and tell them that you will not be attending their order next month. Tell them your father is too ill for you to leave."

Acacia looked at him. "And then what?" she asked. "More of this? I heard you tell Bella that you had a husband in mind for her. You called the man by name. But what about me? You promised me a husband, too."

"But your family believes you are committing yourself to the abbey."

"If I have a marital prospect, I will not have to!"

She snapped at him and he didn't like it. Open-palmed, he smacked her in the face and she gasped, a hand flying to her cheek in surprise. Clayton sat up.

"You will not speak to me like that," he said. "Your future is in my hands, Acacia. I am trying to make you a fine wife for a future husband, but you are not ready yet. There is still much you need to know."

Acacia was humiliated, hurt. "Lily came to you pure," she said. "She did not know anything when it came to pleasing a man. Why must I be taught?"

"Because Lily is useless!" he snapped, lunging out of bed and looking for his breeches. "She came to me useless and cold because she had given herself to another man. To Bentley. Do you not understand? I am trying to mold you so that a future husband will be happy to have you. Do you think I would be so foolish as to pledge you to a friend, to an important man, only to have you embarrass me with your ignorance? You are not a great beauty, woman, so you must have some redeeming talents."

Unfortunately, that made some sense to Acacia. Lowering her gaze, she thought she understood what he was telling her, unaware that it was more manipulation.

"Then I am sorry to have questioned you," she said quietly.

"All of this, I am doing for you!"

Acacia nodded submissively. "I understand, Clayton."

He found his breeches and pulled them on, eyeing her lowered head. With his lust satisfied, he had no more use for her at the moment. In fact, she was only serving to frustrate him.

"Get dressed," he told her. "Go about your business. Mayhap, I will visit you later, after Lily has gone to sleep."

"Aye, Clayton."

Standing up, she quickly found her shift and pulled it over her head as Clayton finished dressing. They were in his private chamber, a room with two entrances – one for him, and one for the servants. When Acacia finished dressing and fled from the servant's entrance, Clayton was left wondering just how long he could keep this charade going.

He had no feelings for Acacia. But he knew, at some point, something would have to give – either he would have to send her to Amesbury or he would have to find her a husband. As the daughter of a duke, she was valuable, much as Belladonna was. But unlike Belladonna, Acacia was not a virgin. That would have to be made clear to any future husband, greatly diminishing her prospects.

But he couldn't think about that now. He'd bedded his first woman since his return to Ramsbury. Tonight, providing Lily cooperated, he would bed his second. But just as he finished on that thought, he could feel his lust rise again. He hadn't had a woman the entire time he was on the battle campaign, and he found that one encounter with Acacia wasn't enough. He needed her again.

He sent his manservant to find Acacia again and send her back to him. He was so involved in growing excited every time he pulled her hair, making her scream, that he failed to hear the sentries on the wall announcing the return of the party from Marlborough.

CHAPTER SEVEN

IT WAS NEARLY sunset when the Belladonna, Dashiell, Lily, and Bentley returned from Marlborough.

Weighed down with merchandise, Dashiell sent the servants into a frenzy as they rushed out to the escort to collect the purchases and take them inside. The final tally had been quite expensive – silk scarves, four cut and loosely basted dresses, hose, hair combs, hair nets, a heavy gold necklace from the goldsmith, and perfume that smelled of flowers.

Most of it was Belladonna's. Something about having Dashiell by her side had turned her into a spending fool. It had been ages since she'd spent such a happy, carefree day, and all of it with Dashiell by her side. He was never anything other than proper, but there was a gleam in his eyes now when he looked at her, a spark that warmed her heart.

She could hardly believe it.

How long had she dreamed that the man might return her feelings? Her strong, powerful, handsome Dash, a man she felt attached to as she'd never felt attached to anyone, ever. It seemed as if he'd always been part of her life and she knew her father loved him also. Dashiell was the son he'd never had, so she knew her father would have been thrilled with the turn of events.

In fact, she wanted very much to tell him, even if he wouldn't understand.

As Dashiell and Bentley disbanded the escort, and Lily went to check on the preparations for the evening meal, Belladonna made her way into the keep to see her father. With the sun setting, the servants were beginning to light the torches on the interior of the keep, which could be very dark without a bit of light.

Belladonna passed servants as they lit the fatted torches in the great iron sconces in the entry, heading up the narrow staircase that led to the floor above. Her father's chamber was there, as was Lily's and Clayton's. Lily and Clayton had separate bedchambers but shared a common chamber between them, yet it was a room Lily seldom visited. Clayton had taken it over and the woman wanted nothing to do with it.

Nor did Belladonna. Any place that had Clayton's stink on it was a place to be avoided. On the level above the entry, she headed for her father's great cedar door. It was at the end of the corridor, as his room overlooked the bailey. The door was always bolted from the inside, mostly to keep the duke from wandering and, not wanting to disturb the man if he was sleeping, Belladonna slipped into a secondary access passage that was used by the servants.

It was a service passage between chambers and it led to a door that opened up into her father's chamber, an unobtrusive door for servants to come and go in silence. But the passageway was very dark as she entered it with the only light coming from a cracked-open door that led into Clayton's chamber.

Belladonna didn't want to see Clayton. She didn't know where the man was, and she surely didn't care, but she had to pass his door in order to get to the one leading into her father's chamber. Quietly, she slipped up to Clayton's door with the intention of closing it when she heard what sounded like a cry of pain.

Startled, Belladonna instinctively peered into the crack in the door to see what was happening in the chamber. A second cry of pain was most concerning, and as her gaze fell on the semi-darkened chamber, she could see movement on the bed beyond.

The coverlet was on the floor and she could see the back of Clayton has he knelt upon the bed. It took Belladonna all of a split second to realize the man was naked and clearly having sex with a woman other than her sister. The cries of pain were coming from the woman in his bed, as he had her hair wounded up in his left hand, tugging on it as he thrust into her from behind. The woman was on her hands and knees, and Clayton was slapping his body against hers.

The smacking sound of flesh was sickening.

When she realized what she was seeing, Belladonna was overcome with shock and disgust. She was about to turn away for, certainly, this was a memory she was going to try for the rest of her life to forget, when Clayton yanked on the woman's hair again and pulled her into a semi-upright position. That was when Belladonna realized that she knew the woman.

It was Acacia.

Belladonna slapped both of her hands over her mouth, muffling the cry of astonishment when she realized that Clayton was bedding her middle sister. He let go of her hair, now holding her by both arms as he pounded into her body while Acacia groaned and cried.

Clearly, whatever was happening was against her will and Belladonna was preparing to rush into the room and brain Clayton over the back of the head with whatever weapon she could find. She was so stunned and horrified that her entire body was tingling; she knew that she had to save Acacia from Clayton's barbaric attack. But as she put her hand on the door to yank it open, fully prepared to risk her life to save Acacia, her sister put both of her hands up and touched Clayton's face as he leaned over to nibble her white shoulder.

"I lied," she said in a tone Belladonna had never heard her use before. "I did miss you while you were away. I missed you dreadfully."

Clayton's response was to bite down on her flesh again, causing her to gasp. But it wasn't a gasp of pain or fear; it was one of pleasure.

Confused, Belladonna refrained from rushing into the room because the situation was becoming clear – whatever was happening,

Acacia seemed to be a willing accomplice. This was no forced sex, no rape. Acacia was actively participating.

Hand still on her mouth, Belladonna stumbled away from the cracked door, shocked to the bone. It was beyond belief; prim and deeply devout Acacia was having sexual relations with Clayton, and willingly doing so. The reality of it hit her like a battering ram.

Belladonna truly thought she might vomit.

Somehow, she found her way out of the passage, heading back down the narrow stairs and into the now brightly-lit entry. But she didn't stop there. Her hands were still on her mouth as she fled the keep, out into the dusk, where the last of the escort party was being dissolved. Bentley had left the area, but Dashiell was still there.

Belladonna headed right for him.

Dashiell hadn't seen her coming. He was talking to one of the soldiers in the escort, a seasoned man who had seen many years of service with Savernake. They weren't discussing the trip into Marlborough, in fact, but the new recruits that were now bedding down for the night in the big training area over near the stables.

The smoke from the cooking fires was already filling the air and Dashiell was commenting on the rag-tag look of the latest recruits. His first clue that someone was coming up behind him was when the old soldier seemed to be looking over his shoulder and not directly at him. That made Dashiell turn around.

Belladonna had her hands over her mouth and was walking very quickly with her head lowered. As the old soldier left to go about his duties, Dashiell reached out to Belladonna when she came near. The moment he grasped her arm, however, she burst into quiet, hysterical tears.

Dashiell was gravely concerned. "Bella?" he asked. "What is wrong? Are you ill?"

Belladonna couldn't even speak. She was nodding her head, unsteadily, but she was sobbing so heavily that Dashiell couldn't make heads or tails out of what she was trying to say. He tried to pull her back over to the keep so they could speak somewhere in private, but she shook her head violently and yanked away from him. Having no idea what to do, Dashiell began to pull her with him, walking in the direction of the troop house and the knight's quarters in the hopes of calming the woman down.

"Bella," he whispered anxiously. "What has happened? Is it your father?"

She shook her head, which gave him some relief. For a moment, he'd been concerned that something had befallen the duke. He continued walking with her, his hand on her arm but refraining from trying to give her any comfort, at least not out in the open for all to see. She was clearly devastated about something and he was desperate to know what it was.

They walked until they passed into the shadow of the great curtain wall and Dashiell saw an opportunity for some privacy. By the time he pulled her over into the darkened area by the wall, she was only slightly less hysterical. Dashiell faced her with great concern.

"Will you tell me what happened?" he asked gently.

She spoke hesitantly. "Oh, Dash," she sobbed. "It… it was terrible!"

"What was terrible, lamb?"

Belladonna was so upset that she didn't even notice he'd used his pet name for her. It had been years since he'd done that and had she been in her right mind, it would have thrilled her. But, at the moment, she couldn't shake the horrific vision she'd just encountered. It was all she could focus on.

"I-I went to see my father," she said, swallowing hard and laboring to breathe. "I-I wanted to check on him to see if his day had been a good one. I was going to use the servant's passage so I could slip in without disturbing him, but when I went into the passage, I saw that

Clayton's door was partially open."

Dashiell suddenly tensed, his grip on her tightening. "Did Clayton do something to you?"

She shook her head because he looked so terribly fearsome at that moment. He frightened her. "Nay," she said quickly. "Not me. But I saw... I saw..."

She was off on a crying jag again, weeping into her hand. Although Dashiell was glad for Clayton's sake that the man hadn't done anything to Belladonna, still, he was deeply curious to know what had her so upset.

"What did you see?" he asked.

Belladonna looked up at him with big, watery eyes. "It is so horrible, I am ashamed to tell you."

"Please. I only want to help."

She took a deep breath as she once again faced a memory she was having a difficult time accepting.

"I saw Acacia," she finally whispered. "She was... with Clayton."

Dashiell didn't quite understand what she was telling him. "With him?" he repeated. "What do you mean?"

Belladonna fixed him in the eyes, deeply ashamed that she was voicing a most unsettling vision. "In his bed," she murmured. "He was... bedding her."

The impact of the words hit Dashiell, washing over him like the ripples in a pond. He went from concerned to astounded all in the blink of an eye. But he didn't react outwardly; he was very good at concealing his emotions, something that served him well in battle and when dealing with men. It was never good for men to know what one was feeling, and Dashiell clung hard to that opinion.

But now... now he hid his shock because Belladonna was already overwrought. Should he become upset, it would only fuel her hysteria. Truth be told, he wasn't surprised to hear any of this, at least not about

Clayton. The man was lower than dirt in his opinion, so to bed Acacia… Clayton had taken himself to new levels of degradation as far as Dashiell was concerned.

The man with limited character had now become immoral, as well.

"I see," he said, his voice calm and even. The hand on her arm began caressing her, comfortingly. "There was no mistake, Bella? The keep can be dark and…"

She cut him off, shaking her head. "I heard her before I even saw her," she said, repulsed by the memory. "She was crying, so I peeked into the chamber to see if someone was injured and saw her as he… I cannot even speak of it, Dash. It is too shameful."

He understood. For her to see something like that, as a woman who had never experienced such intimacy on her own, must have surely been shocking. It was probably even off-putting. His other hand came up and he held her in his gentle grip as she struggled to regain her composure.

"There is no need for you to speak of it to me, or to anyone," he said. "But I am glad that you trusted me enough to tell me. Did Clayton see you?"

She shook her head. "Nay," she said, wiping at her eyes. "Neither one of them saw me."

Dashiell sighed faintly, thinking on the greater implications of the situation. Belladonna had evidently stumbled across a secret and, knowing Clayton, he wouldn't take kindly if he discovered that his indiscretions were known.

Clayton was already an unpredictable man by nature. And as Dashiell once said to Belladonna, he had to fight with the man in battle and needed to keep the peace between them, but this… given that he already thought the man was scum, it was going to be increasingly difficult not to let his emotions overcome his judgment.

"It is good that you were not seen," he said. "But allow me to explain something to you. You and I are in possession of knowledge that I am sure Clayton does not wish to be widely known. Not only would it shame Lady le Cairon, but I am sure Clayton would be quite irate at you for having seen something you should not have seen. I do not want his venom turned on you, for we already know you are on his mind. If he knows what you have seen, it might make the situation… worse."

Belladonna wiped the last of her tears away, feeling comforted by Dashiell's calming manner. But his words concerned and confused her.

"Certainly, I would never say anything to anyone," she said. "I would never dream of humiliating Lily like that. But I do not understand why Acacia… *how* could she do such a thing?"

Dashiell was wondering the same thing of the militantly pious sister. "I do not know," he said, caressing her arms and not even realizing he was doing it. It seemed the most natural of things to do. "The woman is supposed to join Amesbury next month, so to do something like this… I will admit, I am baffled."

Now that the shock of what she'd seen was wearing off, Belladonna was becoming aware of his tender touch, rubbing her arms gently to comfort her. It was enough to set her heart to racing.

"She is the one to tell us that every thought we have is a sin," she said. "If I long for a hair ribbon, Acacia tells me that it is a sin to want for earthly treasures. If Lily raises her voice, then Acacia will say it is a sin for her to be cruel. Everything is a sin to her, so I do not understand how… *why*… she would do this with her own sister's husband. The more I think on it, the angrier I become."

Dashiell lifted an eyebrow. "You are angry for the shame she shall bring upon Lady le Cairon, and that is understandable," he said. "But you are not angry because Lily has feelings for her husband. Remove the shame from the situation and there is nothing left. It is not as if Acacia is hurting Lily in any way."

Belladonna shook her head, reluctantly. "Nay," she admitted. "Lily cannot stand the sight of Clayton. She cringes every time... well, every time he touches her. She has told me so."

Dashiell grunted. "As a normal woman would," he muttered. Then, he realized he'd gravely insulted Acacia in that statement. "What I mean to say is that he has not exactly been kind to Lady le Cairon. You can see that there is no love lost between them."

"But he will be the duke when my father dies," Belladonna whispered, closing her eyes at the horrific thought. "Dash, what is going to happen when he becomes the duke? It will be hell to live here. I will not let him do to me what he's done to Acacia!"

Dashiell looked at her, quite seriously. "I will kill him if he tries," he rumbled. "Make no mistake, Bella. If he so much as looks in your direction, I will kill him."

The conversation was taking a distinct turn from what Belladonna had witnessed to Dashiell's rather strong declaration. Belladonna's thoughts returned to the merchant's yard and how she'd told him she would still dream that they were married. He asked if he could dream with her.

Perhaps it was bold of her to think there was something more to a simple escort to a party, but she very much wanted to believe so. His threat to kill Clayton made her believe that maybe – just maybe – there *was* something more.

"That is sweet of you to be so chivalrous, but if he is the duke, he can act upon his wishes and I will have little to say in the matter," she said. "I was thinking, Dash... do you believe he is serious about marrying me to this Lord Sherston? He said as much last night."

That subject rubbed Dashiell the wrong way. The mention of a marriage between Belladonna and Anthony Cromford was enough to fill his veins with anger. He'd been furious about it last night and he was still furious about it today. But those same words Christopher had spoken to him kept rolling around in his head...

Can you really stand the thought of her being someone else's wife?

Gazing down at Belladonna, he knew he couldn't. He'd spent the past four years dodging around the subject of his feelings for her, of feeling unworthy of such a woman. But Lily's words to him today had changed everything.

She's in love with you, Dash.

God knows, he was in love with her, too. Perhaps it was time to finally show some courage. It had been successful in the merchant's yard so, perhaps, that streak of good fortune would continue where Belladonna was concerned.

"He may be serious, but the match will never happen," he said. "I would not worry over it if I were you."

Belladonna's brow furrowed. "Of course I shall worry over it. I do not wish to marry someone of Clayton's choosing. Can you imagine the horrible husband he would saddle me with?"

Dashiell gave her a half-grin. "I know Lord Sherston. He is not the bad sort, which makes him a surprising choice for Clayton."

She stiffened. "I am *not* going to marry him."

Dashiell's eyes twinkled at her in the dim light. "I know."

"*How* do you know?"

"Because I will not let it happen."

"But how?"

He cocked his head and looked at her. "Tell me something," he said. "If you could choose any husband in the world, who would it be?"

Now, the question was posed to her, one that would make or break Dashiell. He thought he was rather clever by asking her such a thing. He wanted to hear what she had to say.

But to Belladonna, it was an unexpected question and she found herself scrambling for an answer. Truly, there was only one answer, but she wasn't sure how Dashiell would take it. Certainly, he'd flirted with her earlier, and even now he was determined to be her guardian and protector, but that didn't mean he wanted to marry her.

... did it?

She was going to find out.

"I told you that I have often pretended you and I were married," she said. "If I am given a choice, why can I not marry you?"

It was a blunt question she'd turned right around on him. Dashiell no longer thought himself clever for having broached the subject. But the more he thought about it, the more he realized that there was no more perfect question in the universe. He was starting to feel giddy again.

"You would choose me?" he asked softly.

Belladonna hesitated a moment before nodding. "You are not married," she said. "I am not married. Why can we not be married – to each other?"

He realized he was still holding on to her, his hands on her arms. He thought he should probably let her go, for propriety's sake but, then again, he didn't want to let her go. His grip tightened.

"Dreaming we are married is one thing," he said quietly. "The reality is quite another. I am much older than you are."

"So you've told me."

"As the daughter of a duke, you could command a very fine husband."

"I will command the Earl of East Anglia."

She had a point. Dashiell struggled not to let his excitement overrun him. He had to be logical about this.

"And so, you will," he said. "But, truly… you would want an old man for a husband?"

She hissed at him. "Stop saying that," she said. "You are handsome and ageless. I have told you this. Dash, if you do not wish to marry me, simply say so. But you said earlier that you wished to dream with me, so I assumed… I thought it was of some interest to you."

So there it was. He couldn't jest his way out of it, or try to force her to see just how he viewed himself when it came to her. The mood grew serious.

"You are not saying this simply because you do not want to marry Sherston, are you?" he asked.

She frowned. "You asked me who I would choose to marry. It has nothing to do with Sherston."

He stared at her a moment before sighing heavily, a sound of sheer disbelief. "My lady," he said, his voice oddly hoarse. "I cannot put into words how honored I am that you would choose me. Truly, Bella... I wish I could create for you a fine response, but there are no words I can think of that come close to what is in my mind and in my heart. Is marriage to you of some interest to me? It has been since you came of age and I realized how beautiful and witty and compassionate you were. I have long admired you from afar, my lady, and *that* is why I have kept such a distance from you. It is the truth. But if this is what you wish... then with all my heart, I will agree."

The truth had been spoken, and Belladonna was feeling so much excitement that she was lightheaded with it. Usually a reserved and rather mature young woman, and certainly not given to whims, she did something at that moment that was completely out of her nature.

Throwing her arms around Dashiell's neck, she squeezed him tightly.

"Oh, Dash!" she gasped. "I am so happy!"

She nearly pulled him over with the force of her excitement and Dashiell had to put a hand against the stone wall to keep from falling over. But he recovered quickly, laughing low in his throat as he wrapped his big arms around her and held her tightly. Gone was the reserve, the hesitation. Gone were his thoughts of propriety.

Hugging Belladonna – *truly* embracing her – was the best thing he'd ever done.

"You must speak to my father immediately," she told him excitedly. "I know he cannot truly understand what you are saying, but you must have a document drawn up for him to sign that proves he agrees to a betrothal. If you do not, I fear that Clayton will steal me away for Sherston."

Dashiell was only slightly more level-headed than she was. He didn't let her go as he spoke. "I fear there may be more to it than that," he said. "I have an errand to run on the morrow. But I will also go to Winchester Cathedral and speak with the priests. Mayhap, they can advise me on how to proceed."

Belladonna loosened her grip, pulling back to look at the man beneath the moonlight. She'd dreamed of moments like this for so long, and it was difficult for her to realize that what she had hoped and prayed for had finally happened. Dashiell was not only responding to her, but he was holding her… she was in his arms, and it was everything she'd ever imagined it would be.

"Truly?" she breathed. "All the way to Winchester?"

"As I said, I have an errand in the area. It will be no trouble to stop at the cathedral."

Belladonna was overwhelmed with it all. "Oh, Dash… tell me this is real. I am afraid I am going to wake up and realize it was all but a dream."

He smiled at her, his big white teeth gleaming beneath his mustache. "I was going to ask you the very same thing."

"It *is* real."

"It is."

It was her turn to smile broadly. "When will you go to see the priests?"

"I will go tonight if you wish it."

She shook her head. "Nay," she said. "Tomorrow is perfect. You will not change your mind, will you?"

He shook his head firmly. "For the chance to marry you? It is the best thing I could have ever hoped for."

Belladonna was so excited that she was twitching, nodding her head and giggling. Her laughter caused Dashiell to chuckle.

"It will make Jillayne's party so much more meaningful," she said. "I will dance with the man I am to marry. God, I never thought I could say that. Even as I hear it, I still cannot believe it."

"Believe it."

Somewhere across the bailey, they could hear Lily calling to the servants, preparing for the evening meal. Men were rushing across the bailey towards the kitchen yard, while over at the great hall, warm light glowed from the open door.

Still in Dashiell's arms, Belladonna watched her sister moving about in the darkness, instructing the servants. Her thoughts inevitably shifted back to the horrific vision of Clayton and Acacia. It wasn't what she wanted to think about, not at this powerful moment, but she couldn't help it. Faintly, she sighed.

"What are we to do about Clayton and Acacia?" she asked quietly. "I would rather die than see Lily humiliated, Dash."

Dashiell could see Lily moving around, too. He released Belladonna before their amorous embrace was seen.

"I told you," he said. "We say nothing. Not to anyone. I will decide what is to be done about this. But meanwhile, you will not say a word. Agreed?"

She nodded solemnly. "Agreed," she said. "But I will have to face Acacia at some point and, I swear, I cannot even look at her, Dash. I do not *want* to look at her."

His focus turned to Belladonna, realizing how difficult this was going to be for her. She was close to both of her sisters. Reaching out, he took her hand and brought it to his lips for a gentle kiss.

"Be calm," he said in a tone that sent shivers up her spine. "It is possible Acacia was forced into this. It is equally possible that she was not. Until you know the truth, keep calm. Do not treat her any differently. I know that will be difficult. But if your manner towards her changes, she will want to know why. What will you tell her?"

He was right. Belladonna looked at him, her gaze on her hand that was near his lips. His kiss had been so hot, the bristle of his mustache unbearably sweet.

"I will not tell her anything," she said softly. "I suppose you are right. All I can do is keep quiet and pretend nothing has changed."

He kissed her hand again and let it go. "Exactly," he said. "Now, return to the keep and dress for sup. I shall see you in the hall shortly."

"As you say."

"Do you feel strong enough to face what you must?"

"Thanks to you."

She offered him a little smile before heading off in the direction of the keep.

Dashiell watched her go, remaining in the shadows of the wall, trying to absorb everything that had happened in just the past few minutes. Clayton was bedding Acacia, and he and Belladonna had agreed to marry. He almost couldn't grasp it all but he suddenly found himself resisting the urge to run to the battlements and shout his happiness for all to hear.

He felt much like Belladonna did – that he would wake up and it would all have been a dream – but he sincerely hoped God wasn't that cruel. This was a momentous day and he wanted to absorb every single moment of it.

It had been rare in his life that he'd had something to be happy about, but this day was something he'd remember for the rest of his life. It was the day the woman that he'd longed for returned those feelings. It was the first day of the rest of his life and, at forty years and four, he felt as if he were just beginning to live.

With a spring in his step, he headed for the troop house to finish up his duties.

CHAPTER EIGHT

LILY WAS SUPPOSED to be in the keep to change into a clean dress for supper. Instead, she found herself chasing the chickens that had escape from the kitchen yard.

Normally, she would have let the servants chase after them, because chickens left to roam the bailey almost always got eaten by hungry soldiers. But tonight, there were more chickens missing than servants in the kitchen, so Lily found herself chasing down a pair of renegade birds who were determined not to be caught.

It was after dark now, as the sun had set, and Lily found herself over by the armory. She could hear the chickens clucking softly and she was trying to be very quiet about following them. The armory was located in the tower on the outer wall that bordered the kitchen yard, a massive and squat structure with two stories that could be secured from theft or invasion.

Lily could see that the heavily-reinforced armory door was open and a faint glow flickered inside. She could see a shadow moving around in the firelight. The chickens were heading for the open door and Lily knew if she didn't catch them now, she would lose them once they got inside and buried themselves behind the weapons and shields.

Therefore, she picked up her pace, moving swiftly to catch the errant fowl before they made it inside the armory. Skirts hiked up around her knees so they wouldn't make noise, Lily was nearly upon the two fugitives when someone suddenly exited the armory door.

Startled, the chickens scattered, both of them somehow managing to dart inside the armory. It was exactly what Lily was trying to prevent. Frustrated, she came to a halt and sighed heavily.

"Oh, bother!" she said. "Now I shall never find them in that place."

Because of the shadows, she hadn't noticed the man who had come out of the armory, but she most certainly noticed the voice when he spoke.

"I apologize," Bentley said. "Do you want me to help you catch them?"

Pleasantly surprised, Lily found herself looking up into Bentley's handsome face. It was dark enough so that she could only see the outline, but she nodded.

"If you do not mind," she said. "They escaped from the kitchen yard and I was trying to catch them before they made it into the armory."

Bentley grinned, his white teeth gleaming in the moonlight. "They will get lost in there."

Lily nodded, moving past him. "I know," she said. She stepped into the armory and looked around, pointing. "There, over by the rack of pikes. I see one."

Bentley moved in behind her and they both moved towards the wooden racks that housed several sharp, upright poles with blades on the end. But every time they took a step, the chicken would move further away, so Bentley finally came to a halt.

"Mayhap I should rattle the rack and chase him out," he said. "Shall I try?"

Lily nodded, moving back by the door to catch the chicken that would surely come bolting out. When she was in position, Bentley rattled the rack and both chickens came shooting out, running blindly for safety. Lily managed to catch one of them but in the process of trying to grab the other, the chicken in her grasp flapped its wings wildly and she was forced to release it. Both birds went scattering off into the night.

Lily stood in the doorway as Bentley came up on her. "You'd better hurry if you are going to catch them," he said.

Lily held up her left arm with a big bloody scratch on it. "I have lost interest," she said unhappily. "I am tired and hungry, and the servants can do the chasing. I am going inside to tend to this scratch before sup."

"Stupid chickens."

She looked up at him to see that he was laughing softly. A smile spread across her face. "Stupid, indeed," she said. "But I thank you for trying to help."

He dipped his head gallantly. "Anything for you, my lady."

Lily wished with all her heart that such a thing was true. Her smile diminished as she looked up at him, thoughts of rogue chickens fading from her thoughts as the events of the day returned. It was a most momentous day, at least to her. She only hoped Bentley felt the same way.

"About today," she said quietly. "I… I hope I did not make you uncomfortable with what was said, Bent. Truthfully, I spend so much time trying not to think about you that when I had the chance to speak to you, I think… I think I said too much. But it was so good speaking to you again, as we used to."

Bentley started to say something but a heavy pike fell from the rack he'd so recently rattled. He went back over to pick it up from the dirt floor.

"You did not say too much," he told her as he put the pike back and made sure it was steady. "I meant what I said. I miss speaking to you also."

Lily wandered back into the darkened armory. She could hear the longing in his voice, which hurt her heart in so many ways.

"Do you remember the hours we used to spend, simply talking to one another?" she asked, a sad smile on her face. "You and I could talk about anything. I have never had that kind of rapport with anyone, not even my sisters."

He smiled weakly. "I remember."

Lily leaned against the spiral stairs which cut into the corner of the round tower room. "I know we have not really talked since Clayton and I were wed…"

"And for good reason."

She nodded quickly. "I know why," she said. "I know you do not want anyone to think there is anything unseemly with us."

"It would damage your reputation, Lily. You are a paragon of virtue, the future Duchess of Savernake. I would die before jeopardizing your role in life."

Lily heard his chivalrous declaration. It only made her love him more. "And I would give it all up simply to be Lady Ashbourne," she murmured. "If we were to live in a one-room hut, with barely enough to eat and barely enough to keep warm, I would not care because we would be together."

Bentley sighed faintly. "Lily…"

"I do not care!" she suddenly burst. "Oh, Bent, you have no idea how hellish it has been with Clayton. He only wanted the Savernake dukedom; he cares nothing for me. I am only a means to an end. He beds the servants and thinks I do not know, but I do. I am sure you have heard that."

Bentley grunted softly. He'd heard the same thing, praying she hadn't. "Does it matter?"

"Of course it does," she snapped. "While I am a paragon of virtue, my husband is a symbol of debauchery. He'll bed the servants and then expects me to fill his bed. But I can smell the scent of dirty whores on the linens. When I refuse to lay on the same spot where he so recently bedded a servant, he has been known to hit me. Did you know that also?"

Bentley sank back against the wall, dropping his head in a mournful gesture. "Lily, please…"

Lily looked over at him, seeing his slumped shoulders and lowered head, and she realized that she'd burdened the man too much. He looked as if he'd been crushed by her words.

"Oh… my sweet Bentley," she whispered. "I am so sorry. This is not your cross to bear, but mine. I am so sorry I told you that. I should not have. Forgive me."

She started to move away, towards the door, but he stopped her.

"Wait," he said. "It is, indeed, my cross to bear. The woman I love is married to a man I have to look at every day, a man I have grown to hate. Of course I have heard the rumors. Every time I hear a new one, my hatred towards him grows."

Lily shook her head in sorrow. "Then you *do* know."

He nodded, sorrowfully. "I know," he murmured. "But the worst of it is that this vile excuse for a man is touching you in a way that only I should be touching you. Do you know how painful that is, Lily? It guts me. But even as I feel such anguish, it is incomparable to what you must feel. I know that. I only wish I could help you. Every day that passes brings me a day closer to slitting Clayton's throat."

"You must not say such things."

"Why? Of course I entertain such thoughts. The only thing that prevents me from doing it is the fact that, if I do, and you and I are able to be together, a murder would be the basis of our relationship. I am not sure we could survive that."

Lily understood what he meant; their love was pure. A murder, even Clayton's murder, so that they could be together would sully that.

"I could not let you do it," she whispered. "You are too strong and noble a knight to resort to such things."

"Sometimes I wonder."

Lily's gaze lingered on him a moment, watching him as he slumped against the wall over by the rack of pikes. She realized that she wanted something from him and she might never have another opportunity like this. It was wrong, and she knew it, but she couldn't help it.

Quietly, she made her way over to the heavy armory door and pulled it shut, throwing the bolt. When she turned around, Bentley was looking at her with some curiosity.

"Will you do something for me?" she asked him quietly.

He nodded, although it was hesitantly. "What is it?"

"Embrace me."

He looked at her as if she had just asked something horribly painful from him. "Lily…"

"Just an embrace. Please, Bent. I need to feel your arms around me. It has been three years since you have held me and… and I know it is wrong, but surely just a small embrace is nothing much."

"I cannot…"

"Give me the strength to keep living. Just one embrace and I shall never ask you again,"

Bentley stared at her a moment, indecision in his eyes. But then, he unfolded his arms and opened them up to her.

He wanted to touch her as badly as she wanted to touch him.

Lily ran to him, throwing herself into his arms, and he lifted her up off of the ground with the force of his embrace. Lily's arms were wrapped tightly around his neck, her face buried in his shoulder, and he could feel her body rocking with sobs.

God, this was a terrible idea. Bentley knew it was the worst idea possible, like ripping a scab from a healing wound. But he knew in his heart of hearts that this would never heal. He would never be free of Lily, no matter how much time had passed or how hard he tried to keep his mind off her.

Everything about him cried for her, just as everything about her cried for him. Two people in love, who were cruelly torn apart by an underhanded man who was power-hungry. When Lily lifted her head to rub her cheek against his, he turned his head enough to kiss her soft mouth.

He couldn't help himself.

Lily responded instantly, kissing him with all of the pent-up angst and passion she'd been feeling for him these past years. It was a release for both of them, their love finally being demonstrated again, however secretively. But one thing was for certain now; their lips had touched, their bodies were pressed against one another, and the force of their passion was so strong that nothing could tear it apart.

Nothing.

This was their moment in time when, for a brief span, it was just the two of them and no one else. No prying eyes, no propriety, and no restraint. What was happening now was happening naturally, as it was always meant to be, and Lily in particular knew what she wanted.

She wanted him.

Clayton may have had the privilege of taking her virginity, but there had never been any pleasure in being bedded by the man. But now, it seemed completely natural – nay – *right* to know Bentley in the intimate sense. She had always loved him and would always love him, and there might never be another chance like this.

She had to know the man as it was always meant to be.

Even as Bentley kissed her furiously, Lily's hands moved to his tunic, trying to pull it over his head. When Bentley realized what she was doing, he balked, but only for a split second. When the woman's warm hands invaded his breeches and sought out his manhood, now beginning to throb to life, he knew he was lost. He couldn't deny her and, in truth, he didn't want to be denied, either.

His sweet Lily…

Bentley had to pull his tunic off in order to remove his mail coat, which was severely restricting him. Lily yanked at the tunic as he pulled the mail coat over his head, both pieces coming off at nearly the exact same time. He was wearing a padded tunic beneath, but it only went to his hips, so he was unencumbered when Lily unfastened his breeches and they fell to his knees.

There was a sense of urgency now, of passion so fierce that they were nearly frantic with it. He lifted Lily up and she wrapped her legs around his waist, his already-rigid manhood seeking her warm, intimate places. A few well-placed wriggles of her hips and he easily found his mark. She was slick and hot, ready for his entry, and he didn't wait. Holding her tightly, he impaled her upon his manhood.

Lily gasped with the ecstasy of it, realizing for the first time the pleasure of being joined with a man, someone she loved with all of her heart and soul. It was a life-changing experience as Bentley held her tightly, thrusting into her body, and it was everything she knew it would be. This was her moment, something she would remember for the rest of her life, and she didn't regret it. Not in the least.

It was more than she could have imagined.

Their kisses were heated and deep. Bentley turned around so her back was against the stone wall of the armory, holding her legs at his hips as he repeatedly drove into her. Lily's hands found his buttocks, squeezing him, and he found it wildly arousing. With a few more thrusts, he spilled himself deep into her warm and welcoming body, not even concerned that their gasps of pleasure might have been heard. Honestly, he didn't give a damn. Even if Clayton himself came charging into the armory to accuse him of adultery, he wouldn't have cared.

At the moment, he cared for nothing but Lily.

She was gasping for air in his arms, but her lips soon found his again, and the sweet and gentle kisses of lovers resumed, with far more emotion and far less lust. Bentley knew that this would more than likely be the last encounter they would have, if not forever, then for a very long time.

He wanted to make it last.

"Bent?" Lily whispered.

"Aye?"

"Tell me you love me."

"I love you, in this life and in the next."

Lily suckled on his lips sweetly, her legs still wrapped around his body and his male member still buried in her. She rolled her hips against his, feeling his erection as it died down. She'd waited for this moment for so long and, now, she didn't want to lose it. She was clinging to the last wisps of it, feeling it fade, and mourning the loss.

"Are you angry with me for this?" she murmured. "I asked you to embrace me, but this… it was not my intention, truly."

"Nor mine," he said. "It simply happened. I suppose… I suppose love will always find a way, Lily. Right or wrong, it will, indeed, find a way."

She pulled back, looking at him seriously as the torchlight flickered across his face. "And this is wrong?"

He sighed heavily. He wasn't sure how to answer that. "I told you that I would not bed another man's wife when you married Clayton."

"I know."

"But… but I cannot seem to view you as his wife. He married you, that is true, but you do not belong to him."

Lily shook her head, leaning forward to kiss him again. "I only belong to you."

He looked into her eyes, deeply. "I still cannot jeopardize your reputation. As a knight, I would lose all honor in doing so."

Lily knew that. "Then… then this cannot happen again?"

"I should agree with that, but I cannot seem to."

Lily could see how confused he was; the lover versus the noble knight who knew right from wrong. She didn't wrestle with such thoughts, but he did. Kissing him again, one more time, she unwound her legs from his hips and slid to the ground.

"We must do what we feel is right, Bent, whatever that may be," she said softly, watching him reach down to pull his breeches up. "We have denied our love for three years, but it has not gone away. We have not forgotten about each other. Mayhap… mayhap it is wrong to even try to ignore our feelings."

He tied his breeches, increasingly distressed about the situation. "I suppose we can find excuses for what we've done, leaving it up to love, but the reality is that I have bedded another man's wife. It is wrong. Yet… I do not regret it."

Lily put her hand on his cheek in a comforting gesture. He cupped a big hand over it, feeling her soft warmth beneath his palm.

"I love you, Bentley of Ashbourne," she whispered. "I will always love you. But I would never force you to do anything you felt was dishonorable. Tonight, this encounter was just something that happened, and we can accept it as such. I do not regret it, either. In fact, I shall live on it for the rest of my life. But how we conduct our future relationship… I will bow to your wishes in the matter. Truly, there is nothing else I can do."

Bentley pulled her into his arms and kissed her again, deeply. He had no idea what course their future relationship would take, but he did know one thing – that he loved her more than anything on the earth. Lily was everything to him and he wasn't going to lose her, even if she was married to another man.

It was that night that Bentley realized that he had quite a problem on his hands.

CHAPTER NINE

Selborne Castle, Hampshire
Seat of the House of de Nerra

"AYE, I KNEW about John's movements into Scotland. He will push all the way up to the Hebrides if he is not stopped."

Two days after the return from Marlborough, Dashiell was sitting in the lavish solar of Gavin de Nerra, Itinerant Justice of Hampshire. A big man in his fourth decade, he was a wise man with a great reputation, much like his father, Valor, who had had been a much beloved and respected man in England. Valor had passed away the year before, leaving a great legacy for his children to follow, and Gavin was a fine tribute to his father.

He also happened to hate the king deeply, much as his father had. Even as he spoke of the king, his hated for the man glistened in his eyes. Dashiell could see it, like shards of steel ready to cut John's heart out.

"We heard rumor of the king's movements as we were returning home after the battle south of Scarborough," Dashiell said. "It was the de Lohr messenger at Ramsbury that confirmed it only yesterday. He also said something else – that Jax de Velt was killed near Berwick. Have you heard that also?"

Gavin nodded, his movements laced with sorrow. "Archers brought him down."

"Has this been confirmed?"

"I've not heard official confirmation by those who were there, but I have heard de Velt was brought down." He shook his head sharply, as if frustrated. "What was he doing in range of the archers? Ajax de Velt had no need to prove himself in battle any longer. The man is at least twice my age. Who in the hell let him ride into battle?"

They were questions that Dashiell had no answer for. "It is possible that this is only rumor," he said. "It is possible that de Velt is not dead at all."

Gavin looked as if he didn't believe that. "Mayhap," he said. "But rumors of his death are fueling the rebellion. If our allies hated John before, with the rumor of de Velt's death, they hate him even more. This will not bode well for him, Dash. It will mean his end."

It was an ominous prediction, but one Dashiell found hope in. Was it possible these wars would soon be over, spurred by the death of a legend?

"My cousin is calling a meeting of the warlords at Canterbury Castle in May and your participation in it will be key," he said. "I have been told to issue you an invitation and I am quite certain that Chris will speak on this very subject. He and de Velt are friends, you know."

"I know." Gavin nodded seriously, pausing as if looking into the future to see that meeting and all it would entail. "And what of Savernake, Dash? What of your mighty war machine?"

Dashiell knew what he meant in asking that question; it was a mighty war machine with a senile old man in charge. *"Mors in Victoria,"* he muttered. "Victory over death. That is our mantra. The Savernake army stands as strong as it ever has."

"What of Edward?"

So much for Dashiell trying to pretend nothing at all was amiss in the world of Ramsbury. "The duke will insist upon coming, even if he cannot understand what is happening," he said. "I will bring him and try to keep him from disrupting the meeting. You know that everyone will want to see him, my lord. There has not been a battle in the past forty years that Savernake has not played a significant role in, so the warlords will wish to see him. Call it sentiment."

Gavin sighed faintly. "Sentiment, indeed," he said. "I tried to speak with him when we were at Northampton, you know. All he wanted to do was give me communion."

Dashiell smiled, though it was without humor. "He takes his duties as Paul the Apostle very seriously," he said. "We have all been given communion many times. I have personally been baptized at least six times."

It was rather humorous, even if it was tragic. Gavin chuckled softly. "My father adored Edward de Vaston," he said. "I can remember visiting the man in my youth. He was always very kind to my brothers and me, insisting we ride his ponies as the men went into meetings. That made me love going to Ramsbury. I even fostered there for a time."

Dashiell couldn't help but feel saddened by de Nerra's fond reflection of a man who was only a shell of his former self. "I suppose it could be worse," he said. "He could think himself Lucifer and we could all be serving the Fallen One. If the man has to believe he is someone other than who he is, he could do worse than Paul the Apostle."

Gavin planted himself in a big chair near the hearth. The winter weather was cold this day, but it hadn't snowed for weeks, making that land simply appear dead from the freezing temperature. He rubbed his hands together, chilled even in the moderate warmth of the solar.

"Dash," he finally said as he stared into the fire. "I sense that you came here for another reason."

Dashiell eyed the man. "What other reason could there be than to relay the message I was given?"

Gavin continued to rub his hands. "Because I know you," he said. "I have known you for years. You are worried, else you would not have come personally. Why did you make the trip from Ramsbury in the dead of winter to see me?"

It was perceptive of him. But Dashiell only shrugged. "I am worried about Clayton but, then again, he is always a worry."

"Is he growing worse?"

"Worse? Nay. But his ambition is showing, more than ever. That, indeed, causes me worry where the duke's life is concerned."

Gavin turned to him. "Explain."

Dashiell sat forward, his elbows resting on his knees. "It is the same concern I have always had," he said. "I have shared this with you before. Clayton hungers for the dukedom as a starving man hungers for food. The only thing standing between him and his dream is, in fact, Edward de Vaston. The duke is old, that is true, but his health is good even if his mind is not. He could live for ten more years, but if it is up to Clayton, I would not give him such good chances."

Gavin cocked an eyebrow. "You believe Clayton will try to kill him?"

Dashiell drew in a long, thoughtful breath. "That has been on my mind, aye," he said. "He has been known to encourage the duke to walk the battlefields, blessing the dead and wounded."

Gavin grunted unhappily, closing his eyes briefly. "God, did he do that again?"

"At Scarborough."

"And you are here? Who is watching over the duke?"

Dashiell held up a calming hand. "Not to fear," he said. "Before leaving Ramsbury, I dismissed one of the men paid to mind the duke, a man I am quite certain Clayton is controlling. I also posted guards outside of the duke's chamber to monitor anyone coming or going."

"I knew you would be diligent, Dash. I did not mean to question you competence."

Dashiell smiled to let the man known he wasn't offended. "The truth is that I would not put it past Clayton to make a move against the man while I am away."

"The situation is that bad?"

"It is."

Gavin pursed his lips in a manner that suggested the entire idea disturbed him. "God help us all when Edward passes," he muttered. "Clayton le Cairon, Duke of Savernake. If ever a man walked the earth who did not deserve such a thing, it is Clayton."

Dashiell sat up and reached for the wine that Gavin had poured for him when he'd first arrived. "More than you know," he muttered. Taking a drink, he licked his lips and continued. "I have recently been informed that he has taken up with one of his wife's sisters. He is apparently bedding the woman."

Gavin's brow furrowed. "Which one?"

"Lady Acacia, the middle sister."

Gavin sighed, as if relieved. "So long as it is not the youngest."

"Why do you say that?"

"Because Clayton would be a dead man."

Dashiell didn't even ask him to clarify the remark, for he knew what the answer would be. He was starting to feel a bit foolish, realizing that his feelings for Belladonna hadn't been as concealed as he'd hoped. Men like de Nerra had visited Ramsbury often, and they knew the family well. They knew Dashiell well. He supposed that he'd made it easy for them to figure out where his attention was. It was probably the worst-kept secret in all of Wiltshire.

In fact, he snorted.

"Then you know."

"I know that you have had your eye on Lady Belladonna for a few years."

Normally, Dashiell would have denied such a thing. He'd gotten into the habit of denying anything personal when it came to Belladonna, but he knew there was no use in doing so. He was able to acknowledge it now because she felt the same way. As he'd once told

Belladonna, he wanted to shout his happiness from the battlements.

Besides... it felt good to confide in someone, for once.

"Not only do I have my eye on her, but she has agreed to marry me," he said quietly. "Unfortunately, Clayton also has a husband selected for her. Let us be frank, my lord. If Edward dies before I can marry Belladonna, then she will be taken from me. But if I can marry her before that event, then Clayton can do nothing about it. You said that I seemed worried? I am. I have never been more worried about anything in my life."

Gavin was looking at him with astonishment. "Is it true, Dash?" he asked. Then, he broke out into a smile. "God's Bones, I never thought I would hear you speak of the woman in this manner. I was convinced you were going to go your entire life keeping your feelings for her all to yourself. Well done, old man."

Dashiell grinned in spite of himself. "It has only come about recently," he admitted, "but I could not be happier. In fact, I never knew such happiness existed in the world. But all of that is for naught unless I can marry her before Clayton assumes the dukedom."

"Why can't you?"

"Because Edward is not in his right mind. He cannot consent to the marriage."

Gavin rubbed his chin thoughtfully. "Indeed, that is true," he said. "Have you gone to the church with this? Mayhap, the priests can help. You certainly cannot petition the king for her hand, which would be the proper procedure in the absence of a father with the ability to consent."

Dashiell was well aware of the facts. "I thought to go to Winchester Cathedral when I leave here and speak to the priests there. Mayhap, they can offer advice."

But Gavin shook his head. "Not Winchester," he said. "That is John's church and the priests are loyal to him. Nay, my friend. You will have to go to another source."

"Who?"

Gavin finished warming his hands and stood up. "Stephen Langton," he said as he moved away from the hearth. "The Archbishop of Canterbury is the man you must see. He hates John, and he wields much power, and I am certain he can help you with this issue. Do you know the man?"

Dashiell shook his head. "I only know *of* him," he said. "Do you suppose he will see me?"

Gavin poured himself wine. "I am going to Canterbury next week, in fact," he said. "I have business with Langton. I would be honored if you would allow me to present your case to him. Mayhap, I can convince him to approve the betrothal, given the circumstances."

Dashiell stood up, his eyes wide with surprise. "You would do this?"

Gavin smiled when he saw the astonishment in Dashiell's face. "Of course I would," he said. "Before you leave, give me the details of what you wish me to say and I shall do it. And do not look so surprised. Of course I will help you. You are the most respected knight in all of southern England, Dash. Everyone knows what you are up against with a mad liege and a viper like Clayton. If a man was ever facing a tribulation, it is you. Let me see if I can help you. We can do nothing about Clayton, but we can give him one less pawn to use by marrying Lady Belladonna to you."

Dashiell was truly humbled by the man's offer. "I care not for Clayton's delusions of grandeur," he said. "All I care about is Belladonna. I cannot see her married to another, my lord. It would… destroy me."

Gavin could hear, simply by his tone, that he meant it. It was surprising coming from a career warrior like Dashiell. Clearly, the man had deep feelings. He came up beside Dashiell, putting a hand on the man's broad shoulder.

"Then let me see if we cannot prevent such a thing," he said quietly. "I will do what I can, Dash. Meanwhile, you need to keep the duke safe from Clayton's ambition. That is key."

Dashiell nodded solemnly. "I have protected the man with my life for over ten years," he said. "I will continue to do so until the last breath in my body.

Gavin's smile faded, an intense look coming to his dark eyes.

"Let us hope it does not come to that."

CHAPTER TEN

One Week Later

LILY WAS UNUSUALLY happy, and Acacia was unusually sad.

In the week following the shopping trip at Marlborough, and the subsequent realization of an unsavory affair between Clayton and Acacia, Belladonna felt as if there was something very strange in the air when it came to her sisters. It wasn't so much in conversation or in the tone of the words spoken to one another, but more in the way everything seemed to be. The situation as a whole was simply… odd.

Lily was too cheerful for, well, *Lily*. Not that she was constantly grumpy, but she certainly wasn't as happy and laughing as she had been as of late. She laughed at the smallest things and was far too cheerful, even when the lovely pink garment she'd been working on for Jillayne's party was torn by a careless maid. Lily simply shrugged it off and fixed the tear. She didn't berate or scold. Belladonna had watched with shock as Lily let the matter simply roll off her back.

Most puzzling.

And then there was Acacia. Truth be told, Belladonna couldn't even look at the woman. For the first few days after the incident, Belladonna avoided the woman at all costs, but she'd been obliged to speak to her when Acacia had asked about the party that everyone was preparing for.

When the invitation to the great celebration at Chadlington Castle had first come, Acacia had condemned it as foolishness. She'd never really been one for parties, ever, so her response wasn't surprising. But as the week progressed and she watched her sisters sew furiously on dresses and tunics and other finery for the event, she began to grow interested. When she asked Belladonna a direct question about it, Belladonna answered. But that was the extent of her communication with her sister.

She simply didn't want to speak to the woman.

But she did want to speak to Dashiell, and she did quite often. He'd gone to Selborne for a few days and she'd missed him dreadfully. But when he returned, the reunion had been very sweet. He'd kissed her hand and whispered how he'd missed her, which had nearly sent her swooning. They hadn't spoken much beyond that, but it didn't matter. What contact they'd had was deeply satisfying.

Yesterday, she'd had him come to the ladies' solar to try on the tunics she had made for him. He'd been embarrassed by it – so very embarrassed – made worse when Aston and Bentley realized their gruff, insult-loving commander was allowing himself to be primped like a prized pony. But the truth was that they were very happy that the affection he'd always harbored for Belladonna was coming to some fruition.

Still, it was great fun to tease him. Aston had received a fist to the gut for his efforts, but it had been worth it.

It had been a rather perfect week, in fact, for all concerned. If Lily was unusually happy, then Belladonna was unusually ecstatic and Dashiell was very nearly the same. Lily had watched her sister all week. She knew what had transpired between the pair, as Belladonna had told her on the very night they'd returned from Marlborough. Unable to contain her excitement, Lily had whispered it to Bentley, who had whispered it to Aston.

But they weren't the only ones who knew. Servants had noticed, as had others around Ramsbury, and soon the rumors were flying fast and furious that Lady Belladonna and Sir Dashiell were soon to be betrothed. It was all anyone could speak of and, more than once, Dashiell had caught servants grinning at him.

But he would frown, and they would run. Once he'd chased them away, he'd fight off a smile and continue on with his duties. He knew about the rumors, but he had yet to confirm or deny them, and he wouldn't until he received word from de Nerra or the Archbishop of Canterbury.

Now, it was a waiting game.

But not an unpleasant one, as long as he kept busy. The Chadlington festivities were on the horizon and on sunrise of the day they were to leave for the party, Dashiell was already awake, pulling together the escort with the help of Aston and Bentley. He was as excited to attend as Belladonna was, and probably more so. For the first time, he would be her official escort and the thrill he felt went beyond the mere sense of the party. It had solely to do with spending time with Belladonna and little else.

He simply wanted to be with her.

There was a sense of purpose in the air as the entire castle came alive, preparing for the trip. Servants were bringing out the trunks that contained the ladies' possessions, while the quartermasters were seeing to the great array of tents and supplies that would be brought along also. Great supply wagons were brought forth, all of them loaded to the top. An escort such as this required great preparation, and Dashiell wasn't leaving anything to chance.

He also wasn't leaving the safety of the women to chance. He had an enormous escort lined up, one hundred men who were heavily armed and outfitted for the trip. What he hadn't decided on, however, was which knight he would bring with him. Clayton was going, of course, but because Lily was going, Bentley wanted to go, too. The man had never asked, but Dashiell could see it in his eyes.

Ever since that trip to Marlborough, Bentley seemed to pay more attention to Lily than he usually did, a very minor change in his usual habits, but enough of a change that Dashiell noticed. He was torn between admitting the man to the escort so he could be near Lily and leaving him behind to keep him away from her. He knew Bentley tried very hard to maintain a proper distance from Lily, but that didn't seem to be the case any longer. Dashiell didn't want Clayton challenging the man, so bringing Bentley to Chadlington was something he'd not yet decided on.

"Dash?"

A soft, female voice broke into his thoughts as he stood there and mulled over the issue of Bentley. He turned to see Belladonna coming up behind him, her lovely face scrubbed and rosy in the early morning light. She looked so beautiful that he simply took a moment to look at her, drinking in the sight. Every moment he spent with her, even just to look at her, were the best moments of his life.

"My lady," he greeted pleasantly. "You are looking lovely this morning."

Belladonna smiled broadly, a smile of pure joy. "I was hoping you would think so," she said. "And you are looking as handsome as you always do."

Dashiell had no idea how to react to such compliments other than to fight off a grin. "If that is your opinion, then I am honored."

Belladonna could see that she'd embarrassed the man, so she took pity on him and didn't tease him, though it would have been easy.

"I came to wish you a good morn and also to tell you that I have your tunics packed along with the other things I have made for you," she said. "The servants are loading them into the wagon now. I promise you will be the best dressed knight at the gathering."

He eyed her. "Men have never been able to say that I am the best dressed at anything," he said. "I am not a court dandy, Bella. I do not want to look like one."

She laughed softly. "Of course you will not look like one," she said. "But I have made you three new tunics, and they are quite nice."

He dipped his head, rather gallantly. "They are astonishingly beautiful, and being that they are made by your own hand, I shall treasure them all the more. But I still do not want to look like a girl-man."

Her laughter grew. "No one would ever think that. But you *will* be well dressed. As my escort, and my future betrothed, it is fitting that you should be."

She had a point, so he sighed heavily, pretending he didn't like it, when the truth was that he couldn't have been prouder. Reluctantly, he nodded.

"As you wish, my lady," he said. "But know I will only do this for you."

"I know."

"Is that all you came to tell me? That I shall look like a perfumed fool for this party?"

She shook her head, giggling. "Nay," she said. "I wanted to ask you something."

"Anything at all."

"May I give one of your puppies to Jillayne for a present? I am sure she would love one dearly."

He nodded. "Indeed, if you think that is an appropriate gift for a young woman," he said. "Choose whichever pup you like."

She was excited. "Thank you," she said, impulsively kissing him on the cheek before fleeing.

But Dashiell felt that kiss like a brand. It was seared into him, a sensation he relished. But he lingered over it so that he nearly forgot what he needed to be doing, not until a soldier asked him a question and brought him back to the world at hand.

Realizing he had been daydreaming, he began to move quickly, barking at the men to move more quickly in the course of their duties.

When one of the men accidentally toppled a trunk over the side of the wagon, Dashiell flew into full form.

"You sponge-headed dolt!" he boomed. "Don't just stand there; pick it up!"

The men were rushing to lift the very heavy trunk back onto the wagon as Dashiell stood there and glared at them. No one wanted a glaring du Reims. As he moved in to help the men adjust the trunks so the load was even, Aston and Bentley appeared.

Having been in charge of the ensuring the soldier escort was fully armed, they had finished with the men and now came to see if they could help Dashiell since they heard the man bellowing. Both Aston and Bentley were dressed for travel, both of them hoping they would be selected to ride escort to Chadlington Castle.

Even if Bentley wouldn't come outright and ask, Aston would. The party would be full of unmarried maidens and, being an unmarried man, he was keen to see the selection. He approached Dashiell a few steps ahead of Bentley, his young face full of eagerness.

"The men are armed and ready, Dash," he said. "Do you have anything else that needs tending?"

Dashiell shook his head. "I do not believe so," he said. "But you can run a check of the wheels of the wagons before we go. And make sure the quartermasters have extra wheels in the supply wagons before we depart."

Both Aston and Bentley nodded. As they both turned around to carry out the directive, Aston paused.

"Have you decided who is riding escort, Dash?" he said. "If it is me, then I must collect my saddlebags and prepare my horse."

Dashiell could see how hopeful he was, but he could also see Bentley standing behind him, looking as if he'd already been told to remain behind. He simply looked sad. Dashiell felt bad for Bentley, knowing how much he surely wanted to go, but he also thought that it might be best if he did remain behind. They had enough problems with Clayton without adding a knight who was in love with the man's wife and being less careful about showing it.

Just as he opened his mouth to reply, the door to the keep opened and people began to spill forth. The sun was barely over the eastern horizon, so it was still relatively dark, and servants bearing torches were lighting the way.

It was a glowing procession coming out into the early morning. Dashiell could see Clayton at the front of the pack and dressed like a peacock, followed by Lily, who was heavily-dressed against the weather. Surprisingly, Acacia was behind her sister, also heavily-dressed, with Belladonna bringing up the rear.

But Belladonna wasn't alone. It wasn't only the puppy she had in her arms, but her father beside her. She was holding the puppy with one arm and had a grip on her father with the other. Dashiell immediately headed in her direction, but he had to pass by Clayton first. Clayton blocked his path.

"The duke will be coming with us, du Reims," he commanded. "Make a place for him."

Dashiell looked at Clayton, wondering how the duke had made it into the escort party. "This is the first I've heard that he would be going to Chadlington," he said. "When was this decision made and why was I not informed until now?"

Clayton heaved an exasperated sigh. "You are not privy to every family decision," he said, emphasizing the fact that Dashiell was not part of the family. "Lord Chadlington is an old friend of the duke's, so the man is coming with us, whether or not you like it."

"I did not say that I did not like it," he said evenly. "But including the duke means I must make preparations for his safety."

Clayton waved him off. "You have a big enough escort," he said, seeing the gang of heavily-armed men. "Nothing more is required."

"I am in charge of the safety and security of Ramsbury. You will let me make that determination."

Clayton was instantly annoyed with him. "What more do you need?" he asked, almost sarcastically. "You do not intend to bring the entire army simply to protect the duke."

Dashiell wasn't going to let Clayton challenge him. He took a step towards the man and lowered his voice. "I can guarantee that when you are the duke, you will demand more than a one hundred-man escort when you are traveling," he growled. "Therefore, you will afford the current duke, the man who holds the title you so badly want, the same courtesy. I know your attitude is lax when it comes to his safety, but mine is not. Now, go to your horse and stay out of my way. And keep your mouth shut when it comes to the safety of the Duke of Savernake."

With that, he stepped away, bellowing to Bentley and Aston, who came on the run. There was suddenly a good deal of activity now that the duke was traveling with them, and the knights began running for the troop house as still other men headed to the stables to bring forth more horses.

As men moved all around her, Belladonna had seen the entire incident and she had heard it as well. She didn't like it when Clayton and Dashiell argued because she was afraid, at some point, Clayton was going to pull a dagger on Dashiell. She knew that Dashiell tried to keep the peace between them, as he'd pointed out to her, but when Clayton challenged the safety of the duke, that had angered Dashiell and the deadly knight in him came out.

Everyone could see it.

A servant came by and she handed off the puppy, asking that food and water be brought for the dog. As the servant went to do her bidding, she continued to watch Dashiell with some concern as the man organized a larger escort. Clayton was nowhere to be seen, having stormed off after Dashiell's harsh words, and Belladonna hoped that the escort wasn't starting off on a bad note.

All of this extra fuss because the duke would be attending and, to be truthful, she was as surprised as Dashiell was. All she knew was that her father and Clayton had appeared just as she and her sisters were leaving their chambers, and it was at Clayton's insistence that her father was going.

It all seemed strange to her, but she didn't say anything about it. She wondered if Clayton was dragging him along simply to show him off, to show the world how low the Duke of Savernake had sunk. Sometimes, she got that impression from Clayton that he was out to shame her father in front of his peers, which made her very protective of Edward.

Even now, as she stood next to him, she held on to him tightly, as if to shield him from the world. But to Edward, nothing she did registered with him very much. She was sweet and attentive, but it wasn't as if he had the wherewithal to thank her these days. At the moment, he was standing beside her, wrapped in his heavy robes, watching the activity with a simple-looking smile on his face. His eyes, of the fairest blue, were staring off into the darkness.

Belladonna had seen that expression before. Often times, her father simply stared off into nothingness, as if seeing something no one else could. She missed the days when those gentle eyes looked at her kindly and meant it.

"Papa?" she said softly. "Would you like to go back into the keep and sit down until they are ready?"

Edward didn't react for a moment. When he did, it wasn't to answer her question.

"It is the glory of a new day," he said. "I see heaven laid before me."

She smiled faintly. "Why do you say that?"

"Because of the light. Always because of the light."

"But it is dark, Papa."

He turned to look at her. "What is thy name, Angel?"

Her smile faded. "I am Belladonna, Papa. Your daughter."

He stared at her with the simpleton expression on his face, his eyes unnaturally bright. "Daughter?" he repeated. "They died long ago, Angel. Long ago."

Belladonna didn't know what to say. She simply patted his hand. It seemed that her father grew worse every day, for she was certain he still recognized her as of late. But his words this morning suggested there was confusion even in that. It was heartbreaking, truly. As she stood there and held fast to him, waiting for the escort to finish, her father suddenly pulled away from her.

"Papa?" Belladonna ran after him, trying to grasp him by the arm again. "Papa, where are you going?"

He was still strong in his old age, easily pulling away from her. "I am not ready to go to heaven yet, Angel," he said. "I must stay upon this earth. Men are in need of me."

With that, he pushed away from her again and she tripped over her skirts, falling heavily onto the icy ground as the duke charged back towards the keep. Unable to get to her feet fast enough, Belladonna turned in the direction of the escort.

"Dash!" she screamed.

He heard her.

Bent over one of the horses hitched to the carriage, Dashiell's head shot up and he caught sight of Belladonna on the ground. That was all he needed to see in order to rush in her direction. He and Bentley and Aston, among others, were all running towards her as she struggled to her feet, pointing to the keep.

"My father," she gasped. "He's run into the keep!"

Dashiell pulled her to her feet, carefully, as Bentley and Aston went running into the keep after the skittish duke. Dashiell thought he should have gone, too, but he was more concerned with why Belladonna had been on the ground.

"What happened?" he nearly demanded. "Did you fall?"

She shook her head, greatly distressed. "Papa pushed me," she said, watching his eyes widening. "But he did not mean to. He was trying to push me away and I simply tripped."

Dashiell wasn't entirely sure she wasn't covering for a father suddenly gone violent. Given the man's deteriorating mental state, he couldn't be certain of anything. Before he could question her further, Lily and Acacia ran up.

"Bella!" Lily gasped. "What happened?"

Belladonna brushed at her cloak, sweeping off the dirt from the frozen ground. "I tried to grab Papa as he ran off and I fell," she said. "He did not push me; I simply fell. But he was very insistent. He kept calling the escort 'heaven' and he thought I was an angel. He said that he was not ready to go to heaven yet."

Lily looked at her with some distress before bending over to help her brush off the rest of the dirt. Acacia stood a few feet away, simply watching everything without much to say. But Dashiell had a good deal to say.

"Bella," he said, his voice low. "Be truthful with me. Did he push you? You must not be afraid to tell me."

She shook her head immediately. "I swear it, Dash. He did not push me. He was trying to move away from me and I simply fell. But... but he did not recognize me. He told me all of his daughters were dead."

Dashiell sighed heavily at that bit of information, turning as he heard a commotion at the entry and seeing Aston and Bentley emerging with the duke between them. The duke was protesting the fact that he was being removed from the keep against his will, insisting that he needed to remain.

Holding up a hand to beg pardon from the ladies, Dashiell went to the duke and stood in front of the man, ensuring that Edward could see him.

"My lord?" he said. "Do you not wish to go to Chadlington?"

The duke fixed on him and a smile creased his lips. "Dash," he breathed. "My good and faithful son. I cannot go to heaven. Make them understand."

Dashiell nodded patiently, taking the duke from Bentley and Aston. "You shall not go anywhere you do not wish to go," he said. "But we are going to Chadlington Castle. Your old friend, Lord Chadlington, lives there."

The duke blinked as if only just understanding what Dashiell had told him. "Chadlington?" he repeated. Suddenly, it seemed like a good idea now. "I must go there. They must have my blessing."

"Aye, they must."

"And communion. We will have communion."

"Aye, we will."

The duke pushed past Dashiell and started walking towards the escort again. Dashiell motioned to Bentley and Aston to follow the man, and they did as Dashiell and the sisters remained behind and watched. Belladonna walked over to him, her gaze still on her father.

"He responds to you when he will not respond to anyone else," she said quietly. "He has never not recognized me before."

Dashiell could hear the hurt in her voice. He looked at her. "His mind comes and goes, lamb," he said quietly. "He will probably know you in an hour. Who is to say? In any case, he is coming with us. I do not wish to leave him behind if he will become agitated, so we may as well bring him along. He knows Chadlington. It might be good for him."

Belladonna nodded, agreeing with whatever he wanted to do. Dashiell knew best. Looping her hand through his crooked elbow, she and her sisters walked with him back to the escort, where he helped all three women into the fortified carriage that already contained the duke and his minder, Drusus.

Before shutting the carriage door, Dashiell gave Belladonna a wink that Lily saw also and, when the door was closed, Lily simply grinned at her blushing younger sister. It was a sweet moment.

Bentley and Aston were both assigned to the escort now that the duke was coming along. As the sun cleared the eastern horizon, the party of one hundred and fifty heavily-armed men, four wagons, a fortified carriage, ten standard bearers and three fully-armed knights moved from the gatehouse of Ramsbury on their travels north to the brown-stoned castle of Chadlington and a party they would all remember for years to come.

A party that would be pivotal in more ways than one.

CHAPTER ELEVEN

THE PLAN HAD been to stop and camp for the night, somewhere before reaching Chadlington, so the party from Ramsbury would arrive in the morning, with standards flying in the light of day to make a grand announcement of their arrival.

Unfortunately, it didn't quite work out that way.

They'd traveled most of the day at a somewhat leisurely pace until sometime towards midafternoon. A bank of dark clouds rolled in from the west and the temperature began to drop. Dashiell suspected, as did most of the men, that it meant a storm was on the approach, and all of them had been right – as it neared sunset, snow flurries began to fall and by the time they stopped to supper, the snow was falling steadily.

It was quite beautiful, but it was also unwelcome. Dashiell was afraid that if they camped for the night, they would find themselves snowed in by morning, so he made the decision to travel through the night in an effort to reach Chadlington before they were snowed in completely.

This meant that by the time they reached Chadlington at dawn, it was with one hundred and fifty exhausted men, three exhausted knights, an array of exhausted horses, and women who had hardly slept as the carriages had bumped and shimmied over the muddy, snowy road. It had been a long, rough night.

Not exactly the entrance that Dashiell had wanted to make, but it couldn't be helped.

The men of Chadlington couldn't have been kinder in their efforts to help the Duke of Savernake's party find comfort and warmth after so miserable a journey. Chadlington was a large castle with two moderately small wards, meaning the guests for Lady Jillayne's party had to camp outside the walls. But it wasn't just the Savernake party camping; there were several other houses that had already arrived, and the men from Chadlington had spent all night shoveling away snow and spreading straw over the field to the east where the guests would be camping for the festivities.

The Duke of Savernake's party was given the best area to camp in, away from the road but on the upslope so that all water would wick away from the area. As the Savernake men pitched tents and tended to the horses, the Chadlington men built big fires so there would be warmth when they were finished.

Even though Belladonna hadn't slept all night, she was too excited to nap as her sisters and father were doing. The duke was sleeping heavily on one of the long carriage benches while Acacia slept at his feet, getting kicked in the head once in a while as he fidgeted. Lily was passed out on the other bench, but Belladonna stood by one of the windows, looking out over the winter-white landscape as her father's men set up camp.

Smoke was heavy on the icy air, wafting into the carriage, and Belladonna eventually closed the shutters to keep it from filling up the cab. But she was still excited about being there. She very much wanted to see Jillayne, her friend, so she picked the puppy up from where it had been snoring at Lily's feet and, wrapping it up in her cloak with only its head sticking out, she headed out into the frozen world.

Men were working tirelessly raising the tents, their steaming breath bursting like puffs of fog from their mouths as they labored. Since the Chadlington men had shoveled away the snow, leaving a layer of straw upon the ground, it wasn't difficult to walk through the camp. Belladonna was looking for Dashiell, hoping he would take her to the castle so she could present Jillayne with her present.

He wasn't difficult to find.

They were having trouble raising the duke's tent. The ground was frozen because of the weather, and because the duke's tent was so large and heavy, the stakes that they were driving into the ground to hold it were pulling free because they couldn't drive them deep enough.

Therefore, Belladonna stood and watched as Dashiell drove a stake into the ground with a massive, heavy sledge hammer. He was heaving with effort, his hot breath puffing up around him as he worked. When he finished and stood back for the men to secure the tent lines, he caught sight of Belladonna standing several feet away.

Breathing heavily, he immediately went over to her as she stood there, wrapped up in her cloak with the puppy's head sticking out at chest-level. There was a ready smile on his lips as he greeted her.

"Why are you not sleeping like the others?" he asked.

Her eyes twinkled as she looked at him. "I am too excited to sleep," she said. "I came to find you. I want to give Jillayne her puppy and was hoping you could escort me into the castle."

He wiped the sweat from his brow. "Now?"

"Now."

He looked around at all of the activity, specifically at the duke's tent. "We are having a difficult time raising your father's tent," he told her. "I seem to be the only one able to drive the stakes in deep enough. I would be happy to send Bent or Aston with you if you must go now. Would that be acceptable?"

She was disappointed, but she understood. "Certainly," she said. "I am not entirely sure when I shall have the opportunity to give the puppy to Jillayne once the festivities start, so I thought to do it now before the chaos begins."

He grinned. "Chaos, indeed," he said. "I have been told that tonight is the great feast followed by games tomorrow. Chadlington's men have coerced me into both the mêlée and the archery contests of skill."

Belladonna smiled brightly. "And you shall carry my favor for both," she said. "Imagine how proud I shall be when you win everything."

He snorted. "I shall try, my lady."

She shook her head firmly. "You shall *win*, Dash. There is no one in England that can best you, in anything."

Her faith in him was touching. "With you as my champion, surely I cannot fail."

She was pleased that he was seeing things her way. "Of course you will not," she said. "Now, if you will send Bent or Aston to me, I shall be on my way to deliver this puppy."

With a wink, he left her standing for a few minutes while he hunted down Aston, who was the first knight he came across. The man was standing over some soldiers as they repaired a broken axle on one of the wagons, and when Dashiell told him what he was needed for, Aston was more than happy to comply.

Soon enough, Belladonna and Aston were heading for the gatehouse of Chadlington Castle.

CLAYTON HAD SEEN Belladonna, under Aston's escort, heading to the main gate that was built on the western side of the enclosure.

He thought it was a rather perfect situation for what he needed to do.

Clayton had maintained a low profile since Dashiell's tongue lashing before they had departed Ramsbury. He'd gone to his horse and remained there. The entire trip to Chadlington, he had been riding at the very front of the escort, away from Dashiell and the knights who were so against him. He didn't want to talk to any of them, and even when Dashiell made decisions about continuing through the night to avoid being snowed in, he kept quiet even though he didn't want to continue. He wanted to retreat to his tent and sulk, but that wasn't to be.

So, he'd ridden through the night, arriving at Chadlington as exhausted as the rest of them. But he pushed that exhaustion aside when he saw how many people had already arrived for the festivities, as the field to the east of the castle was a veritable sea of tents, and the standards from many different families slapped in the icy breeze.

In particular, he was looking for the banner of Lord Sherston, but he wasn't entirely sure the man would be flying a banner at a celebration he hadn't been invited to. Lord Sherston's home was closer to Chadlington than Ramsbury was, so it was Clayton's hope that once Anthony received the missive, he'd come straight away to Chadlington to await the arrival of the Ramsbury party. Therefore, once they'd arrived at Chadlington, Clayton immediately set out to find Anthony Cromford, Lord Sherston.

Perhaps his future brother-in-law and the last nail in the coffin of Dashiell du Reims.

He'd gone on the hunt while Dashiell and the Ramsbury men struggled to erect tents upon the frozen ground. Clayton never helped with manual labor, anyway, and he could hear Dashiell bellowing all across the encampment, which was normal for the man. He had a big mouth. At least, Clayton thought so. Big mouth and arrogant.

A man he truly hated.

If du Reims wasn't in the picture, then Clayton's life at Ramsbury would be so much easier. He would be king of the castle, even if it wasn't his – yet. And that's what Lord Sherston was supposed to ensure – that Dashiell du Reims would leave Ramsbury if Belladonna was married to another man so that Clayton could be rid of his nemesis once and for all.

God, Clayton could only pray it would happen.

But Lord Sherston proved elusive, at least for the first half-hour of searching. The more Clayton looked, the more he came up empty. In the distance, on the rise against the castle moat, the Duke of Savernake's tents were going up, one by one, and Clayton was growing increasingly frustrated with his inability to locate Sherston.

And then, he had an idea.

There was a town to the west of the castle, a small village, but it did have a tavern. A perfect place for an uninvited lord to linger. As Clayton headed out of the encampment and headed for the town, he caught sight of Summerlin escorting Lady Belladonna entering the great gatehouse of Chadlington.

Summerlin, he could get around. It was du Reims who proved immovable, so Clayton had to strike while Belladonna was with an escort he could intimidate. The town was to the west of the castle, butted right up against it, so it was hardly an effort to enter the main street of the town and make haste towards the only tavern, the Slug and Lettuce.

A nasty little tavern with a nasty little name. Someone must have been drunk when they named it. Of course, it was full of women ready to play lettuce to a paying man's slug but, at this point, Clayton wasn't interested in the whores who seemed interested in him. He was on the hunt for a particular lord that he'd invited to the celebration.

What he didn't know was that the particular lord he sought had seen the Savernake standards enter Chadlington and, even now, he was already in the encampment, looking for a particular lady.

"DASH! DASHIELL DU REIMS!"

Dashiell had just finished pounding in the eighth stake for the duke's tent when he heard someone calling his name. Winded, he turned to see a young lord that he immediately recognized. He tried to hide his shock as he handed the hammer off to one of the nearby soldiers.

"Cromford?" he said, sounding incredulous even though he was trying not to. "Damnation, man, what are you doing here?"

Anthony Cromford, Lord Sherston, was a young and genuinely likable man. As Dashiell had once told Belladonna, Sherston was the kind of man Clayton wouldn't normally associate with. He had an excellent reputation as an honorable knight, but he was also fabulously wealthy and politically ambitious, which was just the type of man Clayton wanted to be allied with.

A man with a hunger for power.

Cromford was a rather short man with a winning smile and flashing brown eyes, and he seemed quite happy to see Dashiell. He extended a hand to du Reims in greeting.

"I see you survived the battle at Northampton," Anthony said, referring to the last time they had seen one another. "'Tis good to see you again."

Dashiell forced a smile at the young knight as he accepted the outstretched hand. "And you," he said. "So you have been invited to this decadent party, too? I was not aware that you knew the House of Chadlington."

Anthony shrugged. "I do not," he said. "Truth be told, I was not invited to the party by Lord Chadlington. I was invited by Clayton. Is he with you?"

A warning bell went off in Dashiell's mind. "He is somewhere around here," he said. "But why should he invite you?"

In Anthony's defense, he was too young and too far removed from the senior command structure of England's warlords to know what most of the older men knew about Dashiell and a certain duke's daughter. He was part of the younger crowd, so his answer was honest in that he had no reason not to tell Dashiell why he'd come.

In hindsight, it was one of the biggest mistakes he would ever make.

"Business, shall we say," Anthony said, grinning. "I suppose he has told you, so I am sure this is not news. He has asked me to come and meet the duke's youngest daughter, Lady Belladonna. Mayhap there is an alliance on the horizon, eh, Dash? Clayton tells me she's the beauty of the sisters. Is she about so that you may introduce us?"

It took all of Dashiell's self-control not to throttle the excited young man. Then, after he squeezed the life from him, he was going to find Clayton and beat his brains out. That was his thought process, and one he would dearly like to act upon, but he knew he couldn't. At least, not for all to see. Therefore, he had to steel himself.

Breathe, man, breathe!

"That is why you are here?" he asked through clenched teeth. "To inspect Lady Belladonna?"

Anthony nodded, unaware how close he was to having his neck broken. "Aye," he said. "Clayton thought this would be a good place to do it. If I do not like what I see, then I can leave and she will be none the wiser. But if I do like what I see…"

He trailed off, wriggling his eyebrows suggestively. Dashiell had to force his balled fists behind his back. Although he didn't blame Sherston for coming at Clayton's invitation, he could see exactly what had happened. Knowing that Dashiell would have circumvented any attempt to see Belladonna had Sherston been invited to Ramsbury, Clayton had invited him to a big event with many people, probably hoping that Dashiell would never even see him.

Cleary, that part of the plan had gone awry as Sherston excitedly came to the Ramsbury encampment looking for Belladonna. Dashiell had no idea where Clayton was and he surely didn't care, because he was going to stop Sherston's interest before it really got started. Taking a deep breath to calm the building rage, Dashiell crooked his finger to

Sherston and began to lead him away from the encampment.

"Come with me," he said quietly.

Gladly, Sherston followed. He followed Dashiell through the Savernake encampment until they reached the south side of the field, away from men where they could be afforded some privacy. When Dashiell felt they were far enough away, he turned to the young lord.

"Anthony," he said evenly. "I am going to ask you a question and I would expect an honest answer."

Sherston was serious. "Of course, du Reims."

"How well do you know Clayton?"

Sherston cocked his head thoughtfully. "We have gambled together," he said. "We have eaten together. We have spent some time together, but not as close friends. Simply as acquaintances. Truthfully, his missive about the lady did surprise me. We do not know each other terribly well."

Dashiell considered that before continuing. "What do you know of his reputation?"

"That he is ambitious."

"Ambitious, indeed," Dashiell muttered. "Anthony, he is so ambitious that he is trying to make a marital match with you to a woman who is already spoken for. He simply does not agree with her match and he is hoping, when the duke dies, that he can take control of her destiny and marry her to you because of your wealth and political connections. That is all he wants you for."

It was rather blunt, and Sherston's brow furrowed. "She is already spoken for?"

"Aye."

Sherston stared at him a moment before sighing heavily. "That is a rather underhanded thing to do," he said, clearly disappointed. "Who is she pledged to?"

"Me."

Sherston's eyes widened. "Oh... du Reims!" he gasped. "I did not know. Had I known, I surely would not have come!"

It was fear causing him to speak, fearful of Dashiell's reaction to his presence. The young man wasn't foolish; he knew what kind of a warrior du Reims was. But in that fear, Dashiell saw an opportunity at that moment that he didn't think he would have. If he could pull Sherston over to his side and to his way of thinking then, perhaps, they could both circumvent Clayton's wishes. It was worth a try, anyway.

"If he did not send the missive to you, it would have been to another wealthy lord," he said. "It just happened to be you. You see, Clayton is threatened by me and because of that, he is threatening to take Belladonna from me to undermine me. Ambition is only the beginning with him, Anthony. He is a vile, petty excuse for a man and when he assumes the Savernake dukedom, it will be hell for us all. That being said, I must ask you a favor."

Sherston nodded eagerly. "Anything, du Reims."

"Go along with him for now. Do not tell him that you and I have spoken. Pretend you are interested in the marital contract, but do not commit to it. I need time and I suspect that you are the only one who can give it to me. Clayton must think you are interested in Belladonna, but you must not act on it. String him along until he demands an answer. Will you do this for me?"

Sherston nodded seriously. "If you wish it," he said. "But for what purpose?"

"As I said, I need time," Dashiell said. "I am awaiting word from the Archbishop of Canterbury. I am afraid if you run to Clayton right now and tell him you have no interest, he will simply invite another less scrupulous lord to court Belladonna, someone who does not have the moral character that you have. If he does that, it will tear Savernake apart. Will you help me?"

Again, Sherston nodded. "Of course," he said. "I will delay him all I can."

Dashiell couldn't have hoped for a better outcome and the relief he felt was palpable. He put a hand on the young man's shoulder. "Good," he said. "Thank you. But know this will not go unrewarded. I shall ever be in your debt, as will the earldom of East Anglia. We will be a much better and much more grateful ally in the end."

Anthony knew that would be a great measure of support for his father and his properties, and he was more than willing to comply with Dashiell's request. There was some kind of a power struggle going on at Savernake and, to be truthful, he really didn't want to get involved. But he had to admit that, for the lady's sake, he was disheartened. He had actually been hopeful of a viable marriage prospect.

"I am happy to help," he said. "But I must say that I am none too pleased to be pulled into Clayton's schemes. I thought this was a genuine offer of marriage."

Dashiell sighed heavily. "It is Clayton's way of undermining my relationship with Belladonna. He will do anything to weaken me, however he can. I support the current duke, as I am sworn to, and Clayton cannot stand the fact that I do. He believes that he should be in command."

Sherston looked at him with disgust. "I did not know such a thing was happening at Ramsbury," he said. "My father will be very unhappy to hear this."

Dashiell held up a hand as if to ease the young lord's growing frustration. "Tell your father if you must, but if I were you, I would not turn on Clayton," he said. "Like him or not, he will be the duke someday and you do not wish him for an enemy."

"I will become an enemy when I turn down his offer of marriage."

"Nay, you will not. Simply tell him she is not to your liking."

Sherston scratched his head in a hesitant gesture. "Is that possible? He said she was a beauty."

Dashiell grinned. "It is *not* possible," he said. "She is an angel. She is the most perfect woman in all of England. You are going to have to lie."

Sherston stared at him a moment before breaking down into quiet laughter. "I am not sure I am that good of a liar," he said. "But if the alternative is earning your hatred, I would rather earn Clayton's."

Dashiell patted him on the shoulder one last time before dropping his hand. "Do this and you shall have my undying gratitude," he said. "You cannot imagine the hell that Clayton has put all at Ramsbury through over the past three years. I could tell you tales of his behavior, but I do not wish to spread gossip. So, suffice it to say it is worse than you can possibly imagine. Thank you for helping me keep the man at bay on this particular subject."

Sherston rubbed his chin, eyeing Dashiell as he did so. "I will do this for you, but you will do something for me."

"You only need name it."

"Find me a bride as lovely and accomplished as your Lady Belladonna."

Dashiell fought off a smile. "Have you met Lady Jillayne Chadlington yet?"

"I have not."

"The last time I saw the girl, she was quite lovely," he said. "As far as I know, she is not spoken for. Tonight, attend the great feast and find me. I will make the necessary introductions and I will ensure there is privacy so her focus will be on you entirely."

Sherston was back to being hopeful again. "With pleasure, du Reims," he said. "And you have my thanks."

"And you have mine."

With that, they separated, with Sherston heading back the way he'd come and Dashiell heading back to finish with the duke's tent.

Damn Clayton! Dashiell thought as he stormed back to the encampment. The more he thought about Clayton's attempt to undermine him, the angrier he became. He knew the man was underhanded, but this went beyond even what he thought Clayton was capable of. Thank God he ran into Lord Sherston when he did; had he not been the one to intercept the man, then the situation would have been very bad, indeed. Trying to marry Belladonna out from under him was a declaration of war as far as Dashiell was concerned.

He'd received the message loud and clear.

CHAPTER TWELVE

Everything was building up to a spectacular first night of the Chadlington celebration.

After delivering the birthday pup to Jillayne, Belladonna was only able to spend a few moments with the woman before she was pulled away by her mother and servants for a final fitting of her party dress. But she took the dog with her, so very happy for her gift. Belladonna's last glimpse of tiny, blonde Jillayne was as she hugged the puppy and kissed it, even as she was pulled away.

Pleased that her friend loved the gift but saddened that she wasn't able to spend a few moments with her, Belladonna had returned to the Savernake encampment with Aston. Once the man had delivered her to the camp, he left her to go about his duties and Belladonna returned to the carriage where her sisters and father were still sleeping. Lulled by the steady sounds of heavy breathing and occasional snoring, Belladonna lay down to rest and promptly fell asleep.

When she awoke, it was to someone knocking on the carriage door. Yawning, she opened it to find Dashiell standing there. He smiled at her and told her that their tents were ready for occupation, so she woke her family and they all staggered to their tents where braziers had been lit and beds had been made. Her father had his own tent, a massive one, while Acacia and Belladonna shared the tent next to it. Lily, unfortunately, was relegated to the tent she shared with Clayton.

They were warm, luxurious accommodations and Belladonna promptly climbed into the bed that the servants had made to try and get a little more sleep before the day truly commenced but, unfortunately, it was impossible because of the noise going on around them.

While some of the soldiers were trying to catch a bit of sleep after the long night, still others were awake, establishing a perimeter around the camp, shouting orders back and forth. The long morning turned into a short afternoon because Belladonna could no longer take the shouting and the commotion. Moreover, she was very excited for the festivities that evening, and sleep simply wouldn't come. Therefore, she rose while Acacia slept like the dead, and began the process of primping for the feast that evening.

Although the three sisters had a veritable fleet of maids, Belladonna preferred to do much of her personal grooming on her own. Unpacking one of her trunks, the one that contained the tunics for Dashiell, she had a servant run the tunics over to him while she pulled forth the garment she intended to wear – a beautiful mustard-yellow damask with silk accents, and a matching shift.

Donning layers of garments did require help. As the sun began to wane in the west, the maids helped her secure the elaborate dress as Acacia finally awoke and decided she should probably dress, too.

As Acacia stumbled about, bemoaning the fact that her dresses weren't nearly as beautiful as her sister's, Belladonna went about styling her hair. She liked to play with hairstyles and she was very good at it. In fact, she had a styling tool that she'd purchased from a merchant who said it had come all the way from Rome, a tube of bronze with a long handle, wooden at the end. When the bronze tube was placed in hot coals for a minute, removed and slightly cooled, wrapping hair around it would curl the hair beautifully.

The bronze curling rod was kept in a satchel along with combs and other hair implements. Belladonna heated the rod in the coals of the brazier and patiently curled her entire head of hair into a cascade of spiral curls. The maids helped a little, but she was determined to do the job herself. With the front of her hair pulled back and bejeweled butterfly combs keeping it neatly pulled back, her hair was positively glorious.

All throughout the encampment now, dusk was falling and the sounds of the night were filling the air along with the smoke from the cooking fires. The herald from Chadlington Castle was walking through the encampment, announcing the feast and inviting guests up to the castle.

As Belladonna finished with her hair, she could hear the man wandering through the camp. Her belly began to twitch with excitement as she thought of Dashiell escorting her to the feast. It would be their first official event together.

Still, she could hardly believe any of this was real. She'd spent so many years pining for the man. Now that her dreams were a reality, she still felt as if it were surreal. Very shortly, Dashiell would show up outside of her tent and he would be dressed in a tunic she made for him herself. Never had a garment been so lovingly sewn. It was enough to send her into giddy fits.

Truly, she never thought she could be so happy.

Outside the tent, she could still hear the herald, so she rushed to the heavy case that held the jewelry. Belladonna's mother had quite a collection, inherited from generations of her family, and all of that jewelry was passed down to her daughters. They wore it whenever they wished, always to pack it back up into the iron-fortified case that would then be put under guard.

As she lifted the top of the case, rubies and emeralds glittered in the weak light of the tent. Belladonna was looking for a particular necklace, one that was strung with fat pearls and a pendant on the end of it that was made of gold, pearl, and amber. It would be perfect with the dress and after some careful poking around, she found it in its satin pouch. Pulling it forth, she put the magnificent piece around her neck and stood back to look at herself in the polished bronze mirror.

With her curled hair and spectacular dress, Belladonna truly felt beautiful. One of the maids presented her with a small pot of beeswax, with a little ocher in it, that turned her lips a faint shade of red when she smoothed it on. It was such a decadent touch, but one that made all the difference in the world. The young woman gazing back at her in the mirror was someone confident and happy.

As Belladonna looked at herself, she was coming to think that she looked older somehow, but this was the woman she'd always dreamed she would become – one that was loved by the man she loved best in the world.

It showed on everything about her.

"Bella, help me," Acacia said, breaking into her train of thought. "This dress is too plain for the feast tonight and I do not know what to do about it. What should I do with my hair?"

Belladonna's happy feelings fled. She turned to her sister, the one she'd been avoiding since that horrible event she'd witnessed. Acacia didn't seem to understand that Belladonna didn't want to talk to her, but before Belladonna ignored her plea completely, she remembered what Dashiell had said about it – *do not treat her any differently, for she will want to know why.*

Perhaps that was true, but it was very difficult to look into Acacia's face and not explode at her.

"Why are you asking me such a thing?" she said with bitterness in her tone that suggested she would not help. "All you have ever done is criticize me when I wear a pretty garment or dress my hair. You have told me that my vanity is a sin, and now you want my help?"

Acacia tried not to look too contrite or too defensive. "Then don't help me," she hissed, turning away. "I will do it myself."

Belladonna knew she should probably feel bad about the situation, but she couldn't bring herself to. She was too disgusted with her sister to be nice to her, even after what Dashiell had told her. As she watched Acacia paw through her mother's jewels, she turned away and addressed one of the maids.

"Send word to Sir Dashiell," she said. "Tell him that I am ready for him."

The maid nodded and fled the tent. As Belladonna went to one of her capcases and pulled forth a finely spun shawl, white in color with an edging of gold thread, she heard Acacia speak.

"Why did you send for Dash?" she asked.

Belladonna didn't look at her as she settled the shawl over her shoulders. Knowing what she knew about her sister and Clayton, she didn't want to tell her anything that might make it back to the man. She knew she could trust Lily, but Acacia was now another matter altogether. She and Acacia had never been terribly close but, now, Belladonna felt as if there was even more of a barrier between them than ever before.

"He has agreed to be my escort," she said stiffly. "One cannot attend a party without one. Who shall be escorting you?"

Acacia looked at her with some chagrin. "I... I do not know," she said. "I suppose any of the knights could. Where is Bent? Or Aston?"

Belladonna couldn't summon one ounce of pity for the woman. "Mayhap, you should have thought about this before you came along," she said. "You did not bring any fine clothing and you do not have an escort. You do not even like parties, Acacia. You have told me in the past that they are nothing but sinful orgies. I do not even know why you are here!"

Acacia was trying not to look too unsure of herself as Belladonna snapped at her. Truth be told, she was here because Clayton was here. She hadn't seen the man in his four months away from Ramsbury when he was on battle campaign, but in the week that he had been returned, Acacia felt as if something between them had changed.

In her mind, something between them had deepened.

He hadn't told her that he'd missed her, as she had told him, but his actions had spoken for him. Clayton had bedded her more than usual, at least twice a day since his return, giving Acacia a sense of comfort and of being wanted, and the truth was that she didn't want him to go to this party without her. If he needed her, she wanted to be nearby, although with Lily sharing his tent, she wasn't sure if such a thing would be possible.

Still, she wanted to be near the man. She was coming to think he needed her, just a bit, and she was coming to be dependent upon him, just in the least. It was something that had never occurred before.

Clayton needed her.

But that wasn't something Acacia was willing to confess to her belligerent younger sister. Beautiful Belladonna, the woman that all men looked at. She envied, loved, and hated her sister all at the same time. Had she been born with Belladonna's beauty, things would have been different. She would have been married already, not telling everyone she was pledging herself to Amesbury as a last resort.

What did Belladonna know of being lonely and unattractive?

"I will not bother you any longer with my foolish questions," Acacia said, turning back to the mirror that a maid was holding up for her. "I shall make do."

"You haven't answered my question. Why would you come to a party when you think it is a sinful orgy?"

Acacia was starting to flush in the face. "What does it matter to you?" she said. "My reasons are my own. You needn't worry about me."

"Then it is not sinful any longer?"

"I do not plan on sinning."

Belladonna simply couldn't keep her mouth shut. Knowing what she did, that was the most ridiculous statement she'd ever heard from Acacia.

"That," she hissed, "is a lie. You are the biggest sinner of all!"

With that, Belladonna turned on her heel and rushed from the tent. She was so angry that she simply couldn't face her hypocritical sister any longer and she was afraid that she was going to say something she would soon regret. Just as she rushed from the tent entry, Dashiell and Aston appeared.

Belladonna quickly forgot about Acacia when she saw Dashiell in the beautiful yellow tunic she'd made for him. It matched her dress and she thought he looked enormously handsome in it. But he also wore a big leather belt with his broadsword at his side, several small daggers, and a chainmail coat beneath it. Not exactly party-going attire.

She burst out laughing.

"We are not going to battle, Dash," she pointed out. "Simply a feast. I do not think you will need your broadsword or mail inside the great hall."

He cocked an eyebrow at her. "Men are as heavily-armed at a feast as they are on the field of battle."

"Then you will not remove your mail?"

He sighed, glancing at Aston, who grinned and looked away. "I would prefer not to."

"Do you really think we will be set upon in the middle of a meal?"

"You will be very sorry I am not armed if we are."

Belladonna chuckled and shook her head. "Is this your idea of *not* being a court dandy?"

"Something like that."

She simply rolled her eyes and went to him, realizing the man was a lost cause. She could never take the knight out of him, nor did she want to. He dressed the same for a great feast as he did for a battle, but if he felt comfortable this way, so be it. Tucking her left hand into the crook of his right elbow, she simply lifted her shoulders.

"Very well, du Reims," she said. "I will not force you to do anything you are uncomfortable with."

She tried to walk, pulling him along, but he remained immovable. "I sense you are displeased," he said.

Belladonna stopped trying to pull him towards the castle, looking up at him with a smile playing on her lips. "This is your personal protest against me turning you into a court dandy, isn't it?" she teased. "I make you a lovely tunic and you load it up with weapons. You are resisting my wishes until the end."

The corners of his mouth tugged. "Kicking and screaming all the way, my lady."

Belladonna was back to chuckling at him. They were still new at this part of their relationship, so she couldn't get too angry about it. Hopefully, someday he'd learn that he could escort her to a party without preparing for a fight, but she doubted it. He was, after all, Dashiell du Reims, and his weapons were part of him. Gently but firmly, she pulled him along and they began to head towards the warmly-glowing castle.

With Dashiell on one side and the heavily-armed Aston on the other, they passed through the encampment as Dashiell's fine clothing drew stares and snickers from the men. One of them even made kissing noises at him, but when he turned to see who had done such a thing, no one would confess. They thought it all quite entertaining to tease the master knight, the one who was always so straight and hard with them. But it was in good fun, and Dashiell knew it, which is why he didn't become irate. He took it in stride.

In truth, he'd never been prouder in his life.

It was with great anticipation that he and Aston escorted Belladonna towards the great hall of Chadlington, beckoned by the smells and sounds, all of them hoping for an unforgettable evening.

For Dashiell and Belladonna, it would be more unforgettable than most.

THE GREAT HALL of Chadlington was a single long room, and a very old room, as Chadlington was a very old castle.

The great hall resembled a Viking long hall, with wooden support pillars and an enormous open fire pit in the center of it. Smoke billowed up to the ceiling, looking for an escape, but it didn't always find one. Therefore, the smell of smoke infiltrated everything along with the smell of dogs, of which there were many. Evidently, those at Chadlington were dog lovers, which explained Jillayne's excitement at the gift of a puppy.

Dogs were everywhere.

In fact, the guests had to wade through a herd of them when they entered. Dashiell and Belladonna were shown to their seats at one of the long tables below the dais, right next to Lily and Clayton, who had arrived before them.

Clayton sat at the very end of the table, ignoring everyone, while Dashiell and Belladonna were seated on the other side of Lily. Aston found his seat somewhere down the table.

Wine was immediately forthcoming, a well-dressed servant shoving a cup into their hands before pouring. As Dashiell's cup was filled, he eyed Clayton and was reminded that he hadn't had a chance to tell Belladonna of his conversation with Lord Sherston, mostly because he'd been busy for the afternoon and Belladonna had been resting. He thought to tell her before the feast, but Aston had accompanied them and he hadn't wanted to spill such secrets in front of the man.

Now, he found himself seated down the table from Clayton, who seemed to be greatly interested in the guests of the hall. Dashiell had a feeling he was looking for Lord Sherston, so he knew he needed to inform Belladonna of his conversation with Anthony Cromford sooner rather than later. Taking a healthy gulp of the sweet wine, he leaned down to her ear.

"I have not had the opportunity to tell you how lovely you look," he said quietly.

Smiling, Belladonna turned to him. "I was hoping you would think so."

"I do."

Her eyes twinkled. "I told you that you looked lovely, too, but you did not want to hear it."

He laughed softly. "If this is how you will wish me to look every time I escort you, then you will have to let me become accustomed to the idea. Too much finery and flattery all at once will cause my heart to seize."

She reached out, fingering the tunic, inspecting her own handiwork when the truth was that she simply wanted to touch him. He felt warm and firm beneath her fingers.

"I would not want for that to happen," she said. "But you look so handsome dressed in a fine tunic. I should think you would want to look this way, always."

"I will look anyway you wish me to."

Belladonna's hand went from fingering his tunic to briefly touching his face before dropping her hand. "You always look handsome and powerful to me, whether or not you are wearing a fine tunic."

Dashiell could feel that wonderful warmth settling between them, the warmth that made his toes tingle and his heart flutter. To think that this beautiful woman was in love with him was still something he was having a difficult time grasping. But by the look in her eyes, he could see that what Lily told him was true. Every second he spent with her now, he *knew* it was true.

He wondered if the look in his eyes bespoke of the same thing.

"You are too kind, my lady," he said softly. "I regret that we have not had much time to speak in the time leading up to this party. We have both been quite busy. I... I have missed talking to you, just the two of us."

Belladonna was back to beaming. "We are speaking now, aren't we?" she said. "And I missed talking to you, too, most dreadfully. When you were gone those few days to Selborne, I surely thought I would die from loneliness."

Her dramatics flattered him but, in that moment, he realized there was yet another subject he needed to discuss with her.

"I understand your longing," he said. "But the journey was necessary. I went to see Gavin de Nerra to discuss certain political matters that should not concern you. But I also spoke to him about you and me, and the inability of your father to approve a betrothal. In fact, I sought Gavin's counsel on the matter. He is a wise man and I trust him."

She was very interested. "What did he say?"

Dashiell took another sip of his wine. "He is going to bring our case to the Archbishop of Canterbury personally," he said. "He is going to plead on my behalf to see if he can obtain the archbishop's approval for our betrothal because of your father's mental condition. Which brings me to something else I must speak to you of."

"Oh? What is it?"

He lowered his voice as much as he could. "I met Lord Sherston today," he said, watching her eyes widen. "He is here at the invitation of Clayton, evidently to look you over. Now, before you become upset, be still and listen to me. I spoke with Sherston and told him the situation, and he was quite appalled to realize that Clayton is trying to use him as a pawn. In fact, he was quite in agreement to decline Clayton's offer of a betrothal to you, but he is not going to do it right away. He is going to delay Clayton as much as he can before giving him an answer."

By now, Belladonna was quite upset but struggling not to be because he'd asked it of her. "But why should he delay?"

Dashiell could see that she was increasingly distressed and, under the table, he reached out and took her hand, holding it tightly in his big fingers.

"I am afraid that if he immediately declines the offer, then Clayton will simply find another lord to accept his offer," he said softly. "I need enough time to receive word from Canterbury about our betrothal and Sherston is going to give us the time we need. He will delay Clayton as much as he can. I have a feeling that Clayton will introduce you to Sherston during our time here at Chadlington. So when he does, remember that Sherston is on our side. Will you do that?"

Belladonna was still troubled, but not nearly as much as she had been. She was simply upset that Clayton had invited Sherston to the celebration, clearly to try and force the man upon her.

"I will," she said, frowning unhappily. "But I cannot believe that Clayton would do such a thing!"

Dashiell shushed her quietly, eyeing Clayton to see if the man had heard her. But Clayton seemed oblivious.

"He is trying to undermine me," he muttered. "But it will not work. Sherston is as disgusted with his attitude as we are. But whatever you do, never let on that Sherston and I have spoken. Clayton must not know that."

She nodded solemnly. "I will not, I swear it."

"Good lass. Now, I think we can enjoy this celebration with some peace of mind."

Belladonna wasn't so sure of that, but he seemed certain, so she swallowed any protests or gripes she had. Dashiell was doing all he could to thwart Clayton's plans and she would have to trust him. She watched him as he drained his cup.

"What you said about the archbishop," she said, going back to the previous subject. "Gavin de Nerra will really plead our case to the man?"

Dashiell held his cup up for more wine, poured by a hovering servant. "Aye," he said. "I could ask for no better advocate. I explained that we must gain approval before Clayton becomes the duke, or all will be lost."

Belladonna's mood began to sink. Thoughts of Clayton trying to control her future, of her father's eventual passing, and of the possibility that she and Dashiell might never wed were weighing heavily on her. Dashiell could see the sorrow on her face and he squeezed her hand under the table.

"Do not fret, lamb," he said quietly. "Clayton will not win in the end."

She nodded. "I know," she said, turning towards him. But the entry to the hall was in her line of sight and her eyes widened at something at the entrance. "Dash! Look!"

Dashiell's head snapped to the hall entry, immediately seeing the Duke of Savernake as he entered the hall with Acacia and Bentley in tow. Men recognized him, and greeted him, and there was a good deal of hand kissing going on as Edward became Paul the Apostle once again and began to bless those in the hall.

Dashiell was already on his feet, rushing towards the duke as Aston, who was closer to Edward, also stood up from the table and rushed to the duke's side.

"Be at peace, brothers," Edward boomed in his unusually strong voice. "Men of God, be at peace!"

Since nearly every fighting man in Southern England knew of Savernake's madness, no one was surprised when he began making the sign of the cross over their heads and muttering prayers in Latin. For Savernake, that had been his usual behavior for some time now. It was oddly comforting and oddly disturbing, all at the same time.

"In nomine Christi, ut benedicat tibi…"

"My lord?" Dashiell said as he came upon the duke. "I was unaware you wished to attend the feast."

Bentley and Acacia were looking at Dashiell with great concern, as if they had been unable to prevent the duke from wandering. Bentley looked positively guilt-stricken.

"Papa awoke from his nap and began to wander the encampment," Acacia said. "Drusus tried to stop him and… and Papa hit him over the head. Bent and I decided to escort him so he would not try to hit anyone else. It was… easier this way, Dash."

Violence was a new thing with the duke, and very surprising for a man who was usually so benevolent. But Dashiell remembered that he'd pushed Belladonna when they were leaving Ramsbury, so perhaps this violence was something they were going to have to contend with now. God only knew how swiftly this madness had claimed the duke, and how every day seemed to bring something new. But Dashiell wasn't looking forward to Edward de Vaston, who was a truly excellent warrior, becoming physically combative.

That could be a definite problem.

"My lord," Dashiell said calmly, trying to force the duke to focus on him. "May I return you to your tent? I will have the servants bring you a wonderful meal. I am sure you would be more comfortable there."

Edward looked at Dashiell, a flash of recognition in his eyes. "My son," he murmured, reaching out to touch Dashiell on the face. "My good and true servant. You must help me bless these men. They are in need of the word of God."

"My lord, I am sure they would be honored, but tonight is a celebration, not a mass. Will you return to your tent with me?"

Edward wavered with uncertainty. "But… where men are gathered, God shall also be there."

"Agreed, my lord. But this is not the time."

Just as Edward seemed to be considering his words, a new element entered the conversation.

"My lord! You honor us with your presence!"

The greeting came from behind Dashiell and he turned to see Lord Chadlington approaching with his arms outstretched, as if to embrace Edward. But Edward simply lifted a hand and made the sign of cross.

"Peace be with you, my son."

"But my lord, it is *me*. It is Bruce!"

"I bless you in the name of the Father, Bruce."

That wasn't the response Lord Chadlington was looking for. He came to a confused halt, looking at Edward rather curiously. Dashiell, seeing that the lord was somewhat at a loss, spoke quietly to the man.

"His mind is consumed by madness, my lord," he muttered. "Surely you have heard tale of this. He believes himself Paul the Apostle. It would be wise of you to treat him that way. The Duke of Savernake, as you knew him, no longer exists."

Lord Chadlington looked at Dashiell in shock, but quickly recovered. Although he had supplied men for the rebellion against the king, a bad back and bad hips had prevented him from fighting himself. Therefore, he hadn't known the extent of Savernake's madness even though he had, indeed, heard the rumors. He addressed Edward far more carefully.

"My-My lord," he said, indicating the high table where his family was sitting. "Will you sit with us? We would be honored."

Dashiell wasn't entirely sure that was a good idea, a situation that turned awkward when Edward completely ignored the request and wandered over to the nearest table, lifting his hand and uttering blessings to the men. The soldiers were eyeing him with some confusion until Dashiell began to silently indicate for them to cross themselves, as one would normally do when receiving a blessing from an apostle.

Some of the men began to respond, encouraging those around them to cross themselves also. Soon enough, the entire table was crossing themselves as Edward gave them his blessing.

Paul the Apostle had found a flock.

"Stay with him," Dashiell muttered to Bentley. "I will be sitting at the other table and will watch the situation. If you need me, I shall come. Try not to let him hit anyone."

Bentley wriggled his eyebrows at him, not looking forward to spending the evening trailing the mad duke around. But Dashiell had no intention of doing it because he wanted to spend the evening with Belladonna and he wasn't about to let Edward ruin it. He'd been waiting for four long years to enjoy a meal and perhaps a dance with Belladonna, so he turned for the table to return to her, hoping the duke wouldn't spoil his evening and the evening of others.

"Dash?"

Dashiell heard the soft female voice, turning to see Acacia standing beside him. He forced a smile.

"My lady?"

Acacia pointed over to the table that contained her sisters. "Will you take me with you?"

Dashiell held out an elbow to her and she took it, latching on tightly. As they turned to head over to the family, Dashiell caught sight of the end of the table.

It wasn't how he left it.

Lily, Belladonna, and Clayton were there, but so was someone else. Dashiell could plainly see Anthony Cromford standing at the end of the table, and it was clear that he was in conversation with Belladonna as Clayton mediated. Clayton seemed pleased, Sherston interested, and Belladonna reluctant. Introductions were taking place.

So, the moment had come.

Breathe, Dashiell told himself. He was in control of this situation so there was no reason for him to become irate about it. However... he knew that Clayton would be expecting him to become irate. He knew that for a fact. If he didn't react the way Clayton wanted him to, then the man might be suspicious. That meant Dashiell was going to have to do exactly what his gut told him to do – rage. With Acacia on his arm, he stormed up to the table and practically pushed Acacia down into a seat.

"Lord Sherston," he addressed Anthony in a tone that would make most men quake in their boots. "I did not know you were here, also. It is agreeable to see you again."

Anthony's head snapped to Dashiell but he kept a polite tone. In fact, it was the same tone Dashiell had heard from the man earlier when they were speaking in confidential conversation – a tone that suggested he was not afraid of the man who had just used a sharp tone with him.

"Dash," he greeted calmly. "It is good to see you."

"Did your father come with you?"

"Nay, he did not. It is difficult for him to travel in his old age."

Dashiell hoped that Sherston realized his sharp attitude was all an act; given their earlier conversation, he would assume so.

"A pity," he said, softening his harsh stance ever so slightly. "He is a man of wisdom and good conversation."

Sherston nodded. "He is, indeed," he said. Then, his gaze moved over to Belladonna. "And he would have found a great deal of pleasure in being introduced to Lady Belladonna and Lady le Cairon."

So much for softening his harsh stance. Even though Dashiell knew this was an act on Sherston's part – at least, he truly hoped it was – he still didn't like the way the man looked at her. But that was his jealousy talking; he didn't like the way any man looked at her. He stood back and indicated Acacia.

"And this is Lady Acacia, another de Vaston sister," he said. "She has no escort this evening that I am aware of. Mayhap you would be so kind as to provide her with that honor."

It was clear that he was trying to divert Sherston from Belladonna. As Acacia flushed violently to the suggestion, Clayton spoke.

"Lord Sherston is here to meet Belladonna," he said firmly. "I told you that I had Lord Sherston in mind for her, du Reims. What a happy coincidence to find the man here so I could make the necessary introductions."

It was a shot directly over Dashiell's bow. As Dashiell turned to Clayton to verbally eviscerate the man, Sherston moved away from the pair and went directly to Belladonna, claiming the seat beside her that had been formerly occupied by Dashiell. He leaned in to the woman rather provocatively and whispered in her ear.

"Slap me in the face," he murmured.

Belladonna jerked back, her expression full of shock and outrage. "Good Sir, you…"

Again, Sherston leaned forward and shoved his face into the right side of her head. "Slap me," he muttered again. "Do it quickly!"

Startled, Belladonna did as he demanded. Lifting a hand, she slapped him across the face as hard as she could. Sherston's head snapped sideways and he looked at her as if she had just grievously insulted him. In a huff, he stood up and marched past Clayton.

"I do not care how beautiful she is," he hissed at Clayton. "No woman will treat me like that!"

With that, he stormed off, leaving Clayton open-mouthed. But just as quickly, Clayton ran after him to soothe the man. The last Dashiell saw, they were heading over to the northwest corner of the hall where Clayton was trying to apologize and Lord Sherston was pretending to be horribly upset. Dashiell had to fight off a smile as he returned his attention to Belladonna.

"He must have said something quite terrible to you," he said, surprisingly calm.

Wide-eyed, Belladonna simply nodded. "He… he did."

Lily was looking at her sister with a great deal of shock. "What did he say, Bella?" she asked.

Belladonna didn't want to tell her sister the truth, so she leaned forward and whispered the first thing that came to mind, something terribly shocking and crude that she'd once heard from a maid. It was the only thing she could think of. As Lily gasped, appalled, Belladonna stood up and made her way over to Dashiell.

"I do not feel much like feasting this night," she said to him. "Will you take me back to my tent?"

Dashiell gazed down at her, wondering what Sherston had actually said to her. He couldn't really tell if she was upset or if she was simply acting the part.

"You cannot let that ruin your evening," he said. "You have been waiting for weeks to attend this celebration. Do not leave because of what some fool said."

Belladonna reconsidered, at least for the sake of her sisters, who were still looking at her with shock. She was trying to play whatever game Sherston and Dashiell were playing because Dashiell had asked her to. So, perhaps, leaving a party she very much wanted to attend was, in fact, premature. After a moment, she nodded.

"Very well," she said. "But you will sit with me. Do not leave my side again."

"I swear, I will not."

When they'd reclaimed their seats and trenchers were beginning to be brought forth by the servants, Dashiell leaned over into her ear.

"What did he say to you?" he whispered.

Belladonna turned in his direction, making sure to keep her voice down. "He asked me to slap him."

"He did?"

"Aye."

Dashiell thought on that; there was great approval in his eyes. "That was wise," he muttered. "Now, Clayton will spend all night trying to apologize to him and the both of them will leave us alone. That was a brilliant move on Sherston's part so he will not be expected to entertain you."

"Then I did the right thing?"

"You did. But one question."

"What is it?"

"*What* did you tell your sister?"

Belladonna nearly choked on the wine she had just sipped. Daintily, she wiped her mouth with her fingers as Dashiell lifted his cup to his lips.

"I told her that he said he was seeking a warm haven for his heated rod."

Dashiell choked so hard on the wine he was drinking that it came out of his nose.

CHAPTER THIRTEEN

THE DAY FOLLOWING the dumping of snow dawned bright and spectacular.

On the field to the north of the castle, a small army of servants was clearing away the quickly-melting snow and spreading straw all around to help with the moisture, because very soon, the first game of the day would be played upon the field.

Already, the participants were starting to gather under the bright winter skies. Houses from as far north as Nottingham were participating, and men who were exhausted and with great aching heads from too much drink the night before were collecting around the edge of the field. The first event was to be the mass competition, a mock battle where there would be two teams fighting against one another.

The rules were simple enough. The battle went one of two ways – men could either fight on teams or it could be one giant fight where it was every man for himself. Sometimes these mass competitions were fought on horseback and sometimes on foot, and if a man was captured or stunned, he could be ransomed back to his men. It could be quite profitable, which was why so many men were willing to participate and chance getting their brains beaten in for the opportunity of obtaining some wealth.

Last night, the herald of Lord Chadlington announced at the feast that this particular mass competition would be fought on foot, as horses and sharp weapons were not allowed, and it would be every man for himself, which made it rather brutal and very exciting. Dashiell, Aston, and Bentley had already formed a group. They would help each other out in the hopes of being the last three standing. Clayton was left on his own and not invited into their group even though he spent the rest of the night trying to convince Lord Sherston to be his ally. Sherston rightfully declined, and Clayton was without anyone.

But such was the nature of the game.

At this early hour, the encampment of guests was buzzing with activity as men ate their morning meal and dressed for the coming game. Squires were busy making sure weapons were in the best possible repair and ladies were donning their finery.

Inside the tent she shared with Acacia, Belladonna was already dressed. She was wearing a beautiful blue woolen gown and a matching cloak that was lined with rabbit fur. Her hair, still curly from the night before, had been braided and now hung over one shoulder as she stood in the middle of the tent as the maid finished putting on her shoes. She wore doeskin boots this morning to keep her feet warm.

Acacia was also dressing on the other side of the tent, looking for something warm and stylish from her sister's collection of clothing. The two women hadn't said a word to each other all night and, even now, Acacia didn't even ask if she could wear something of Belladonna's. She was simply doing it.

Belladonna ignored her.

Once her shoes were on, however, the sound of the world outside of the tent drew her to the tent flap, where she stood and watched the encampment mill about. Maids brought in food to break their fast, but Belladonna wasn't hungry. She was too excited. The anticipation soon became too much to bear and she quit the tent, going on the hunt for Dashiell.

Today was to be their day of glory.

He wasn't hard to find. His tent was adjacent to the duke's tent, meaning he was close at hand should he be needed. As soon as

Belladonna left her tent, she could see him with Bentley and Aston, all of them crowded around a heavily-smoking fire, mostly dressed, as the squires finished buffing out marks and scratches on their weapons.

Dashiell had his back to her and she smiled at the sight of him; his auburn hair was glistening in the morning light, his fine figure of broad shoulders, narrowed torso, and big legs producing pleasing lines. Surely there was no one more magnificent to look at. Just as she summoned her courage to call to him, someone grasped her by the arm.

"You are up early," Lily said, her breath hanging in the air in the freezing temperatures. "Have you broken your fast yet?"

Belladonna shook her head. "Not yet," she said. "I am too excited to eat."

Dashiell heard the chatter, turning around to see Belladonna and Lily standing several feet away. He smiled, waving them over.

"Come, ladies," he said. "Join us. Bent says that he is still drunk from last night, Aston is complaining that he had no lovely women to dance with, and I am evidently the only one who is feeling well this morning."

As Belladonna laughed at him, Lily looked at Aston in mock outrage. "*I* was dancing last night," she said. "Are you saying that I am not lovely?"

Aston held up his hands to soothe the angry woman. "I meant outside of the House of de Vaston, of course," he said. "Besides... you did not dance with me, else I would have nothing to complain over."

Lily tried to maintain her outrage, but she couldn't quite do it. She grinned at the knight. "'Tis well and good for you that you have changed your story," she said. Then, she looked at Bentley, sitting on a stool with his head leaning on one hand. "And no wonder you are still drunk. Every time I saw you, you were downing another cup of wine."

Bentley smiled weakly at her. "It was good wine."

"Is it a good headache?"

He snorted. "Not *that* good. Mayhap I indulged a bit too much."

Lily's gaze upon him was loving. There was no other way to describe it. But Belladonna wasn't looking at her sister; she had eyes only for Dashiell.

"You indulged a good deal also," she said to him. "I am surprised you are not feeling as Bent does."

Dashiell wriggled his eyebrows. "I am stronger than he is," he said. "I can drink any man in England under the table."

Next to him, Bentley made a choking sound. "I have seen you lose a drinking game or two," he pointed out. "Remember at the tavern in Marlborough when your cousins were passing through town? You sat on one side of the table, the de Lohr brothers on the other, and you three drank a strong spirit that came all the way from Rome. I had never had anything like that in my life. Do you remember how powerful it was? It was like drinking lightning."

Dashiell put a hand on the man's aching head, petting it as one would pet a dog. "Precious darling," he said with mock sympathy. "Did it burn a hole in your precious little throat?"

Bentley shot Dashiell a look to kill, but Aston was giggling like a fool. "I remember that," he said. "It put David de Lohr to sleep after one cup, but Dash and Chris continued drinking to see who would be the last one standing."

"And you shall be the first one falling if you continue that story," Dashiell threatened.

But it was too late. Belladonna wanted to hear the story. "Do not stop, Aston," she said. "What happened?"

Dashiell was glaring threateningly at Aston, who wisely moved out of his range and went to stand near Belladonna, effectively putting her in between him and Dashiell. Taking his life in his hands, he continued.

"Neither Dash nor Chris could stand up, but they continued to sit and drink the stuff," he said. "It was a matter of pride. They were so drunk that they were holding on to the tabletop to keep from falling, and Dash only lost the game because Chris reached over and pushed him. Had he not pushed, Dash would not have fallen."

Belladonna was greatly enjoying the tale. She looked at Dashiell. "What a terrible thing for your cousin to do."

Dashiell shrugged, full of regret. "I would have done it to him had I thought of it."

She laughed softly, now noticing that Lily had gone to stand next to Bentley, asking him if she could do something to help his head. The tone she used was so soft, so sweet. Somehow, it reminded Belladonna of the mess with Acacia and Clayton, and her poor eldest sister roped into a marriage with a man everyone hated. Lily didn't deserve such a thing; she deserved a life with sweet Bentley, a man worthy of her. Her good humor faded.

"Mayhap, there will be a chance for you to redeem yourself in the future," she said to Dashiell. "Meanwhile, you have a chance to prove yourself today in the games. I can see that men are already gathering at the field."

They were situated on a rise, so the competition field in the distance was easily seen. Indeed, there were men already gathering as Chadlington people prepared the field. The sun was rising over the land, and the snow from the previous day was still glistening white although, in some areas, it had melted and mixed with the dirt to produce mud. Still, everything looked beautiful and crisp for the most part.

"Aye," Dashiell said as he observed the distant field. "We are nearly ready to go down there ourselves."

Belladonna pointed to the western side of the field. "There are lists," she said. "I want a good seat to watch you when you destroy everyone."

Dashiell wanted her to have a good seat, too. It was a matter of pride with him. He'd never had a favored lady in the stands cheering for him, so this was a momentous day for him as well. His gloves were tucked over the hilt of his broadsword and he pulled them forth.

"We will go there shortly," he told her as he began to put his gloves on. "But I must check on your father first to ensure he is adequately attended while we are away. Will you go with me?"

Belladonna nodded, gathering her skirts so they wouldn't drag in the mud, as Dashiell finished pulling on his gloves and took her politely by the elbow to escort her to her father. They made their way away from the others, heading towards the duke's tent only to come face to face with Clayton as the man emerged from it.

Immediately, Dashiell was on his guard.

"What were you doing in there, le Cairon?" he asked.

It was evident that Clayton was surprised to see him. Dashiell always put him on the defensive and, this time, was no different. The confrontation was immediate.

"I came to see if the duke wants to go to the tournament field," he said defiantly. "What are *you* doing here?"

Dashiell was growing very weary of Clayton, his belligerence and his lies. "I am preparing to go to the field and came to see to the duke's health before I do," he said. "It is a good thing I came when I did. Under no circumstances is he to go to the tournament field, le Cairon. Do you understand?"

Clayton frowned. "You cannot make that decision for him."

"I can and I will. The Duke of Savernake wandering among men who are engaged in mock combat is a recipe for disaster. He could be badly injured, or worse, although I know that is your ultimate goal, Clayton. It will not work this time."

Clayton began to turn red in the face. "You are as mad as the duke is."

Dashiell could feel his anger rise but with Belladonna beside him, he didn't want the conversation with Clayton to go any further. He'd already said too much.

"We shall see."

Without another word, he pushed past Clayton and into the tent, where the duke was snoring soundly and Drusus, his minder, had a look of extreme relief upon seeing Dashiell. As Belladonna went to go check on her father, Dashiell confronted the minder.

"What did Clayton want?" he asked in a low voice.

In spite of the cold temperatures, Drusus wiped sweat from his brow. "He wanted me to rouse the duke, my lord," he muttered. "He wants the man dressed and on his feet for the tournament."

Dashiell's jaw ticked, fighting down his anger. "The duke is not to go near the tournament field," he growled. "You know what will happen – he will wander onto it and get himself killed."

Drusus nodded nervously. Then, he dug into his pocket and pulled forth four pieces of tarnished silver. When Dashiell looked at him curiously, Drusus put the money into Dashiell's hand.

"Sir Clayton gave it to me, my lord," he said, his voice trembling. "He told me that it was for my troubles."

"What troubles?"

"Dressing and preparing the duke, my lord."

Dashiell stared at the money, realizing exactly what it was for. It was meant to buy Drusus' loyalty and, more than likely, his complicity. Dashiell had removed one minder who had been loyal to Clayton, and now the man was trying to buy the other.

Dashiell knew what he had to do.

"You will stay here," he told Drusus calmly. Then, his attention turned to Belladonna, who was now going through the trunk sitting near her father's bedside, looking for warm clothing. "My lady, remain here a moment. I will return very shortly."

Belladonna simply nodded. She had no idea where Dashiell was going and if she did, she probably wouldn't have stopped him. She probably would have cheered him on.

Quitting the duke's tent, Dashiell went on the hunt. It didn't take long to find Clayton back at the tent he shared with his wife, collecting his possessions for the coming mass competition.

All Clayton would remember of that moment was that Dashiell burst into his tent without a word and, suddenly, everything went black. When he finally came to, groggy and with loose teeth, he noticed four pieces of silver had been thrown onto the ground beside him.

The stakes of the struggle between him and Dashiell had grown. Dashiell was on to him. But to Clayton, none of that mattered. The attack, he vowed, would not go unanswered. Rising slowly, he waited until the world stopped rocking before making his way back to the duke's tent.

Dashiell would pay.

DASHIELL BARELY MISSED getting his head knocked off.

The mass competition was pure and utter chaos, much more than he'd expected. Usually, there was a good-natured hint to this event, but this morning saw no evidence of such good-natured camaraderie. It was literally a boiling, nasty mass of men trying to knock each other's heads off, and gangs of knights were roaming around, beating down those who were without such a gang. Individual knights were being summarily destroyed.

In the midst of all of the fighting, however, Dashiell couldn't help but notice that Clayton hadn't made it to the field. After he'd knocked the man silly and threw the money he'd paid Drusus at his feet, he hadn't given Clayton another thought as he'd headed to the tournament field with Belladonna, Lily, Bentley, Aston, and several other senior soldiers who wanted to witness the spectacle. Such an event was only meant for the knights and nobility, so the rank and file soldiers had to watch from the sidelines and place wagers on the winner amongst themselves.

Events such as this were great fun.

Dashiell assumed that he'd injured Clayton badly enough that the man didn't feel up to competing. It was either that, or he was fearful to show his face, afraid that Dashiell would do more than punch him in the nose this time.

Therefore, Dashiell didn't worry too much about him because he needed to focus on the event, which was inherently dangerous. Overzealous competitors had been known to greatly injure men. And as the mass competition began, it was clear that this event would be no exception.

It was a brawl.

So far, Dashiell, Bentley, and Aston had managed to capture six fairly wealthy knights and one earl's son, a young man who was thoroughly enraged that he'd been manhandled by Dashiell. Once the men had been subdued, there was an entire contingent of Savernake soldiers at the edge of the field who happily took the captives from the Savernake knights and tied them up, keeping them caged until the bout was over and they could be ransomed.

It was already a rich haul.

"Dash!"

A shout came from Dashiell's right and he turned to see Lord Sherston heading in his direction. Having a fairly massive club in his hand, he lifted it as Sherston approached, but Sherston put up his hand to ease Dashiell's battle-ready response.

"Nay, Dash," he said, huffing with exertion. "I came to ask if I could join your group. A man on his own is on borrowed time out here."

Dashiell thought about it, but only momentarily. Since Clayton wasn't anywhere to be seen, it didn't matter if Sherston allied with them. Dashiell had wanted to make sure Clayton would have no suspicions that he and Sherston were in league with each other. But if Clayton wasn't around, then it wasn't an issue.

"Tuck in with us," Dashiell motioned the man over. "We have been able to accumulate quite a score."

Lord Sherston rushed over, taking a stand beside Dashiell. "Thank you," he said. "I thought I was going to be eaten alive for certain."

Dashiell was watching the field now, as they were back over in a corner so he could better assess the mass competition as a whole. The muddy field had streaks of blood in it from men who had been beaten by the roving mobs. There were at least three of them now, and they were starting to beat on each other to see which gang was the strongest.

"I intend to win this, Sherston," Dashiell said. "You had better be prepared to fight until the death."

Sherston grinned. "I am prepared, my lord. I have a solid club that I stole. Someone put spikes in it, in fact."

It was then that he looked at Dashiell and Bentley and Aston's clubs; they were all spiked, all stolen from men who had tried to brain them. He ended up laughing.

"I see we are all prepared to do our worst," he said. "God help our opponents."

Dashiell looked out over the field again. He did take his eyes off the distant gangs for a brief second, long enough to look in the lists to see Belladonna, Lily, and Acacia sitting there, cheering them on. At least Belladonna and Lily were; Acacia was simply sitting there as if bored.

But all Dashiell wanted to do was make sure Belladonna was safe and secure; he'd been glancing into the lists ever couple of minutes since the event started. But now, he returned his focus to the mass. The event was drawing to a close, and he intended to be the last man standing.

It was time to end it.

"I would prefer that God not help them," he said. "I intend to be very wealthy by day's end and I cannot do that if God is not on my side. Therefore, with His help, we must organize and end this."

"What do you have in mind, Dash?" Bentley asked over his shoulder.

Dashiell was pointing to the group of about six knights who seemed to be defeating everyone else. "See them?" he said. "That is a group of knights from Wendlebury. They fought one battle against the king and no one has seen them since. Rumor has it that they have defected to John and, from what I have seen, they are not only capturing men to ransom, but they are crippling them. All of these men have fought against the king, so that tells me there may be some truth to that rumor."

Bentley had his eyes on the group of six knights, currently pummeling a couple of men who were putting up a valiant fight.

"I've seen them," he said. "I saw them put a Malmesbury knight down so brutally that the man had to be dragged off the field. They could not even ransom him because he was bleeding so badly."

"I wonder why the field marshals aren't disqualifying them," Aston wondered. "Surely their tactics are unethical."

Dashiell cocked an eyebrow. "Mayhap they are unethical, but they are not illegal," he said. "You know that nothing is illegal in something like this, and you must trust your opponents to be somewhat chivalrous in their treatment of you. But these men… they have no such chivalry or morals."

"Then what do we do?" Bentley asked.

Dashiell's gaze was fixed on the group of ruffians. "We use the element of surprise," he said. "We attack them while they are focused on that smaller group. They are going to come after us next and I do not intend to stand here and wait for them to move. We must attack them first."

It seemed like a logical plan, so the four of them prepared for the coming fight. Moving along the northern edge of the field, they had to fight off a few random knights, beating down each of them in succession and leaving it to the Savernake soldiers to collect them and pull them in with the rest of the captives.

Closer still, they came. There weren't many men on the field now, making their movements more obvious, and the people in the lists began to shout encouragement, cheering them on. Dashiell didn't dare turn to see if Belladonna was watching him, but he was certain she was. In the few times he'd looked to her, she had been looking straight at him, so he knew instinctively that she was watching him.

Now, he was about to make her terribly proud.

But that was before a booming voice suddenly echoed on the field, startling Dashiell enough that he stopped stalking the Wendlebury knights. He recognized the voice; God help him, he did. And by the time he turned to the source, Edward was making his way onto the field, holding up his hands and giving a blessing to the men in mock-battle.

"By the power of God given me this day, I absolve you of your sins, all of you, poor wretched creatures given whim to earthy sins!"

"Christ," Dashiell hissed. "He's going to get himself killed."

He was already on the run, heading for Edward, who was between the group of Wendlebury knights and the group of Savernake knights. Dressed in heavy robes, Edward was like a beacon, drawing every man who wanted to extract a massive ransom right to him.

Dashiell could see that. He could see that Edward already had the attention of nearly everyone on the field, and he ran faster than he'd ever run in his life. By the time he reached Edward, who was making the sign of the cross in the direction of the lists, a few of the Wendlebury knights had reached him also.

At that point, Dashiell did the only thing he could do. He tackled the Wendlebury knights with the force of a runaway horse, plowing into them and sending at least four of them straight into the mud. As the group descended into throwing punches, Dashiell bellowed at Aston and Bentley.

"Get him out of here!"

Aston grabbed Edward and yanked the man towards the edge of the field as Bentley and Sherston went to help Dashiell. Somewhere, he'd lost his club, but his fists were doing serious damage. Bentley and Sherston jumped in with their clubs and began beating the Wendlebury knights, beating them for all they were worth. They might have been outnumbered, but they weren't going to go down without a fight.

But they weren't the only ones drawn in to the battle.

Sitting in the lists, Belladonna and Lily saw when their father entered the field, and it was Lily who saw Clayton standing several yards back from the edge of the tournament field, trying to conceal himself in the spectators. But he was quickly forgotten when Dashiell and Bentley went to fight off the predatory knights as Aston struggled to remove the duke from the field. Being that the duke was a big man, and healthy, he didn't like being roughly handled, so he began to struggle against Aston as the man tried to save his life.

That was all Belladonna and Lily needed to see. Suddenly, they were bolting up from their seats, rushing from the lists and running towards the edge of the field where Aston was literally fighting with Edward now, who was confused and agitated. As Lily rushed to help Aston with her father, Belladonna ran to the edge of the field to see about Dashiell and Bentley.

She simply couldn't leave them on their own.

Aye, it was foolish of her to want to help Dashiell, but the man had compromised himself trying to save her father. Belladonna didn't know where her father had come from, or why he'd suddenly appeared, but the fact remained that he had, and Dashiell had done what he was required to do –

Save him.

There were groups of spectators at the edge of the field, men who were simply observing or men who had been in the fighting but had somehow managed to emerge without being captured. There were men with clubs in their hands and those without, but Belladonna was fixed on those with the clubs. In fact, as she ran past one of the men, she yanked the club right out of his hand. She kept running, pushing past observers who tried to grab her to prevent her from running onto the field.

But it didn't work.

With a cry of pure anger, of pure anguish at her beloved Dashiell being beaten by horrid knights, Belladonna made it onto the field and began swinging the club at the heads of the men grappling with Dashiell.

The first man was smashed right in the face, destroying his nose and teeth. As blood spurted and he fell off Dashiell, Belladonna brought the club around again at the man on Dashiell's back and hit him on the back of the neck. It wasn't enough to really hurt him, but it did get his attention. By the time he turned around to fight back, her club was already sailing in a downward motion, catching him in the face. As he fell away, Dashiell was free and he leapt to his feet.

Seeing Belladonna on the tournament field was inarguably the most frightening thing he'd ever seen in his life. Four of the six Wendlebury knights were down and injured, leaving the remaining two for Bentley and Sherston. Dashiell didn't even give thought to continuing the fight; he rushed at Belladonna, threw her over his shoulder, and ran from the field as fast as his shaking legs would carry him.

Bentley and Sherston were declared the winners a short time later. It was an exciting end to a most exciting mass competition.

CHAPTER FOURTEEN

BELLADONNA KNEW SHE was in trouble.
She knew this because Dashiell hadn't said a word to her other than telling her to remain in her tent and not leave. It wasn't so much what he said but *how* he'd said it. She knew that he would be terribly angry at her if she disobeyed, so she didn't. She simply sat on a stool near the brazier, warming herself, as the sounds of the encampment went on outside.

Acacia hadn't returned from the lists. She had no idea where her sister was, and Lily hadn't made an appearance, either, leaving Belladonna to believe that, somehow, she was being punished. Maybe Dashiell was keeping everyone from her, like some terrible solitary confinement. But as she sat there and stewed, the tent flap moved aside and a familiar figured stepped through.

"Are you well, Bella?" It was Jillayne, her fair face wrought with worry. "God's Bones, when I saw you rushing the field, I nearly fainted!"

Belladonna was relieved to see at least one friendly face. Standing up, she went to grasp Jillayne's outstretched hands.

"I am well," she assured her petite, pretty friend. "No harm done."

Jillayne forced a smile. "What happened?" she asked. "Why did you rush out to the field?"

Belladonna's smile faded. "I am not entirely sure," she said, and it was the truth. "I saw my father out there, and suddenly there were men rushing towards him… I thought he was going to be killed. I had to help him. I had to help them all."

Jillayne squeezed her hands. "Your father is well," she said. "I have just come from his tent. My father is with him now, as are some of your father's men. They are all seeing to him and he is well. Sir Dashiell asked me to come and sit with you so that you are not alone."

So... he wasn't furious at her? At least, Belladonna could hope that was the case. She pulled Jillayne over to the stool where she'd been sitting, pulling up a second stool for herself.

"Sit," she told her friend. "I am glad you've come to visit. We did not have a chance to speak yesterday when I brought you the pup."

Jillayne's face lit up. "He is a sweet animal," she said. "He slept with me last night. My father already says he wants to breed him to our dogs to create very fine hunting stock."

She seemed very excited about it and Belladonna was pleased. "They are very good dogs," she said. "The knights of Savernake sell them to lords at a good price."

Jillayne grinned. "I have my own fine stock now and I did not have to pay for it," she said, watching Belladonna giggle. "It has been a long time since we last saw one another, Bella. I did not know your father... I mean, I did not know he was so... sick."

Belladonna's smile faded. "It started about three years ago," she said. "It has gotten worse every day. In fact, the day we left for Chadlington, he did not even know me. That has never happened before. I suppose that is why I rushed the field – he seems to have no sense of danger. I am not ready to lose my father yet."

She wasn't ready to lose her father yet, for a variety of reasons. Firstly, because she loved him, but secondly because his death would mean Clayton would inherit the dukedom. There was panic in that thought. But Jillayne was sympathetic.

"My grandsire went mad in the last year of his life," she said. "It is difficult when they do not realize something is wrong."

Belladonna smiled weakly. "My father believes he is Paul the Apostle," she said. "That was why he was on the battlefield. He was blessing the men."

Before Jillayne could reply, the tent flap moved again and Lord Sherston abruptly appeared. He was looking at Belladonna but politely acknowledged Jillayne, seated near the brazier.

"My lady?" Sherston addressed Belladonna. "I apologize if I am interrupting, but I was given permission by Dashiell to inquire on your health."

He is on our side. Belladonna remembered what Dashiell had told her and in spite of the oddity of her introduction to Lord Sherston last night, she smiled politely at the man.

"You are not interrupting, my lord," she said. "And I am doing very well, thank you."

He remained in the tent opening, making no move to enter. "That is good news," he said. "What you did was quite brave, my lady. I commend you for it."

Belladonna wasn't too sure she should be congratulated, considering the chaos that had been going on. "It was foolish, I suppose, but when my father entered the field… I was greatly afraid for his life. I needed to help him. And Dash and you and the others – you were being set upon by fiends. I simply could not stand by and watch that happen."

Sherston smiled at her. The lady was not only beautiful, she was brave. He was coming to regret having told Dashiell he wouldn't accept the proposal, but it was a regret he was going to have to live with. He was a man of his word.

"Your father does not have a scratch on him," he said. "You did, indeed, help him. And you helped Dash, too. Had you not beaten back those men, he might have been seriously injured."

She flushed, ever so slightly, glancing at Jillayne, who seemed to be fixated on Sherston. She was staring at him with a greatly interested expression.

"Dash has not spoken to me since the incident, so I would not know how he fares," Belladonna said. Then, she shifted the subject. "My lord, do you know Lady Jillayne Chadlington? It is her celebration we are attending. It is her day of birth."

In fact, Sherston had been waiting for this introduction. He'd hoped to have it last night, but he'd been occupied with Clayton for most of the night in order to keep him away from Belladonna and Dashiell, so the introduction Dashiell had promised him never came. But here it was, in a private setting no less, and he had to admit that he was quite taken with Lady Jillayne's petite beauty.

"My lady," he said, bowing his head gallantly. "It is a pleasure to make your acquaintance. I am Anthony Cromford, Lord Sherston."

Jillayne flushed prettily; she was quite adept in the art of feminine flirtation. "It is an honor, my lord," she said. "May I congratulate you on winning the mass competition?"

Sherston grinned. "It was purely by chance, I assure you," he said. "Luckily, Lady Belladonna gave us the advantage we needed to secure the victory. I would be proud to take her into battle with me any time."

Belladonna was mortified, but in a good-natured sense. As she shook her head firmly, and Jillayne giggled, another body came to stand next to Sherston.

Dashiell had finally made an appearance.

"How are things with the duke?" Sherston asked him. "No ill effects?"

Dashiell was bruised and beaten, and his right eye had a hint of dark shadows around it, but he was otherwise whole enough. His gaze was on Belladonna.

"No ill effects," he said. "But Clayton is nowhere to be found. Have you seen him?"

Sherston shook his head, slowly. "Nay," he said, "but I would be willing to wager that if I walk this encampment and the outlying area, he might very well find *me*."

That was probably true. Clayton wanted something from Sherston, and considered him an ally, so Dashiell nodded his head.

"Would you mind?" he asked.

"Not at all," Sherston replied. "When I find him, where would you have me take him?"

"Where are you staying?"

"In town, at the only tavern."

"Take him there. I shall join you at some point soon."

Sherston simply nodded. Then, he turned to Jillayne and dipped his head once more.

"My lady," he said. "It was a great honor to know you. I hope to see you again, very soon."

Jillayne smiled prettily and Sherston quit the tent. When he was gone, she turned to Belladonna.

"He is so handsome," she gasped, but then realized that Dashiell was still standing in the tent opening. Feeling somewhat foolish, and thinking that she should probably leave, Jillayne rose from the stool and made her way to the tent opening. "Good day to you, my lord."

Dashiell simply bowed his head to her as she slipped out. Once she was gone, he stepped into the tent and closed the flap.

Now, a heavy silence settled. Was he angry with her? Was he not? Dashiell remained silent as Belladonna stood there, watching his every move. The anticipation of his anger was setting her on edge.

"Well?" she finally said. "If you are going to become angry with me, get on with it."

He sighed faintly. "I am not angry," he said. "God knows, I should be. But I find I cannot muster the strength. I am simply glad that you were not injured."

Belladonna was distressed to realize that he seemed subdued. Beaten, even. She didn't like that appearance on the man, not in the least.

"I am sorry that I ran onto the field," she said, "but when I saw my father... and when I saw you fighting with all of those men trying to save him, all I wanted to do was help. I could not sit by idle and watch something terrible happen."

He simply nodded his head. Then, he saw a pitcher half-full of wine sitting on a small table and he went to it, picking it up and drinking straight from the pitcher. He drank most of it before lowering the pitcher to the table and wiping his mouth with the back of his hand.

"It was foolish of you," he said, heading wearily for one of the stools. "You could have been gravely injured, or worse."

"I know."

"Do you have any idea the terror I felt when I saw you swinging that club?"

"I am sure it was considerable."

"Considerable?" he repeated, his tone tinged with anger in spite of him telling her he had none. "That does not come close to…"

He was cut off when he lowered himself onto the stool and it immediately collapsed, dumping him onto his back. As he grunted in surprise and, perhaps, a bit of pain, Belladonna ran to him.

"Did you hurt yourself?" she gasped.

Flat on his back, Dashiell looked up at her. After the mass competition that morning and the battles he'd been through, for her to show concern with a broken stool seemed utterly ridiculous. He started to tell her so when he suddenly started laughing.

It was too ludicrous to believe.

When Belladonna saw Dashiell laughing, she began to see the humor of the situation, too. The man had just grappled for his life, and managed to remain somewhat upright, before being dropped by a broken stool. It was faulty furniture that finally sent him to the ground. Plopping onto her buttocks beside him, she laughed until she cried.

Dashiell, too, was laughing tears. Pushing himself into a sitting position, which took a great deal of effort, he wiped at his eyes as he gazed into Belladonna's face. She was sitting right next to him so when he sat up, they were very close. The laughter faded as her near proximity had an impact on him.

He didn't feel like laughing anymore. Reaching out, he cupped her face with his bruised, scarred hand.

"I was never so proud as I was today, knowing you were watching me from the lists," he said quietly, caressing her cheek with his thumb. "It was a perfect day and I would have been victorious had your father not made an appearance."

Belladonna leaned her cheek into his hand; his touch was like magic. "I do not understand how or why he came to the field," she said. "When we left him in his tent, he was sleeping soundly. But when he appeared on the field, he was alert and warmly dressed. As if he had planned to attend all along."

Dashiell had much to say on the subject, since he'd just left the duke's tent. Lily was there, still trying to keep her father calm, as was Lord Chadlington. Bentley and Aston were there, but they were simply there to ensure that the duke didn't try to leave his tent again. They were also there to prevent Clayton from coming into contact with him.

Lily had told Dashiell that she'd seen Clayton lingering on the edge of the field at the time her father made his appearance, which led Dashiell to believe that Clayton had orchestrated the entire thing. In fact, he was certain of it. Such things had happened before, too many times to count, only this time it was different.

It was going to be the last time.

With a heavy sigh, Dashiell dropped his hand from Belladonna's cheek.

"It was Clayton," he said after a moment. "I was not going to tell you about this, but since I believe it was the motivation behind

Clayton's actions, I must. When we went to visit your father before the tournament, Drusus told me that Clayton had given him money."

Belladonna's brow furrowed. "Money? For what purpose?"

Dashiell cocked an eyebrow. "So that Drusus would do what Clayton wished," he said. "Drusus returned the money to me and I went to Clayton with it. In fact, I knocked him out with a blow to the face and threw the money beside him. Did you not notice that Clayton did not make the tournament?"

Belladonna's eyes were wide with surprise. "I did, but I did not care, and I did not ask Lily about it," she said. "He did not come because you beat him?"

"I beat him because he is trying to force Drusus into doing his bidding when it comes to your father," Dashiell said. "Bella, Clayton wants your father dead. He used to be subtle in his attempts, but he is no longer subtle about it. Ever since we returned from the battle campaign, he has been quite obvious in his actions."

Belladonna was greatly disturbed by what was happening with her father. "Clayton wants to be the duke so badly that he will do what he can to ensure my father's death," she murmured. "Dash... what happens if my father dies before the Archbishop of Canterbury can sanction our betrothal?"

Dashiell could see the fear in her eyes. "Not to worry," he said. "I will prevent whatever Clayton is trying to accomplish. But I think our betrothal is only part of it, to be truthful. I believe that Clayton simply wants the dukedom and its riches. His greed is starting to overwhelm him."

Belladonna pondered that for a moment. "You must protect my father, Dash," she said, angst in her eyes. "Not because I simply do not wish for Clayton to become the duke, but because I love my father. He is a great man."

He could see how much she was worried and he shifted so he could put his arms around her. He pulled her close, his big hand on the back of her head.

"He is a very great man," he said quietly. "And I will do what is necessary to protect him, up to and including killing Clayton. Now that Clayton is showing his true colors, I will show mine. I will kill him before I let him make another attempt on the duke."

His words gave Belladonna a good deal of comfort but being in Dashiell's arms gave her far more than simple comfort. He was dirty, and smelled of mud and grass, but she didn't care in the least. She wound her arms around his neck and buried her face in the side of his sweaty head.

"I trust you," she whispered. "And I adore you, Dash, for everything you have done for my father and for my family."

The mood of the tent had gone from one of concern over the events of the day to something hot and smoldering all in the blink of an eye. Dashiell could feel Belladonna's hot breath against his ear and it sent bolts of excitement running through him. Instinct began to take over; this sweet, beautiful woman loved him and he knew he loved her with all his heart. He'd never been this close to her, at least not in the manner in which they were embracing each other, and he followed that instinct that told him to taste her. Something inside his head was screaming at him. Shifting his head, he began to deposit soft and tender kisses on her jaw.

Belladonna gasped when she felt the first kiss. It was an innate reaction to something she'd been dreaming of for years. In fact, she was having difficulty breathing as he tenderly kissed her flesh. Turning her head slightly, Dashiell's mouth was suddenly in front of her and their lips met with such force that Belladonna audibly grunted.

But that was nothing compared to what Dashiell was feeling. Belladonna was sweet and hot, incredibly delicious. Her sweet scent filled his nostrils as he suckled her lips, tasting her, acquainting himself with her.

He could have very easily lost himself in an even deeper kiss, but he wasn't oblivious to the fact that they were in a tent, and anyone could enter at any moment.

Still, it wasn't enough of a fear to cause him to release her right away. He'd been waiting for this moment for a very long time and he wasn't going to relinquish it until he was ready.

He might never be ready.

His hands went to her head, holding it between his two enormous palms as he kissed her with a passion he never knew he could feel. He'd had women before, but not like this. Never like this. He held her head in his hands as his lips devoured hers, and then he pulled her close to him once again, so forcefully that she grunted as he forced all of the air out of her lungs.

"Christ," he hissed, loosening his grip. "Did I hurt you? I did not mean to."

Belladonna had a dazed look about her. Her lips were red and chaffed from his bristly mustache having scratched her tender skin.

"Nay," she said, swallowing. "You did not hurt me at all."

He stared at her a moment, trying to determine what he was really feeling. When he exhaled, it was a ragged breath.

"This is all so new," he murmured. "Even now, as I have duties hanging over my head, all I want to do is take you in my arms. I want to kiss you until you swoon and I want to hold you until the sun sets, and longer even than that. I do not want to leave this moment in time. Even saying such things makes me sound like a silly, besotted fool."

She smiled, her hands going to his face. "It makes you sound like a man who has found happiness," she said. "There is no shame in that."

He lifted an auburn brow. "Mayhap not," he said. "But I have gone through my entire life thinking love was something that only the weak succumbed to. Now… I am not so sure that is true."

Belladonna gazed into his eyes, the color of blue that was so deep, it was nearly lavender. "Then I am weak," she whispered. "You have made me weak and I do not care."

Nor did he. Dashiell took her into his arms again, pulling her close as his lips slanted over hers. The kiss was hotter this time, something that made Dashiell's heart pound and his loins grow warm. All he could think of was her soft flesh beneath his calloused hands, and her hair, when he kissed her neck that smelled of flowers. Everything about her was soft and fragrant, things he'd dreamed of but had never truly experienced.

Now, he was.

"Bella," he whispered against her flesh. "If I told you that I loved you, would you believe me?"

She gasped; he heard her. He stopped kissing her long enough to look her in the eye only to see that she was tearing up. Thinking he'd said something terribly wrong, he opened his mouth to apologize but she put her fingers over his lips, silencing him.

"I have waited so long to hear those words," she whispered, "for I have loved you for as long as I can remember, Dash. So very long."

A smile spread across his lips, tremulously, and he leaned forward to kiss her once more, simply because he could. He wanted to kiss her every day, as much as he could, for the rest of his life because it was something that seemed more natural to him than breathing. Just as he wrapped his arms around her to pull her close, they both heard commotion outside of the tent.

Dashiell released Belladonna so quickly that he ended up rocking back on his heels, losing his balance, and falling on his buttocks right next to the broken stool. Belladonna lurched to her feet about the time the tent flap pulled back, spilling forth Lily and Bentley.

Instantly, their focus changed. Lily looked as if she had been weeping and Belladonna immediately went to her as Bentley looked at Dashiell, sitting on the ground.

"Clayton is back," Bentley muttered. "You had better come, Dash."

For a man who was thoroughly exhausted from the events of the day, Dashiell moved to his feet fairly quickly. "When did he return?"

Bentley sighed heavily; he was incredibly unhappy. "A few minutes ago," he said, keeping his voice down because Lily was so upset. "He's in a foul mood. Evidently, he saw Lord Sherston and Lady Jillayne walking together through the encampment, and he is in a rage about Sherston paying attention to someone other than Belladonna."

Dashiell's eyebrows lifted in surprise. "He said that?"

Bentley nodded. "He did," he said. "Not to anyone in particular, but he was mumbling about it when he returned to the duke's tent. Aston was at the door and told him to go away, so Clayton hit the man in the face. When I intervened, he tried to hit me, too, but I shoved him away. Then, Lily and Acacia got involved and he slapped them both. God help me, Dash… it was all I could do to not kill him."

Dashiell rolled his eyes. He couldn't believe what he was hearing. Already, he was moving from the tent, mentally preparing himself to take on Clayton.

"Why did you not bring Acacia with you?" he demanded. "You left her with him?"

"She would not come."

Dashiell growled. "Foolish wench," he said. Then, he eyed Bentley. "Why did you not kill him, Bent? I would not have faulted you."

Bentley eyed Lily. "Because Lily asked me not to," he said. "She pulled me from the tent, away from Clayton, who was trying to provoke everyone. Aston is still there, as is Acacia, but Clayton is combative. You must go to him."

Dashiell was already so angry he could hardly see straight. It was a struggle to maintain his composure.

"I will," he said. "But you will remain here with the women. If Clayton is on a rampage, I do not want them unprotected. And I do not want you around Clayton right now if he is targeting you somehow."

"I believe he is targeting Lily more than me."

Dashiell put a hand on the man's chest to keep Bentley from following him. "Bent," he commanded softly. "Stay here. I will return."

Bentley paused at the tent opening, watching Dashiell as the man headed to the duke's large tent. The past few minutes had been an absolute nightmare with Clayton, so Bentley found himself praying that Dashiell would either find the strength to deal with the man or the strength to kill him.

All Bentley knew was that if Dashiell didn't do something about the bastard, then he would.

It had come to that.

CHAPTER FIFTEEN

"You!"

Dashiell had hardly set food in the duke's tent when Clayton was shouting at him.

"This is all your doing!" the man raged. "You have no power, du Reims! How many times must I tell you that Savernake belongs to me? You will not interfere!"

It was an instant battle and Dashiell sized up the room before engaging. The duke was lying on his bed and Acacia was sitting next to the bed, cowering from Clayton's rage. Drusus was in the corner, watching everything fearfully, while two of Dashiell's senior soldiers and Aston stood just inside the tent opening.

As Dashiell stood there and pondered the scene, it all seemed to pass before him in slow motion. For a split second, everything was lethargic and surreal. The past three years suddenly flashed before his eyes; Dashiell had spent that time circumventing Clayton's plots and generally trying to ensure the man didn't destroy the Savernake dukedom. It had been a lovely, peaceful place to live before the event of Clayton and his scheming father, and all Dashiell wanted to do was maintain that peace in the wake of a man who wanted to greedily consume everything. For Lily's sake, and for the sake of everyone, Dashiell had genuinely tried to keep the peace.

But after the events of today, he was no longer going to do that.

He was furious. Bloody furious that Clayton had tried to kill the duke, yet again. At this moment, he decided there wasn't going to be a "next time". For all of their sakes, and for the safety of the Duke of Savernake, Dashiell had to take action.

It was time.

"Savernake does not belong to you," Dashiell said, moving in Clayton's direction. He pointed to Edward, napping in his bed. "It belongs to *him*. It never belonged to you. You came to Ramsbury three years ago and stole what did not belong to you. And now you are trying to hasten the duke's death so you can assume what should have never been yours in the first place."

Clayton was so angry that he was pale, a sheen of sweat on his upper lip. "Is that so?" he snarled. "Then who should it have gone to? Bentley of Ashbourne? He hasn't the lineage to assume such a thing!"

"And you do?" Dashiell shot back. "Your father was a bachelor knight who married a woman with a small inheritance. He took that money and gambled it away. When he heard that the Duke of Savernake's eldest daughter was unwed, he brought his only son to Ramsbury where you both convinced a man who was losing his mind that you would be the best possible husband for the heiress. It did not matter to you that she was in love with another man and that the duke approved the match. You lied and cheated your way into a betrothal and I am quite certain, if examined by the church, would have been found lacking. But you married Lily so swiftly that there wasn't time for an appeal. So… the low-life son of a low-life father married the girl and inherits the dukedom."

By the time he was finished, the impact of his words hung in the air, the reality of the situation permeating everything like a cloying stench. It was heavy and ugly. Clayton simply stood there, quivering with anger. He didn't bother denying anything.

"You are a stubborn fool, du Reims," he finally hissed. "Everything belongs to me and all of the rationalization in the world will not change that. Legally, and in the sight of God, Savernake belongs to me. *I* am the heir. If Edward is no longer able to make decisions, then command of this dukedom must fall to *me*."

"You are not fit to utter the name Savernake much less assume the responsibility of it."

Clayton twitched, as if ready to throw a punch, but he thought better of it. He wasn't going to throw a punch at Dashiell because he knew he would lose in the end. Therefore, he started to move away from the man, out of arm's range, as he spewed his venom.

"When I am the duke, I am going to throw you out of Ramsbury," he seethed. "You have challenged my authority for the last time, do you hear? Edward's daughters all belong to me and I shall do with them as I please. Did you think that introducing Lord Sherston to Lady Jillayne would change that? The man has been offered Belladonna's hand and he will accept it!"

Dashiell tracked him as he moved across the tent. "I have no idea what you are speaking of."

"Do not lie! You know exactly what I mean!"

"Whatever makes you think I introduced them?"

"Because that is something you would do! You are trying to distract Sherston, but it will not work! He wants Belladonna!"

"Did he tell you that?"

"Of course he did!"

Dashiell was fairly certain he was lying. He hoped he was, at any rate. He knew Sherston, but not too terribly well, so it was possible for the man to go back on his word. Dashiell hoped that wasn't the case.

"Then if he wants Belladonna, what was he doing with Lady Jillayne?" Dashiell asked, taunting him.

Clayton's entire face was twitching with rage. "Because *you* forced them together. You introduced them!"

Dashiell didn't like being called a liar, and he didn't like how the situation was now turned on him as if he had to defend himself. It was

Clayton's way of taking the focus off of him, but it wasn't going to work.

"I do not wish to talk about something as insignificant as Sherston," he said. "I want to talk about you. Where were you today when the duke wandered out into the mass competition?"

Clayton's lip twitched in a menacing manner. "I do not have to answer to you."

Dashiell folded his big arms across his chest. "When it comes to the safety of the duke, you do," he said. "I am told that you were seen on the fringes of the field at the same time the duke appeared on the field. You did not show up for a competition you were scheduled to compete in, and suddenly the duke appears in the middle of the fighting, just as he appeared in Driffield, and Northampton, and a half-dozen other battles."

"I had nothing to do with those!"

"Yet you gave Drusus four coins so he would do your bidding when it came to the duke."

There was no use in refuting that and Clayton knew it, but he tried. "I never said anything about the duke. I gave Drusus the money because…"

"Because you were trying to buy him, just as you bought Simon, whom I dismissed."

Clayton's twitching was growing worse. "You cannot prove anything."

Dashiell's gaze lingered on the man. He didn't speak for a moment, but it was intentional – the longer he remained silent, simply staring at Clayton, the more nervous the man became.

"Then tell me something," he finally said. "Where were you today while the competition was going on?"

Clayton was glaring at him but he seemed to be having difficulty making eye contact. "I… I was in camp."

"After I knocked you to the ground, what did you do?"

Dashiell's voice was loud, almost mocking, and Clayton flared. "It is none of your business what I did!"

Dashiell was finished playing games with the man. "I will tell you what you did," he said. "You came back to the duke's tent and forced Drusus to dress the man. Drusus can confirm this."

Everyone turned to look at the minder, standing back in the shadows. When he saw all eyes upon him, he was startled by all of the attention. Fearful of Clayton, he kept his focus on Dashiell.

"He... he had me dress the duke, my lord," he stammered.

Dashiell's tone with Drusus was considerably softer than it had been with Clayton. "Did he tell you why?"

The minder shook his head fearfully. "He told me to dress him, my lord," he said. "I did not ask why."

"But it was Clayton who forced you to dress the duke and then took the man from the tent."

"Aye, my lord."

Dashiell looked back at Clayton, his expression somewhat droll. "Now we know what you did when you were supposed to be on the field of competition," he said. "You came here, forced Drusus to dress the duke, and then took the duke down to the field, knowing full well that the man could easily be injured or killed by the competitors. There is no use in denying it. Therefore, I will make the assumption that in your actions, you deliberately tried to kill the duke. That is attempted murder, Clayton. I have put up with your attempts to put the duke in harm's way long enough. I will no longer tolerate your threat against him."

Clayton was turning red in the face. "If the duke wants to see the competition, then you have no right to deny him. If it was up to you, you would keep the man caged like a beast for the rest of his life!"

"I keep him in his chamber, or in his tent, for his own safety and you are well aware of that," Dashiell said. "But somehow, you have found a way to release him time and time again, hoping he will meet his death so that you may inherit his dukedom. I will tell you now that this will not happen again."

Clayton wasn't sure what that meant, but he knew he didn't like it. "You cannot give me orders and you cannot prove anything. It is the wild speculation of a madman!"

Dashiell didn't answer him. He turned to Aston and the two soldiers behind him. "Remove him," he commanded. "Take him to my tent where you will bind him. He is now my prisoner. I want no less than six guards on him at all times. When we get him back to Ramsbury, his new home will be the vault."

Aston rushed Clayton with the greatest of pleasure as Clayton yelped in frustration, in fear, when he realized what Dashiell was doing. He tried to run but he didn't get far; Aston had him around the neck, throwing him to the ground, as the soldiers pounced on him.

As Clayton twisted and bellowed, the soldiers restrained him and pulled him to his feet. Clayton kicked and fought.

"Unhand me!" he roared. "You cannot touch me!"

Dashiell ignored him as Aston and the two soldiers dragged him out of the tent. He could hear Clayton cursing and screaming as he was taken back to Dashiell's heavily-guarded tent.

The threat, finally, was neutralized.

It was a powerful moment. In hearing Clayton's extreme distress, Dashiell could only feel relief. Relief that the duke would now be safe and relief that, perhaps, they could all resume a somewhat normal life again now that Clayton's behavior had finally gotten him into trouble. Dashiell had overlooked too many transgressions, thinking he could handle Clayton in his own way, but the truth was that with Clayton growing bolder, the situation had become dire.

When they returned to Ramsbury, Dashiell was going to bring

Clayton up on attempted murder charges and seek out Gavin de Nerra to see what justice could be served. Perhaps, it would mean Clayton spending the rest of his life in the vault and forfeiting the dukedom even though he was married to the heiress. That might prove tricky, so Dashiell was determined to seek out de Nerra as soon as they returned home.

Meanwhile, Savernake could return to normal.

The soft sound of weeping jolted Dashiell from his thoughts and he turned to see Acacia sobbing into her hands. He immediately remembered what Belladonna had told him, of Clayton bedding Acacia, and he could see in that instant that it was absolutely true. Acacia had just seen her lover subdued and was understandably upset, so if she'd meant to keep the affair a secret, her tears had given her away. Dashiell didn't have much sympathy for her.

"My lady?" he said politely. "Mayhap you should return to your own tent now. It would be better for you there."

Acacia's head jerked up, her eyes red and watery. Her mouth worked, as if she wanted to say something to him, but the words wouldn't come. Gathering her skirts, she ran past Dashiell and out of the tent.

Now, it was just Drusus remaining, along with the duke. Dashiell looked up at Drusus, seeing that the man appeared greatly relieved. Drusus was a simple man, but he was honest, and Dashiell knew he was fearful of Clayton. He lived in fear of Clayton probably more than most because every time he obeyed Clayton, because he had no choice, he risked Dashiell's anger. It surely must have been a hellish existence, and Dashiell wasn't unsympathetic.

Finally, Dashiell's gaze moved to Edward, who was sleeping heavily upon his traveling bed. It was a fine piece of furniture, made by Savoy artisans. All of this angst and madness because of an old man who had lost his mind.

It was sad, truly.

Dashiell bent over the duke just to make sure he was well, putting a hand on the old man's forehead in an affectionate gesture. He loved the man like a second father, and all of the madness with Clayton had been distressing. God willing, the duke would be safe now and able to live out what was left of his life in peace. Come what may, Dashiell was going to do his best to ensure that happened.

Removing his hand from the duke, Dashiell glanced up at Drusus. "I will send more soldiers to guard the duke," he said. "You will not leave him, not ever."

Drusus nodded firmly. "Aye, my lord."

"And you will not let him leave this tent. If he has a notion to wander, then send one of the soldiers for me."

"Aye, my lord."

Dashiell headed for the tent opening, feeling more peace and calm than he had in a very long while. He could still hear Clayton screaming, now something about the bindings being too tight. Dashiell could only shake his head. As far as he was concerned, Clayton wasn't getting nearly what he deserved, but it would have to do for now. The threat was neutralized and that was all he cared about.

But those thoughts were quickly distracted as he heard angry voices coming from the tent that Belladonna shared with Acacia. Specifically, he could hear Belladonna's voice.

And she was clearly unhappy.

AFTER FLEEING HER father's tent, Acacia headed for the tent she shared with her sister. She could hear voices in there and, stifling her sobs with her hand pressed over her mouth, she stumbled into the tent.

Belladonna was there, as were Lily and Bentley. In fact, Bentley was sitting on the ground as Lily and Belladonna stood over him, with Lily tending to a cut over his right eyebrow. It was a fairly substantial cut, something he'd gotten on the tournament field, but there was dirt caked into it that Lily was trying to clean out. Belladonna held a bowl of warmed wine, used to clean it, while Lily scraped away with a cloth.

"He arrested him!" Acacia gasped.

Belladonna, Lily, and Bentley looked up at her.

"Who was arrested?" Belladonna asked.

Acacia was nearly hysterical. "Clayton!" she said. "Dash had him arrested! Did you not hear the screaming?"

Truth was, they had. Belladonna had even peeked her head from the tent to see Clayton being dragged away by Aston and some other men. Her first reaction had been shock, as had Lily and Bentley's, but that was only momentary. Elation followed.

However, knowing what Belladonna did of her middle sister's relationship to Clayton, she showed no interest at all in what her sister was clearly upset over.

"Thank God," she muttered as she turned back to the task at hand. "I am so glad Dash finally arrested him. I hope they beat Clayton to death for all of the pain and sorrow he has caused us."

Acacia's eyes widened. "Can you be so cruel?" she said. "What Dash has done is... is...."

"Is better than Clayton deserved," Belladonna fired at her angrily. "Do you seriously intend to defend Clayton? Three years of hell from that man and you honestly think to defend him?"

Acacia was emotionally unbalanced. She had tears spilling over her cheeks as she stared at her sister. "You heartless woman," she hissed. "Dashiell is a criminal for arresting him. I will go to the king and tell him what Dashiell has done!"

By this time, Lily turned to her sister, a scowl on her face. "What do you care what becomes of him, Acacia?" she demanded. "He is certainly no concern of yours. I, for one, am more relieved than I can say. I thank God that Dash had the courage to do it. He will always have my undying gratitude."

Acacia blinked as if startled at Lily's response. It was so... cold. But she had expected it. Clayton was her sister's husband, a woman who never loved him nor understood him. Acacia had been Clayton's only salvation in a world where everyone hated him and as she looked at Lily, she began to feel unreasonable jealousy and hatred. She'd never felt that before, not in the entire year that Clayton had been bedding her.

But now... now, she felt it.

How she hated Lily for being married to her lover.

"This is all your fault," she growled.

Lily truly had no idea why her sister was so excited over Clayton. "*My* fault? What did I do?"

Acacia jabbed a finger at her. "You did not love him," she said, her voice trembling. "Had you only shown him a measure of compassion and respect, others would have, too. But you showed him disregard and everyone saw that he was unworthy of their respect. It was *you* who did this to him!"

Lily was genuinely taken aback. "You are mad," she said. "You know that I never wanted to marry him. You know he tricked Papa into the betrothal. How can you say such things to me?"

"Because you treat him no better than a dog!"

"He *is* no better than a dog!"

Acacia made a choking sound. "Wicked," she hissed. "You are wicked and sinful. And I know why!"

Lily rolled her eyes. "Shut your lips, Acacia," she said, turning back to Bentley's wound. "I will not listen to you any longer."

"*Him!*" Acacia pointed at Bentley. "It is because of him! You still love him, and he has prevented you from loving your husband. It is wicked, I say!"

Belladonna had stood by silently, watching her sisters argue, but she could no longer remain silent when Acacia started accusing her sister of adultery. She knew exactly why Acacia was unleashing on Lily and she wouldn't stand by and watch it happen. As Lily's face turned red and she turned to Acacia to scream at her, Belladonna put herself between her sisters and focused her fury on Acacia.

"*You* are the wicked one!" she shouted. "How dare you accuse Lily of such deceitful things when it is you who are deceitful!"

Acacia was wild-eyed with rage. "Shut your mouth, you little pimple! This does not concern you!"

Belladonna wouldn't back down. "It does, indeed," she said. "Where Clayton is concerned, it concerns us all, but you more than any of us. Back at Ramsbury, I *saw* you with Clayton as he bedded you. Did you think it was a secret, Acacia? Of course it wasn't. I saw him as he... as he *touched* you in a way he should have only been touching his wife. You were warming his bed like a whore, which is exactly what you are. You are angry at Lily because *you* are her husband's whore!"

Lily's eyes widened as she faced Acacia with her mouth hanging open. "He – he bedded you?" she gasped. "Acacia, is this true?"

Acacia's face had gone from an angry red to a sickly white. She stared at her sisters, stepping backwards and almost tripping on her skirts. She was struggling to answer when Lily suddenly rushed at her and slapped her, hard, across the face.

"Answer me!" Lily screamed. "Are you Clayton's whore? Is that why you are defending him?"

Dashiell picked that moment to appear in the tent opening and it was clear from his expression that he had heard everything. Acacia was nearest him and he reached out and grabbed her by the arms when she tried to bolt.

"Easy, lady," he told her. "Be calm."

But Acacia turned into a wildcat, digging her nails into Dashiell's arms but creating no damage because of the heavy clothing he wore. Still, she tried to scratch him and pull away.

"Let me go, you beast," she snarled.

Lily wasn't finished with her sister. She ran up behind her and grabbed her by the hair, yanking savagely.

"You... you hypocrite!" she cried. "How long have you been warming my husband's bed and shaming me in the process? *How long*?"

By this time, Bentley was on his feet and Dashiell called to him over the heads of the fighting women.

"Remove Lady le Cairon to her tent immediately," he told him. "Keep her there."

Bentley was on the move, pulling Lily's hands out of Acacia's hair, which was no easy feat. He had to unwind it from her angry fingers, and she refused to let go. She pulled and yanked, and Acacia screamed. Belladonna finally rushed forward to help Bentley and Dashiell separate them.

As Bentley dragged Lily from the tent, Belladonna more or less took Lily's place by slapping Acacia on the head.

"How could you do that to her?" she cried. "All this time you have been telling all of us what sinners we were when you were the biggest sinner of all. God will punish you for this, Acacia. You are going to hell!"

Acacia had gone from defiant to sobbing pitifully. She'd stopped fighting Dashiell and simply stood in his grip, weeping.

"It is Lily's fault," she sobbed. "She left Clayton to fornicate with Bentley!"

Still, the woman refused to take responsibility and Belladonna balled up her fist, ready to take another swing at her. She was enraged beyond her capacity to control it. But when Dashiell saw the balled fist, he reached out to stop her.

"No more," he told her steadily, pushing her hand down. "She will suffer greatly, but not by your hand. Leave her punishment to God."

Belladonna looked at him and he could see tears pooling in her eyes. After a moment, she simply burst into tears and turned away.

Dashiell wasn't entirely sure what to do with Acacia, but he couldn't leave her here where Belladonna might start beating on her again. Everything had deteriorated so badly that he wasn't sure what to do. All he knew was that he had to separate the women and ensure they were calmed.

Everything had deteriorated rapidly.

"Dash?" Aston burst in through the tent, crashing into the back of Dashiell. "What is all the shouting about? What happened?"

Dashiell looked over his shoulder at the man. "Where is Clayton?"

"In your tent as you requested. He has twelve guards on him and he is bound hand and foot. He is not going anywhere."

"He is secure?"

"Most definitely."

Dashiell directed Acacia over to the edge of the tent and pushed her down on a small chair. "Sit," he commanded softly. "Do not move. Do you understand me?"

Acacia simply cried, not acknowledging him, so he hesitantly released her. When she didn't try to run, he returned to Aston and lowered his voice.

"We cannot remain here," he muttered. "Everyone is in turmoil; Clayton, the sisters, the duke – everyone. The celebration has turned into chaos for us and I cannot, in good conscience, remain. We must return home immediately."

Aston eyed Belladonna and Acacia at opposite ends of the tent, weeping. "What happened?" he asked, confused. "What was all the shouting about?"

Dashiell simply shook his head. "Later," he said quietly. "Pass the word. We are moving out immediately."

"What about Lord Chadlington?"

"I will make up an excuse. Go and do as you are told."

Aston quit the tent without another word, heading out into the bright blue day beyond. On what should have been a beautiful day of celebration, for the party from Ramsbury, it turned into something pivotal. Clayton was under restraints, Acacia was hysterical, Lily had just found out her husband was bedding her sister, and Belladonna…

Dashiell looked at Belladonna, sitting on the unbroken stool with her back to him. She was calmer now, quietly wiping her tears away, and his heart genuinely broke for her. She'd been so excited for this celebration and it had all gone so terribly wrong. Everything had spiraled out of control.

Dashiell could only hope that returning to Ramsbury, and the sense of peace they would have without Clayton on the prowl, would make up for a most disturbing and eventful trip to Chadlington.

Now, everything had changed.

CHAPTER SIXTEEN

Ramsbury Castle
Late April

SPRING WAS COMING.

Belladonna could smell it in the air. The heavy snows from winter had melted away and the land was beginning to turn green once again, although the weather was still very cold at times. Still, the land and sky had a fresh feel to them, signaling the approach of a warmer season.

At Ramsbury Castle, things had been very different for the past two months. As Belladonna passed from the kitchen yard and into the keep, she found herself reflecting on the past fifty-one days since their return from Chadlington. She'd counted every one of those days, because every single day she woke up expecting the events with Dash, and Chadlington, and Clayton, to have been a dream. She kept expecting to wake up to a world that was just as it had been for the past three years, but every morning Dashiell would greet her with a discreet kiss that told her she was not dreaming.

Her love for Dashiell, and his love for her, was very real.

Real and growing.

It was like heaven. Belladonna never knew she could be so happy. But even in her happiness, there were things around her that were very different – Clayton was imprisoned in the vault of Ramsbury, where he had been since the day they returned from Chadlington, and Acacia had, indeed, committed herself to Amesbury when the time came.

Since their return from Chadlington, Acacia had locked herself in her chamber and remained there, only emerging to travel to Amesbury on the designated day without a word to either sister. She wouldn't speak to Dashiell, or Bentley, but she would speak to Aston. She blamed Lily for her troubles, and for Clayton's troubles, and Lily refused to even acknowledge Acacia's accusations, so her departure to Amesbury was met with no great fanfare. Lady Acacia Eleanor de Vaston left for Amesbury Abbey, and barely a word was said about it.

That had been four weeks ago and, with Acacia's departure, the last of the uneasiness for the inhabitants of Ramsbury seemed to go with her. The mood, for the most part, was back to normal.

People were happy once again or, at the very least, at peace.

"M'lady!"

Someone was calling to Belladonna before she could step inside the keep and she turned to see one of the kitchen servants heading in her direction. Politely, she paused as the woman in dirty woolens and frazzled hair rushed up to her.

"M'lady," the woman said. "We've got a side of pork we must cook because if we don't, it'll go bad. Can we prepare it for the men tonight?"

Belladonna shrugged. "Why ask me?" she said. "Did you ask Lady le Cairon?"

The old woman nodded her head. "We asked this morning, but she didn't give us an answer," she said. "If we don't cook it, it will spoil."

Belladonna lifted her shoulders again. "Then go ahead, I suppose," she said. "Where is Lady le Cairon?"

"We've not seen her, m'lady."

"She must be around, somewhere."

The old servant simply nodded her head and rushed off again, heading back towards the kitchens. As Belladonna watched her go, she happened to catch a glimpse of Dashiell and Bentley on the battlements near the top level of the armory.

Instantly, her heart swelled at the sight. She paused a moment, shielding her eyes from the bright sunshine as she watched Dashiell move across the battlements in conversation with Bentley. He was in a tunic she'd made for him, dyed nearly the color of his auburn hair, and she thought he looked exceptionally handsome in it.

Belladonna had to smile when she noticed that he wasn't wearing mail underneath it. Since the Chadlington celebration, he genuinely tried to dress to please her, wearing the tunics she would make for him but not hiding them with mail coats or hoods, or any other type of protection. He would, however, wear a belt with a sheath for his broadsword, or he'd have daggers or other weapons shoved into the belt, but he was genuinely trying to please his favored lady, which touched Belladonna immensely. He was starting to look a little more like a gentleman, or a court dandy as he called it, and a little less like a warrior armed to the teeth. It was the look of a man in love, and who was loved.

It was a wonderful transformation.

As Belladonna stood there watching him, he caught sight of her and lifted a big hand in greeting. She waved back, eagerly, and Bentley caught sight of her, too. He waved at her and she waved back. Truly, Belladonna liked Bentley a great deal. She always had. Now that Clayton was in the vault, he seemed happier because Lily was happier.

Oh, Belladonna knew they loved each other. They always had, and it was something that was established. But even though Clayton was in the vault, Lily and Bentley had maintained a completely proper relationship with one another as they did even when Clayton had been roaming free.

Nothing had changed on that account, at least as far as Belladonna could see, but the pair did seem more at ease around each other. They smiled more. But Belladonna thought it was a terrible pity they still couldn't be together.

Tragic, even.

In fact, that was on her mind as she continued on into the keep, looking for a sister she hadn't seen in a while. Preparations for the evening meal were well under way, something Lily was usually heavily involved in. Wandering to the upper floor where Lily's chamber was, she knocked softly on the door.

"Lily?" she called.

No answer. Again, she knocked. "*Lily*?"

Then, she thought she heard a voice, so she opened the door into Lily's resplendent chamber. She was greeted by the smell of rushes as she entered, but also the smell of something else – something rank. She could see her sister lying on her side on the bed and as she approached, she saw Lily vomit into a bowl.

Belladonna rushed to her sister's side.

"Why did you not send for me?" she asked gently, noting that the other smell she'd sensed upon entering the chamber was the vomit. There was quite a bit in Lily's bowl. "How long have you been like this?"

Lily wiped at her mouth with a cloth she had in her hand. "It does not matter," she said. "It will pass."

Belladonna frowned. "If you are ill, then I must send for a physic," she said. "Was it something you ate?"

Lily put her hand on Belladonna to ease the woman. "Nay," she muttered, rolling on to her back, exhausted. "It was nothing I ate, Bella."

"Then what? Clearly, a sickness of some kind."

"Nay, not a sickness. I… I have been trying to keep this from you, but I am afraid I cannot keep it a secret much longer."

Belladonna was confused as well as concerned. "Secret?" she repeated. "What are you talking about? Let me go to the kitchens and bring you something to settle your stomach. Broth, mayhap? Or a bit of bread?"

Lily shook her head, but the mere mention of the food was enough to cause her to heave into her bowl again. There wasn't anything in her stomach, so she mostly dry heaved. When she was finished, she lay pale and panting on her bed as Belladonna took the bowl from her and set it on the table next to the bed.

"Lily," she said softly, putting her hand on the woman's forehead. "Please let me get you something to…"

Lily cut her off. "Do not say it," she begged. "Do not speak of food. Not now. Mayhap, I will be stronger later."

Belladonna was genuinely perplexed. "You needn't worry about anything," she said. "I will see to the meal tonight. You must rest if you are going to be well again."

Lily grasped her hand, weakly. "It will take a long time for me to be well again, I think."

"Why would you say that? How long will it take?"

"About seven months, I should think."

Belladonna still wasn't grasping what she was being told. "Seven months? Why seven months?"

With a sigh, Lily put Belladonna's hand on her belly, making sure that her sister realized there was a nice, round bump there. When Belladonna stared at her sister's belly, starting to realize what she meant, Lily spoke softly.

"That is when my child will be born," she said quietly. "I am with child, Bella. It is the child causing the sickness."

The news hit Belladonna hard and her hand flew to her mouth, stifling the gasp. "Oh… Lily!" she whispered through splayed fingers. "But… but you said the pessaries from the apothecary would prevent such a thing!"

Lily's hand found her way onto her belly, caressing it lovingly. "This is not Clayton's child," she whispered. "It is Bent's."

Belladonna's mouth popped open, her eyes widening in shock. "*Bentley* is the father?"

Lily nodded. Then, the tears began to come. "I do not care what you think of me," she wept. "Acacia was right. She was right when she said I have always loved Bentley and this child was conceived in love, Bella. Had Clayton not come along, I would be married to Bentley now and this would be our first child, and I would be rejoicing. I would be so happy that it would put all other happiness to shame."

She was starting to weep, which caused Belladonna to tear up. It was such a terrible, tragic situation that she simply couldn't help it. She gripped her sister's hands tightly.

"I know you love him," she said. "I have always known. But you and he… you hardly look at one another, so I never knew that… oh, Lily, this is truly his baby?"

Lily nodded as tears streamed down her temples. "I do not know what to do," she said. "Clayton will know it is not his."

Belladonna's brow furrowed. "But why? He is your husband and…"

Lily interrupted her. "Bella, I have not lain with my husband since before he left for the battle campaign to the north," she said. "Not since last autumn, when he forced himself upon me. When he returned home two months ago, I managed to avoid him until Dash put him in the vault. Therefore, he will know this child is not his."

Belladonna was shocked to the bone at the dilemma, horrified for her sister and the woman's reputation, but more horrified at Clayton's reaction. The man was in the vault but, at the moment, that didn't much matter. He would be a husband shamed, a future duke whose wife was to bear a child that was not his.

The implications were staggering.

What should have been a joyful time in life for Lily and Bentley could turn into something dark and horrible. Belladonna felt a good deal of panic on her sister's behalf.

"You must not worry," she said, trying to reassure the woman. "Mayhap you can go away to have the child. Mayhap you can go to a town where no one knows you and have the child there. No one has to know, Lily. Surely there is a way."

Lily was struggling to still her tears. This was a secret she'd kept since she realized she was expecting a few weeks ago, when her stomach would lurch at odd times of the day, with or without a prompting of food. Some days she was fine and some days, like today, she was ill. But the one thing she had felt constantly was fear.

She was positively terrified.

"Mayhap there is a way," she said, wiping at her eyes. "I thought that I might take a small home by the sea and wait until the child was born. I could simply say that I was ill and needed to go away. You would support me in this, of course."

Belladonna nodded eagerly, stroking her sister's dark head. "Of course," she agreed. "Anything you wish. But… have you told Bent?"

Lily shook her head sadly. "I do not wish for him to feel this burden. It is mine and mine alone."

Belladonna squeezed her hands. "You are so wrong," she insisted softly. "You know that Bent loves you. This is *his* child, Lily. You must tell him."

Torn, Lily simply lifted her shoulders, unable to do more than that. She knew her sister was right, but she wasn't sure she could bring herself to agree. She knew Bentley was an honorable man and he would want to do the honorable thing, but given that he couldn't marry her, it would tear his noble heart to shreds.

It was a terrible situation all around.

As the sisters sat there and held hands, pondering the uncertain and frightening future for Lily and her baby, they could hear the sentries at the gatehouse announcing visitors. Belladonna turned towards the lancet window that faced over the bailey, hearing the commotion.

"I did not know we were expecting any visitors," she said. "Did you?"

Lily sighed heavily and tried to rise. "I did not," she said. "I must see who has come."

Belladonna pushed her down onto the bed. "Nay," she said firmly. "I will see who has come. I will return to you when I know, I swear it."

Lily still wasn't feeling very well and she wasn't sure she could even make it down to the bailey, so she had to let her sister take charge. Defeated, she simply lay there.

"Return to me quickly," she said.

Belladonna kissed her hands and stood up. "I will."

Lily lay there, listening to Belladonna's footfalls fade away. She wasn't thinking about the visitors or the fact that she was unable to perform her chatelaine duties. Her mind was centered on the child in her belly and the complications that it brought. They were the same thoughts she'd been having since she realized she was with child, the same chaotic fears she had been entertaining.

What will happen when Clayton finds out?

What will happen to me?

God, what will happen to my child?

In a time of her life that should have been her happiest, all she could feel was devastation.

DASHIELL HAD BEEN standing on the battlements when the incoming party had been sighted.

He had men stationed at the gatehouse with very fast horses, just for an occasion such as this. Ramsbury was surrounded by open plain for the most part, so their line of sight on the road leading to the castle was about a mile. At that distance, they couldn't make out any details, so Dashiell had riders stationed at the gatehouse to be the eyes for the sentries.

Two riders took off, racing down the road and heading for the incoming party. Dashiell and Bentley watched curiously for at least one of the riders to return with information, which happened very quickly. As the rider approaching, flying at full speed, he came near the gatehouse, shouting the identity of the approaching party.

De Nerra... Canterbury...

Now, Dashiell and Bentley made haste down to the gatehouse to greet their incoming guests. Truth be told, Dashiell was surprised to see de Nerra, but it wasn't completely unexpected.

In the week following the return from Chadlington, Dashiell had sent de Nerra a missive about Clayton. He explained that the man had tried to kill the duke by releasing him on the mass competition field and, based on that action – which was the last in a long line of similar actions – he'd arrested Clayton and the man was currently being held in the Ramsbury vault.

At this point in time, what Dashiell did was perfectly justifiable. Clayton had made one too many attempts to assume the dukedom and Dashiell had every right to lock the man up to protect the duke. The complications would come when the Edward passed away and Clayton would assume the title. Dashiell needed de Nerra's wisdom on the matter, but he'd expected a missive from the man and certainly not a visit. More surprising still was that the banners of the Archbishop of Canterbury were flying with him. So clearly, this was a very touchy incident, enough to warrant a visit from Stephen Langton himself.

Knowing that the Itinerant Justice of Hampshire and the Archbishop of Canterbury were about to make an appearance, Dashiell sent his men into a frenzy cleaning up and making room in the bailey of Ramsbury for what would be a considerable entourage. He also sent men rushing into the keep to inform Lady le Cairon that she would need to prepare for guests.

Everyone at Ramsbury was moving with a purpose as the entourage came closer, moving rather slowly up the road to Ramsbury as clouds began to gather overhead. It had been a lovely day, with hardly a cloud in the sky. But this time of year, the weather could be unpredictable, and from that black clouds forming overhead, Dashiell knew they were in for a storm.

He hoped it wasn't indicative of the message de Nerra and Canterbury bore.

As Dashiell and Bentley stood in the gatehouse, soon joined by Aston, Belladonna emerged from the keep and made her way across the bailey as the wind began to pick up. The sky continued to darken as she headed for Dashiell and the open portcullis of the gatehouse.

The soldiers and servants seemed quite busy as she closed the gap. In fact, she had to move out of the way as one soldier ran past her and almost plowed into her. By the time she reached Dashiell and his knights, she was looking curiously at the busy bailey.

"God's Bones," she said. "What on earth is happening that men should be running around in such a frenzy?"

Dashiell smiled at her. "We have important visitors," he told her. Gavin de Nerra is riding with the Archbishop of Canterbury."

Belladonna looked at him in surprise. "The archbishop is here?" she asked. "I… I did not know you had asked him to come here, Dash."

He shook his head. "I did not," he replied. "All I have done is send word to de Nerra about Clayton's incarceration. I did not expect him to come to Ramsbury, but he has, and he is evidently bringing Stephen Langton with him."

Belladonna peered through the gatehouse, down the road leading to the castle that was relatively straight. She could see the party approaching in the distance, flying colorful banners.

"Then the archbishop is not here to discuss our betrothal?" she asked.

Dashiell took her by the elbow and turned her around for the keep. "I am sure that will be discussed," he said. "But my suspicion is that they are here because of what happened with Clayton. But do not fret; I am sure our betrothal will be discussed also. Therefore, I need you to return to the keep and tell Lady le Cairon that we are expecting important guests. She will need to make all due preparations for the evening meal and also for their lodging."

Belladonna thought of her ill sister, lying in bed and hardly able to move. "I will do it," she said quickly. "Lily is… ill. She is not feeling well, so I will attend to her duties."

Bentley, who wasn't standing too far away, heard her.

"Lady le Cairon is ill?" he said. "What is the trouble?"

Belladonna looked at the man, unable to tell him the truth. But she was nearly bursting with her concerns and fears, so much so that it must have been in her expression. Dashiell saw it, although Bentley did not.

"Her stomach," she said after a moment. "It is nothing. She will be fine."

With that, she turned away and began moving quickly towards the keep. But a word from Dashiell brought her to a halt.

"My lady?" he called after her. "Bella? Wait a moment."

Belladonna came to a halt, turning to look at the man and trying to make it seem like she wasn't trying to hide something. He had a way of looking at her that seemed to bore into her very soul.

"What is it, Dash?" she asked as he came near. "I have much to attend to and very little time to do it."

"Since when do you not have time for me?" he asked softly.

Her shoulders slumped as she eased her stance. "I am sorry," she said. "I did not mean it the way it sounded. Of course I have time for you, always."

He smiled at her. "That is good to know," he said. "But something changed in your face when you mentioned Lily. Is her illness serious?"

Belladonna found that to be a ridiculous question, all things considered. But she was also very upset over it, a burden she didn't want to assume all on her own. Perhaps, if she shared it with Dashiell, he could think of something. Perhaps, he could advise Lily on what she should do, because he was a very wise man. God only knew, Lily needed help.

With that in mind, she lowered her voice.

"Nay, it is not serious," she said, her expression bordering on miserable. "But… Dash, she told me something today that frightens me to death. I am terrified for my sister."

His brow furrowed. "What is it, lamb?"

"I will tell you, but you must swear to me that you will not say a word to anyone."

He was growing concerned. "I swear. What is it?"

Belladonna reached out, putting her hand on his arm and Dashiell clasped a big hand over it.

"Lily is with child," she whispered.

"I see," he said quietly, failing to see why she was frightened. "She is positive?"

Belladonna nodded, tears stinging her eyes. "She is."

He paused. "This cannot be terrible news, lamb," he said. "The birth of an heir is cause for celebration."

She blinked, tears spattering on her eyelashes. "You do not understand," she whispered. "The child is not Clayton's – it is Bentley's."

Dashiell didn't outwardly react but, inside, he was stunned. As was usual with him, the worse the crisis, the calmer he became. He could see that Belladonna was full of brimming emotion and he didn't want to break the dam. Therefore, he refused to give her any hint of what he was feeling. Instead, he squeezed her fingers.

"And she is certain of this?"

Belladonna nodded, wiping at her eyes. "She says that she and Clayton have not… she has not been with him since last autumn, before you left on battle campaign," she said. "She says the child is due in seven months, so Clayton will know the child is not his. I am so frightened for her, Dash."

Now, Dashiell could understand why. Lily wasn't his sister and, truth be told, he was deeply concerned for her as well.

"Does Bentley know?"

Belladonna shook her head. "She does not want to tell him. She says this is her burden alone."

He grunted. "That is hardly true," he said. "If a child has been created, clearly, two people were involved."

"I know," she said, sadly. "Whatever shall she do, Dash? She needs help."

He lifted an eyebrow at the enormity of that understatement. "She does, indeed," he said, lifting her hand to kiss it because she was so upset. "But I am not sure I am the one to come up with a solution. This is Lily and Bentley's problem, not mine."

Belladonna's eyes filled with tears. "Please, Dash," she said. "You are so wise. Clayton will know the child is not his and surely he will tell everyone. All of England will know that my sister conceived a child by a man who was not her husband. Please… please think of something. Please help."

It really wasn't his problem, as he said, but he could hardly deny her. She was turning to him for help and he wouldn't disappoint her.

"As you wish," he said, patting her hand again. "You must let me think on it. But you must not tell anyone else, do you hear? You are right to be afraid because this is a serious problem. Where is Lily now?"

"In her bed. She was vomiting when I left her."

Dashiell sighed. The problem with pregnancy was that, at some point, people were going to know. Lily wouldn't be able to hide her condition forever.

"Then go about your tasks, the ones you were going to do in her stead," he told her. "Everything will be all right, lamb. We will greet the archbishop and Lord Gavin, and we will deal with our immediate problems before we deal with Lily. For now, she is safe. No one will know she is with child because I just saw the woman this morning and would have never guessed it, so her problem is not immediate. We must deal with one thing at a time."

"Then you will think of something?"

He hesitated. "I will," he said, "but you must convince Lily to tell Bentley. If she does not tell him, I will. It is not fair to him to keep this from him."

Belladonna nodded. Knowing she had his help on such a terrible subject gave her great comfort. She was feeling better already.

"I will tell her," she said. "She will listen to me."

He winked at her as he dropped her hand. "Go, now," he told her. "You have duties to attend to. I will bring Lord Gavin and the archbishop into your father's solar, so please provide them with refreshment."

Belladonna had many things to complete, which was good. It kept her mind off Lily's problems, at least for the moment. Dashiell said he would think of something and she trusted that he would.

Smiling gratefully at the man, she turned for the keep, running through the order of business she needed to accomplish. First to the kitchens to tell the cook to expect guests, and second to have refreshments brought to her father's solar. But just as she stepped into the keep, the clouds let loose and it began to rain.

In hindsight, Belladonna should have taken it for a sign of things to come…

Stormy.

CHAPTER SEVENTEEN

Somewhere on the road through Wiltshire, de Nerra and his party picked up a traveling band of minstrels, who were now playing loudly and festively in the great hall of Ramsbury.

Dashiell knew this because he could hear them all the way across the ward. Even through the patter of rain, the faint strains of music as the great hall filled with men trying to stay dry as the thunderstorm pounded overhead could be heard. But in the solar of the Duke of Savernake, everything was warm and comfortable as Dashiell held counsel with Gavin de Nerra and Stephen Langton, the Archbishop of Canterbury.

Considering Stephen Langton was well into his sixth decade, he was an elderly man who didn't often travel. Because of that, Dashiell had to admit that he wasn't glad to see him. Only a very serious subject would get the man out of Canterbury and on the road to Wiltshire, so he wasn't a particularly welcome sight.

But he didn't let that reluctance show as he greeted the man, and the archbishop was quite amiable in return. He appeared weary, that was true, but after a long journey that was to be expected. Dashiell also greeted Gavin, and the man seemed glad to see him. But he wouldn't state his reasons for coming before they were someplace secluded; in this case, the duke's solar.

That fact worried Dashiell even more.

Once they entered the solar and there was some privacy, the archbishop immediately asked to see his old and dear friend, the Duke of

Savernake. Dashiell sent Aston for the duke and while they were waiting, small talk floated around. Refreshments were brought in, by none other than Belladonna herself, and she greeted the archbishop and de Nerra politely. But all of this was a stalling tactic, a build up for what was soon to come.

When Belladonna and the servants quit the solar, and it was only Dashiell, Bentley, de Nerra, Langton, and a few trusted de Nerra knights and ecclesiastical advisors left, the archbishop ate an entire piece of bread with butter before coming to the point of his visit.

"Sir Dashiell," he said, licking his finger of the butter that remained. "I know you were not expecting such a great group to descend on you this night, but you have some serious issues that must be addressed, and I believed they were important enough to do such things in person."

Dashiell nodded. "Of course, my lord," he said. "And your visit to Ramsbury is always welcome, expected or not."

The archbishop accepted a cup of warmed wine from one of his men. "I am honored," he said. "I have visited here many times in the past to see my friend, Edward, and I know he trusted you greatly, du Reims. I am told his madness is worse now and that is why I have come. It is why I have sent for him. I want to see for myself."

Dashiell suspected that was the case. "You are welcome to see him, my lord," he said, "but do not be troubled if he does not recognize you. He recognizes few people these days."

"Does he still believe he is Paul the Apostle?"

"Still, my lord."

Langton digested that. "A pity," he finally said, seemingly truly saddened. But he only lingered on thoughts of his friend for a moment before facing the issue at hand. "It seems you have a few items to deal with here at Ramsbury, so I will address them one at a time. Firstly, de Nerra tells me that you wish to marry the youngest daughter of the duke but the man, in his current mental state, cannot give permission.

Is this true?"

Dashiell nodded. "It is, my lord," he said, feeling the need to plead his case. "I am not sure how much Lord de Nerra told you, but I feel that I am a worthy candidate for the daughter of a duke. I am Viscount Winterton, the hereditary title of the heir to the earldom of East Anglia. When my father dies, I will inherit the earldom. I have much to offer Lady Belladonna, not the least of which is my deep affection and respect for her. To be frank, my lord, the lady and I love one another. We have for many years. It is my most earnest desire to marry her."

Langton listened to him carefully. "That is what de Nerra told me," he said, glancing at Gavin. "He also said he wonders what took you so long to plead for the woman's hand."

Dashiell gave him a lopsided grin. "Fear," he said frankly. "Fear that she would not wish to marry such an old man. Imagine my delight when I was proven wrong."

Langton grinned, revealing long, yellowed teeth. "Then I am delighted for you," he said. "And you need not give me your resume, du Reims. I knew your grandfather. He was a great man, and I personally believe you will make an excellent match for the lady."

Dashiell tried not to feel overwhelmingly hopeful, spurred on by the archbishop's words. "It is possible to have the church's blessing, then, given the mental state of the duke, my lord?"

Langton nodded. "It is," he said. "But I must see my old friend and decide for myself if he is able to give consent. If he is not, then I will give it for him. But I must make that decision myself. Is that clear?"

Dashiell nodded. "It is, my lord."

"I will also speak with the lady to ensure she is not being forced into this."

"I shall bring her to you at your convenience, my lord."

Langton seemed content that Dashiell understood the process and was agreeable to it. "Marriages are not the domain of the crown, du

Reims, as much as the king and those before him believed it was. It is the jurisdiction of the church, as every holy union is. Therefore, I will give permission if my questions are satisfied."

Dashiell was so relieved that he was nearly weak with it. He glanced at Gavin, who was smiling at him. It was a knowing little smile that suggested their victory was only a breath away. But before they could begin rejoicing, Langton spoke.

"There is one more question," he said. "Has the lady had any other suits?"

Dashiell wasn't sure how much Gavin had told the archbishop of Clayton and his intentions, but when he glanced at the man, he saw Gavin nod faintly. That told him that the subject had been brought up, so Dashiell had no choice but to tell the truth.

"None that have come seeking her, my lord, but there is a… situation," he said. "The duke's eldest daughter, Lily, married Clayton le Cairon three years ago. You have been to Ramsbury at least once since that time, as I recall, so I believe you have been introduced to Clayton. Clayton has someone in mind for her and he has contacted this man, but the man knows of my offer for the lady and has agreed to refuse Clayton's offer."

Langton's expression hardened. "I have met le Cairon, but I do not know him personally," he said. "However, I have been told all about him from David de Lohr, in fact. He does not like the man, nor does anyone else who knows him. Power hungry is the way he has been described to me. What business does he have taking it upon himself to broker a marital contract for the duke's daughter?"

Dashiell sighed heavily. "He believes it is his right, since he will be the duke upon Edward's death."

Langton was deeply displeased. "It will be if she is still unmarried when Edward dies," he said. "But it is not his responsibility now, as much as he tries to make it such. De Lohr told me how le Cairon coerced the marriage to Edward's heiress and he also told me of le Cairon's repeated attempts to put the duke in harm's way, hoping he will be killed so that le Cairon can inherit the dukedom. Do I speak the truth so far, du Reims?"

Dashiell nodded solemnly. "You do, my lord."

"And now I am told that you have arrested him and put him in the vault?"

"I have, my lord."

"Explain to me the catalyst for this decision."

Dashiell felt he was being put on trial, but it didn't bother him. He knew he had done the right thing and he had every faith in his judgment of the matter.

"We have endured three years of le Cairon putting the duke in harm's way, my lord," he said. "At first, he was subtle about it. He would leave a door open, or pay a servant to look the other way while the duke wandered off. He insisted that we always bring the duke on battle campaigns, although part of me agreed with that. The Duke of Savernake has been a warrior for a very long time and his reputation is beyond compare. He inspires the men who see him. But le Cairon insisted he come on a battle march for purposes other than inspiration."

"Explain."

Dashiell shrugged. "As I said, he would leave a door open and let the man escape, and then call it an accident," he said, "but in battle, he would purposely allow the man to wander into the fight because the duke believes he must bless the men. In this past campaign against John, I caught the duke wandering the battlefield no less than four separate times and every time, it was traced back to le Cairon. But two months ago, we attended a celebration at Chadlington and le Cairon was blatant in his attempt to put the duke in danger. The duke barely came away with his life and I determined that in order to preserve the man's safety, I could no longer permit le Cairon to retain his freedom. That is what it boils down to, my lord – Clayton le Cairon has made numerous attempts on the duke's life and, as the duke's captain, I have to put an end to it once and for all. What le Cairon has done is nothing short of attempted murder."

Langton was looking to Dashiell with great distress as he realized the full scale of le Cairon's treachery. After a moment, he sighed heavily.

"I had heard as much from de Lohr," he said. "But I wanted to hear it from you. If all of this is true, why did you wait so long to arrest him?"

Dashiell knew that question would come. "Because in the beginning, he was very subtle, my lord," he said. "He blamed everything on a 'mistake' or an 'accident'. At first, we believed him but, very quickly, we came to realize his true nature. He was clever in his attempts to hide his movements against the duke but, as of late, he made no such attempt to hide anything. When he became so bold, and I have witnesses to attest to his boldness, I had the proof I needed to act."

Langton understood. "This is most distressing," he muttered, shaking his head. "Then you did the right thing, du Reims. Le Cairon is in the vault and he is going to remain there as long as I have anything to say about it. But you do realize this creates a problem when Edward passes away. There will be a succession crisis for the dukedom and it is very possible that, without an heir, it will revert to the crown. The de Vaston family is a royal relation, after all."

Dashiell knew all of that and he nodded reluctantly. "Edward's ancestor, Gilbert de Vaston, was a cousin to William the Conqueror through his mother Herleva of Falaise," he said. "It was William who awarded the dukedom to Gilbert."

"Then John will want it back if Clayton does not inherit it."

"But Clayton has committed an act of attainder, my lord," de Nerra spoke up. The law was his jurisdiction. "By making attempts on the duke's life as he has, he has committed great crimes. But by committing an act of attainder, he forfeits the title and cannot pass it to his heirs, if any. That means his wife will lose her title, and her inheritance. The family will lose everything."

Dashiell knew what that meant; he'd known, from the beginning. "They will essentially be destitute," he said. "Savernake will revert to the crown, meaning John can give it to any favored ally he chooses, including any of those mercenary scum he seems so fond of. It is a very real possibility that Savernake's mighty army will be under John's command at Edward's death."

The weight of that reality hung in the air, an outcome that no one wanted to see. It was a truly horrific thought that Savernake, and her powerful war machine, should be given to an ally of the king, and someone not born and bred in England. As bad as Clayton was, John was worse. Langton sighed, deep in thought.

"So it comes to this," he said, looking between Dashiell and Gavin. "Do you want Clayton in command of Savernake, as a man loyal to the rebellion, or do you want John in command of it? Either prospect is appalling, so you must decide which is the lesser of the evils."

Dashiell felt as if he'd been hit in the gut. He could feel his stomach roll at the thought of such a horrific choice. Before he could speak, however, Langton continued quietly.

"There is something else you should know, du Reims," he said. "The king held a meeting last month in Oxford between his agents and the rebel leaders, de Lohr and de Winter included. You may or may not be aware of the contention between John and the pope at this time but, as a fighting man, I am sure you know that the pope has had his issues with John. The king, historically, does not have the pope's support in this battle for his crown. But my sources tell me that the pope has made a decision in that regard – to support his rule or not to. John is waiting for this decision. If he gains papal support, then you will lose my support, unfortunately. I cannot go against the pope and the church will lay down its arms. If that is the case, it is more important than ever that Savernake not revert back to the crown. I am sure you understand this."

Dashiell listened to the information seriously. "I was not aware of the meeting," he said. "I should have been. Savernake has been at the forefront of this rebellion."

Langton nodded patiently. "Savernake has, but Christopher de Lohr felt it best, given the circumstances with Edward, that the duke not attend. He did not want John's agents seeing the powerful Duke of Savernake's madness. For all the king knows, Edward de Vaston is still leading his armies, and that is a strong factor for the rebellion."

Dashiell understood, but he wasn't happy about it. Any meeting with the king's agents should have been shared with him, as the head of Savernake's armies.

As he looked to Gavin to see what the man's reaction was to all of this, the solar door opened. Everyone turned to see Edward coming through with Aston on one side and Drusus on the other.

"Ah," Langton said as he stood up, stiffly. "My old and dear friend."

Edward had the same glazed look on his face that he usually had. As Langton came near him, he seemed to recognize him, briefly, but that recognition was quickly gone.

"Blessings, my son," he said to Langton. "Go with God."

He made the sign of the cross before Langton, which was hugely ironic considering who Langton was. But they'd been through this before, at least once, so when Edward offered his hand to Langton, the man kissed it.

"You are looking well," Langton said, looking Edward over carefully. "Do you know who I am, my lord?"

Edward looked at him, momentarily confused, before the confusion rippled away. "We are all men of God," he said. "Do you love God?"

"I do."

"Then you shall inherit His kingdom."

Langton tried to speak concisely, hoping something might break through the fog of madness enshrouding Edward's mind. The last time he had seen his old friend, Edward had recognized him. But this man did not. It was like looking at a shell of a man he'd once known and loved.

"My name is Stephen Langton," he said. "I am here because this man wishes to marry your daughter. Edward, do you know who this man is?"

He was pointing to Dashiell, who came up to Edward so the man could look him in the face. A flicker of recognition in Edward's eyes turned into a smile as he reached out, putting both hands upon Dashiell's face.

"My son," he whispered. "My Dash."

Dashiell glanced at Langton, who was pleased to see at least some recognition for a man who had served Edward closely for twelve years.

"Aye, this is Dashiell," Langton said. "Dashiell wishes to marry your daughter, Edward. Do you approve of this?"

Edward's smile faded as he stared at Dashiell, looking at him through eyes that no longer sparkled with the life Edward once had. It greatly saddened Dashiell to look into the face of a man who truly had no idea of the life, or people, going on around him.

"My daughter," Edward said.

"Aye, your daughter," Langton said, looking at Dashiell for the name. When Dashiell told him, he repeated it. "Belladonna. Your daughter, Edward. Dashiell wishes to marry her."

Edward simply gazed at Dashiell as if he hadn't heard Langton. He dropped his hands from Dashiell's face and turned away.

"A man will leave his father and mother, and be joined to his wife," he muttered. "They shall become one."

Langton followed him as he wandered. "Indeed, they shall," he said. "Do you give your approval for Dashiell to marry Belladonna?"

He was met with silence, confusion. When Edward finally spoke, it was with great angst. "I absolve you of your sins, all of you, poor wretched creatures given whim to earthy sins," he said. "Go with God!"

He lifted his hands as he wandered, now mumbling to himself. Langton followed him for a few moments, trying to speak to him, before giving up entirely. Finally, he turned to Dashiell.

"I am hungry," he said, disheartened by the state of his old friend. "Feed me, du Reims, and bring Lady Belladonna to the feast so that I may speak with her. Let me be assured this is what she wishes and if it is, you two shall have my blessing."

It was all Dashiell could do to contain his delight. "Aye, my lord."

As Gavin and Bentley took Langton from the solar and headed to the great hall where the minstrels were still playing loudly, Dashiell and Aston rounded up Edward and, along with Drusus, coaxed him back to his chamber, where his supper was already waiting.

Once Edward was locked in, safe and sound, Dashiell turned to Aston with such an expression of joy that Aston was actually startled by it. But three softly uttered words from Dashiell's lips told Aston everything he needed to know about the expression and the joy, in Dashiell's heart.

Perhaps the meeting with Langton had been stressful, disheartening even, but there was one good thing that had come out of it.

Dashiell could hardly control himself.

"She is *mine*."

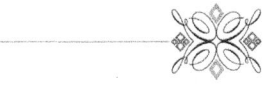

CHAPTER EIGHTEEN

Knowing that Dashiell was meeting with the Archbishop of Canterbury over the fate of their betrothal did nothing to ease Belladonna's nerves.

She was as nervous as a cat, trying desperately not to show it. There was so much that needed to be done that she had to force herself to focus on her tasks, from making sure more meat was put on to boil to accommodate their guests, to ensuring that rooms were prepared for the archbishop and the Itinerate Justice of Hampshire.

In fact, once the refreshments were prepared and delivered to the solar, by Belladonna herself, she then took it upon herself to personally inspect the guest chambers. Ramsbury had such a large keep that the entire top floor was dedicated to servants and guests. There was a roomy chamber for the Itinerant Justice, but Belladonna put the archbishop in Clayton's former chambers, which were quite luxurious.

Clayton's chambers simply sat these days and gathered dust for want of an occupant, so she made sure the servants cleaned up the rooms and put fresh linens on the bed. The mattress wasn't too musty, stuffed with goose feathers, so she didn't go about re-stuffing it on such short notice, but she did make sure the servants sprinkled the mattress with dried lavender to freshen it up.

Once that was finished, she was heading to her father's chambers to check on the man when she saw Aston removing him from his chamber. Aston was very patient with her father, and her father seemed to both recognize and trust him. So she watched as Aston and Drusus took Edward down to his solar to see his old friend, the Archbishop of Canterbury.

While her father was out of his room, Belladonna had the servants clean it and sent someone to fetch her father's supper. Her final step was to peek in on Lily, who was sleeping heavily, so Belladonna pulled a coverlet over the woman and left her alone. She would check back on her sister later. Leaving Lily's darkened chamber, she headed back down to the great hall.

It was full of men, some she recognized and some she didn't, all of them trying to stay out of the rainstorm, which was now lighting up the sky with bolts of lightning. It made for a rather spectacular display and Belladonna paused before entering the hall through the servant's alcove, gazing up into the sky and watching the flashes of light.

The great hall was packed with men. It was smoky and smelly, and dogs roamed in packs, scarfing scraps from the straw-covered floor. Belladonna came in through the servant's entrance, noting the food that was set out on platters in the alcove as harried servants rushed to serve the masses.

On the dais, she spied Dashiell, Bentley, and several other men she didn't recognize. One of them was even sitting in her father's seat, which traditionally was held empty for him. The realization irritated her, but Dashiell was at the table so she assumed he had a good reason for putting a guest in Edward's place. In fact, the closer she came to the dais, the more she realized that the man in her father's place was the archbishop.

No longer entirely irritated, for she knew Dashiell had seated the archbishop in the duke's seat as a sign of respect, Belladonna made her way to the table.

Dashiell was the first to see her and he stood up quickly, making his way to her through the dogs and crowd of men. Once he reached her, he held out his elbow to her with a smile.

"Greetings, lamb," he said. "I was about to send for you. The archbishop has some questions for you."

Belladonna took his elbow, holding fast to him. "What questions?"

Dashiell tried to lower his voice as much as he could, given the noisy room. "He is about to approve our betrothal and wishes to make sure you are not being forced into it," he said. "Tell him what is in your heart and when he approves, I shall ask him to marry us tonight."

She looked at him, eyes wide. "Tonight?" she repeated, shocked. But that shock was quickly replaced by delight. "Truly, Dash?"

"Truly."

Belladonna was thrilled. She was so thrilled that Dashiell couldn't help but notice that she was leading *him* to the table, one step ahead of him, as the men at the table turned to acknowledge her. She was, once again, introduced to de Nerra, whom she had met earlier in her father's solar, and Dashiell had her sit next to the archbishop, in Lily's usual place. Belladonna smiled timidly at the old man with the long, yellowed teeth.

"My lady," the archbishop greeted. "It is agreeable to see you again. You have my compliments for a delicious meal."

Belladonna's smile turned genuine. "Thank you, my lord."

"I also saw your father earlier. He seems in good health."

"He is, my lord."

"I am deeply saddened by his mental state."

Her smile faded. "As we all are, my lord," she said. "The father I have known and loved all of my life is no longer with us."

The archbishop nodded to her statement. "I must agree," he said. "You are aware that is part of the reason I have come to Ramsbury, my lady. There is much taking place here and I had to see Edward for myself."

"I understand, my lord."

The archbishop's gaze lingered on her for a moment before he reached for his cup of wine. "I am sure you do," he said. "But I must speak to you also. You are aware that Dashiell du Reims wishes to marry you."

Belladonna glanced at Dashiell, sitting next to her. He didn't react to the archbishop's question, but she smiled at him nonetheless.

"I wish to marry him, also, my lord," she said. "It has always been my heart's desire."

The archbishop could see the glow in her expression as she said it. That told him more than her words ever could. So if there had been any doubt in his mind that the lady was, perhaps, being forced into this, they were summarily dashed but that one, simple expression.

She had the look of a woman in love.

"I see," the archbishop said after a moment. "Then you are agreeable to this?"

"I am, my lord. With all my heart, I am."

The archbishop's gaze moved from Belladonna, to Dashiell, and back again. Then, he lifted his shoulders.

"I have nothing more to say," he said. "It seems as if the lady is agreeable, so my blessing is given. Du Reims, you may, indeed, marry the lady."

Belladonna shrieked with excitement, completely forgetting herself and kissing the archbishop on the cheek before throwing herself on Dashiell and nearly knocking him off his chair. But he managed to keep his balance, wrapping his big arms around her and hugging her tightly as she squealed excitedly.

The archbishop watched the excited display with a chuckle before turning to de Nerra. "I do not believe she is pleased about this," he jested.

De Nerra was watching the pair, quite thrilled for his friend. "My lord, I believe you have just made two people wildly happy," he said. "For myself, I should like to thank you. Dash is a man who has worked very hard for England and I am thrilled you have permitted the man to find his happiness. I have seen many marriages, most of them unhappy, a few of them merely satisfied, but even fewer where there was a love match. This, my lord, is a love match."

The archbishop could see that. "Then I am pleased for them both," he said, turning to see that another course of food was being served to him by a nervous servant. "Ah, what is this? Something more delightful."

The happy couple was forgotten as he delved into a stuffed egg dish. The same egg dish was placed before de Nerra, and everyone else at the table, but de Nerra was watching the lady and Dashiell in an extraordinary display of affection. It was joy personified.

Love match, indeed.

As de Nerra mulled over a successful betrothal, Belladonna didn't care that she was openly hugging Dashiell for the entire room to see, and Dashiell didn't seem to mind. But she was squeezing him so hard, and wriggling around excitedly, that she ended up smacking him in the nose. He laughed and eventually pushed her back down into her chair as he looked around her to get Langton's attention.

"You have my deepest gratitude, my lord," he said. "You have no idea how long I have waited for this moment."

The archbishop's mouth was full of egg stuffed with breadcrumbs and cheese. "According to de Nerra, a long time, indeed," he said. "I will consider this meal your betrothal celebration, then. We shall eat and drink to the happy couple and a prosperous marriage for the future Earl and Countess of East Anglia."

He lifted his cup, as did everyone at the table. They had heard the conversation between the lady and the archbishop for the most part, and they most certainly saw her joyful reaction to the blessing for her marriage to du Reims.

Since the entire high table was lifting their cups, men in the hall began to see it and lifted their cups, too. It filtered through the room and men began shouting for a blessing, or a word from the archbishop, so Langton was forced to speak to the room.

Stiffly, he stood, as his old body simply wasn't what it used to be.

"Good men of Savernake," he said loudly, as someone told the minstrels to stop playing because the music abruptly ceased. "My good and true men, you are witness today to a joyous celebration. A betrothal has been struck between Dashiell du Reims, Viscount Winterton, and the Lady Belladonna de Vaston. May their marriage be prosperous, generous, and kind to them both."

With that, he drank, and the entire room went mad with the cheers of Savernake soldiers, most of whom had been aware of Dashiell's love for the duke's youngest daughter. It was, in fact, the worst kept secret at Ramsbury. But now that it was out in the open, with the blessing of the Archbishop of Canterbury no less, they were free to shout congratulations to the happy couple at the high table. When Dashiell took Belladonna's hand and kissed it gallantly, the room filled with a deafening roar.

It was a very happy moment for a family, and their retainers, who hadn't known much happiness as of late. The mood was gay, the men full of drink and food, and the atmosphere was one of great celebration, so much so that no one really noticed when the door to the great hall swung open and men began to enter.

It was only when Dashiell caught sight of the latest arrivals that the smile vanished from his face. He could see men approaching, men that he knew well, but men that had not been expected. In fact, his heart sank at the sight of such great and noble warriors, his friends and, in some cases, his cousins.

God help him.

He knew their arrival could not be a good thing.

"We were prepared to go to Canterbury next month to meet with you and the allied commanders, Chris. I did not know you would be coming to Ramsbury."

The softly-uttered words came from Dashiell. They had left the great hall and were back in the duke's solar, a room that reeked of power and of warfare, as the old walls had heard the planning of many a battle over the years.

Indeed, they were about to hear of one more as Dashiell and Bentley, along with the archbishop and Gavin now sat in the room with some of the most powerful warlords in all of England.

Christopher de Lohr and his brother, David, were soaked to the skin from having traveled in a heavy rainstorm. Christopher was accompanied by his eldest son, Curtis, merely a squire at his age but a very big lad with his father's build and intelligence. Along with Christopher and David came the usual array of de Lohr knights, men who had served the House of de Lohr for many years.

Although Dashiell wasn't surprised by the usual de Lohr knights, he was surprised by the other warlords that had accompanied the de Lohr brothers – Marcus Burton, for one, a man some men called the third de Lohr brother, whose feats of strength and bravery were legendary. Gart Forbes had also come with them, a mountain of a man with a great bald head, a mean streak, and a spotless reputation.

But it was the last man of that impressive group that surprised Dashiell the most, a knight by the name of Bric MacRohan. Bric was an Irish knight, a legacy knight sworn to the House of de Winter, and the man throughout England known as *Ard Trodaí*, or the High Warrior.

As good as the de Lohrs were, and Burton and Forbes, these were older men who had already cemented their reputation and preferred to lead men more than actually participate in the heavy fighting. But

MacRohan was a beast of a knight who was fearless in battle, more than anyone Dashiell had ever seen. He'd seen the man literally walk into the heat of fighting as if he were walking through a lovely meadow, showing no concern that his life might possibly be in danger. If there was a dirty job to do, or one with the least chance of success, MacRohan was the man for the job. He would volunteer for it, and happily so.

Dashiell greatly admired him his courage.

And it was this group of knights who had come to Ramsbury, some of the greatest England had ever seen. While Dashiell was pleased to have them, he was also very wary of their presence, which was why his softly spoken words were met by serious expressions. Christopher, with his second cup of warmed wine in hand, spoke in response.

"That meeting has been called off, Dash," he said. He looked to the group around him. "We are still heading to Kent, but for another purpose now. You, and your army, will come with us."

Dashiell glanced at the group, who all appeared quite solemn. "As you wish," he said. "But what is happening? Why have the plans changed?"

Christopher sighed heavily. "As you know, John has marched into Scotland. He had to roll over Jax de Velt to get there."

"I heard," Dashiell said. "Is it true that de Velt was killed?"

Christopher didn't say anything for a moment. "It is," he finally muttered. "But it was a glorious death, I am told. Ajax de Velt has passed into legend, and he will be remembered with honor. But I, for one, will miss my friend."

It was a sad note on a sad passing. "I am sorry for you, Chris."

Christopher shrugged. "All warriors must die," he said. "It was simply his time, I suppose. But the fact remains that his death shall not go unanswered. John *will* pay."

It was an ominous statement. "Where is he now?" Dashiell asked.

"Still in Scotland," Christopher said. "He has taken all of Alexander's holdings in Northern England and any supporters of the Scot king have also had their lands confiscated. John is unstoppable now, Dash, and in order to combat him, we must do the unthinkable."

"What?"

Christopher looked at him. "Prince Louis of France is preparing to sail for England as we speak," he said quietly. "He is bringing his army, and his father's army, with him."

Dashiell hadn't expected that answer. He looked at his cousin as if he hadn't heard right. "Louis is coming to England?" he repeated. "You have invited the French?"

Christopher nodded, but it was clear that the weight of command was wearing heavily on him. "We have little choice if we are to survive," he said. "Dash, I know this looks like treason, but I assure you, it is not. We have a man on the throne of England who has turned this country into a quagmire of poverty and despair. I do not have to tell you that. We are fighting for our freedom, our children's freedom, and the happiness of England. Certainly, those are simple terms, but it is the truth. John has grown too powerful with his mercenary army. Men are fighting for the King of England that do not belong here. If John wins, those same men will infiltrate our lands, and our lives, and take places of position in our country. It will be a disease we will not be able to rid ourselves of. Do you understand that?"

Dashiell could see the anguish in Christopher's expression, something he'd never seen from the man before. His cousin was one of the most powerful warlords in England, a man with a long history of service to the crown, and not one to panic in any event. Everything he did had a greater purpose. The fact that he was advocating the French army to aid the rebellion told Dashiell just how serious this all was.

"Of course I do, Chris," he said quietly. "But inviting the French to fight with us…"

"We are simply bringing in our own mercenary army."

Dashiell wasn't quite seeing it that way. "But once the French are here, will they return home easily?" he asked seriously. "Or will they want rewards from us in the form of our women and properties?"

"It is possible."

"Then you are replacing one disease with another."

"We have no choice."

Those were powerful words. With a heavy sigh, perhaps one of disgust, Dashiell turned away and headed to the table where the wine was. He found he needed it. As he moved, he passed near MacRohan, who wasn't unsympathetic.

"Dash," he said in his heavy Gaelic accent. "I have thought the same as you have. The French are looking for a foothold in England and by inviting them to side with us against the king, we are giving it to them. But ask yourself this, lad – would you rather have a Teutonic mercenary as your neighbor, or a French lord?"

Dashiell looked at the man. Truth was, he adored Bric and they had a long-standing friendship. He also trusted him implicitly, as he did all of the men in the room. But the thought of knowingly allying with the French against the king was something he was having a difficult time stomaching. After a moment, he simply shook his head.

"So we must choose the lesser of the evils," he said. Then, he looked to the archbishop, sitting near the hearth. "It seems to me that this is a day for such choices."

Langton couldn't disagree. "The history of mankind is full of such decisions, du Reims," he said. "It is not unusual."

Christopher caught on to the fact that there was something more going on at Ramsbury, something he'd walked in to. "My lord, although it is always a pleasure to see you, I did not expect to find you here," he said to Langton. "What is happening with Savernake that requires your presence?"

Langton glanced at Dashiell before speaking. "I was called here on another matter," he said. "De Nerra and I were. It would seem that du Reims has arrested Clayton le Cairon for an act of attainder against the Duke of Savernake. The man has tried to murder him to gain his title and his wealth, and du Reims has arrested him."

As the others looked to Dashiell in surprise, it was David who smacked his open palm with a fist. "God be praised," he said with satisfaction. "Finally, Dash. You finally did it."

Dashiell nodded, pouring wine into his cup. "I have, after Clayton made a very bold attempt against the duke," he said. "But along with his arrest comes a problem of succession. With Clayton in the vault, and under charges, he cannot inherit the dukedom. That means it reverts to the king, and if the king wins this war against his nobles, then it is very likely a Teutonic mercenary – or another lord of John's choosing – will be given Savernake and all of her wealth. That, my friends, would be a very bad problem for us to have."

It was clear from David's expression that he hadn't thought of that. Much like the rest of them, he had only been thinking of saving Edward's life and ridding themselves of Clayton. But the truth of the matter was that Edward would die one day and there would be no one to inherit his title and lands. As Dashiell had said, it would be a very bad problem.

"No matter what, Savernake cannot fall into the hands of the king," Langton said. "It would be a disaster for us all. Du Reims and I were discussing that very issue today, but now that you have all arrived, I have a proposition that might work to our advantage."

Dashiell was curious. "What is it, my lord?"

Langton was a very learned man, a very wise man. He didn't give advice that he didn't think through carefully.

"Since we do not wish for the dukedom to revert to the crown, the only alternative is to restore Clayton," he said. "It is the lesser of the evils I spoke of earlier, du Reims. I fear that Clayton *is* the lesser of the evils in this case. It is my suggestion we keep him in the vault for the rest of Edward's life, but once Edward passes on, we release Clayton and inform him that the dukedom is his, with stipulations."

Christopher came to stand next to Dashiell, listening very closely to what the archbishop was suggesting. "What stipulations?" he asked.

Langton was to the point. "He assumes the dukedom, but it is only through our good graces," he said. "He is expected to abide by our wishes and he cannot make a major decision without our approval. If he does, then we break all alliances with Ramsbury. We lay siege to the castle and claim it. By this, I mean it will become an outpost of the Earls of East Anglia and du Reims is placed in command. He will be supported by the House of de Lohr, of course, and the House of de Winter."

It was a very bold proposal, but one that would assure the dukedom remained intact for the most part. Dashiell listened very carefully to the proposal, mulling it over just as the others were.

"I have fought with Clayton before," Marcus Burton said from his seat near the window. A big, brooding man with brilliant blue eyes, he had a long history as an enemy of the king. Edgy and fierce, he was not a man to be crossed. "I know his father, and I knew Clayton before he married the Savernake heiress. He and his father do not live very far from my seat of Somerhill Castle in South Yorkshire. I knew of them for the most part, an ambitious family with a greedy father and an even greedier son. The marriage to Savernake's heir was calculated, as we've always known, and I cannot imagine that Clayton would readily accept any conditions to his rightful assumption of the dukedom. The man will do what he pleases, regardless."

Dashiell wasn't hard-pressed to agree. "Marcus is right," he said. "He does not respond well to threats. I should know, as I have been threatening him for the past three years. What he does fear is anything physical – I have had to beat him on occasion and that is the only thing that makes an impact."

"Then use it," Christopher said grimly. "Use that threat, Dash. We will give Clayton back his dukedom but if he betrays us, in any fashion, it will have lethal consequences."

It was probably the only thing that would work, but the thought of returning the dukedom to Clayton made Dashiell feel ill.

"Oh, God..." he finally mumbled. "We are going to have to give it back to him, aren't we?"

Langton cocked a bushy eyebrow. "Unless you want the next Duke of Savernake to be a Teutonic mercenary."

Dashiell sighed heavily. "I do *not*," he said. "I do not believe any of us do."

Langton nodded wearily. "Then it is settled," he said. "Unhappily, it is. But the matter of you attending your cousins and the rebellion when they meet Prince Louis on the shores of England is not. What say you, du Reims?"

They'd come back to the original subject and Dashiell looked at the archbishop. "Do you support this move with the French, my lord?"

After a brief hesitation, Langton nodded. "I do."

Dashiell ran a hand through his hair thoughtfully, as if that gesture would help him make a decision. He had the largest army of any of them, second only to Christopher, so he knew his participation was key. But, truthfully, there was only one real decision he could make.

"I trust my cousin," he said after a moment. "If Chris believes this is the only way, then I trust him. Savernake will support Louis' arrival. So will East Anglia; I will ensure that my father sends men to Kent as well."

"How many men will that be?"

"I have almost two thousand men here at Ramsbury, plus my father's army is nearly the same size."

"A sizable force, indeed."

Dashiell nodded, thinking on his father's reaction to all of this.

Talus du Reims was a man of reason, but his impatience sometimes got the better of him. And, he hated the French with a passion. As Dashiell pondered his father, the big and frightening figure of Gart Forbes emerged from the shadows behind him and put a trencher-sized hand on Dashiell's shoulder.

"There is nothing else you could do, Dash," Gart muttered. "There is nothing else any of us can do. John, and his mercenaries, must be purged from England and this is the only way. There is an old saying – my enemy's enemy is also my friend. I fear that is how we must look at the French arrival."

"We must look at it another way, too," Christopher said.

All eyes turned to him. "How?" Dashiell asked.

Christopher's blue eyes glittered in the weak light of the solar. "Vengeance for de Velt."

That was the most powerful reason of all, at least with this group. Vengeance for a friend could be a powerful motivator. Without much more to say on the subject, Burton and Forbes moved over to the table where the warmed wine was, pouring themselves full measures and drinking deeply. David and Christopher soon joined them.

All but Dashiell, of course. He was still pondering the situation and the events of the day as a whole. It had truly been a momentous day, one he would forever remember. The day he was betrothed to Belladonna, the day that he realized Clayton would, indeed, have to inherit the dukedom, and the day he learned that the French were coming to England's shores to help them in their battle against the king.

Aye, a momentous day, indeed.

"Could you men stand to hear some good news for a change?" Dashiell turned to the group as they drained the wine. "You are, mayhap, wondering why Canterbury is here."

Heads turned to him, with Christopher peering over his shoulder where Langton was seated next to the hearth, warming himself in front of a mighty blaze.

"That had crossed my mind," he said. "I assume it was because of Clayton's issue?"

Dashiell shrugged. "There is more."

"What more?"

Dashiell looked at his cousin, his eyes twinkling in the firelight. "Do you recall the conversation we had at Driffield about a certain young lady?" he asked. "A daughter of a duke, in fact."

Christopher's tired face lit up. "I do," he said. "Lady Nightshade, isn't it? What is her name again?"

Dashiell started to laugh. "Belladonna," he said. "You asked me a question on that day at Driffield. Do you recall?"

Christopher shook his head. "I do not."

"You asked me if I could stand the thought of her married to another man."

"And?"

"And I cannot. That is why I have asked the archbishop for his blessing on our betrothal. Since the duke cannot give it, I have asked permission from the church and it has been granted. The lady and I are to be married."

A great cheer rose up from Christopher and David, David going so far as to rush his cousin and sweep him up into a big hug, no easy feat considering Dashiell's size.

"God be praised," David said. "I was wondering if you would ever declare your intentions. Your father will be delighted."

Even as David hugged him, Dashiell accepted Gart's outstretched hand in congratulations. "Aye, he will be," he said. "My younger brothers are already married, and I do believe he was worried that I should never wed. It will be a great relief to him."

As everyone congratulated Dashiell on his betrothal, Bentley came forward as well. He'd been standing on the fringes of the discussion, listening to some of the most powerful men in England discuss serious issues that would affect them all.

He'd been on the fringes since de Nerra and Canterbury had arrived earlier in the day, watching and listening in case Dashiell needed him. So much had been discussed, and so much had happened on this day. It had been quite eventful, not the least of which was Dashiell's betrothal to Belladonna.

It was a rather bittersweet moment for him, to be truthful. He and Lily had been verging on a betrothal when Clayton had interfered, so he understood well what it was like to love a woman and not be able to have her. It made him long for those days before Clayton's arrival, days when he and Lily were free to show their love.

But those days were long gone.

Still, he was happy for Dashiell. When the others moved away from Dashiell and back to the table with the wine on it, Bentley came forward with a weak smile on his lips and congratulations on his tongue, but such words were never meant to be. The sounds of screaming suddenly filled the air and everyone froze, shocked at the sound.

But their frozen state was only momentary; Dashiell bolted from the room, and everyone bolted after him with the exception of Canterbury. He was moving slower but, still, he was moving, all of them rushing towards the sound of screaming on the floor above.

What they found would change the course of their plans, permanently.

CHAPTER NINETEEN

WITH DASHIELL IN her father's solar along with the other important warlords that had so recently arrived, Belladonna was left at the dais with Aston, whom Dashiell left behind to oversee the men and the fortress while he was in conference. When Aston left the great hall to go to the gatehouse, Belladonna also left to go see to her sister. She very much wanted to tell Lily about the betrothal, excited to share such wonderful news with her sister.

It was such a surreal moment in Belladonna's life. Finally, she was betrothed to the man she loved and even as she made her way to her sister's chamber, she felt as if she were walking on air. It was still storming outside but, to her, it was the most beautiful day she had ever experienced. Nothing could change that.

So many non-important things were crossing her mind as she headed to Lily's chamber – what dress she would wear for her wedding, for example, and how many children they would have. Belladonna had always wanted a large family, so she thought eight or nine sons would be a good number. But then she giggled when she thought that she might have to adjust that number after having given birth for the first time. She'd seen servant women in labor to bring forth their children, and it seemed to be quite painful.

Aye, perhaps she would decide how many more children to have after the first one.

Thinking of children turned her thoughts back to Lily, who was now expecting her first child. Belladonna wasn't as frightened as she had been when she'd first been told, now more concerned with what needed to be done about it. She knew that Dashiell would do the right thing, for all concerned, so she didn't worry anymore.

She trusted Dashiell completely.

Lily was awake when Belladonna arrived in the chamber, and Belladonna spent several minutes telling the woman about everything that had been discussed that day and of the important visitors at Ramsbury. Lily was groggy and still not feeling well, so her happiness with Belladonna's betrothal was minimal. She simply wasn't up to it.

Still, Belladonna knew Lily was happy for her even if she wasn't able to fully show it. She briefly thought of Acacia, expressing to Lily that she wished she could share the news with their middle sister. They spoke of Acacia for a few moments, wondering how she was getting along at Amesbury and trying not to speak ill of her. After the anger and the fighting had died down, they found that they missed their sister.

In the end, she was still part of them.

Odd how time and distance had eased their fury with her; no matter what Acacia had done, she was still their sister. Her blood was their blood. Lily made the comment that Clayton was unworthy to separate her from her sister, which sounded to Belladonna like she was willing to forgive Acacia somewhat.

But time would tell. Given the situation, Belladonna wasn't entirely sure *she* could forgive Acacia. The woman had seemed more than willing to side with Clayton, on everything, and that was something she couldn't seem to get over.

But it was of little matter. In truth, Acacia hadn't sinned against her, only Lily, so she would do whatever Lily felt was best. Belladonna was just about to leave Lily to her rest when they both heard servants scuffling in the passage between the rooms and raised voices that sounded concerned.

There was thumping, as if something had dropped, and they heard more voices, now lifted in panic. Having no idea what was happening, Belladonna left Lily with the assurance that she would return to tell her what was going on and followed the sounds of the servants. Very quickly, she realized that the noise was coming from her father's chamber.

The door was wide open and there was a great deal of commotion going on. Entering her father's room, Belladonna immediately witnessed her father lying on the floor and Drusus pounding on the man's back.

Startled, she ran to her father as the man lay on his stomach on the floor. Drusus pounded on his back a couple of times before rolling him onto his back, and that was when they both saw the man's face.

It was blue.

Belladonna screamed.

"What has happened?" she cried, laying her head on her father's chest. He wasn't breathing, but she could hear rattling. "Drusus, what has happened? Why isn't he breathing?"

Drusus was in a panic. He began to push on the duke's chest, as hard as he could, and Belladonna screamed at him to stop.

"What are you doing?" she shrieked. "He is not breathing!"

Drusus had sweat pouring off of his bald head. "He is choking!" he told her, rolling the duke onto his side again and pounding the man on the back. "He shoved great pieces of bread into his mouth and could not swallow it all. He is choking on it!"

Belladonna was horrified. She stumbled back, ending up on her buttocks, as Drusus continued to pound on the duke, but to no avail. The man wasn't breathing, and his face was blue as his sightless eyes stared off into space. She wanted to help but didn't know how.

He was choking to death in front of her.

With a grunt of determination, of effort, she helped Drusus roll the duke back onto his stomach so the man could apply pressure to his back, trying desperately to use whatever air was in Edward's lungs to push the lodged food out of his throat. Five or six heavy pushes, and nothing was coming forth. When Belladonna didn't think he was working hard enough, she shoved him away and practically jumped on her father, trying to force him to expel what was in his throat.

But there was no movement, no matter how hard she tried. Belladonna realized that she was watching her father die.

"*No!*"

It was a scream heard throughout the keep. As Belladonna dissolved into hysterics and continued pounding on her father's back, the sounds of thunder could be heard. It was a stampede, the sound of boots against the wood flooring and a herd of armed men suddenly bolted into the room. Belladonna looked up to see Dashiell leading the charge and she pointed to her father.

"Help him!" she cried. "He is choking!"

The group of men swarmed over them. Belladonna found herself pushed out of the way as the group of them lifted the duke up, using their strength to hold him aloft and point his head downward while Dashiell beat on the man's back, struggling to dislodge what was in his throat.

But it was to no avail.

"What is he choking on?" Dashiell demanded.

Drusus was near tears. "Bread, my lord," he said. "He shoved it all into his mouth before I could stop him, and he could not swallow it all."

Bread. When mixed with water, or saliva, it formed a hard ball that would be difficult to remove. But Dashiell and the others tried; God help them, they tried for long minutes upon long minutes. They even started shaking the duke, trying to shake it loose, but the more time drained away, so did the duke's life.

It was a horrifying scene.

Belladonna had no idea how long they had been trying to save her father from choking. It seemed like hours when it was really only minutes. She sat on the floor, weeping as she watched the terrible scene, realizing that Lily had wandered into the room also and now stood over by the open door, sobbing at the sight.

Belladonna staggered to her feet and rushed to her sister, and, together, the two of them clung to each other as they watched Dashiell, Bentley, and several other men try to save their father's life. Bric MacRohan even punched Edward in the gut with his big fist, hoping that would dislodge the mass, but there was no response at all.

Finally, after a good deal of shaking and thumping on the man, they lay him back to the floor where Dashiell put his ear to Edward's chest and listened.

There was nothing.

With a heavy sigh, Dashiell closed his eyes tightly for a brief moment before lifting his head and looking to the anxious faces around him. He shook his head, a brief movement, but one that conveyed to them that Edward de Vaston, Duke of Savernake, was no longer a part of the living. They had been unable to save him. When Langton realized his old friend was dead, he bowed his head and began to perform the last rites over the supine body.

It was a solemn moment, flooding the room with enough grief and despair to fill a moat. Bric, Gavin, Christopher, David, Gart, and Marcus stood over the duke, deeply regretting that they'd been unable save him. For men used to victory, and success, it was a difficult thing to come to terms with.

But the truth was that Edward was already dead when they came into the room; it had been the hero spirit in all of them that had tried to snatch Edward back from the jaws of death. Feeling guilty even though they shouldn't have, they bowed their heads as Langton intoned the ritual over him, but Dashiell and Bentley were looking to the women standing in the doorway, weeping and clinging to each other.

It was a shattering sight to see. It was Dashiell who finally moved, heading towards the pair, his sorrowful gaze was on Belladonna.

"I am so sorry, lamb" he whispered. "He is gone."

Belladonna broke down into painful sobs, falling into his arms, as Lily went to her father and knelt beside him. Taking one of his hands, she clutched it against her chest, trying not to look at her father's purple face.

"Go, Papa," she whispered. "Go where you can be strong and proud again. Go where your mind is sound again. We will miss you, but it is better this way."

Such painful words, words not lost on the warlords gathered around Edward's body. As Lily wept softly, with her father's hand clutched to her chest, she felt a big hand rest on her shoulder, trying to give her some comfort.

It was Christopher, his heart breaking to see the daughters of the duke so distraught. Having daughters of his own, he was rather partial to them. He felt deeply for their loss.

"I am sorry, my lady," he muttered. "This is a difficult loss to accept, for us all."

But Lily lifted her tear-stained face to him. "That man we came to know the past few years... that was not my father. He would not want you to remember him that way."

Christopher removed his hand from her, sympathy in his expression. "I will remember Edward de Vaston as a man with a quick laugh and a kind manner. But on the field of battle, there was no one greater."

Sniffling, Lily struggled to her feet, helped up by Christopher and David. "I think my father began dying three years ago when his madness overcame him," she said, looking down to his cooling corpse. "Every day, his mind left him just a little more. It was a very long farewell for a man I loved dearly. As much as I have been dreading this moment, now that it is here… I am actually relieved for him."

"Why?" Christopher asked.

She looked at him. "Because our family motto is *mors in victoria*," she said. "I cannot explain my feelings except to say my father has found victory over death. Victory because death has set him free from the madness that trapped him."

It made perfect sense to them all. Lily's tears returned as she stood over her father and silently wept. The men moved away to give her some privacy, but Langton remained, whispering prayers over the body of his old friend. But as Lily stood there, quite alone, Bentley walked up beside her.

He knew he shouldn't. God knows, he was well aware of it. But he couldn't simply stand by and watch her grieve alone. He had to comfort her, in some way, so he simply came to stand beside her.

After a moment, he reached out and took her hand, holding it tightly. When Lily looked up and saw that it was Bentley, her beloved Bentley, her tears returned with a vengeance and she buried her face in his chest.

Bentley hesitated for a brief moment before wrapping his arms around her. To hell with propriety.

He was going to comfort her.

The only sounds in the room now were those of the gently snapping fire in the hearth, and Lily and Belladonna's weeping. Everyone else was stone-silent, seemingly frozen in place, stunned at the swift and unexpected passing of the Duke of Savernake. But as the shock began to wear off and reality settled, it was Christopher who finally looked over at Dashiell, standing in the doorway with Belladonna in his arms.

"We were only just speaking of this," he said hoarsely. "Discussing the duke's passing and what must happen when he does. Christ, did we somehow curse him by even speaking of such a thing? Did *we* do this?"

Dashiell knew it was more a rhetorical question than an actual plea.

Faintly, he shook his head. "Nay," he said. "We did not do this. It was an accident. Speaking of his death did not cause it."

"But now he is gone," Langton said, his gaze fixed on Edward. "It is true. We were only just speaking of the future without Edward and now, suddenly, we must face it. Are we ready to?"

Dashiell knew exactly what he meant; *Clayton*. Someone had to go tell Clayton that he was now the duke. God, Dashiell didn't even want to think about it with the duke not even cold at his feet. But it was either accept Clayton as the new duke or John would regain control of Savernake, and Dashiell would not allow that while there was breath left in his body. As distasteful as it all was, now, they had to face it.

This had been a day of monumental decisions and life-changing events, and Dashiell was struggling to process it all. But one thing was for certain; he couldn't dwell on it. He had to make decisions and make them quickly. Quietly, he shut the chamber door and faced the men in the room.

"And so, it comes," he said, struggling against his grief. "What we have feared has come to pass. Clayton is now the Duke of Savernake. But we will not tell him so until morning, until the army is ready to leave the gates. Bentley, find Aston and the two of you began preparations. I want every able man armed and ready to depart by dawn. Is that clear?"

Bentley nodded sharply as he released Lily. "Aye, my lord."

"Good. Be on your way."

As Bentley quit the chamber, heading off to rouse the mighty Savernake army, Dashiell turned to Langton.

"You have given my lady and me permission to wed," he said. "I will ask you then to marry us now, without delay. The lady and I shall be husband and wife when I tell Clayton he has assumed the dukedom. I will not leave that detail to chance."

Langton understood. "Very well, du Reims," he said. "I will perform the mass before this night is out."

"You will perform it now, if you please. There is no time to waste, and my night is full from this point forward. I have a duke to bury, another one to swear fealty to, and an army to muster."

Langton looked to Belladonna, who was looking rather surprised by Dashiell's declaration, but not resistant. In fact, she looped her arms through Dashiell's right arm, her cheek resting on his bicep affectionately. Although there wasn't time for the proper procedure that usually accompanied a wedding, that didn't truly matter in the end. Langton would speak the words that would make Dashiell and Belladonna man and wife, a union that would bind them together, forever. He looked to de Nerra, standing near Edward's supine body.

"Will you bring me my prayer book?" he asked. "It seems that I have a wedding mass to perform and I do not know where my possessions have been taken."

Gavin swiftly and silently left the chamber, leaving the others lingering over a dead body, now whispering among themselves about what was to come. It was fortunate they had a plan, which was most fortuitous considering Edward's sudden death left them all shocked and saddened. Dashiell finally sat Belladonna into a chair near her father's hearth and returned to the others, gathered around Edward's body.

"Help me put him onto his bed, if you will," Dashiell said quietly. "Let us get him off the floor."

Between the six of them, they gently picked Edward up and put him onto his bed as Drusus, still weeping softly, smoothed the covers for him. Dashiell closed the duke's still-open eyes, pulling the coverlet over his face so his purple features wouldn't disturb Belladonna. She'd already seen too much, and the lingering state of her father's corpse wasn't something she needed to continue to view.

"What would you have us do, Dash?" Christopher asked him quietly. "Does anything need to be done that we can assist with?"

Dashiell tried to think beyond the immediate needs of the night. "I would like to bury Edward before we leave on the morrow," he said. "I will need help with the arrangements. There is a small chapel to the southern side of the hall where generations of de Vastons have been buried. If we put men on digging the grave, we can bury him before the sun rises. I do not want to leave his burial for his daughters to handle because we have gone off to war."

Christopher and David both nodded. "We'll put men on it," Christopher said. "We shall also see about a temporary coffin of some kind. Edward can receive a grand burial some time when you return and there are no wars but, for now, let us get him in the ground with proper prayers. That will have to suffice."

"Thank you," Dashiell murmured sincerely, putting a hand on Christopher's arm.

As his cousins moved to arrange for the duke's burial, Gart and Marcus were left standing with Dashiell.

"And us?" Marcus asked. "What do you need of us, Dash?"

Dashiell looked at the old warriors, men that had seen so many years of so many battles. His respect for them was fathomless.

"I have asked Bent and Aston to muster the men, but it is a big army," he said. "Your help would be deeply appreciated in helping assemble them and making sure no detail is forgotten. I am to be married tonight and I fear my focus will be on my bride for most of the night. Come the dawn, however, we shall all make our way into the vault to inform the new Duke of Savernake of his title and of our expectations. But until then, we've a busy night ahead of us."

Marcus nodded and turned away as Gart put a meaty hand on Dashiell in a show of sympathy. As the two of them lumbered from the chamber, Bric wandered up beside Dashiell.

The big Irish knight stood silently next to him, a mute support of Dashiell and what he had faced that night. Dashiell turned to look at the man; Bric had hair that was so blond it was white, and eyes of a blue color so pale that it was silver. Those silver eyes were looking at the women on the far side of the chamber.

"It has been quite a day for you, Dash," Bric finally said. "You are a man of great strength, greater still when in crisis. Even so, I am sorry you had to go through this, lad. 'Tis most shocking for the daughters."

Dashiell was looking at the women, too. Lily was over with her sister, once again, as the two of them sat before the hearth, holding hands.

"They are strong," he said quietly. "You have no idea how strong they are. They've had to be strong since their father lost his mind and Lily's husband has been trying to kill him. Truthfully, I blame myself for everything we have gone through."

Bric looked at him, surprised. "Why would you say that?"

Dashiell glanced at him. "I should have killed Clayton the minute he came through the gates of Ramsbury. He was looking for hospitality and I should have given it to him with the end of my sword."

Bric grinned. "You may still," he said. "We are heading into another battle, Dash. Much can happen when the fighting starts."

Dashiell knew exactly what he meant. "That is what I am afraid of after arresting Clayton and holding him in the vault for so long. I am afraid that, once released, he will have a sword aimed at my back."

Bric's smile faded. "Not as long as I am around, lad. I'll run him through if he so much as looks in your direction. And that's a promise."

A weak smile creased Dashiell's lips, a smile of gratitude. Bric slapped him on the shoulder before departing the chamber, off to assist Marcus and Gart with preparations for the army.

In spite of the horror of the day, Dashiell felt truly blessed by his close circle of family and friends. He was so much more fortunate than most. But that feeling of gratitude was tempered by the sight of Lily and Belladonna, huddled together in their grief.

The sight gave Dashiell such sadness, but with that sadness was also the joy in knowing he would soon be a married man. He only wished that it would be under better circumstances, but that couldn't be helped. He would take Belladonna for his wife this night and, for at least a few hours, he was going to block out everything else.

For tonight, and for everything he and Belladonna had fought so hard for, they deserved at least that.

An hour later, in Edward de Vaston's lavish solar, the Lady Belladonna de Vaston married Dashiell du Reims, Viscount Winterton, in front of friends and family, all of whom had waited for this day nearly as long as Belladonna and Dashiell had.

It was a bittersweet and tender moment in the midst of a day that all of them would remember for the rest of their lives.

CHAPTER TWENTY

"Lily?"

It was a hissed whisper coming from her door. Lily, exhausted from the events of the night, was just laying her head down when she heard the hiss again and realized that it wasn't coming from her locked bedchamber door, but from the servant's entrance near the hearth. A hidden door that led to the servant's passage was open and an enormous, dark figure was entering.

Alarmed, she sat up. "Who –"

A soft hiss cut her off. "It is me," Bentley whispered. "I am sorry to startle you, and Dash would be furious if he knew I was here, but… I had to come. I do not know if I shall see you before we depart and I had to see you before I go."

Lily calmed rapidly when she realized who it was. Tossing off the coverlet, she rose to her feet. "I am glad you came," she said. "Bella told me that many great men came to see Dash tonight but she did not tell me why. I can only guess from the actions in the bailey and what I heard in my father's chamber that war is on the horizon."

Bentley nodded, coming to stand at the end of her bed. "War, indeed," he said. "John is moving through England and Scotland, destroying everything in his path. The rebels have allied with the French and we are going to Kent to rendezvous with their fleet."

Lily's eyes widened with fear. "The French?" she gasped. "And then what will you do?"

"Reclaim England from John and his mercenary army."

Lily's gaze lingered on him in the darkness for a moment as she processed that terrible scenario. "Then… you could be gone for a very long time."

"Aye."

With a faint sigh, she sat heavily on the edge of the bed. "Oh, Bentley," she murmured. "This is terrible news. These wars could go on for years and years, now with France involved."

Bentley took a few steps towards her, sitting down beside her on the bed. "It is possible," he said. "It is equally possible that with French support, we can overcome John and his mercenaries once and for all."

Lily looked up at him, the handsome lines of his face. "You will take great care, won't you?" she asked. "I could not bear it if anything happened to you. I would not want to live."

Although Bentley had no real intention of touching her when he'd come to say goodbye, his natural weakness for the woman caused him to reach up and cup her face with one of his big hands.

"Nothing will happen to me," he assured her. "But even if it does, then know that my life on earth was something joyful because of my love for you. It is true that circumstances have not favored us, but the love I have for you will endure forever, Lily. You must honor that love by living every day as the proud, beautiful woman I know you to be."

Lily's eyes were filling with tears as he spoke. He was so noble, so strong, and her heart was breaking into a thousand little pieces at the thought of not seeing him again. But it was also breaking for another reason.

The child she carried.

Lily had vowed not to tell Bentley. As she'd told her sister, she felt this was her burden alone. But the more she looked at him, the more she realized that wasn't true. He had a right to know. Perhaps it would help him endure these terrible battles looming on the horizon to know that his love with Lily had come to fruition. Perhaps, he could help her decide what to do now that Clayton was the duke and she was pregnant with another man's child. Lily didn't want to die at Clayton's hand, and she didn't want Bentley's child to die.

Perhaps, at the moment, it was best to tell him everything.

"Before you go, I must tell you something," she whispered. "I am not sure this is the right time, but I do not believe I will have another chance, so I must do this. Forgive me, Bent, but I have an enormous burden that I must share with you. I need your wisdom and guidance on the matter."

Bentley looked at her seriously. "Of course," he said. "You need not even ask. What is your trouble?"

This was the moment Lily had dreaded. She wasn't entirely sure what to say, so she didn't try. Instead, she stood up and removed her robe, leaving her clad only in a heavy sleeping shift that was voluminous enough to not show the outlines of her body.

"Give me your hands," she murmured.

Bentley did, and Lily pressed them against her belly, which was a firm bump set within her pelvis. As soon as he realized her blossoming belly, a pregnancy, his eyes widened and he looked up at her with shock. Lily smiled weakly.

"It is your child," she whispered. "I have not been with Clayton since late last year, so there is no possibility this child is his. Also, whenever he forced himself upon me, I had pessaries from the apothecary in Marlborough that were guaranteed to prevent conceiving a child. I used them every time because I did not want a child with him. But with you… I used nothing. This is the result."

Bentley was clearly in shock. He kept his hands on her belly, finally moving his fingers so he could feel more of her belly. She wasn't very big at all, but he could definitely feel the firmness of her womb.

"A… a child?" he finally muttered. "*My* child?"

Lily nodded. Watching the shock and reverence on his face warmed her soul, more than she could have ever imagined, but realizing what a terrible bind they were in caused the tears to fall.

"I was not going to tell you," she wept quietly. "I was simply going to go away and have the child and not burden you with such a thing, but now… you are leaving for battle, Bent, and it is possible you will not return to me. I did not want you to go away not knowing of this life we have created together. No child was every conceived with such love. But Clayton is now the duke and he will know this child is not his. I do not know what to do. Please help me."

The horror of the situation closed in on Bentley. She was absolutely right; Clayton would not be kind to her if he discovered this pregnancy. In fact, knowing the man, he could very well hurt both her and the child and call it justice. With that terrible thought, Bentley wrapped his arms around her and pulled her against him, his face buried in her belly as he held her tightly. Lily wrapped her arms around his head.

"Do not fret," he told her fervently, feeling the woman he loved in his embrace, carrying a child they had conceived together. *His child.* Oh, God, he couldn't let Clayton harm her! "Let us think through this calmly, Lily. All is not lost."

Lily trusted him; she had to. In truth, it felt so good to share this burden with him, knowing he would think of something. He was brilliant that way.

Bentley released her from his embrace and sat her down beside him, holding her hands as he wiped away her tears.

"Clayton has been in the vault for the past two months, so he does not know about this pregnancy, nor will he," he said firmly. "You have not visited him, have you?"

Lily shook his head. "Never."

"Good." He sighed, his mind working swiftly. "I think you said it best when you said that you needed to go away to have this child. If you remain here, there will be unfathomable consequences."

"I know."

Bentley began to think of all the places to send her, places where she would be safe, at least until she had the child and he could return for her. Truly, there was only one place he could think of.

"My father has a spinster sister who lives in Dorset, in a village called Weymouth," he said. "It is by the sea. It is far enough away that no one would know you and my aunt would take great care of you and of the child."

Lily liked the idea of going far away where no one would know her or question her. It was something she'd thought of before. "What will you tell your aunt?" she asked. "What I mean to say is what will you tell her about me? Who I am?"

"My wife," Bentley said without hesitation. "I will tell her that you are my wife and our marriage was forbidden, so she must take the greatest care of you. She will understand. You can have the child in peace."

It all sounded so wonderful and Lily was trying not to become too excited or relieved about it. "But what of Clayton?" she asked. "I cannot simply leave and not say anything. He may even suspect you are somehow involved. What if –"

Bentley shook his head, putting his fingers over her lips. "You can leave a missive telling him that you had to go away for your health," he said. "He cannot possibly know the truth. When your health is restored, and the child born, you can return to Ramsbury."

She frowned. "Without my baby? Bent, I will not leave my child behind."

He was not surprised to hear that. In truth, he was glad. It meant she had more love for her child than her position as the Duchess of Savernake. Not that he ever doubted her, but it was still good to hear.

"You have two choices, as I see it," he said quietly. "You can leave the child in Weymouth with a good family and return to Savernake to assume your position as duchess. Clayton never need known why you really went away."

Lily's expression was dark. "I do not like that choice," she said. "What is the second choice?"

His gaze was intense. "You can remain in Weymouth with the child and I will ask Dash to release me from my oath to Savernake. I will join you there, and we shall live as man and wife for the rest of our lives."

It was a surprising answer, but one that lit her up from inside. Her brave, noble knight was willing to surrender his entire life for her. Lily put her hand up, touching his face.

"Is it true?" she murmured. "You would give up your life for me?"

"You would give yours up for me."

"It is true, but I am miserable in my life, Bent. It is easier for me to do it. But you… you have position and prestige with Savernake. That is asking a great deal for you to walk away from it."

He smiled faintly. "You will let me worry about that," he said. "Nothing is more important than being with you, Lily. You and our child. I would defy God himself for such a privilege."

The matter, as far as Lily was concerned, was settled. She would rather give up a thousand dukedoms than spend one more day as Lady le Cairon. Living a lie as Lady Ashbourne was much more to her liking. Therefore, she kissed Bentley deeply and they fell back on the bed, enjoying the last few moments that they would share together for a very long time.

Clothing came off, falling silently to the floor, and when Bentley finally joined his body with hers, it was with great tenderness and longing. It was engrained into their very souls that they would be together, forever, come what may.

Clayton or no Clayton, dukedom or no dukedom, nothing could ever separate them.

When Belladonna should have been sleeping, she found that she couldn't.

It was late, so late that she had no idea what time it really was. She thought it might have been sometime after midnight, but one would have never known by the activity in the bailey.

The entire area was lit up with torches, giving the vast grounds of Ramsbury Castle an eerie glow. Men were moving about in the bailey below and she could watch them from her window. She could see Dashiell, her husband, as he went about his tasks that needed to be completed, which mostly included yelling orders at men who needed to complete their own work. She could see the other great knights moving in the darkness, taking care of tasks that Dashiell had asked of them.

In all, she'd never seen Ramsbury so busy, and most especially in the middle of the night. The great army, which hadn't seen any activity for the past couple of months, was being assembled and the gatehouse was open as they spilled out into the land beyond because the bailey was getting so full.

Belladonna knew that several powerful men had arrived that evening, the Archbishop of Canterbury included, but what she didn't realize was that Christopher de Lohr had brought his mighty army from Lioncross Abbey Castle, merging it with Marcus Burton's Somerhill army near Cirencester, and then with Gart Forbes' troops from Dunstan Castle as soon as they entered Marlborough.

It made for a massive amalgam of manpower. At the moment, an army of about five thousand men was encamped outside the walls of Ramsbury and the smoke from hundreds of cooking fires mingled with the storm, which was intermittent throughout the night.

But Belladonna couldn't think about armies or men, or great knights or battles at the moment. All she could think about was

Dashiell and that she was spending her wedding night watching him pull together the Savernake army so they could depart on the morrow.

It was difficult not to feel sorrow at that.

Dashiell had told her he would return to her at some point during the night, and she waited with excited nervousness for that moment. It was all happening so fast and she was struggling to keep her wits about her.

After the wedding, which seemed to pass in a blur, Dashiell had taken her up to her chamber, leaving her with a kiss and a promise that he would return. Belladonna went into her chamber and, with the help of a pair of maids, built a roaring blaze in her hearth and selected a lovely dressing gown to await her husband in.

She still couldn't believe that she and Dashiell were finally married. She'd dreamed of it for so long that now that it had happened, it seemed wholly surreal. But that could describe her entire relationship with Dashiell – she'd pined away for the man for so long that when they actually did declare their mutual affection, everything seemed to happen with lightning speed.

But she couldn't have been happier. As far as she was concerned, her dreams had come true, and tonight was the night she and Dashiell would know each other as husband and wife.

Since her mother had died when she was young, it had been Lily who had informed her of the ways between men and women. Curiosity had driven Belladonna to ask questions that Lily was too embarrassed to answer, so she often found herself asking questions of the older serving women, including the cook. She knew how dogs mated, for she had seen it before, especially when Dashiell and Bentley and Aston were breeding their hunting dogs. She'd often watched before Dashiell had chased her away, angry that a young maiden should be so interested in breeding dogs.

The thought made her grin.

Therefore, she knew more than most young virgins about the mating of men and women, or at least the general idea of it, but other than several passionate kisses from Dashiell, she hadn't experienced any pleasures of the flesh and Dashiell had never pushed himself on her. He was too much of a gentleman for that.

But tonight, things would change.

Belladonna very much wanted to know Dashiell as a woman knows a man. She wanted to feel his hands on her, his muscular body against his. She wanted to be as close to him as she possibly could, and the mere thought was enough to set her heart to fluttering. She could only hope he would feel the same way.

Something told her that he would.

So, she prepared for him. She bathed in rosewater and rubbed her skin with oil that smelled of flowers. It made her skin soft and moist. She also set out water for Dashiell to wash in when he arrived, thinking that he might want to do such a thing before he touched her. Wouldn't he want to wash the stink of the men and horses off of him? She thought so, anyway. She hoped he didn't think she'd put out the water and soap because she thought he smelled badly.

That wouldn't be any way to start off their married life together.

With everything set out, she waited. And waited. As the night continued on, past midnight and into the early morning hours, Belladonna remained standing by the window, hoping for a glimpse of her husband now and again. He'd told the men at their wedding that he intended to be occupied with his wife on this night, but it was clear he had duties that were more pressing than even she was. But she wasn't offended by it. She knew he would come to her when he could.

At some point, Belladonna moved away from the window because it began to rain again. Closing the oiled cloth covering, she went to sit by the fire and wait out her husband. But the night dragged on and Belladonna was more tired than she realized. She must have fallen asleep because when next she was aware, it was to Dashiell's soft voice in her ear.

"Come along, lamb," he said as he bent over and scooped her up out of the chair. "To bed with us both."

Sleepy, she yawned in his face. "I did not realize I had fallen asleep," she said. "I was waiting for you."

He smiled as he deposited her onto the bed, the same bed she'd slept in since she was a child. It was big and comfortable, and more than enough for the two of them.

"I am sorry to keep you waiting," he said as he began pulling off his gloves. "We are mobilizing an army in a very short amount of time, so there is much to do."

Belladonna lay down on the bed, desperately trying not to fall asleep again. "It is fortunate that your cousins are here to help you."

Gloves tossed aside, he unfastened his belt, laying it carefully on the back of a chair. Removing his broadsword from its sheath, he went to prop it up on the wall next to the head of the bed.

"Indeed, I am," he agreed. "They have many men with them who have also been a great help. But let us not speak of them tonight. I will be dealing with them for the foreseeable future so, at this moment, I only wish to speak of us, Lady du Reims."

Belladonna grinned, a sleepy gesture. "I never thought I would hear that name where it pertained to me."

"Nor I," he admitted as he untied his tunic.

"When did you know?"

He eyed her as he removed his hauberk and damp tunic, heading to the hearth to lay them out to dry. "Shall I be honest?"

"Please."

"The day we went to Marlborough those months ago. Do you recall? You were so angry at me that you told me not to speak to you."

Belladonna laughed softly. "I remember."

"That was the day I knew I would marry you."

"But how? I would not even let you speak to me."

"I will tell you, but you must promise not to become angry."

"I promise."

He didn't reply for a moment as he continued undressing. He wasn't wearing all of his protection on this night, only pieces of it, so the mail coat came off after the tunic. Having dressed himself for so many years, all he did was bend over slightly, pull out the arms, and he was able to get it over his head. That, too, ended up by the hearth, over a chair so it could dry out.

"When we were riding into the town, Lily came to speak to me," he finally said. "I do not know if you remember this, but she did. During the course of the conversation, she told me you were in love with me. Once I knew that, it was easier for me to pursue you."

Belladonna did, indeed, remember that trip into town, and she remembered clearly when Lily had ridden to the front of their escort to talk to Dashiell.

"She told you that?" she said, sitting up in bed. "Then she lied to me. I asked her what she had spoken of, and she gave me some silly answer. She never told me she said such things to you!"

He gave her a half-grin as he pulled off his undertunic, a heavily-padded tunic that was sticky with sweat. When it came off, the only thing he had left was a thin linen tunic underneath.

"She told me you were in love with me and if my feelings were the same, then I had better make them clear. So, I did." Belladonna scowled at him, but he held up a finger to her. "You promised you would not get mad."

She had. Frustrated, she lay back down on the bed. "Just wait until I see Lily again."

"What are you going to say to her?"

"I do not know yet, but it will be terrible."

He laughed softly and pulled off the thin tunic, the last layer between his flesh and the open air. "Do not berate her too much," he said as he moved to the water in the basin that she had set out for him. "Were it not for her, I would still be hiding in fear of my feelings for you, so you can thank her for what she did."

Once he pulled his tunic off, Belladonna forgot all about her meddling sister. The firelight was glistening off of his muscular form as she lay there and watched him wash his hands and arms. In truth, in all the years she had known him, she had never seen him naked from the waist up, so it was something of an eye-opening experience.

He was absolutely magnificent.

He had big, muscular arms, so firm and tight that she could see the veins running through them. His shoulders were very broad, his neck and chest defined and as muscular as the rest of him. He had a soft matting of hair on his chest, something she thought rather alluring, and when he turned to dry off his skin, she could see scars on his arms and torso, but they did not take away from all of that male beauty.

"You have scars," she said, rather dreamily. "You have been fighting battles for as long as I have known you, but I have never seen your scars."

He glanced up at her as he washed off his face. "I have many," he said. "But I was certainly not going to show them to you."

"Why not?"

"Because that would have been unseemly and improper."

"But they are just scars."

He eyed her. "You do not seem to have any concept of how a man behaves around a maiden he is not betrothed to because we have had this conversation before, many times."

"I know."

"You even became angry with me for it, somehow thinking that I did not wish to be seen with you."

"You are my husband now. You have to show me everything, improper or not."

He froze in the midst of drying off his face, casting her a long look. When he resumed drying, he was fighting off a grin.

"You," he said slowly, "are bold and reckless, Lady du Reims. I could never say this before, but I can now – I like it. I like it when you are bold and reckless with me."

She laughed, laying on her side and watching him as he finished washing his torso and drying off. When he finally tossed the linen towel aside, he made his way towards the bed where she was laying. There was something soft in his expression as he gazed down at her.

"I wish we had more time for this," he said quietly. "I wish we had all of the time in the world but, alas, we do not. We must consummate this marriage and then I must leave. It hurts my heart to even say it."

Belladonna's expression was full of longing and sadness as she looked up at him. Scooting over on the mattress, she patted the bed beside her.

"Lay with me," she whispered.

He didn't hesitate. He was in his dirty breeches, however, and didn't want to bring that filth onto their marriage bed, so he quickly pulled off his boots, untied the top of his breeches, and slid them right off his body.

Shocked at the speed in which the man stripped off his clothing, Belladonna realized he was nude but the firelight was behind him, so she couldn't really see much of the front of him as he climbed into bed, pulling the coverlet up over them. His arms went around her, and a leg draped over her hips, pulling her as close to him as he possibly could.

"You have no idea how long I have waited for this," he murmured, kissing her forehead. "It does not seem possible, yet here we are. You are my wife. I have never been prouder of anything in my life."

Belladonna snuggled against him, her cheek to his naked chest for the first time. He smelled of the pine soap she'd put out for him, his flesh soft and warm. It was heaven. It was everything she'd ever hoped it would be and more.

"This is our moment, Dash," she whispered. "Whatever comes, whatever our future holds, I will remember this moment as the most beautiful moment of our lives. The moment when I became yours, and you became mine. But I think that, somehow, I have always belonged to you. There has never been another man for me and there never will be. Only you."

His answer was to kiss her, long and hard and deep. The more he suckled, the more aroused he became, his hands in her hair as he inhaled and breathed and tasted everything about her. She smelled sweet, like flowers, and when she rolled onto her back, he ended up in the dominant position on top of her.

Nothing had ever felt more right in his life.

It was dark beneath the coverlet as his hands moved aside her robe, untying the sash and pulling it open. When their naked flesh touched, he groaned with pleasure, savoring the moment as his manhood throbbed to life. He wanted to take his time with her, to savor every touch and every kiss but, at this moment, the consummation was more of a statement than an act of passion – he had to claim her in every way, to mark her with his seed, so Clayton could never again use her as a bargaining pawn. As of this night, she was Lady du Reims, the future Countess of East Anglia, and he needed to ensure that nothing could ever change that.

She was virginal and delicate and soft. Just like brand new snow, pristine and white, and he would be the first and only man to touch it. He ran his hand up her torso, feeling her silken flesh and experiencing more lust than he ever knew possible. She seemed to purr like a kitten when he kissed her, and his kisses moved down her neck, to her shoulder, and down her chest. Belladonna seemed comfortable with everything until his hot, wet mouth closed in over a tender nipple. Then, she bucked as he suckled her furiously, a big arm wrapping around her as her body to still her movements.

He could feel Belladonna trying to pull away from him, perhaps startled by this intimate new experience, but he held her fast, nursing on her tender breasts, running his tongue over flesh that tasted like flowers. Dashiell could feel her hands at his head, her fingers winding into his thick auburn hair. Truly, he had her exactly where he wanted and he wasn't about to let go.

He moved on.

His free hand moved to the tender core between her legs and she gasped with surprise when he wedged his big body in between her legs and fingered the dark curls. She was wet, her body already preparing to receive him, and the realization had his heart pounding and his erection as hard as it had ever been.

Tenderly, he stroked her virginal lips, all the while either nursing at her breasts or kissing her belly as he tried to ease whatever nerves she might have. But it seemed to him that she was not only relaxing beneath him, she was enjoying it. The more he stroked her pink, wet folds, the more her hips would thrust forward as if trying to capture that searching finger.

Therefore, he inserted a finger into her to satisfy that hunger her body seemed to be experiencing, the inherent need to feel a man between her legs. Belladonna gasped at the intrusion, groaning softly as he thrust in and out of her, mimicking the lovemaking they would soon be making.

But Dashiell would not delay any longer; he needed his manhood inside of her in the worst way. He had to consummate this marriage and satisfy that part of him that saw this as a necessary duty. *Duty!* God, no… it was his pleasure. His fingers were still in her as he tossed the coverlet back, exposing them both to the cold night air.

Now, he could see her beautiful body bathed in the firelight. She was full of breast, slender of waist, and her legs were parted to receive him. Very quickly, he removed his fingers and placed his erection at her threshold, coiling his buttocks and thrusting into her. With that action, she naturally started to tighten in fear. He could feel it. Kissing her gently and whispering words of encouragement, he coiled his buttocks again, thrusting hard this time. He felt her maiden's barrier break as he gathered her up into his arms.

Beneath him, Belladonna was impaled on his big body, perhaps the most shocking and wonderfully powerful sensation she had ever known. Instinctively, she wound her arms around his neck as he thrust into her warm and wet folds. There was some pain at the first, but he was moving inside of her powerfully as her body accepted him, and the pain soon vanished.

All Belladonna could do was hang on to him and experience something she had waited all of her life for, finally belonging to Dashiell in every sense of the word. His skillful movements were creating something of a fire in her, something that seemed to be sparking low in her belly. Every time he thrust into her and pushed his pelvis against hers, the fire grew.

Dashiell knew what he was doing, building a fire in her loins that was growing to a fevered intensity. When her first climax came, she screamed out as much in surprise as in pleasure, and Dashiell put his mouth over hers to suck in all that pleasure to feed his own. It spoke to the very core of his manhood, experiencing something so powerful with the woman he loved. He could feel her tremors around his manhood, milking at him and demanding his seed, and he held out as long as he could.

It was truly something to behold.

But soon enough, he succumbed to the bone-jarring passion he was feeling for her and he released himself deep, imaging that his seed would find its mark on this night. A son from Belladonna would be the greatest gift he could possibly imagine. In fact, his release was so powerful that he bit his lower lip from the sheer pleasure of it.

He could taste his own blood.

Several long moments passed with only the sounds of heavy breathing in the chamber. Flat on her back on the mattress, Belladonna was pinned beneath Dashiell, but it was with the utmost pleasure. Her arms were around him, and his arms were around her, and nothing was more important than this moment in time.

It was what she had wished for, as long as she could remember, and finally, her wish was a reality. It was such a beautiful moment that it brought tears to her eyes and when Dashiell pulled back to look at her, he saw tears streaming down her temples.

"Bella?" he asked, greatly concerned. "Are you well, lamb? Did I hurt you?"

She smiled at him through her tears. "You did not hurt me," she whispered. "I am fine. I am simply overcome with the beauty of the moment. I love you, Dash, more than the heavens love the stars."

He smiled in return, kissing her nose, her cheek, and finally her lips. "And I love you," he murmured against her mouth. "You are my heart, Bella. Without you, I cannot live, nor can I breathe. You are what beats inside of me. I consider myself the most fortunate man who has ever lived."

Belladonna reached up, running her fingers through his thick hair. She was looking at him, drinking in his face, memorizing it for the months of separation to come. A finger moved over his bristly mustache, something that was so iconic with him.

"I wish you did not have to go," she murmured.

"As do I."

"Can I come with you?"

He smiled faintly. "I will put you with the infantry if you do. You can fight with the best of them."

She giggled. "I would rather stay in your tent and cook and clean for you. I could wash your clothes and make sure you are rested."

He cocked an eyebrow. "If you come with me, I will most definitely not be rested. I will spend all of my time just as we are now."

It was a kind way of telling her she could not go with him. He wasn't sure if she was serious or not, but better not to encourage it. He didn't want to spend his last hour with her denying her wishes as she begged.

Belladonna sensed that and, in truth, she wasn't entirely serious with her request. But she missed him already.

"Then I shall wait for you here," she said. "I shall watch the horizon every day for your return. Not a moment will go by without me thinking of you and wishing you were with me."

He shifted so that he was lying beside her, facing her in the weak light of the room. "As will I," he said, putting a big hand on her head and stroking her hair. "But I shall also look towards our future with hope and joy. You and I have a great life to live, together."

Belladonna was feeling content and sleepy after their coupling, but trying desperately to stay awake. She didn't want to relinquish one moment to something as ordinary as sleep. Laying her head against his chest as he wrapped his big arms around her, she sighed with satisfaction.

"Tell me of your father," she said. "I have never met him, you know. Do you think he will like me?"

Dashiell grinned as he thought of his father, the mighty and powerful Talus du Reims. He was a warrior, from a long line of warriors, a gruff man with a heart of gold.

"He will love you," he said confidently. "My mother passed on years ago, but my grandmother is still alive. She is extremely old but the last I saw her, she still retained her mind. Her name is Cantia and I adore her."

"Cantia? That is a lovely name," she said. "Does she live with your father?"

"She does. You will love her, too. In fact, my entire family will adore you, so you needn't worry. But I do have a confession."

"What?"

He sighed heavily. "I told you that I have younger brothers," he said. "Laurent is two years younger than I, and Torsten is the youngest. They are both married and, the last I heard, they had nothing but daughters between them. That means it is up to you to produce a son."

She snorted. "Must we speak of this already?"

"Probably not, but I suppose I should tell you now rather than later."

Belladonna started to laugh. "I have been told the ways of men and women, but no one has told me how I should force my body to have a son over a daughter."

"Is that so?"

"It is."

Dashiell grinned as his arms tightened around her. Already, he could feel himself growing hard again, his body electrified by the woman in his arms.

"I think it all has to do with how many times I can bed you in a night," he said seductively. "The more I bed you, the more chances there are of us having a son."

She craned her neck back, giving him such a disbelieving expression that he burst out into soft laughter.

"I think you are simply trying to take advantage of me, sir," she said.

He rolled over her, his big body on top of her once again as his mouth latched on to her tender earlobe.

"I would never do that," he murmured.

Belladonna giggled and gasped as he suckled on her earlobe and, soon enough, he was acquainting himself with her tender body yet again, gently taking his wife a second time.

It was the best night of their lives.

CHAPTER TWENTY-ONE

Due to the fact that he'd been kept in near darkness for months on end, Clayton shied away when men bearing torches entered his cell. The light hurt his eyes and he pressed back into a corner, trying to get a look at who, exactly, had come for him.

He didn't even know what time it was much less what day. He'd tried to keep track for the first month but, after that, he simply lost interest. Nothing held interest for him anymore and when he saw armed men entering his cell, he was quite certain he was about to be executed. When he saw Dashiell standing in front of the group, he was positive.

This was to be his last day on earth.

"Well?" he demanded. "What do you want, du Reims? I've no time for your idiocy so if you have come to taunt me, be gone with you. You bore me."

Dashiell couldn't even muster the energy to shake his head at the man's belligerent attitude; *this is to be the next Duke of Savernake*, he thought with disgust. With a heavy sigh, he fixed on Clayton.

"I have not come to taunt you," he said. "I have brought men of power with me. We have a message for you and you will listen."

Clayton snorted, keeping his face turned away from the bright torches. "Get out," he growled. "I do not want you here."

"Edward is dead."

That drew a reaction from Clayton. Suddenly, he wasn't so belligerent. Lifting his head, his weakened eyes squinted in the torchlight as he looked at Dashiell.

"He is?" he asked, astonished. "What happened?"

"He choked to death."

Clayton's mouth popped open in surprise. "My... God. Is it really true?"

"It is."

"I am sure all of Ramsbury is in mourning now."

Dashiell had absolutely no patience for his mock-sympathy, or whatever he was displaying. He turned to look at Langton, standing beside him.

"This is the Archbishop of Canterbury," he said. "This is Stephen Langton. He has something to say to you and you will listen closely."

Clayton stared at the man in the darkness.

"My lord," he greeted warily. "What do you want of me?"

There was suspicion in his question and Langton took a step closer, eyeing the weasel of a man who would now shoulder a very powerful dukedom. He'd spent all night agonizing about it but, in the end, he still maintained his original decision.

Either Clayton or John...

"I have come to discuss a life choice with you," he said frankly. "I want you to look around your cell at the men who are here and understand that I am supported in what I shall say to you. If you do not recognize these men, I will tell you who they are – the Earl of Hereford and Worchester, Christopher de Lohr. The Earl of Canterbury, David de Lohr. Sir Marcus Burton, Lord Somerhill. Sir Gart Forbes, Lord Tivington. Sir Gavin de Nerra, the Itinerant Justice of Hampshire. We also have Sir Bric MacRohan, Captain of the Guard for the House of de Winter. You will further recognize men you serve with here at Ramsbury – Viscount Winterton, Dashiell du Reims, Sir Bentley of Ashbourne, and Sir Aston Summerlin. Do you know and recognize these men?"

Clayton was looking around the cell now that his eyes were adjusting to the torchlight. "I do," he said.

"Excellent," Langton said. "Then when we speak to you of issues, you will understand the seriousness of it."

"What issues?"

"Be still and I will tell you."

Clayton backed down from his usual abrasive manner. When Langton saw the subdued behavior, he continued.

"You are in this vault because of an act of attainder," he said. "You are charged with attempted murder against the Duke of Savernake. Do you understand these charges, le Cairon?"

Clayton didn't want to admit anything, but he found himself staring at the Archbishop of Canterbury, perhaps the greatest ecclesiastical mind of his time. The man was also well versed on the laws of the land. That being the case, Clayton was careful in how he proceeded.

"I understand that du Reims has brought these charges against me," he said. "But I've not had a trial. I have been kept in this filthy hole to rot at his whim."

Langton had little patience for his denials. "Everyone knows what you did in order to gain the marriage to Savernake's heiress," he said. "And everyone knows you have been trying to murder the duke since that very day. There is no use in denying the charges, for every man in England knows them to be the truth. I could very easily have de Nerra order your execution based on the testimony of many witnesses. You *do* understand that, don't you?"

Clayton was starting to feel cornered. "If you are going to do it, then get on it. Why carry on so?"

Langton cocked an eyebrow. "Because we are here to strike a bargain with you."

Clayton thought that sounded both strange and encouraging. "What bargain?"

"With Edward dead, you are the new Duke of Savernake," Langton said. "It is your right, as the husband to the heiress. But given you have committed an act of attainder, that right can just as easily be stripped from you. If you do not agree to our bargain, it will be, without hesitation. Therefore, you will listen carefully, le Cairon."

Now Clayton was bloody curious about all of this. "I am listening."

Langton continued. "We will restore you to your full title, but with conditions. Firstly, you will not have freedom of rule or of decision. You will answer to the Earl of Hereford and Worcester, the Earl of Canterbury, Gavin de Nerra, Dashiell du Reims, or myself. You cannot make a move or a decision without our approval. That is the first condition. Do you understand and agree?"

Clayton frowned. "But *I* am the duke."

"Only under our good graces. As I said, we can strip that from you at any time for the crimes you have committed. Either you accept our terms, or you lose the dukedom. It is that simple."

Clayton realized this wasn't going to be an easy thing. He could see that these men, some of the most powerful in England, intended to control him one way or another.

He fully understood that they had evidence against him; although he would never admit it, he knew they had enough evidence against him to execute him. However, he wanted his freedom. He wanted to be the Duke of Savernake, and these men were willing to strike up a bargain with him so that he could be.

But he was coming to see that it wouldn't be on his terms.

"Go on," he grumbled. "What else?"

"You have no command or power over the army or over your wealth," Langton said. "Du Reims will continue to command the army and de Nerra and I will administer your wealth. If you want to spend money, you must gain our permission. If you want to raise taxes on your lands, you must gain our permission. If you want to do anything that has to do with administering your lands or wealth, you must gain our permission. Are we clear so far?"

By this time, Clayton was turning red in the face. "But I am the *duke!*"

"In name only. You shall be powerless. If you want your freedom, these are the conditions."

Clayton was outraged. When he forced himself into a marriage with Lily those years ago, this was not what he had anticipated. He'd anticipated wealth and status. He'd fought and schemed for three years to get what he wanted, only to fail at the end. Now, just when it seemed as if he would finally receive his due, it was an empty version of his most ardent desire. What he was getting was a title with nothing behind it.

No glory, no power. Just the title.

"You cannot do this to me," he said through clenched teeth. "It is *my* right."

Langton lifted an eyebrow. "Who are you going to complain to?" he asked. "John? He would laugh in your face and strip you of your title, leaving you penniless. Do you know how badly he wants to get his hands on the Savernake fortune? Go to him and complain, and you will discover just how much he wants it. Now, if you want the title, as you so badly do, you must agree to our conditions. You have no choice."

Clayton could see that. Now, he understood why all of these powerful men were crowding into his cell – it was a show of force. They were showing him what he would be up against should he refuse their bargain or, worse still, accept it and go back on his word.

He knew he was cornered, but for a man whose ambition had clouded every aspect of his judgment, he couldn't admit it. To agree to their terms would be to surrender everything. But on the other hand, he was a smart man. He could agree to their terms yet still carve out a measure of power and wealth for himself. He was good at that, wasn't he? Fooling men and getting what he wanted in the end? It had worked with Edward de Vaston – it would work with this group.

They thought they had him where they wanted him, but Clayton would prove differently.

He would win in the end.

"Very well," he finally spit out the words. "You have my agreement."

Langton could see in his eyes that he didn't mean it, not in the least. There was something glittering in Clayton le Cairon's eyes that bespoke of a man who would lie, cheat, and steal to get what he wanted. He'd already done that, and if Langton was any judge of character, he was going to do it again.

He knew, in that instant, that they were going to have trouble with the new Duke of Savernake.

"Swear your oath to me," Langton said. "Swear to me on God's holy name that you will adhere to the terms of this bargain."

"I swear."

The glitter in Clayton's eyes was still there. He was taking a vow he never intended to keep. But Langton didn't refute him; he wouldn't lower himself to argue with a liar.

But he knew, in that instant, that something would have to be done.

"The army is departing in less than hour," he said as he turned away. "Your horse will be prepared, and your armor and weapons will be brought to you here. You will dress and ride out with army."

Clayton looked at the group with some concern. "Where are we going?"

"You will be briefed on the way."

With that, the men filtered out of the dank, damp cell, leaving the new Duke of Savernake locked inside, yelling after them how unfair they were for keeping him there.

But he was ignored. They'd accomplished what they had set out to do, but instead of feeling satisfaction, all most of them could feel was depression that such a man now held a prestigious dukedom.

But none was more depressed than Langton. He was coming to wish he'd never made the proposal, that he had come up with another solution. But there *was* no other solution. As the group trickled out of the vault and into the early morning beyond, Langton hung back, motioning to Christopher and Bric as he did.

While the others continued on, including Dashiell, Langton came to a halt and pulled Christopher and Bric into a huddle.

"That man is lying upon his oath," Langton said quietly. "We are going to have trouble with him. I can see it in his face."

Christopher cocked an eyebrow. "If you believe that, then we will not release him," he said. "He can remain in that cell and rot."

Langton shook his head sadly. "It is an unpleasant business sometimes when dealing with a man who would deliberately ruin the lives of others," he said. "My dear friend Edward was a great man. He deserves a better heir than the one he received. If only for Edward's sake, and the sake of his children, I should like to right what has been wronged."

"What do you have in mind?" Christopher asked.

Langton simply shook his head, seemingly miserable over the situation. "Mayhap... mayhap it is time for an intervention. Dashiell said it best – le Cairon came to Ramsbury looking for hospitality and should have been met with a sword to the gut. Had he done that, we should not be facing the situation we are now. Mayhap, it would have been the best thing to do, for all concerned."

Christopher and Bric glanced at each other, suspecting the solution that Langton had in mind, but he was unable to be plain about it. As a man of God, men's souls were his business. So was the protection of the righteous.

But even Langton could see that there was only great suffering ahead if Clayton le Cairon assumed the dukedom. It would be hell for all of them and, sometimes, in a situation like that, there was only one choice to be had, for the good of all. Bric actually voiced what they were all thinking.

"We are heading into battle, my lord," he said casually. "Many things can happen in battle, in fact. A man can enter into a fight and never emerge from it. I have been known to make sure of such a thing."

Langton and Christopher looked at Bric. "Then... such a thing is possible with le Cairon?" Langton asked seriously.

MacRohan's silver eyes glittered in a deadly fashion. "Not only possible, but probable," he said. "As you said, the wrongs should be righted. Edward de Vaston deserved better. Everyone at Ramsbury deserves better."

An understanding settled, one that had great impact on the three of them. *A plot.* Nay, not a plot... *justice.*

"Le Cairon is married to the heiress," Christopher said, looking at Langton. "The title rests with her. She can always marry again should her husband die."

Langton closed his eyes, refusing to acknowledge that they were discussing outright murder. "She can marry someone worthy," he said softly, "for this man is not. I can see Satan in his eyes."

"I've thought the same thing at times."

"Dashiell must never know about this conversation. He must be blameless."

"Aye, my lord."

"In fact, no one must know about this conversation. MacRohan, be on your way."

"Aye, my lord," Bric said quietly.

With that, he turned away, heading off into the night. The High Warrior wasn't afraid of the nasty, but the necessary jobs. Rather than let anyone else dirty their hands, Bric MacRohan was willing to assume the risk and pay the price.

He was a man with the true heart of a warrior and, in this case, he was willing to do what needed to be done to save all of them from a man who had been trouble all of his life. Most importantly, he'd be saving his friend, Dashiell, from a continued hellish existence. Poor Dashiell had spent three years living with a serpent, but if Bric had anything to say about it, that serpent was about to be quashed.

In truth, Bric had seen how Clayton had responded to the terms put forth, and he, like every man there, knew Clayton had been lying when he'd agreed to them. There had been no question. He knew that Clayton would do all he could to push his boundaries and assert himself. The struggle of Savernake, and the struggle of the rebels in general against a king they did not support, was bad enough without conflict from within.

Therefore, he felt no remorse in offering to eliminate a liar, a cheat, and a man who had tried many times to commit murder.

No remorse at all.

SHE WAS AWAKENED with a kiss.

Belladonna opened her eyes to the sight of Dashiell leaning over the bed, his face outlined in the dim light of the hearth. She smiled sleepily.

"Have you come back to me already?" she asked, reaching up to pull him down to her. "How long has it been since you left me?"

He grinned as she tugged on him, bracing his arms on either side of her as he kissed her again.

"It has only been two hours," he said. "The army is ready. We are riding out and I have come to say farewell."

Her smile vanished, and she was suddenly quite lucid. Rubbing her eyes, she sat up. "Already?"

"Aye."

He pulled her from the bed and into his arms, trying not to jab her with what he was wearing. He wished it was his flesh against hers but, unfortunately, he was in full battle gear. All he could do was put his arms around her and embrace her with the things on his body meant for death.

But Belladonna didn't care about the mail or the weapons, although his sheathed broadsword smacked her in the leg when he hugged her. She only cared for the fact that this was the moment she had been dreading.

He was leaving.

"Oh, Dash," she breathed, gazing up into his face and trying sincerely not to weep. "I do not want you to go."

He gave her a gentle squeeze before releasing her, cupping her face in his two big palms. "I know," he murmured. "I do not want to go, either, but I must. We knew this moment would come."

Belladonna nodded sadly. "We did," she said. "Will you at least write to me? Will you let me know how you are and what is happening?"

He sighed heavily. "I am not sure if that is wise," he said. "I will be in the heart of what is happening, privy to information and locations that we will not want John's loyalists to know. If they capture a messenger from me to Ramsbury, it is possible they will torture the man for information."

Her heart sank, but she understood. "Very well," she said. "Then… you will not send me any word at all?"

"I fear that I cannot, lamb. You will simply have to assume that I am well and that I shall be returning home to you as soon as I can."

Belladonna struggled against the depression that provoked. "As you say," she said. "But before you go, have you thought about what we are to do about Lily and her problem? I must know what you think we should do."

He nodded. "I have, somewhat," he said. "The good news is that Clayton is going with us. He is now the Duke of Savernake, but with severe restrictions on that position. He must answer to a committee of men, and he truly cannot make any decisions on his own, so the title he wanted so badly is completely empty. All that aside, he is going with the army and he will be away for a goodly while. That means you do not have to do anything immediate with Lily. If she wants to go away, she can, but there is no rush for her to do so. She will have time to plan and find a place that suits her."

Belladonna was relieved to hear it. "God be praised," she muttered. "Clayton will be away from Ramsbury and Lily will have room to breathe."

"At least for a while."

"How long do you think you will be gone?"

"It is difficult to say, but my suspicion is that this will be the last great push between the king and those who oppose him. I do not see this ending for several months, at least, mayhap even long enough for her to have the child and send it away."

Belladonna felt better that her sister would have some time to determine what she truly wanted to do, but saddened that it meant Dashiell would be away from her for an unknown length of time.

Several months, at least.

"Then I will help Lily determine what needs to be done," she said. "And I shall pray every day for your safety."

He kissed her, deeply this time, before gently releasing her. He just stood there a moment, looking at her, drinking in her beautiful face. There was so much sorrow in his heart that it was difficult to contain it. All he knew was that his heart was breaking to have to leave her so soon after their marriage.

He missed her already.

"You are my adored one," he said softly. "Never doubt for one moment that my love for you is stronger than the ages. I swear to you that I will return to you, Bella. Nothing can keep me from you, not even death."

She smiled tremulously. "I love you so," she whispered, standing on her toes to kiss him one last time. "There will not be one moment of the day when I am not thinking of you and praying for you."

When he kissed her one last time and moved for the door, she followed. But he quickly stopped her.

"It has started to rain again," he said. "I do not wish to remember you standing in the rain as I ride away. I want to remember you here, warm and safe. It is a memory I will hold dear."

Belladonna couldn't reply for the lump in her throat, but she nodded simply to please him. Dashiell touched her face one last time before quitting the chamber, shutting the door softly behind him.

It was then that Belladonna let the tears come, collapsing on the bed to weep softly at the thought of her beloved Dashiell riding into battle yet again. It was far too much for her to take.

But in the same breath, she realized that she hadn't given him a favor, something for him to remember her by, so she suddenly leapt up from the bed, rushing to her wardrobe and flinging open wide the doors. She had to give the man something of her, something to hold close on the cold nights ahead. On the peg nearest her was a yellow brocade gown, with a pattern of decorative ovals woven into it. Yanking it off the peg, along with the shift that went with it, she tossed them both onto the bed.

Quickly, she stripped off the robe she was wearing and pulled on the shift. It had long sleeves, snuggly fit for warmth, and over that she pulled on the yellow gown. It was heavy, with sleeves that draped to the ground, an elegant gown fit for the wife of a viscount and the daughter of a duke.

Her hair was already somewhat dressed, as she still had the golden circlet in her hair from her wedding hours early, so she did nothing more than run a brush through the golden-red waves, quickly, all the while hunting for her shoes. She found a pair of red slippers in the wardrobe, so she pulled them on hastily. The last thing she grasped was a red silk scarf, putting some of her scented oil on it, before making haste down to the bailey.

The sun was just starting to rise as she rushed from the keep and out into the wet bailey, which was swarming with men. It wasn't raining at the moment, and the men were all moving in an orderly fashion out of the gatehouse, in columns that marched solemnly into the wet-shrouded land beyond.

Unfortunately, she didn't see Dashiell. Belladonna was distraught that he might have already departed the gatehouse but she couldn't be certain since there were so many mounted men still in the bailey, so she dodged her way through the masses, heading straight for the gatehouse itself.

The west side of Ramsbury's gatehouse had steps and a raised entry, so Belladonna ran up the stairs, putting her in a perfect position to watch the men streaming beneath the raised portcullis and out onto the road beyond.

Anxiously, she watched for any sign of Dashiell, but so far all she had seen were infantry. So many men passed by her, some of them lifting a hand to wave to her, as the duke's daughter, and she lifted a hand to wave back. In days past, she and her sisters would perch themselves right on this staircase and watch the men depart Ramsbury. It was almost a tradition. But this morning, she was here for one man and one man alone.

And then, she saw him.

His helm was on, the lance in his right hand flying a standard of the amber and yellow Savernake colors. He was also wearing a heavy cloak against the inclement weather, a garment that was also of the dark amber background with small, yellow Savernake tridents embroidered into it. He was bringing up the rear of a group of mounted cavalry, and she waved the red silk scarf in the air, wildly, until he saw her. Then, he spurred his fat dappled-gray warhorse in her direction.

"Bella?" he asked, concerned. "What are you doing here, lamb? I told you that it was wet and I did not wish my last memory of you to be…"

She cut him off as he came near. "I know," she said quickly. "But I remembered that I forgot to give you a favor, something to keep by your heart, always. I could not let you go without a piece of me, Dash."

With that, she looped the red silk scarf around the upper portion of his left arm, tying it on tightly. Dashiell had pulled his excited steed to a halt, watching her face as she tied the favor on and made sure it wouldn't slip. She seemed determined to secure it tightly and he let her. He simply remained still while she fussed with the tie until it was to her liking.

"There," she said, lifting her eyes to his. "Now, you may go. Godspeed, my love."

He smiled faintly at her as the bright red scarf waved on his arm. "Thank you for this glorious gift," he murmured. "I will treasure it always."

With that, he spurred his warhorse onward and Belladonna watched him trot out into the cold morning beyond. A good portion of the army filled in behind him and she watched until she could no longer see him.

But it didn't matter. He was in her heart as surely as if he were in her arms. She could still see him, feel him, and taste him, and it was something she would hold to her for the rest of her life, come what may.

Godspeed, my love…

CHAPTER TWENTY-TWO

September
Newark, the Midlands

IT WAS CHAOS.

The battle of Newark Castle was in full swing and men were fighting with a ferocity rarely seen. On a bright autumn day that, under normal circumstances would have been lovely and peaceful, men were killing each other and taking great pleasure in it.

The king was boxed up in Newark Castle, which had the rebels frothing at the mouth. They wanted John, and they wanted him badly, so much so that they'd laid siege to Newark Castle with so many men that it looked like the population of a great city had ganged up around the old castle walls. Siege engines were hurling flaming projectiles over the walls and the Earl of Wolverhampton, Edward de Wolfe, had brought a great battering ram that his men, hidden behind archers bearing great shields, were using to try and damage the gatehouse enough so that men could start infiltrating the castle.

It was sheer madness, and that had only been the first day. But on the second day, things changed dramatically.

There were two fronts to the battle – around the castle itself and then a raging war in the fields to the east of the castle. While de Wolfe, Marcus Burton, Gart Forbes, and other warlords bombarded the castle, Savernake, along with de Winter, the Earl of Lincoln, Christopher and David de Lohr, William Marshal, and the king's half-brother William Longespée handled the mass of mercenaries in the open ground, an enormous army that had come down from the north to try and free the king.

But it had been a hard fight.

The mercenaries, fighting for the sheer pleasure of fighting, were brutal in their tactics. Already, Dashiell had seen them cut down several excellent knights and then cheer with glee when they were bathing in their blood. Even for seasoned warriors, it had been shocking. Therefore, the mounted knights were being shadowed by infantry because the mercenaries were specifically targeting the mounted men and the commanders of the infantry, hoping to cut the head off the rebellion so the infantry would scatter.

But it wasn't working; the infantry was protective of their commanders, Dashiell included, and after a particularly brutal fight that had lasted for several hours with a gang of mercenaries from Franconia, Dashiell and his men found themselves backing off somewhat so the men could have a few moments of rest. Pulling out their bladders of watered wine or flat ale, they drank deeply and took a moment to simply breathe, watching the fighting going on around them.

"Du Reims!"

Dashiell heard his name, turning to see a knight riding towards him astride a big bay warhorse with a huge gash on one leg. Given that he'd spent all morning trying to fend off fools from trying to kill him, Dashiell had his broadsword lifted as the man came near. But when he flipped up his visor, Dashiell gratefully lowered the sword.

"Sherston," he said with relief. "I did not know you were here."

Anthony Cromford grinned, his young face sweaty and grimy. "Aye," he said. "I rode in with the Earl of Lincoln. It's quite a mess we find ourselves in, isn't it?"

Dashiell snorted. "You could say that," he said. "It has been a while since we last spoke. How is your father?"

Sherston nodded. "Well, thank you," he said. "He wanted to come with me but, alas, he has an ailment of the joints that makes it so he can hardly hold a knife much less a sword."

"Ah," Dashiell said, raising his helm as he leaned forward on the saddle. "It is difficult to grow old. After watching the duke in his elderly years, I do not think I am looking forward to it, but it is better than the alternative."

Sherston laughed softly in understanding. "It is better than being dead," he agreed. But his smile quickly faded. "I have been looking for Clayton. Is he around here?"

Dashiell's smile vanished. Clayton was not his favorite subject to discuss, especially as of late. In the five months since leaving Ramsbury, Clayton had proved himself to be an absolute nightmare. He'd been given Edward's traveling tent, his attendants, and all of the trappings of the Duke of Savernake, and he'd done nothing but abuse what kindnesses he'd been given. He openly railed against Dashiell and anyone else who opposed him, and even now, he'd taken a contingent of overworked soldiers near the heart of the fighting because he was determined to prove himself a glorious warrior and a worthy duke.

Truly, everything about him had been a nightmare and Dashiell, as well as the other warlords, were at the end of their patience with him. But Sherston didn't know that, so Dashiell tried to be politely neutral when answering.

"If you want to speak with the Duke of Savernake, he is over towards the west, seeking glory," he said. "Or I can just as easily relay a message to him. He is not the most pleasant individual these days."

Sherston lifted his eyebrows. "I heard," he said. "News travels. I am very sorry about Edward's death, du Reims. He was a well-loved man. And what you now have in his place… as I said, I am very sorry."

Dashiell nodded. "As am I," he said. Then, he eyed Sherston for a moment. "Is this about the betrothal to Belladonna?"

Sherston shrugged, averting his gaze as he wiped at his sweaty face.

"In a sense," he said. "I shall be truthful, du Reims – I must refuse Clayton's marital offer. I cannot hold off any longer, even though I know you wanted me to give you time. But I simply cannot hold off."

Dashiell's lips twitched with a smile. "You do not need to," he said. "I married Belladonna before we left on campaign. But I am curious, what is so pressing that you must refuse now?"

Sherston gave him a rather comical look. "Because I married Jillayne Chadlington."

Dashiell burst out laughing. "God be praised," he snorted. "I had not heard. Congratulations, my friend. My wife will be very pleased to hear that her friend, Jillayne, has married such a fine young lord. Truly, it is good news."

Sherston smiled in return and started to reply when an arrow suddenly hit him in the neck. As he toppled from his horse, he and Dashiell were suddenly surrounded by a mass of fighting men. It was instant turmoil, and Dashiell was in a panic to get to the young lord as he lay upon the earth, bleeding to death.

Leaping from his warhorse, Dashiell began to fight his way through men whom he realized, to his horror, were wearing the colors of William Marshal.

And they were trying to kill him.

Greatly puzzled by the savagery of allied troops, Dashiell fought fiercely, reaching Sherston on the ground and trying to fight off the men that were stepping on the fallen knight. He saw the flash of a big broadsword in his periphery and brought up his weapon only to realize that it was Aston, fighting off more Marshal men that were trying to kill him.

"Aston!" Dashiell bellowed. "What has happened?"

Aston was exhausted and distressed. "Marshal and Longespée have turned against us," he said. "They have flanked us to the east and west, and de Lohr has suffered major casualties. Now they are coming after

Savernake."

Dashiell was shocked, but he didn't have time to dwell over it. His life depended on his ability to accept what he'd been told, and accept it quickly. Two allied rebel armies, once having sided with John, were now apparently in the king's fold again. *Damnation!* Dashiell thought.

The world was collapsing.

"How are the other armies?" Dashiell asked Aston. "De Winter and Burton and the rest? Are they suffering heavy casualties also?"

Aston nodded. "We are being crushed, Dash."

Those were ominous words, and Dashiell had to think quickly. The lives of his men, and potentially every man in the rebellion, depended on it. Bending over Sherston, he could see that the young man was dying; an arrow had gone through the right side of his neck, straight through to the other side, carving a nasty path through his flesh with a serrated arrowhead. It was a mess.

But Dashiell wasn't going to give up. Sherston was looking up at him, utter fear in his eyes, and Dashiell couldn't let the man down.

He wouldn't.

"I am going to put you on your horse," he told the young knight. "The horse will find its way out of this. All you need do is hold on. Do you hear me? Just hold on."

"My father," Sherston said, trying to speak even though his throat was destroyed. "You must tell my father."

"I will."

"And Jillayne…"

"She will know how glorious you were in battle, Anthony, I swear it."

Sherston was gurgling, unable to breathe because blood was in his lungs now. He coughed, spraying blood onto Dashiell, as both he and Aston lifted him back to his horse. More arrows were flying overhead and men with swords were trying very hard to kill each other. It was absolutely harrowing.

Once Sherston was thrown over his saddle, Dashiell turned the horse towards the north, where there seemed to be less fighting, but the horse was terrified and wouldn't run. It was then that Dashiell saw the banners of Longespée, now attacking de Winter men, and Dashiell knew in that moment that if he didn't do something, and do it quickly, they were all going to die.

In truth, he knew what he had to do.

There was little choice.

"Aston," he said. "Pass the word to de Lohr, de Winter, and the others. Tell them to retreat. This is a battle they cannot win. Tell them that Savernake will hold the line to cover their retreat, but tell them to get out of here. They must run."

Aston looked at him, a flash of pain crossing his features as he realized what Dashiell was suggesting. They couldn't all retreat because, surely, the Marshal and Longespée armies would follow. It would mean more slaughter. But if one army was willing to stay to hold the line, just long enough for the others to get away safely, then at least some of them would be saved.

Savernake had to make the sacrifice.

"Aye," he finally said. "I'll send word."

Dashiell could see the disappointment in Aston's face and he reached out, putting a hand on the man's arm. "It will be all right," he said. "Go, now. Spread the word. And our men must move over to the east to push back on Marshal and Longespée. Where is Bentley?"

"I saw him nearby. He is around here somewhere."

"Find him."

As Dashiell was issuing orders to Aston, both of them failed to see a scenario brewing behind Dashiell. There were men fighting all around them, creating enough of a distraction that both of them failed to see Clayton as he came up through the fighting masses.

He was on foot, his sights set on Dashiell, who had his back turned to him. It didn't take a genius to realize that Clayton was stalking him, once again giving in to the urges that told him to kill men who were in a stronger position then he was. First, it was Edward, and he'd tried for years to kill the man. Now, it was Dashiell.

Clayton hated him with a vengeance.

In fact, as Clayton saw it, Dashiell was the cause of all of his troubles. It had been Dashiell who had prevented him from killing Edward, and now it was Dashiell who was preventing him from enjoying what he saw as his right.

With Dashiell out of the way, there was nothing standing between him and the glory of Savernake, which belonged to him. Clayton had spent the past seven months, ever since Dashiell had him thrown into the vault of Ramsbury, stewing over a bastard who had denied him his entitlement.

But today... today, that was going to change.

Men fell in battle all of the time, and Dashiell du Reims would be no different.

So, Clayton moved up behind him, an ax in his hand, one he had taken from the hands of a dying Marshal man. With the ax planted in Dashiell's back, everyone would know that he had been killed by an enemy soldier. At least, that was the plan.

But the reality of it was much different. What happened occurred within the blink of an eye.

As Aston turned away from Dashiell, on his way to carry out Dashiell's orders, Clayton knew it was time to act. He pushed through the fighting masses, ax lifted. He was going to plant the thing right between Dashiell's shoulder blades. But suddenly, there was a body between him and Dashiell, and Clayton ended up planting the blade of the ax into Bentley as the knight put himself between Dashiell and the man who wanted to kill him.

As Bentley went down, Dashiell turned around to see Clayton behind him, looking down at Bentley in outrage. How dare the man foil his plans! But Dashiell never had the chance to retaliate – one minute, Clayton was snarling at him and in the next, the man's head was on the ground near his feet. His body remained upright for a few long, morbid seconds before Bric MacRohan gave it a kick and pushed it to the ground.

Dashiell found himself looking into Bric's deadly expression, and the bloodied sword in his hand, realizing that MacRohan had just killed Clayton.

God, it all happened so fast that Dashiell was struggling to process it, but as the screaming and dying went on around him, he knew he couldn't linger on it. He had to move. Suddenly, MacRohan was lifting Bentley up, shoving the wounded man into Dashiell's arms.

"Get him out of here!" he bellowed. "*Move!*"

Orders from the High Warrior weren't mean to be disobeyed. Dashiell put his hands under Bentley's arms and began dragging the man out of the fighting as Aston, who had seen the sequence of events, raced back to Dashiell's side, grabbing the reins of Sherston's frightened horse in the process.

Together, the two of them shuttled the injured warriors out of the heat of the fighting, heading for the fringes of the battlefield where the wounded were gathering. They left them with the physics and the priests who were tending to the dead and dying. Bentley survived his initial wound, but Sherston did not.

But, like all great heroes, Dashiell and Aston raced back into the heat of battle, determined to hold off the onslaught as the wounded rebel armies retreated. The last anyone saw of them, they were fighting for their lives against impossible odds.

Such tales of glory would be told for generations to come.

CHAPTER TWENTY-THREE

Early October
Amesbury Abbey

IT WAS WELL and good that she worked in the kitchen, for it gave her access to things most postulates would not have access to.

In this case, it was a tool for her salvation.

Acacia had spent the months since her arrival at Amesbury in torment. Her life was in shambles when she arrived at the abbey, made worse by the fact that Amesbury was a strict order that didn't believe in much more than praying and sleeping, and even sleeping was considered a sin. Conversation was prohibited unless it was the reading of scripture.

In truth, it had been nothing as Acacia had expected. All she wanted to do was read her bible and walk in the garden but, instead, Amesbury turned into a lesson in the harsh realities of piety. The nuns in charge were old and shriveled, and had no patience for a duke's daughter who had been pampered her entire life. Acacia slept little, was constantly cold, and she had been assigned to the kitchens to work when she was not praying.

For a woman wrought with depression and insecurities, the hoped-for haven at Amesbury was a fate worse than death.

With little choice in the matter, Acacia worked in the kitchen, cleaning dirty vegetables for an old cook who liked to throw things at her when she didn't work fast enough. She prayed through chattering teeth and cried herself to sleep nightly. She wanted to go home, but she was quite certain her sisters didn't want her. She had ruined her relationship with them, and they were against her, so she knew she could not go home.

But her prayers soon became requests for Clayton to come and save her from this hell, and take her someplace where she could be warm and happy again. The postulates were not allowed to write or send missives, so Acacia would have to rely on God to whisper in Clayton's ear to tell him what she needed.

She was still convinced, even after all of these months, that Clayton needed her. He wanted her – *surely* he missed her. Therefore, she knew that he must come for her at some point.

But that point never came.

Months passed. In spite of the fact that Acacia was hardly eating anything, her belly began to grow and her menses stopped. It wasn't until the child in her belly began to move around that she realized she was with child, *Clayton's* child, and panic seized her. In the many times Clayton had bedded her, conceiving a child had never occurred to her, either through stupidity or ignorance, or both. But it should have.

God help her, it should have.

After that, her prayers turned to tear-filled pleas to God to kill the child in her womb. She couldn't stand the shame of bearing a bastard but, more than that, it complicated the situation so terribly. Lily would certainly never forgive her if she returned home with Clayton's child in her arms, and everyone at Ramsbury would know she had fornicated with a man who was not her husband. Perhaps they wouldn't know it was Clayton, but they would know she had been bedded by some fool who had left her with his child. It would make any potential marriage impossible unless she lied, and convinced everyone else to lie, that she'd been married before, but her husband had been killed.

Yet… she knew it was impossible.

Acacia had no direction in life, no one to turn to, and returning to

Ramsbury was not an option. She had burned her bridges there and, truth be told, she wasn't sure she wanted to mend them. She wasn't certain there was any point to it. But seven months away from home, toiling away at Amesbury, had taught her something – she knew she could no longer face what her life had become. She could no longer face what she'd done to herself.

Clayton was never coming for her. She knew that now. He hadn't needed her as he said he had and, as the days passed, she came to understand she'd been lied to. He'd lied to her about everything and she'd ruined her relationship with her sisters over it.

She couldn't live with the shame.

Therefore, she took something from the kitchens that night after supper. A small copper knife, very sharp, and one she used to cut vegetables with. Now, this little knife would be her way out of her predicament. After the postulates were sent to bed that evening, Acacia lay on her bed at the end of the dormitory, listening to the sniffling and the snoring of the other postulates, and pulled out her little knife.

The embarrassment, the depression, ate at her until she could no longer think straight. She had to end what she had created. Dragging the sharp part of the blade across both wrists, she cut as deeply as she could.

Blood, bright red, dripped down her flesh and onto the thin woolen cover she was allowed. But through it all, Acacia remarkably kept her mouth shut. No cries of anguish, no gasps. She simply closed her eyes and, as the tears fell onto her musty straw mattress, she imagined better days when she was young and free, and her father was without his madness, and Clayton had yet to marry Lily.

These were the best days of her life, when she and her sisters still loved one another and there wasn't anything to come between them, not bad judgment nor jealousy nor men. It was just the three of them, and she missed that desperately.

In the end, Acacia knew she'd been wrong, but she simply didn't know how to fix it. Instead, she clung to old memories, even as a strange buzzing filled her head and she grew progressively weaker. Blood soaked the mattress, spilling out onto the dirt floor. By the time it was discovered before dawn, it was too late.

The Lady Acacia de Vaston had passed on from one purgatory to another.

CHAPTER TWENTY-FOUR

Mid-October
Ramsbury Castle

GIVEN HOW WET the spring and summer had been, by the time autumn came, the weather was remarkably dry. The sky was a brilliant blue and a scattering of clouds crossed it, pushed along by a gentle breeze. It was colder now, with the hint of oncoming winter but, for the most part, the weather had been delightful. It was, perhaps, the only delightful aspect of Ramsbury these days.

The army was still away, still battling the king and his band of mercenaries. In the beginning, those at Ramsbury received word from time to time from people passing by, perhaps merchants or noblemen looking for lodging for the night, who spoke of the French fleet that had come ashore in May and how the rebels now held most of southern England.

But that didn't mean Savernake's army came home to roost because there was some peace in the south. On the contrary, Savernake's army, along with de Lohr and de Winter and the rest of them, were pushing the king and his mercenaries out of the country, with battle after battle, now pushing northward to reclaim lands and properties the king and his mercenaries had held. As Dashiell had told Belladonna, there would be no missives forthcoming for fear they would fall into the wrong hands, so any news Ramsbury received was purely by chance.

At first, the lack of information had been torture. Months passed and the absence of news from Dashiell had been devastating for

Belladonna and Lily. To combat the anxiety, they kept busy. They tended the puppies, the keep, and the poor. They were the benevolent benefactors of Ramsbury, holding fast to the few tidbits of news they were gleaning from their visitors and rumor.

But as the summer had arrived, a kind of numbness overcame them when it came to the lack of news. They'd learned to live with it. Summer days passed and, finally, more news came by way of a traveling merchant. There was fighting in the Midlands now, with the king bottled up in Newark Castle. The rebels were on the cusp of victory, it seemed, and Belladonna and Lily were comforted. Their men would soon be home.

But devastating news was soon to come their way.

In October, a cart from Amesbury arrived at Ramsbury, delivering the remains of Acacia. She had killed herself, an exhausted and bitter old nun said, and they would not bury her at Amesbury. She had sinned in death, as well as in life, and they wanted nothing to do with her.

The old crone proceeded to inform the sisters that Acacia had been with child and had undoubtedly killed herself over the shame of such a thing. After that, she would say no more. Leaving the casket at the gatehouse, the procession from Amesbury hurried away as fast as they could, leaving nothing but sorrow in their wake.

It had been a shattering revelation for Belladonna and Lily to realize what Acacia had done. A serious quarrel with their sister, one that time and forgiveness should have resolved, was now never to know resolution. Acacia had seen to that. If only she'd been able to reach out to her sisters with her sorrows, if only they had reached out to her to heal the rift... Belladonna and Lily simply couldn't fathom what the price of their anger had brought them. Acacia was dead.

And then... there was the child.

That was perhaps the most shocking news of all, and the sisters could only assume it was Clayton's child. But Lily, in particular, was in no position to judge Acacia for what she'd done considering that she, too, carried the child of a man to whom she was not married. Lily wished with all her heart that she could tell Acacia that she forgave her, but there would be no forgiveness now as a quarrel with her would never be mended in this life.

It was something she and Belladonna would now have to live with.

All fights, hatreds, and anger were forgotten on the day Acacia came home. The sisters had wept over the coffin of their beloved sibling even as the sentries at the gatehouse lifted it up and took it over to the chapel where, most recently, their father had been buried. That was where they intended to bury Acacia no matter how she had met her death. Surely God would be forgiving to a woman who clearly felt she had no other option.

Dashiell had left two hundred men behind at Ramsbury to protect and defend it, and he'd left a very old sergeant in charge, a man who had served Edward for nearly his entire reign. Joachim was the old sergeant's name, and Belladonna and Lily had come to include the old man in their decisions, mostly because he was wise and seemed to think much as their father had.

When it came to Acacia's burial, they discussed it with him and old Joachim was under the impression that no matter what Acacia had done, her father would want her buried with him. Therefore, a fresh grave was dug in the ground of the chapel of Ramsbury, right next to Edward, and Acacia was laid to rest next to her father. It was the last act of mercy that the sisters could give her.

And that had been their lives for the past seven months. There had been heartache, but there had also been days of normalcy, something that was desperately need. Yet, there were also pressing issues that grew more pressing with time – Lily was not too far from giving birth to her child and, for the past several months, she and Belladonna had discussed the many things she could do so that Clayton would never know of his wife's condition. Belladonna had told her of Dashiell's recommendations, and Lily had told her of Bentley's.

At first, Lily was leaning heavily towards running off to Weymouth to live with Bentley's spinster aunt. In fact, that had been her plan until Acacia had been brought home in a wooden box. After that, she didn't seem to have much inclination to leaving, instead, sitting in her chamber and sewing garment after garment for her baby.

Belladonna would sit with her a good deal of the time but whenever she spoke of leaving for Weymouth, Lily didn't seem too keen on it. Although she wouldn't discuss her feelings on the matter these days, Belladonna suspected that Lily simply didn't want to leave her sister or her home. Acacia's death had done something to her, perhaps forcing her to realize just how precious her love for her family was. Lily and Belladonna had grown closer in the past several months and Lily became very emotional when it came to leaving.

She simply didn't have the heart to do it.

But time was drawing close and if Lily was to travel to Weymouth, she had to do it soon. She didn't want to be caught out on the open road having her child. Running out of options, she mentioned to Belladonna that she was considering having the child at Ramsbury and then giving it to the servants to tend. That way, she could be near the child yet still at home, where the people she knew and loved were. Clayton would never know a servant's infant was his wife's child, because the man never lowered himself to speak to or even acknowledge the servants.

He would never be the wiser.

In truth, it made perfect sense to Belladonna and she even went so far as to take old Joachim into her confidence to explain the situation, hoping the old man would have some suggestions for her. He did, in the form of recommending his own wife to tend the infant and tell everyone it was their grandchild.

When Lily heard of the plan, she wanted to meet Joachim's wife, who lived in the village in a tiny cottage and not on the grounds of the castle. She was a beer wife, supplying beer to the taverns in the village, and old Heddy immediately took a liking to Lily, and Lily to her. It seemed like a perfect situation.

It was a plan that brought Lily and Belladonna a great deal of comfort and, nowadays, everyone seemed more at ease than ever before. It made the fact that there had been no recent news of the army's movement easier to bear and on this mild October day, the sentries at the gatehouse announced the arrival of a lord and his daughter, who had stopped to seek shelter for the night.

Belladonna, who had been feeding the dogs, with several of the grown puppies from the spring litter now to feed, heard the noise from the gatehouse and left the dogs to go to the bailey to greet the visitors.

The pair had quite an entourage of wagons, and ten heavily-armed men, who the Savernake soldiers separate from the caravan. They normally stripped all weapons from visiting soldiers. As the wagons were moved away, leaving the lord and his daughter standing in the middle of the bailey, Belladonna greeted them politely.

"Good afternoon, my lord," she said. "I am Lady du Reims. May I ask your business?"

The lord dipped his head politely. "Lady du Reims," he said. "I am Lord Corston and this is my daughter, Clarimund. We are traveling from Reading to Bath and hoped to seek shelter for the night."

Belladonna nodded. "We would be happy to provide you with shelter," she said, "but there is a tavern in town that might also prove comfortable."

Corston shook his head. "I am bringing goods back to Bath and have a good deal to protect," he said. "It would be difficult to do that in a livery. Is our presence of great inconvenience, my lady?"

Belladonna shook her head. "It is not. Please come with me and I shall take you to the hall to rest while I have a chamber prepared for you."

Lord Corston grasped his tiny daughter by the elbow as they began to follow Belladonna across the bailey, towards the dark-stoned great hall.

"Truly, travel has been quite easy these days," he said, simply to make conversation. "The land is peaceful this far south. None of the madness that I hear is happening to the north."

That drew Belladonna's attention. Since all of the news they'd had in the past several months had been from passing travelers, she wondered if Lord Corston could tell her anything new.

"It has been peaceful here," she agreed. "You said you just came from Reading?"

Corston nodded. "We were in London before that, on a purchasing trip. I own a merchant shop in Bath."

"Would you show me some of your goods before you leave? Mayhap, I should like to purchase something."

"It would be an honor, Lady du Reims," he said. "What castle is this, by the way?"

"Ramsbury Castle."

Corston looked around at the massive walls with very few soldiers about for such a large place. "It seems rather empty," he said, pointing to the battlements. "Such a large fortress should be heavily defended, I should think."

Belladonna glanced up to the battlements. "Our army is away."

"Fighting against the king?"

"Aye."

Corston's manner seemed to demure. "It has been an ugly business, to be sure," he said. "It was all we heard of in London."

By this time, they had entered the mouth of the hall. It was somewhat dark and cold beyond, with a few servants sweeping the hearth or scrubbing down the tables. Belladonna led her guests to the long feasting table next to the hearth and asked one of the servants to start a fire once the ashes were all swept away. She sent another servant for bread and wine before turning back to Corston.

"It should be warm in a moment," she said. "What did you hear about the wars? In London, I mean. What were people saying?"

Corston sat heavily, a weary sigh emitting from lips. "Have you not heard about the king, then?"

"Heard what?"

"He is dead."

Belladonna's eyes widened. "Nay," she said, shocked. "We've not heard much here, unfortunately. Our army is fighting against the king and the commanders told us they would not send us any word, fearful it would fall into enemy hands. We have had to rely on travelers like you to tell us what is happening. The king is dead, you say? When did this happen?"

Corston nodded. "Last month," he said. "A sickness of the bowels took him, but it was after a very nasty battle, evidently, one in which he gained victory over the rebel army. But only momentarily. You said your army was fighting against the king?"

"Aye."

Corston lifted his eyebrows ominously. "From what I heard in London, the battle near Newark Castle was very bad for the rebel cause," he said. "That is where John died, you know. At Newark. Are you aware that William Marshal and the king's half-brother, William Longespée, had turned against the king?"

Belladonna really knew nothing about it. Dashiell had never told her of such things and she'd never asked, so all of this was new information.

"I had not heard," she admitted. "My... my husband never really spoke of the politics of the rebellion. But I do know that William

Marshal has always served the king, as did his father. I find that astonishing that he should betray John."

The wine and bread came, accepted gratefully by Corston and his daughter. Corston took a heavy drink before replying.

"Marshal's betrayal was short-lived," he said. "He and Longespée sided with John once again in the end, but their defection was not anticipated by the rebels. When those two turned on the rebel army, it was a slaughter at Newark, so I am told."

"What do you mean?"

Corston took another long drink of wine, smacking his lips. "The rebels were caught off-guard," he said. "I met a man in London, who had been at Newark, and he told me that some of the great armies were severely damaged – de Lohr, de Winter, and Lincoln among them. Have you heard of them? Very old and great families. In any case, as these great families are being beaten down by the traitors Marshal and Longespée, another army sacrificed itself so they could pull free. This army put itself between the rebel army and John's loyalists long enough for the wounded rebel army to escape. It must have been a sight to see."

A warning bell went off in Belladonna's mind. She didn't know why it should, but something told her she didn't want to know the name of that sacrificial army. It sounded like something a noble commander would do, laying down his life so that others would live. It sounded very much like something Dashiell would do. With the greatest reluctance, she asked the fatal question.

"Who was the martyred army?"

"Savernake, I think."

Belladonna's breath caught in her throat. She heard the name – *Savernake* – but it took her several long moments for the reality to sink in. Then, she began to feel lightheaded.

"Sav… Savernake, you say?" she breathed.

Corston was oblivious to the tone of her voice. He was too busy finishing off his wine. "Aye."

"How long ago?"

"Mere weeks, so I heard," he said. "It is a sad story, truly. I've heard of the Savernake army; I think every man in England has. A mighty army, I'm told. If what they did was true – and they sacrificed themselves so the rebels had a chance to retreat – then it is a great and noble sacrifice, indeed. But for them to fall to traitors like Marshal and Longespée is an unfitting ending at best."

Belladonna found herself gripping the table so she wouldn't fall to the floor; the room was beginning to sway.

Sacrifice...

The word was ringing in her head as if someone had struck a bell. There was an odd buzzing in her ears, reverberating, singing out that terrible word that the merchant had so callously spouted.

Sacrifice...

"And... and you say that you are certain of this?" she asked, her voice oddly hoarse.

Corston was into his bread now, chewing loudly. "As I said, I met a man in London who said he was at Newark when it happened," he said. "Unless the man was lying. But it is true that John has died and now young Henry is upon the throne. That is cause enough for the rebels to ease their onslaught, only now, they have to contend with the French, who do not wish to leave our shores. If you ask me, the rebels should have never brought them here in the first place."

The man was rattling on with no idea what damage he was doing. Every word out of his mouth was like a dagger to Belladonna's heart. The more he spoke, the more injured she became until, finally, she stood up, greatly unsteady on her feet from the news spinning around in her head.

"I... I will see to your chambers," she said, her voice trembling.

"Thank you, Lady du Reims," he said as she turned away. "Ramsbury Castle... I have heard this name before, but I cannot place it. May I ask whose residence this is?"

Belladonna came to a halt, heart pounding, panic filling her veins. She stood there, weaving unsteadily. "The residence of the de Vaston family," she said. Then, she turned to look at him. "The Dukes of Savernake."

Corston stopped chewing and his eyes widened. "Saver –" He swallowed hard, bolting to his feet when he realized what he had done. "My lady, I did not know. Please forgive me for... God's Blood, forgive me for being so ignorant. I did not know this was the seat of the Savernake army."

Belladonna couldn't help it; her eyes filled with tears. "It is," she whispered. "The men you speak of... those are *my* men. My husband."

Corston was devastated. The man looked positively ill. "Forgive me," he breathed. "I have not heard how they fared after the battle, only that they saved the retreating army by fighting off John and his mercenaries. Surely... surely some have fared well. Surely the army is still intact for the most part. They have not returned home yet?"

He was trying to undo the damage he had done, but it was too late. Belladonna shook her head, quickly wiping away her tears so this fool of a man wouldn't see them.

"Nay," she said. "I will go and see to your chambers now."

With that, she ran off, running from the hall and leaving Corston and his daughter utterly shattered over what had happened. Corston's daughter began to weep softly as Corston sat down and poured himself another cup of wine. He drank the entire thing on two gulps.

Meanwhile, Belladonna was struggling not to become hysterical, running for her sister's chamber in the keep. By the time she entered the tall, dark foyer of the keep and headed up the narrow stairs, she was openly sobbing. She burst into Lily's chamber and nearly frightened the woman to death.

"Bella!" Lily gasped, pricking herself with her needle because she was so startled. "What is the matter with you?"

Belladonna was trying very hard to catch her breath, trying to bring forth the terrible words that would cause Lily to understand just how awful everything was. Rushing to her sister's side, she fell to her knees and buried her face in Lily's swollen lap.

"A-A lord and his daughter are here," she sobbed. "They-they are seeking shelter for the night. The-the lord said he had just come from London and he heard that the Savernake army sacrificed itself to save men who were being destroyed by the king's army. He said they are martyrs!"

Lily went pale. "Sweet Mary," she breathed. "It cannot be true."

"It is!"

Belladonna was so hysterical that Lily had to grab her by the hair in order to pull the woman up so that she could look at her.

"Bella, *stop!*"

"They're dead!"

Lily slapped her sister across the face, hoping to jar her out of her hysteria. The sharp sound coupled with the sting did the trick; Belladonna gasped and her hand flew to her left cheek, already turning red from the force of Lily's slap. But the wild sobbing stopped as Belladonna realized she'd been out of control. Still, the tears fell as she looked at her sister's ashen face.

"I am sorry," Lily murmured. "Bella, you must get control of yourself. Tell me what happened."

Belladonna swallowed, laboring to think clearly. "The lord told me that John's army was beating the rebel army because William Marshal and William Longespée had turned on the rebels," she said, her voice trembling. "He said that some of the rebel armies were being destroyed and that the Savernake army fought off the king's men so the beaten rebels could retreat."

Lily looked at her with such horror in her expression that it was like a blow to the gut. "Oh, God… no," she whispered. "When did this happen?"

"He said only a few weeks ago, at most. He was not for certain."

As Belladonna dissolved into quiet tears, Lily simply sat there and stared at her. She simply couldn't accept that Dashiell and Bentley might never be coming home. And what of Clayton?

Was he never to come home, either?

Lily was torn, greatly torn, with all of the feelings stirring within her breast. If Clayton met his death on the field of battle, then he was never returning. God, she felt so wicked for praying that was true, hoping God wouldn't punish her by taking Bentley away from her, too.

Lily's mixed feelings ran deep.

But Belladonna's feelings weren't mixed at all. She was only thinking of Dashiell, the strong and glorious commander of Savernake's army. Covering the retreat of his friends, of his cousins, sounded so much like something the man would do. That was why men loved him so much. They knew Dashiell du Reims would always do what was true and right, for everyone. But sometimes, that true and right attitude meant that Dashiell put himself secondary to other men.

Belladonna prayed that this wasn't one of those times.

"Bella," Lily said as she tried to wrangle her emotions. "Sit down, sweetheart. We must speak of this and you must be calm."

Belladonna closed her eyes, tears popping from them. "I do not know if I can be."

Lily sighed heavily. "You must," she said. "You married a knight, Bella. You must know that something like this could always happen."

"But what about Bent?" Belladonna wept. "Do you not fear that he, too, will never return?"

Lily's composure took a hit, but she held fast. "Of course I do," she said. "But weeping like a child will not bring him back to me, one way or the other. Do you think Dash would be happy to see you falling to pieces? I do not think so. He would want you to be strong. They would both want us to be strong."

She was right. Belladonna's heart was breaking as she realized that Lily was right; she needed to pull herself together. She was shaming Dashiell with her behavior. He would want her to be strong and she was failing at it miserably.

Now, she was ashamed. Dashiell du Reims' wife should be the strongest woman in all of England, not the weakest.

Do you think Dash would be happy to see you falling to pieces?

Of course, he wouldn't be. He deserved better.

Taking a deep breath, Belladonna tried very hard to stop her tears. It was the most difficult thing she'd ever had to do in her life, but it was important. She wanted to make Dashiell proud, in everything she did. For him, she would be the strongest woman she could be, even in the face of such terrible news. Wiping the tears from her face, she turned to her sister.

"You are correct, of course," she said. "Forgive me. It will not happen again."

Lily watched her youngest sister take a seat, sitting stiffly, trying so hard to be brave. In truth, Lily was only marginally composed herself.

"Now," she said. "I will speak with this lord myself, but we must remember that what he heard was only rumor. Did he witness any of this first-hand?"

Belladonna shook her head. "Nay. He said he heard it from a man in London who said he witnessed the battle."

Lily nodded shortly. "But men tell tall tales sometimes. We know that they can create a terrible situation where none existed."

"That is true."

"Mayhap it is not as bad as the lord has told you."

"There is that possibility," Belladonna said. "Mayhap we should send a couple of the men into the towns in the area and see if they can discover anything about this battle."

"That is a very good idea. Ask Joachim to select two men to do that."

"I will," Belladonna said, feeling better now that they were taking some kind of action to get to the core of the truth. It was certainly better than living with the fear of the unknown. "I will ask him right now."

Lily smiled encouragingly at her. "Good lass," she said. Then, she set her sewing aside. "I suppose I should see to the evening meal. We have guests, after all."

Belladonna reached out, pulling her sister up from her chair. Lily's belly was quite enormous with Bentley's child and things like sitting and standing often needed assistance. Belladonna took her sister's arm as they headed for the chamber door.

"Oh!" Belladonna suddenly remembered. "I forgot to tell you that our visitor is a merchant. He is coming from London with wagons heavy with goods. There may be something we wish to purchase from him."

Lily looked at her with interest. "Is that so? Then I am very interested to see what he has. Mayhap, he has something my baby can use."

Belladonna smiled weakly. "That baby has more clothing and blankets than I do."

Lily simply rolled her eyes, knowing her sister was right but defiant in her stance. Her baby would have the best, and the most, of everything and she didn't care what others thought. But as they reached the doorway, she came to a stop and faced her sister. They looked at each other, the realization of what might be the course of their future evident on their faces.

"Come what may, you and I will be together, forever," Lily said softly. "Mayhap our men will come home. But if they do not, then we are united, Bella. Come what may, we hold the Savernake dukedom in our hands. And this child… if it is a boy, he will inherit the dukedom, as my son. Our hope lies in him."

Belladonna drew strength from her sister. She didn't want to think of a future without Dashiell. She hated the idea that their life together was over before it had even begun, but what Lily said was true – she'd married a knight, and death was always a possibility. She'd been living in denial all this time, ignoring that potential.

She couldn't ignore it any longer.

No matter what, she would live her life in a way that would make him proud.

"Come what may," she agreed softly.

Lily touched her gently on the cheek before the two of them continued down to the great hall where their guests were.

CHAPTER TWENTY-FIVE

TWO DAYS AFTER the event of Lord Corston and the news he bore, Ramsbury was once again facing a peaceful day as the sun rose over the dew-kissed fields and the road outside the castle was being traveled by farmers heading to Marlborough for the coming market on the morrow.

As they'd planned, Belladonna had asked Joachim to send two men out to neighboring towns to find out what they could about the battle at Newark Castle. Contrary to the calmness she'd promised Lily, Belladonna had been struggling against the hysteria that seemed to come in waves. Some moments, she was fine. But in other moments, tears would come and she had a very difficult time fighting them off. It was the fear of not knowing the truth that had her emotions in turmoil.

The fear that she had lost her reason for living.

On this morning, Belladonna had fed the dogs in the dog pen, noticing that they were all getting quite big and hairy as winter approached. There were several of them, too, so she was thinking that she might put out the word that she was selling some of the Ramsbury fine hunting hounds, prize dogs for any savvy lord. It was either that, or the dogs were going to bust out of their pen and take over the entire castle. They were sweet dogs, but they ate far too much.

The kitchens were working to full capacity this morning, baking bread for the day and preparing for the coming meals. Lily had been down early to supervise the daily schedule but now she'd gone back to bed, as she had as of late. She was exhausted much of the time as the child grew, and Belladonna suspected they would have a baby soon. Joachim's wife concurred and had even taken to sitting with Lily, singing to her or simply talking to her, as Lily spent most of her time in bed.

After feeding the starving mutts, and passing an eye over the kitchen as the servants worked busily, Belladonna found herself wandering over to the chapel. She wasn't sure why, but she felt drawn there. Her mother and father were there, and now Acacia, and there had been times the past few months when she had simply come to sit and think. Sometimes, she prayed, but mostly, she sat and thought about her life and her future. It seemed more important than ever now that news of Savernake's defeat was heavy on her mind.

The chapel was cold and dark at this hour as the shadows from the outer walls prevented light from coming in through the windows. It smelled heavily of fresh earth, even though it had been a few weeks since Acacia had been buried next to her father. Belladonna wandered into the chapel, with the fine altar her father had made in Paris, shipped across the channel and then brought by horse cart to Ramsbury.

It was made from cedar wood, much like her father's chamber door, and the twelve apostles were caved upon it, with Paul and Peter being larger figures. As Belladonna gazed at the altar this morning, she began to wonder if her father had thought he was Paul the Apostle in the last years of his life because of these larger carvings. Her father had never been particularly religious, at least not enough to imagine himself an apostle, so she wondered if the grand cedar carvings had anything to do with it.

Oddly enough, she missed those days of her father blessing the men and giving communion to everyone multiple times because he'd forgotten he'd done it before. She missed the days of seeing Dashiell walking about Ramsbury with that proud swagger he seemed to have. The days before they were courting were such exciting days; her heart would flutter wildly at the sight of him and even though he wasn't nearly as friendly with her as he had been when she was younger, it was still a thrill to talk to him, to sit next to him at sup, and to hear him hurl insults at the men.

Bumbling pisswit!

She grinned as she thought of the knight with the endless insults.

God, she missed him.

Tears stung her eyes but blinked them away. She tried not to think of a world without Dashiell, but she told herself that even being his wife for a night would be worth a lifetime without him.

Yet… it was a lie. She was selfish. She wanted the man for the rest of her life, by her side, and she wanted to hear him scream at the soldiers and call them bumbling pisswits or sponge-headed dolts for the rest of her life. This fine, noble man who had fought for the good of England, for the good of them all, didn't deserve death at the hands of traitors, against a king who wasn't fit to wear the crown.

But that was precisely what she was facing.

Honestly, she didn't think she could stand the pain.

Dash, where are you?

Moving to the altar, she knelt in front of it, bowing her head as the tears began to fall. She prayed harder than she ever prayed in her life, praying that Dashiell would come home to her. She'd sworn to be strong for Dashiell's sake, but in moments like this, when there was no one else around, she let the tears fall freely. The pain was too great not to.

She wanted her husband back, safely.

Belladonna spent most of the morning in prayer, kneeling in the dirt, praying for Dashiell's safe return and the safe return of Bentley. She didn't want to be unreasonable and ask for the entire army to be returned whole and sound, so she was specific about Dashiell and Bentley. As much as Lily pretended to be strong, Belladonna knew the woman was broken inside at the thought of Bentley dying.

She could see it in her sister's eyes.

As the morning inched towards the nooning hour and the sun had risen enough so that sunlight streamed in through the thin, lancet windows of the chapel, she began to hear the sentries at the gatehouse taking up the cry.

Someone had arrived at Ramsbury. The cries were faint and Belladonna ignored them for the most part. She didn't want to be bothered while she was in prayer, but then she realized that if she didn't answer the call, the servants would go on the hunt for Lily, and Lily was not to be disturbed.

Perhaps, it was another traveling lord, looking for shelter for the coming night. Perhaps, he might even have news about the battle at Newark. With that in mind, Belladonna rose to her feet, brushing the dirt from her gown from where her knees were resting on the floor of the chapel. Without much enthusiasm, she headed out of the chapel.

The sun was overhead, bright and shining, and she shielded her eyes as she walked towards the gatehouse. She could see men all around the gatehouse and, finally, men were heading in her direction. She couldn't see who they were because of the angle of the sun, but when they drew closer and she dropped her hand from her eyes, she abruptly came to a halt.

Coming towards her were the two men sent to the neighboring towns to discover news about the Savernake army.

Belladonna couldn't seem to move towards them. She simply stood there, her heart in her throat, as the two men approached her, followed by Joachim. When they came to within a few feet of her, they bowed sharply.

"Lady du Reims," one man with a bushy white beard spoke. "We have good news, my lady. We were nearing Swindon when we saw the Savernake banners. The army looks to be coming home, my lady."

Belladonna was so shaken by the news that she staggered a bit as Joachim rushed to her side, grasping her arm.

"Are you well, my lady?" he asked, concerned.

Belladonna waved him off. She was solely focused on the two men who had seen the army. "They are heading this way?"

The men nodded. "Aye, my lady," he said. "We saw the banners. We rushed back with the news."

Belladonna's hand was at her throat as she struggled to keep her breathing on an even keel. "You did not go to them?" she asked. "You did not go to see if the rumors were true?"

The men shook their heads but they were looking at each other, uncomfortably. "My lady," the man with the white beard said, "it seemed to us that the army was much smaller than before. And… they were moving in groups, not all in one formation."

Belladonna had no idea what the meant. "What do you mean by groups?" she asked. "Is that strange? Is something wrong?"

Beside her, Joachim spoke. "It could be that that the healthy men are at the head of the army, my lady, and the wounded are following behind at a slower pace."

Belladonna digested that, but it did nothing to slow her pounding heart. If anything, she was feeling more apprehensive than ever before. "Knights," she managed to say. "Did you see any mounted knights? Did you see my husband?"

The men shook their heads. "We were too far away, my lady," white-beard replied. "We saw the standards and that was enough. We knew you would want to know. They should be here within the hour; at least, the first part of the army. They are coming home, my lady."

They are coming home.

Belladonna could hardly believe it. She thanked the men and, with shaking legs, made her way back to the keep. She had to tell Lily that the army was returning. Finally, they would know everything they needed to know. By the end of the day, Belladonna would either be a widow or safely in her husband's arms.

She prayed it was the latter.

Oddly enough, there was some encouragement in the realization that the army was nearly home. At least they would know what had happened, in the end, and those men who had left the castle those months ago would return to their home and to those who loved them. Aye, there was an odd comfort in that and, by the time Belladonna reached Lily's chamber, she was quite calm about it.

Today, they would know the truth.

Lily was sitting up when she arrived, stitching a bumblebee on the little tunic in her hands. She glanced up and saw her sister entering her chamber.

"I heard the sentries," she said. "More visitors?"

Belladonna shook her head. "Nay," she said. "The army has been sighted. They should be here within the hour."

Lily dropped her sewing, her eyes wide at her sister. "My... God," she gasped. "Truly? They are returning?"

Belladonna nodded. "Aye," she said calmly. "Their standards have been identified."

Lily's breathing began to come in rapid heaves. "Bentley," she whispered. "And... *Clayton*. Bella, he cannot see me like this. You *know* that. We thought... Sweet Mary, we thought the army would be gone until this child is born. Now it is too late to run!"

Belladonna nodded. "I know," she said calmly, "but Clayton will not see you. We will hide you and I will tell Clayton that you took ill and left to the seaside for your health. You know he will not care, and he most certainly will not look for you. When it is safe, Bentley will take you away."

Lily's eyes filled with tears as she looked at her sister. "What if he does not return?"

"Then someone will take you away. Please do not worry, Lily. All will be well, I promise."

Now, the roles were somewhat reversed. Lily was close to panic and Belladonna was calm. With the help of a few maids who were sworn to secrecy, and who knew of Lady le Cairon's condition, Belladonna took Lily to a chamber on the top floor where the servants and visitors slept. It was two adjoining rooms, with one heavily-fortified door, and the maids were in a frenzy moving all of Lily's possessions up to it.

With Lily safely tucked away pending the arrival of the army, Belladonna's apprehension was growing. Her palms were sweating and her mouth was dry but, on the exterior, she seemed unusually calm. She returned to her chamber to wait out the return of the army but found she couldn't stay there. She saw Dashiell at every turn; on her bed, standing by the hearth – everywhere. His ghost filled the chamber.

Fretfully, she fled back to the chapel, seemingly the only place she had any comfort. Gazing at that beautifully carved altar, it seemed most appropriate to pray, and pray she did. Falling to her knees in front of the altar, she began to pray furiously.

Time passed. It was slow, like the trickle of a stream, meandering with no real destination. Belladonna felt as if she were riding upon it, like flotsam, floating along with time as she waited for Savernake's army to return and the news that her husband was either dead or alive. Just when she lost herself in the timeless ritual of prayer, the faint cries of the sentries started up again.

The army was coming through the gates.

Her heart leapt into her throat. Tears sprang to her eyes but she fought them off as hard as she could. She wanted to be proud and strong when the men came to tell her that Dashiell had been killed in battle, or she wanted to be proud and strong when he walked into the chapel in person. She planned what she was going to say to him, to tell him how much she loved him and how much she had missed him. She would tell him that her love for him had only grown over time.

There were so many things she wanted to tell him and she prayed she would have the opportunity.

More shouting went on and, soon enough, she began to hear men other than the sentries calling to one another, meaning someone had entered into the bailey. Grooms were being brought forth from the stables and she could hear servants moving about outside of the chapel. In fact, dust was blowing in from the bailey, in through the open chapel door from the feet that had stirred up the dust of the bailey.

At some point, Belladonna lost the ability to pray. She simply knelt in front of the altar, her eyes closed, listening to every shout, every bit of movement from the bailey beyond. She heard Joachim as he spoke to someone, but she couldn't hear a response.

Until a voice came from the open doorway.

"Lady du Reims?"

Belladonna knew the voice. God help her, she knew it. Opening her eyes, she turned slowly to see Aston standing in the open doorway.

He looked beaten to hell. His blond hair was dirty and unkempt, his face stubbled, and he had a big healing gash on the side of his neck. The sight of him did not do her heart good. In fact, she could feel herself cowering, but she resisted with all her might.

Be strong!

"Aston," she said, slowing rising. "You… you have returned."

"Aye, my lady."

"Is my husband dead?"

Aston shook his head. "Nay, my lady."

So much for being strong. Belladonna burst into tears, her hands flying to her mouth to keep the sobs at bay, but it did little good. She sounded as if she were dying, breathing heavily as she sobbed at the same time. She ran at Aston.

"Where is he?" she demanded. "Take me to him!"

Grasping her by the arm, Aston led her out into the bailey, into the remnants of the once-great Savernake army. Everything, and everyone, was in shambles. Men were missing arms, eyes, and limbs. They were leaning on their fellow soldiers for support. To Belladonna, they looked like the walking dead and her eyes widened at the sight.

"My... God," she gasped. "Then it was true. The battle at Newark... it was true."

Aston had her by the elbow, leading her towards a group of wagons over near the gatehouse.

"You were told about Newark?" he asked.

She nodded, looking at the utter devastation of the men around her. "A passing merchant told us," she said. "But he had only heard rumor. Aston, what happened?"

Aston sighed heavily. "Destruction," he mumbled. "We were facing off against John's mercenary army near Newark and the odds were even until William Marshal and William Longespée changed loyalties. That weighted John's army heavily against us. We would have been able to make adjustments had it happened before the battle, but it happened during. We didn't know who our enemies were until they started cutting men down. They boxed us in on the east and west flanks and, when we realized that, we knew that someone would have to remain behind to fight so the more damaged units could get away. Dash led us into that battle, my lady. I have never seen anything like it in my life."

Belladonna could hardly believe the utter devastation she was seeing among the once-mighty Savernake army.

"How many men did we lose?" she asked, her voice dull with sorrow.

Aston had his sights set on a particular wagon that had been moved over near the armory. He headed towards it.

"We left here with almost eighteen hundred men," he said. "We lost almost nine hundred, including Clayton."

Belladonna looked at him in shock. "Clayton is dead?"

"Aye," he said. "So is Lord Sherston. Surely you remember him."

"I do," she gasped. "What happened?"

Aston sighed heavily. "He was hit by an arrow in the neck. Dash tried to save the man, but we were fighting for our own lives at the time and it was... harrowing. I hope I never see such a thing again."

Belladonna was swept with sorrow over the loss of Anthony Cromford, a man who had been truly kind to her and Dashiell in their hour of need. It was difficult to hear of the death of a genuinely compassionate man.

"I am so sorry," she murmured. "He was a very kind man. And my husband? Is he well?"

Aston was closing in on the wagon he'd been looking for. "He has been injured, but it has not stopped him," he said. "But Bentley... he has been badly wounded."

They reached the wagon, but Belladonna was still looking at Aston until someone suddenly grabbed her. She yelped with fright until she realized it was Dashiell, and his arms were around her so tightly that she couldn't breathe. Her tears returned with a vengeance as she grabbed hold of him, inhaling his dirt and his musk, never in her life experiencing anything so sweet or satisfying.

He was home!

"Dash," she wept. "You've come back to me!"

Dashiell had her so tightly that he was in danger of crushing her. "Aye," he said, his voice raspy. "I told you I would. And I have never loved you more than I do now, at this very moment."

Belladonna squeezed and squeezed, incapable of doing anything else, until she finally released him, at least so she could look him in the face. She was met by a very weary-appearing man with a massive gash across his face that ran from the corner of his nose all down the right side of his face and down his jaw. Someone had put stitches in it, big and black catgut stitches, and Belladonna gingerly touched the terrible wound.

"My sweetest love," she murmured. "Does it hurt much?"

He shook his head, looking down at her. It took her a moment to realize there were tears in his eyes. "Nay," he whispered. "It simply makes the old man look older. Now uglier. But I am alive."

"That is the most important thing," she said fervently. "You are still the most handsome man I have ever seen and I love you madly."

"Still?"

"More than the heavens love the stars."

That seemed to trigger something in him, something deeply emotional, and Dashiell kissed her deeply, listening to her soft weeping. There was such joy in her tears, such adoration in her touch. Together, they embraced away months of separation, and of fear and longing. It was happiness beyond description. But even as Belladonna rejoiced over the return of Dashiell, she caught sight of someone lying supine in the bed of the wagon.

It was Bentley.

The tall, dark, and handsome knight barely looked like himself. His hair was long and dirty, and he had a full beard upon his face. He was covered with blankets but, from the color of his pasty face, he was quite ill. A gasp of sympathy escaped her lips.

"Bent," she murmured. "What happened to him?"

Dashiell was looking at the man, great sorrow in his expression. "An ax," he said. "It caught him in the back. He has hovered near death since that time and the physic did not expect him to survive this long, but he has. The man has a strong will to live."

Belladonna's hand flew to her mouth. "Poor Bentley," she breathed. "Where is the physic now? Why is he not here, with him?"

"We lost our physic to the de Winter army. They had more casualties than we did."

"So you have been tending Bentley yourself?"

"As much as I have been able. I have tended my share of battle wounds in my life, but this... this is beyond any skill I possess. That Bent has survived this long is a miracle."

He seemed too horribly depressed about it and Belladonna looked him. "Lily is an excellent healer," she said softly. "She has learned much from the apothecary in Marlborough where she used to purchase her pessaries. In fact, we must send for the apothecary right away. Mayhap, he will know how to help Bent."

"It would be wise. I have done all I can."

Belladonna put her hand on his arm, sympathetically. "You are the wisest, strongest man I know," she said softly. "I am sure Bent is only alive because of you."

That seemed to bring on more depression from Dashiell. "He is wounded because of me," he said. "Bent took the ax that Clayton was aiming for me. He put himself in harm's way and the next thing I realized, Bric MacRohan cut Clayton's head clean from his body, but not until after Clayton sunk the ax into Bentley's back. What Bentley did, he did to save me. I... I cannot watch him die, Bella. He has survived this long and I swear, I cannot watch him die."

Belladonna was beside herself with the details of Bentley's injury and Clayton's graphic death. She could see such pain in Dashiell's eyes, so she didn't press him about anything he'd just told her, not Clayton's attempt on his life nor MacRohan's rescue. None of that mattered now, not with Bentley as a casualty.

Somehow, she felt that Dashiell was crying out to her for help, as if he were too bone-weary and muddled from the rigors of war to make one more decision. He'd come home for peace, and she was going to give it to him. For all of these men, who had suffered and fought for one another, she was going to do what a wife of the noble and powerful Dashiell du Reims would do.

She was going to be worthy of him.

"We will do all we can to help him, I swear it," she assured Dashiell, laying a warm, tender hand on his cheek. "This man saved your life and I cannot watch him die, either. Quickly, now, we must get him inside."

Men began to move as she ordered them about, putting Bentley onto a large woolen blanket and using it as a stretcher. As Aston remained in the bailey with the army, Dashiell and Belladonna followed Bentley up to Lily's chamber, where Belladonna put the man on Lily's bed. Leaving Dashiell with Bentley, she ran up to the upper floor for Lily.

The floor was virtually empty, dimly lit. Belladonna ran straight to the door of Lily's new chambers and tried the latch, only to realize that Lily had locked it. She pounded on the panel.

"Lily!" she called. "It is me! Open the door!"

Quickly, the door was unlocked and Lily's anxious face appeared.

"Where is he?" she hissed. "Is he asking for me?"

Belladonna shook her head, but her expression was full of joy and sorrow at the same time. "He is dead," she said. "He was killed when he tried to kill Dash. But, Lily... it was Bentley who saved Dash by taking the ax meant for him. He is badly wounded. You must come!"

Lily was gripping the door for support, startled to the bone by reports of Clayton's death. "Clayton... he is *dead*?"

Belladonna nodded swiftly. "Aye," she said. "You no longer need fear him. He can no longer hurt you, not now – not ever."

Lily let out a sound that was something of a grunt or a groan, something that suggested complete and utter disbelief as well as relief. Perhaps it was joy in its purest form. In any case, she reached out and grasped Belladonna.

"Is it true?"

"It is. I swear it is."

Lily's eyes filled with tears even as delight spread across her lips.

"Oh… Bella!"

But Belladonna couldn't let her become too happy about the situation. "Save your joy for later," she said, grasping the woman by the hand pulling her along. "Bent is here and he is in need of healing. I told Dash you had learned much from the apothecary you are so fond of, but it is possible that Bent needs a real physic. He is in very bad shape, Lily. The physic that tended him did not believe he would survive this long, but he has. He is fighting for his life."

Lily's head was still spinning with news of Clayton's death, but Belladonna was correct – she couldn't give in to the relief and joy of it now. She needed all of her focus for Bentley, who was more important to her than anything else in the world. She was too overwhelmed to feel grief at his injury. Having not seen the man, she had no idea how dire his prognosis was and, true to form, she was strong and immovable, like a rock. She knew what she had to do.

The moment Belladonna told her of Clayton's death, she knew exactly what she needed to do.

"Bent will not die," she said firmly as they headed down the narrow stairs, with Belladonna in front of her to make sure she didn't fall. "He will live. And with Clayton dead, I am free to marry again, this time with a man of my choosing."

"You are."

"Then I choose Bent. He shall marry me now and our child will be the legitimate heir to the dukedom of Savernake."

They came to the bottom of the stairs and Belladonna looked curiously at her sister, but she could see that the woman was completely serious.

"But… Lily, he is injured," she said gently. "Before you can marry him, you must help him. Dash said that…"

Lily cut her off. "Bentley should have been the Duke of Savernake," she said. "He would have been had Clayton not interfered. Bella, if the man is going to die, let him die as my husband. Surely, loving Dash as you do, you can understand that."

Belladonna did. Had the Fates not been kind to her, she would have faced just that scenario – a short marriage to a man she desperately loved. Nay, she didn't blame Lily in the least. In fact, she completely understood.

"Then go to him," she said softly. "He is in your chamber. I will send for a priest from Marlborough. I will also send for a physic – you know the one? He nursed Papa through his illness last year when he had that terrible cough. I will bring them both here. If the physic cannot help you heal Bent, then the priest can at least perform the marriage ceremony and give the man last rites."

Lily had an expression on her face that Belladonna had never seen before. It was full of hope and of dreams, things that could not be shattered.

"He will *not* die," she said as if she had God's ear. "He will be the next Duke of Savernake, the way he should have always been. For the suffering Bent has gone through, watching the woman he loves marry another man, surely… surely God will not let it end this way. Surely He will be merciful."

Belladonna didn't argue with her. She seemed completely convinced and Belladonna would not be so cruel as to dash her sister's beliefs. The woman had so many dashed that, in this case, it was completely unfair not to support whatever dream she wished for. If it was for her beloved Bentley to survive, then so be it.

Love could perform miracles.

In fact, Bentley of Ashbourne did survive, although his recovery was slow. Two days after his return to Ramsbury, the priest from St. Peter's Church in Marlborough performed the marriage mass that saw the Lady Lily de Vaston le Cairon wed Bentley of Ashbourne, who took his wife's family name upon their marriage and became Bentley de

Vaston, Duke of Savernake. It was a way for the de Vaston name to continue, and not uncommon when there were no male heirs. And when Lily bore a son nearly a week later, he was christened Merrick Edward Dashiell de Vaston, Earl of Collingbourne, the hereditary title for the male heirs to the dukedom of Savernake.

All was well in the world again.

With the birth of a new heir, and the joy of a new duke who was most worthy of the title, Ramsbury gradually returned to the happy place it had been before the event of Clayton le Cairon. What sadness there had been was soon forgotten, and Bentley and Lily, Dashiell and Belladonna spoke of Edward and Acacia with fondness, as time had the ability to soften one's sorrowful memories until only the joy of family could be remembered. There was no mention of Edward's madness or of Acacia's weaknesses. There was only affectionate remembrance. Clayton's name was never mentioned again, and there were no reminders of him, as his body had been left at Newark to be buried in an unmarked grave.

Bric MacRohan, in fact, had seen to that.

But with all of the happiness and contentment at Ramsbury, there were none happier, nor more content, than Dashiell and Belladonna. It was a marriage made in heaven, and there were those who swore they had never seen a couple more in love. They were rarely apart because, quite literally, one could not survive without the other. They were two souls that functioned as one and, in time, there were stories to be told of Dashiell du Reims and his unwavering love for his darling wife.

Life soon came full circle for the pair when, near Easter of the following year, Belladonna discovered she was expecting their first child. Upon telling her husband, the man wept with joy.

I love you more than the heavens love the stars.

And Dashiell's love for Belladonna went even deeper than that.

The love they shared was immortal.

EPILOGUE

Year of Our Lord 1223 A.D., December
Thunderbey Castle, seat of the Earls of East Anglia

"THIEVES! RUFFIANS! I am under attack!"

The cry came from an old man, lying in his bed, as three young boys leapt onto the mattress and banged on him with wooden swords. They had found the swords where their mother had hidden them. She was usually very good at hiding them, but they were sneaky – sometimes, they even spied on her. If she discovered that they had, she would spank them unless their father came to their rescue. But Papa wouldn't go against Mama so, often times, they had to endure the spanking.

Still, the contraband swords were fun while they lasted.

"Wicked bandits!" the old man cried as the eldest boy, six-year-old Tobin, smacked him with the flat part of the sword. "Fiends!"

He grabbed the oldest boy with the auburn hair, who screamed with both delight and anger when his grandfather began to tickle him mercilessly. His cries brought his two younger brothers, five-year-old Beckett and three-year-old Callen, to his rescue. The du Reims siblings defended each other to the death, even against a grandfather who liked to tickle with old, bony fingers.

The bed was a sea of rolling, fighting, screaming children and one laughing grandfather when Dashiell walked in. He'd heard the yelling when he'd entered the keep and now he stood in the doorway, chuckling at what he saw, until his father noticed him.

"You are the father of these monsters," he accused. "How can you live with yourself?"

Dashiell leaned against the doorjamb, folding his big arms across his chest. "It is simple," he said. "They take out their aggressions on you. And do not act as if you hate it. You would die of misery if my children did not pummel you daily."

Talus opened his mouth to reply, but a flying tackle from little Callen cut him off. The child had hit him right in the gut and he grunted as air escaped his lungs. Wrapping the boy up in a big hug, he kissed the blond head, listening to the child scream unhappily. It was like music to his ears.

"These are my fondest days," Talus said as he released the struggling child. "These three remind me so much of you and your brothers that it is frightening."

"So you have told me."

"And I mean it," he insisted. "I love my granddaughters, of course, but they do not try to kill me like my grandsons do. Ah! It is the best of life!"

Dashiell simply laughed, watching his father as he wrestled with the boys. Talus had been ill this past year, with poison in his chest that the physics could not remedy. So it was the general consensus that Talus du Reims wasn't long for this world, and that was why Dashiell let his boys jump on him. His father had such little joy these days and if rough children gave it to him, then Dashiell was happy to comply.

In fact, he'd come home to Thunderbey Castle two years ago at the request of his father, who was just beginning to enter into his health crisis. He wanted his heir home, he'd written, and Dashiell had made the difficult decision to return home. It had been traumatic for Belladonna to leave her sister, and her sister's children. Since all of the de Vaston and du Reims babies had been born around the same time and had grown up together, it had been like splitting up one large family.

Tobin was a year younger than Merrick de Vaston, and then Beckett had been born, followed by two more sons from Lily and Bentley, until Callen was born. Six boys, all cousins, and all within just a few years of each other had made for a rather madcap household until Dashiell had made the decision to move his family back to Thunderbey Castle where his only daughter had been born about six months after their arrival.

Now, Dashiell and Belladonna and their four children lived with Talus in mighty Thunderbey Castle while Dashiell's brothers manned two of the outposts for the East Anglia earldom. It was a lovely arrangement that saw Dashiell see his brothers quite often, men he adored, and Belladonna had come to love them also. She was also quite close to their wives. In all, the return to Thunderbey had been a good move, but Dashiell knew that Belladonna missed Ramsbury and her sister.

Which was why he had a surprise for her this Christmas. He'd invited Bentley and Lily to spend the Christmas season with them at Thunderbey. Even now, the Duke of Savernake and his family were heading to the wilds of Suffolk for a holiday celebration. It had been difficult for him to keep the surprise, but he wanted to see Belladonna's face when she saw her sister for the first time in two years.

It would be his Christmas present to her and he didn't want to spoil it.

But he had to admit that he was more than a little concerned with how his sons would react to seeing their cousins again. Merrick had two younger brothers, Jasper and Ashbourne, whom they called "Ash", and from what Bentley said, his boys were nearly as out of control as Dashiell's were. Not exactly out of control, but certainly lively. He hoped his father would have a good Christmas, too, with six wild boys jumping on him instead of just three.

It would certainly make things interesting.

"Dash," his father said, hugging Callen when the child wrapped his arms around his head and squeezed. "When are Bentley and his wife arriving? Have you told Bella yet?"

Dashiell put a finger to his lips in a silencing gesture, looking out into the stairwell landing behind him to ensure his wife was nowhere to be seen.

"She does not know," he whispered loudly. "And you will not tell her and then pretend you are too ill to listen when I come to scold you."

Talus was being smothered by his grandsons as he tried to have a conversation with his son. "I will not tell her," he insisted. "I was simply asking."

"Do not ask," Dashiell said. "She will hear you. You know she hears everything."

"What do I hear?"

Belladonna was coming up the stairs behind Dashiell, carrying their toddler daughter on her hip. Little Rosalyn du Reims was the exact image of her father with auburn hair and eyes so blue they were nearly lavender. Dashiell reached out to take his beautiful daughter from her as she came to the top of the stairs.

"Everything," Dashiell answered her as he kissed his daughter's head. "You hear everything."

Belladonna cocked an eyebrow at him before peering into the chamber. "And I could hear the yelling going on up here down in my solar," she said. "I came to see what the fuss is about, but now I know. I wonder where my boys found their swords."

It was a question for Dashiell, who cleared his throat rather guiltily, but it was Tobin who answered.

"Bull wanted us to fight him!" he insisted, pointing the wooden sword at his grandfather. "He says it will make him well again!"

Bull is what they called Talus, because when Tobin had been very young, he'd heard men address his grandfather as "Earl". Somehow, that became "Bull", and all of the offspring called Talus by that name, including the daughters of Dashiell's brothers. The name Bull had stuck, and Talus was quite proud of it.

But Belladonna shook her head to her son's assertion. "I seriously doubt jumping on the man and hitting him with your swords will make him well again," she said as she entered the chamber and held out her hand. "Give them to me, Tobin. Now."

Tobin's face fell as he looked at his father, who nodded his head. With a huge frown, Tobin handed over his sword, took Beckett's and handed that one over, but when it came to Callen, the lad had no intention of turning over his sword. He scampered off the mattress and hid under the bed.

"Callen du Reims," Belladonna said. "If you do not come out from underneath that bed, there shall be no sweets for you at sup. Do you understand?"

Callen began to cry and because Callen was crying, Talus leapt to his grandson's defense. "Please, my lady," he begged. "He is just a little boy. His sword makes him happy. You cannot take it from him."

Belladonna had a difficult time refusing Talus. He was a sweet man who reminded her very much of her husband. She went to him and kissed him on the head.

"I can and I will," she said. "All armies must have discipline, and this army is no different. If I do not have discipline with my boys, then I have lost control. Would you agree with that?"

Talus wasn't beyond bargaining with her on behalf of his beloved grandsons. "I would," he said. "But surely there is a compromise to be found. If I tell you a very special secret, will you agree to let them play with their swords for a little while longer?"

Dashiell heard his father. "Papa, don't you dare."

Talus ignored him. "Well? Your husband has a very big secret he has been withholding from you. I will tell you if you agree to let the boys keep their swords."

Belladonna looked at her husband. "A secret?" she frowned. "What have you been keeping from me, Dashiell?"

It was rare when she called him by his full name and Dashiell looked at his father with great irritation. "See?" he said. "Now you have made her angry with *me*."

Talus snorted at his son. "That is no concern of mine," he said, returning his focus to Belladonna. "Well? Do we have a bargain?"

Belladonna eyed the old man, trying to see if he was bluffing, but since Dashiell seemed irritated, she wisely presumed he wasn't. She handed the swords back to Tobin, who was thrilled.

"Now," she said, folding her arms expectantly. "Tell me."

With a very sly smile, he lifted up the linens on his bed. "Lads," he said. "Get in, quickly, so your mother may not get to you."

There was a good deal of squealing as Tobin, Beckett, and Callen dove beneath the bed linens, giggling and squirming all the way. When they were safely out of their mother's range, Talus simply lifted his shoulders.

"It seems I have forgotten," he said, pulling the coverlet over his head. "Mutiny! Rebellion! Do not give in to her, lads!"

The bed was alive with squealing, frolicking children and one crafty old man. Belladonna fought off a grin as she turned to her husband.

"I have been fooled," she declared. "My wrath will be severe when they least expect it."

She said it rather loudly so the naughty boys on the bed could hear. But Talus was trying to make a tent out of the swords and the coverlet, ignoring her completely, so she simply shook her head and turned away.

"Never bargain with a sick old man," Dashiell told her. "He has nothing to lose because he knows you will not punish him."

Belladonna shrugged. "Now you tell me," she said. Then, she eyed him. "What is this secret you did not want him to tell me."

Dashiell grinned. With his daughter in one arm, he put his free arm around Belladonna, pulling her close. Bending down, he slanted his lips over hers for a gentle kiss. But with her, any kiss was immediate arousal. He kissed her again, longer and firmer this time, but she put her hand up, her fingers on his lips.

"You shall not use kisses to have your way," she murmured, a twinkle in her eye. "Tell me the secret or no more kisses for the rest of the day."

He looked wounded. "You would do that to me?"

"I would."

"You are a cruel woman."

"Aye, I am."

He grinned. "But I like you this way," he said. "As for the secret, I was saving it for the Christmas holiday. Would you truly have me tell you now? It is supposed to be a gift."

Belladonna cocked her head. "If it is a gift, then you do not have to tell me."

His smile broadened. "It will be the best gift you have ever received."

She gazed into his eyes, into that face she knew and loved so well. The past eight years had been the best years of her life, married to a man she adored more with every breath she took. The wise, patient, and loving husband was also a wise, patient, and loving father, and Belladonna loved to watch him with their children. In many ways, he reminded her of her own father, and how kind and gentle he'd been with his children. She knew she was very fortunate to have had two such wonderful men in her life, men who had shown her the true meaning of family, of devotion, and of love.

She was the most fortunate woman in the world.

"Nay," she whispered, her eyes glittering at him. "*You* are the best gift I have ever received. Nothing can compare."

Even though she'd told him no more kisses, he stole one from her, anyway. "I love you, lamb."

She smiled. "And I cannot imagine there is anything you could give me that would be any more precious than what I already have."

Belladonna would maintain that opinion for the rest of her life, although a visit from her sister and Bentley a few days later came close to being nearly the best gift she'd ever received. Christmas that year was full of love and joy, and as Bentley and Lily, and Dashiell and Belladonna watched their children play in the big solar of Thunderbey, it seemed that this moment in time, for all of them, was in the true spirit of the season.

Family. Devotion. And a love that spanned the ages.

It was the stuff legends were made of.

THE END

The children of Dashiell and Belladonna	*The children of Bentley and Lily*
Tobin	Merrick
Beckett	Jasper
Callen	Ashbourne "Ash"
Rosalyn	Elowen
Chasen	Elyn
Stellan	
Aria	

ABOUT KATHRYN LE VEQUE

Medieval Just Got Real.

KATHRYN LE VEQUE is a USA TODAY Bestselling author, an Amazon All-Star author, and a #1 bestselling, award-winning, multi-published author in Medieval Historical Romance and Historical Fiction. She has been featured in the NEW YORK TIMES and on USA TODAY's HEA blog. In March 2015, Kathryn was the featured cover story for the March issue of InD'Tale Magazine, the premier Indie author magazine. She was also a quadruple nominee (a record!) for the prestigious RONE awards for 2015.

Kathryn's Medieval Romance novels have been called 'detailed', 'highly romantic', and 'character-rich'. She crafts great adventures of love, battles, passion, and romance in the High Middle Ages. More than that, she writes for both women AND men – an unusual crossover for a romance author – and Kathryn has many male readers who enjoy her stories because of the male perspective, the action, and the adventure.

On October 29, 2015, Amazon launched Kathryn's Kindle Worlds

Fan Fiction site WORLD OF DE WOLFE PACK. Please visit Kindle Worlds for Kathryn Le Veque's World of de Wolfe Pack and find many action-packed adventures written by some of the top authors in their genre using Kathryn's characters from the de Wolfe Pack series. As Kindle World's FIRST Historical Romance fan fiction world, Kathryn Le Veque's World of de Wolfe Pack will contain all of the great storytelling you have come to expect.

Kathryn loves to hear from her readers. Please find Kathryn on Facebook at Kathryn Le Veque, Author, or join her on Twitter @kathrynleveque, and don't forget to visit her website and sign up for her blog at www.kathrynleveque.com.

Please follow Kathryn on Bookbub for the latest releases and sales: bookbub.com/authors/kathryn-le-veque.

Printed in Great Britain
by Amazon